PRAISE FOR SCOTT THORNLEY
AND *ERASING MEMORY*

"An all-too-human sleuth with otherworldly gifts, MacNeice seems a character worth revisiting... Thornley has two more MacNeice books on the way, but with Thornley's eloquence and his character's appeal, the two should be at the beginning of an even longer run." — *Toronto Star*

"The reader is... compelled to go on, in part because that killer, if not a superior, twisted mind, is a first-class jerk and we love to see such people get their comeuppance."
— Philip Marchand, *National Post*

"Thornley's intelligent and evocative prose, combined with his depictions of complex police investigations, brings to mind one of Canada's most prominent, bestselling crime writers, Peter Robinson." — *Quill & Quire*

"For crime fiction junkies, Scott Thornley's first novel, *Erasing Memory*, a beautifully written police procedural set in a fictional version of Hamilton, just whets our appetite for more.... Please tell me this is the first of a series."
— Stevie Cameron, author of *On the Farm: Robert William Pickton and the Tragic Story of Vancouver's Missing Women*

"MacNeice is a splendid addition to the pantheon of [literary] detectives... A first-class mystery." — *Vancouver Sun*

PRAISE FOR SCOTT THORNLEY AND *THE AMBITIOUS CITY*

"Terrific...Thornley blends history into a really good cop-shop story...Read this and then look for the first MacNeice book, *Erasing Memory*." — *Globe and Mail*

"No writer grabs the violent new zeitgeist more firmly than Scott Thornley with his second book, *The Ambitious City*." — *Toronto Star*

"Captivating...Along with a terrific plot, Thornley produces prose that is both hard-hitting and thoughtful... I'm already anticipating MacNeice's next investigation." — *Edmonton Journal*

PRAISE FOR SCOTT THORNLEY AND *RAW BONE*

"This is stellar police-procedural writing that takes in characters, history, and, most of all, place. Dundurn is beautifully and sordidly rendered in all its glory as MacNeice tracks a killer with a message...Those who like solid clue-hunting will love this series." — *Globe and Mail*

PRAISE FOR SCOTT THORNLEY
AND *VANTAGE POINT*

"A really good, twisty whodunit that also has an art-world background. One of Thornley's best."   —*Globe and Mail*

"In the Toronto writer Scott Thornley's fourth and most accomplished novel featuring Mac MacNeice, he puts readers on edge in the opening pages and leaves them hanging out there until the authentically spectacular windup."
—*Toronto Star*

"[MacNeice is] one of Canada's best-loved fictional detectives, whose insight-laden conversations with his deceased wife and fascination with bird calls herald the kind of oddball investigative savant whom readers adore."   —*Booklist*

"If you read only one mystery this year, make it this one."
—*Oakville Beaver*

MIDDLEMEN

MIDDLEMEN

A MacNEICE MYSTERY

SCOTT THORNLEY

SPIDERLINE

Published in Canada in 2023 and the USA in 2023 by House of Anansi Press Inc.
houseofanansi.com

House of Anansi Press is committed to protecting our natural environment.
This book is made of material from well-managed FSC®-certified forests,
recycled materials, and other controlled sources.

House of Anansi Press is a Global Certified Accessible™ (GCA by Benetech)
publisher. The ebook version of this book meets stringent accessibility standards
and is available to readers with print disabilities.

27 26 25 24 23   1 2 3 4 5

Library and Archives Canada Cataloguing in Publication
Title: Middlemen : a MacNeice mystery / Scott Thornley.
Names: Thornley, Scott, author.
Identifiers: Canadiana (print) 20230197701 | Canadiana (ebook) 2023019771X |
ISBN 9781487011505 (softcover) | ISBN 9781487011512 (EPUB)
Classification: LCC PS8639.H66 M53 2023 | DDC C813/.6—dc23

Cover image: (goshawk): Milan Zygmunt / Alamy Stock Photo
Series design: Alysia Shewchuk
Book design: Lucia Kim

*House of Anansi Press is grateful for the privilege to work on and create from the
Traditional Territory of many Nations, including the Anishinabeg, the Wendat,
and the Haudenosaunee, as well as the Treaty Lands of the Mississaugas of the Credit.*

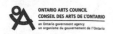

With the participation of the Government of Canada
Avec la participation du gouvernement du Canada |

*We acknowledge for their financial support of our publishing program the Canada Council
for the Arts, the Ontario Arts Council, and the Government of Canada*

Printed and bound in Canada

MIX
Paper from
responsible sources
FSC® C103567

In Memoriam
John Bienenstock
1936–2022
A visionary researcher, immunologist,
and beloved friend.

Secrets are those places we cannot find
　　on a map
because no road is paved to go there.

　　—Jean-Pierre Larocque, Montreal, 2022

[PROLOGUE]

MACNEICE CHOSE THE LEFT BANK, WHERE HE AND KATE HAD FIRST met, not because he was still searching for her shadow — he hadn't been to Paris since her death, and that was long ago — it was just that he felt most at home among Kate's haunts. He wanted to wander familiar streets and melt away the crime scenes that had defined his life in Dundurn.

There was, however, one lingering task from his last case that he couldn't erase. he had to retrieve the portfolio of grisly staged photographs of murder victims from the Parisian gallery that had unwittingly offered to exhibit them. A week into his stay, he placed a call to the gallery and left a message with his name and the number of his hotel.

The next morning, MacNeice emerged in search of a croissant and strong coffee. He nodded to the desk staff, who greeted him cheerfully with "Bonjour, Monsieur MacNeice," and walked toward the breakfast room.

The hotel's concierge, Jean Vernaz, stood at the bar with a look of concern. "Monsieur MacNeice, un moment, s'il vous plaît," He walked the taller man back several steps. "You have two women in the lounge . . . They are . . . quite exceptional."

MacNeice wondered for a moment what the concierge meant by exceptional, but he suddenly understood. "Je suis désolé, Jean; it's okay."

"You know them? They are very famous in Paris, maybe infamous . . . I don't know."

"One is slender and chic and somewhat sad; resembles Jean Seberg?"

"Oui, c'est ça. With black hair, not blond."

MacNeice said he was expecting them, even though he wasn't.

They were sitting on the sofa facing the fireplace, locked in quiet conversation. Chanel Bourget wore a white linen blouse, slim-fitting tan slacks, and matching tan slip-ons. The throw cushions had been pushed aside, and against them she'd tossed a brilliant red scarf and a purple leather briefcase. On the glass table before them were two coffee cups, Chanel's vivid red lipstick imprinted on one. She was facing her partner and appeared to be wiping away a tear as MacNeice arrived.

They'd probably drawn stares from passing guests; Carmen's arm was draped tenderly over Chanel's shoulder, while Chanel's hand lay casually on the older woman's knee. A large square portfolio sat next to a vase of pale pink roses so perfect you'd swear they were silk.

The older woman spotted him; she squeezed Bourget's shoulder and nodded in his direction. Chanel turned and launched herself off the sofa, sending her sunglasses skidding across the parquet floor. Picking them up, MacNeice said, "Bonjour, Chanel," and held out his hand. She brushed it aside, threw her arms around his neck, and held him close. He inhaled a scent so subtle that he could only assume it was the spring fragrance that comes with being a Parisienne.

"Je suis très contente que tu sois venu me voir." She shook her head. "I'm sorry. I say how happy I am that you came to see me."

Taken aback by Chanel's enthusiasm, MacNeice gave her the glasses. "It's wonderful to see you. Please introduce me."

The other woman stood and thrust out her hand. "Carmen Weitzman. Thank you, Detective MacNeice, for saving the life of my beloved."

MacNeice registered the soft touch of her hand; he'd expected a stockbroker's vise grip. He smiled, enjoying how quickly his assumptions could be proven wrong. "You're welcome. Though her life was actually spared by her captor."

Tall and curvy, Carmen wore a tailored grey suit with electric blue pinstripes, a deep purple shirt, and, below her trouser cuffs, shimmering blue socks tucked into a pair of near-black oxfords.

Chanel patted the couch. "Please, MacNeice, sit with me." She smiled openly and appeared half her age; she'd had no reason to smile in Dundurn. Carmen went in search of fresh coffee for three.

Ninety minutes and several cups later, MacNeice led the women to the hotel's entrance. Chanel had wept several times during their meeting, and while she'd glanced at it frequently, the portfolio remained untouched. It, and all it represented, seemed to exude a power over her, but she didn't want to know more about the creator of the images it contained other than what she'd known when rescued from the farmhouse.

As they stepped outside, Chanel turned back to MacNeice, pointing to the portfolio under his arm. "What will happen to that?"

"It'll be filed away in an evidence room . . . and possibly never opened again." He smiled tenderly. "Your role, Chanel, will never be forgotten. Not by you, and not by me."

She swallowed hard, nodding to regain her composure. "Merci, MacNeice . . . I *do* owe my life to you. I will never forget."

He watched as they strolled up rue Dauphine. Fifty yards on, she looked over her shoulder to see if he was still there — so he waved. Chanel pirouetted, raising her hands to her lips in a prayer-like gesture, before swinging around again and continuing on.

Back in the hotel, he again went off in search of breakfast as an antidote to the caffeine speeding through his bloodstream.

It wasn't long before his mind started unravelling their affectionate parting. What if, his brain teased, Bourget had made a copy, or a dozen copies, of Venganza's stunning homicidal photographs — for private collectors? MacNeice put a generous helping of the hotel's strawberry jam on a piece of croissant, but he left it on the plate because his mind wasn't finished. What if Chanel's intimate knowledge of the artist's technique — of killings doubling as works of art — only added to their value?

MacNeice's frontal cortex broke the thread, recalling his old friend John Michaluk: "Mac, it's like the two most famous words in sport... *You never know.*"

[1]

"RUN, JACK, RUN!" THE COMMAND WAS URGENT, ANGUISHED, AND final. Jack was frozen by the explosions illuminating the forest and the desperation of the command, causing him to betray the instinct to respond to a threat he couldn't see. He started to run, hesitated, then turned back. Another explosion — a blinding flash — and the ground erupted. Something hot pierced his leg. The path he'd taken into the woods was no longer an option. He swung about and ran off into the night.

Jack hurtled through a colonnade of trees standing silent like soldiers, each laying claim to the slate sky above. He leapt over the fallen ones, was lashed by the limbs of young saplings and torn by needle-sharp buckthorn. Slipping sideways on the moss-covered rocks, he kept going. Driven by panic and terror, he flushed birds out of hiding and tore past their startled yellow eyes.

As he ran, his panic was replaced by a desire to seek help — to get home. His natural ability as a sprinter took over. While he couldn't run flat out forever, he quickened his pace to the point where each footfall barely touched ground.

Reckless running cost him. Losing his footing on a shale embankment, he tumbled into a gully, and while scrambling for purchase, he stumbled again. When at last he gained traction, he raced onward with such determination that his remaining fear dissolved. In the darkness, Jack relied on his other senses. Smell and sound would have to do what sight could not.

Somewhere behind him came the report of another explosion. Jack kept running. He had no idea how far he'd gone or where he was. He simply trusted he'd find the way home.

Emerging from the forest, he was confronted by a wall of corn waving drunkenly in the night breeze. He stepped cautiously into the first row and ran for twenty yards — then, acting purely on instinct, he reversed direction and picked up speed. He would run to the end of the field, or, if necessary, the end of his breath.

Jack burst out of the cornfield into a drainage ditch and then onto a highway. A car horn blasted; its lights startled him and — before he could react — a fender grazed his hip, throwing him hard against the other side of the ditch.

Gasping for breath, he lay on his side as more cars passed. Within minutes, adrenaline and tenacity got him up again. Limping badly, Jack still believed he'd make it home.

In pain, his heart racing, Jack loped along the shoulder.

Drivers honked their horns, worried he might dart in front of them.

He ran on, giving only fleeting glances to the silhouettes of barns and houses, the mist-covered cars and pickup trucks. He was certain he'd come upon a sight, a sound, or a familiar scent.

But—time slides. It's never accounted for in the tick-tock-tick of a second hand. It slides, passing by unnoticed like a stranger on the street.

Had Jack known the moment he was spent—had he slowed to the point where he was walking, then stopped and fallen? Had he paused to ease the pain in his hip, check the bleeding from his leg, or just to gather strength to carry on? Whatever the reason, he eventually lay down on the gravel shoulder and, moments later, closed his eyes.

Though greatly diminished, his senses continued to track the sounds of engines, of night-birds and crickets and frogs calling between the waves of traffic. He noted a radio somewhere in the distance before its sound dwindled, pushed sideways by the wind.

The passing vehicles left exhaust-infused gusts to buffet and soothe him; the smell of dusty, dewy weeds comforted him. But as Jack's breathing slowed and his chest stopped heaving, all those sounds and scents, like consciousness itself, faded—and his body finally surrendered to the dark.

[2]

"**H**EY, THERE. YOU OKAY, PAL?"

"He dead, Bert?"

"No ... but pretty banged up." The dog lifted its head but couldn't summon the strength to stand. Exhausted, its snout dropped slowly to the gravel, its eyes wide with fear or confusion. Bert saw the pool of blood around its hind leg. What hadn't been absorbed by the gravel formed a gelatinous ruby shadow. "Al, grab that blanket from the trunk. We'll take him over to Redsell's."

"The horse and cattle guy?"

"Yeah. He'll either fix him up or put him down." By now the dog was moaning softly. Bert settled him on the blanket, then withdrew a hand. "Christ! His back's covered in blood and some kinda gore."

Al leaned over. "Jesus, Bert, that looks bad. Hey, you got a post hammer back there — why not give it a whack on the head?"

Bert looked up. "Sure, Al...long as you do the whacking."

"I'm juss sayin' to put it out of its misery. I can't do it; I'm a specifist."

"Pacifist. We'll take him to Redsell. I need to ask him some questions anyway." Wrapped in the blanket, the dog's body went limp. "Don't you die on me now."

It was dark inside the clinic, but Redsell's pickup was there, so Bert rang the night bell. Moments later the reception fluorescents came to life.

"Seven o'clock, an early start for you..." A tall, slender man with tousled blond hair and blue eyes opened the clinic door. "We open at eight. Does this need dealing with now?"

"I think you'll tell me."

Chris Redsell let them in, locked the door, and led them through to the operating room. He lowered a large circular lamp and gently removed the blanket. On a table meant for horses and cattle, the dog looked tiny and defeated. Its eyes blinked several times against the light, and it struggled to get up. "Easy...easy. Let's just have a look at you." Redsell was calm and reassuring; the dog sighed, closed its eyes, and dropped back to the table.

"We'll take a microchip reading, but first I'll check these wounds. There's a coffee machine next door. Make three; black for me."

Waiting for the machine to brew, the two men looked at the photographs of large animals on the wall. "I guess they're his happy customers," Al said, peering closely at a Holstein.

"Yeah, some are thoroughbreds from Fort Erie. He's one of the track's go-to vets."

When they returned, Redsell was washing his hands and the dog was still. "I've given him a sedative; that hind leg needs some work." He finished drying his hands and pulled on a pair of surgical gloves. "He's seen the wars—his name's Jack."

"You got that from the microchip?" Al asked.

"No. From that dangle-jangle on his collar." Redsell called them over to the table, where his scalpel and instruments lay gleaming on a tray. "But this is interesting..." He pointed to a large area of matted blood on Jack's backside. "There's no injury here. That blood isn't Jack's. He's got a nasty contusion on that hip, like he was hit—but the flesh there isn't torn, so I don't know what that belongs to..."

Looking closer, Bert asked, "What are those confetti things?"

"Shattered bone—again, not his. If I had to guess, something awful happened and Jack just ran himself out getting away from it. He was losing blood—a lot of it splattered on his belly and the back of his front legs," Redsell said. "I'll also test that blood and bone, so give me a couple of hours."

[3]

RETURNING FROM THE WINE GROWERS ASSOCIATION, BERT AND AL were surprised to see two cruisers and an unmarked car outside the clinic. Al's chin dropped into his neck. "This doesn't look good."

Inside, they were immediately confronted by two cops in flak jackets, one with his hand resting on his sidearm. "What's your business here, gentlemen?"

"We brought in an injured dog earlier." Bert didn't have to say another word; one of the cops turned and walked away. The receptionist offered an eye-roll in Bert's direction. He interpreted that as something big about to drop on the morning's good Samaritans.

The cop reappeared and waved them over. "In here," he said. Inside were two more uniforms and a plainclothes detective who introduced himself: "Gerry Steiner, Detective Sergeant, Patrol Support." The uniforms didn't bother to look up.

Redsell was standing behind the operating table, sipping a coffee. "I'll just give Bert and Al an update," he said. "Jack's fine. Something zipped through that hind leg, nicked the tendon, missed a blood vessel, and didn't hit the tibia. I patched it up and did an X-ray of his hip; nothing's broken, but I'm sure it hurts like hell. The rest of the blood and those tiny bone fragments are human. Dundurn's chief pathologist is on her way."

"What the hell?" Bert threw his hands on top of his head. "I mean — *what the hell?*"

"Exactly. Microchip identifies his owner as Dr. Evan Moore; lives over by Jordan Harbour."

"We called; no answer." Steiner watched both men. "Moore's name doesn't mean anything?" Al and Bert shook their heads. "Tell me about the dog; where'd you find him?" Steiner leaned against the wall, his hands slid casually into his pockets like he was watching a Little League game, one that didn't include his kid.

Bert gave a quick overview of why they'd been on the road. His vineyard had taken years to break even, and now, with five seasons in the black, he wanted to expand his output and had purchased another hundred acres from a grape grower. "I was taking the signed deed over to the Wine Growers Association for registration. Al's my field manager; we were on Highway 8, just past Vineland, when I spotted the dog on the shoulder and pulled over to take a look. I wanted to see Chris over here anyway..."

"Concerning?"

"A veterinarian's opinion — about using goats to mow between the vines to keep the weeds down."

"Not bad as one idea," Redsell said.

"I'd appreciate you taking these officers to where you found him." Steiner paused, then asked, "Which way was he headed — Dundurn or Niagara?"

"Niagara...but when you mention Jordan Harbour, he wasn't that far away...eight to ten miles, give or take."

"Going home..." Steiner said softly.

Once they'd left, he turned to Redsell. "Tell me about this breed — how fast can they run?"

Redsell's brow furrowed and his lips curled up in a smile.

"Okay, stupid question." Steiner nodded. "Put another way, how far could he get from where this happened to him?"

"Top speed upwards of thirty to thirty-five miles per hour, but not for long. He's a Lab-whippet mix — his legs and that upswing from chest to abdomen are the giveaway — that just means he's smart and fast." Redsell stroked the dog's head. "As for how far...well, he's exhausted and not just from blood loss. I think he ran through the night."

Steiner processed the information, "Okay...let's say he averaged ten miles per hour over the course of, what, four hours?"

Redsell moved his hand to the dog's shoulder. "No question, he could do that. Apart from that wound and a sore hip, he's in great shape."

"Forty miles sounds incredible to me."

"Yeah, well, I'm pretty sure he was motivated."

"So, Doc, we put an X on a map where they found him and make that the centre of a circle stretching out forty miles. Caught in that are subdivisions, towns, industrial parks, forests, orchards, vineyards, downtown Dundurn..." Steiner shook his head at the vastness.

Redsell shrugged. "Pretty much. The only thing I can say with certainty is that Jack was happy and healthy before this happened. And that, because it didn't rain overnight, there'll probably be a blood trail."

"Right..." Finding it hard to believe it would be that simple, Steiner tried to imagine the logistics of such an operation. "Are you set up to keep him here, just till we locate the family?"

"Not really. As you can see..." He drew Steiner's attention to the large belt harnesses and chains mounted to the ceiling with pulleys. The examination table was immense and the X-ray machine cantilevered like an enormous square-eyed robot from the wall. "We treat large animals here; we don't have crates for family pets. Right now there's a nurse prepping a horse with a hernia. Jack can't stay here, but I'll keep him calm until the pathologist is finished. Once she gives the nod, we'll clean him up, let him shake off the sedation fuzzies, and then he's over to you."

"Richardson will be here soon, but what do you suggest *we* do with him?"

"I'll modify a goat cone to keep him from getting too curious about the wound. His hip just needs time." He looked down at the bandage. "But, first thing, contact the family. Failing that, I guess, take him to a shelter." To Steiner that sounded like a death sentence, and the vet's stoic shrug seemed to confirm it. "I've given him an antibiotic injection, but that leg will need daily care for at least a week."

[4]

THREE MEN SAT AT THE CIRCULAR TABLE IN RIVIERA AUTOMOBILE Restoration's soundproof windowless office. It was half past four in the morning and they were listening to a violent, decibel-shattering thumping outside their door. The source was a sodium hydroxide bath—a dip-'n'-strip. The tank was louder than usual, and the torrent of caustic soda was stripping something not listed in the manufacturer's specifications.

The dip-'n'-strip was a contained tsunami designed to remove paint, primer, and rust from a fender. Only in this case, it was stripping and dissolving flesh, muscle and tendon, cartilage and organs, until only the largest bones remained, each with the structural integrity of a bread stick. Adding greatly to the din was a robust exhaust system powered by

twin turboprops—an exaggeration, but not by much. As
testimony to the dangers of such an aural assault, six pairs
of ground-crew sound-dampening headphones hung nearby.

"For every living and dead thing, there was a first breath,
and there was, or will be, a last. Earth sheds its human skin
willingly. And, as we mortals take the stage with a breath,
we do so unaware of our assumptions about the coming
journey. We simply—innocently, ignorantly—go forward
confidently in our untouched beauty."

Clarence Blow scanned the faces of the other men to confirm they were listening. "And yet, arriving at that moment
when life finally leaves us, we tend most vividly to feel a rush
of guilt, sorrow, regret, and grief for our largely unearned
pride. Most of us don't end our days basking in gratitude
for the life we've had." Looking at their heavy brows, he
realized he was wasting a decent, thoughtful oration. But
he was determined to go on. "As for joy and tenderness and
love—when we're teetering above that infinite void, we see
those qualities wistfully, as through a veil. But that was not
the case this evening..."

Clarence smiled as a fresh thought arrived: "Shuffle
two letters of *veil* and you have *evil*. Isn't that amusing?" He
could see that the men before him weren't remotely amused.
More's the pity, he thought. *Dolts; dulled, dull, a Middle English
word that first appeared in the 1540s.* While reaching for the
wine, he accidentally nudged the sawed-off shotgun resting on the table. The bottle was empty; Clarence tapped it
several times with a gloved finger before standing up. He
smiled again: "I'll fetch another." As he opened the door,
the banshee's wail filled the room.

When it closed behind Clarence, Pete started up. "I'm

tellin' you, man, the smoking end of that piece was at nine o'clock for half an hour. Ten minutes ago, it was at nine-thirty. Look at it now, Johnny—twelve o'clock. It's pointed at me."

Johnny reached over to turn it away.

"Don't. Don't! He'll know. Be cool like nothing's happening—but watch out for me."

"Okay. Though maybe nothing is actually happening..."

Pete turned on him. "You're wrong—that's not a fuckin' Ouija board or spin-the-bottle. He's not that Russian guy bending forks with his mind; it's a piece and he definitely moved it."

"I don't know what you're freaking out about. We're his team." Johnny studied the barrel of the shotgun as if it might move on its own, maybe this time in his direction.

"I'm tellin' you, he's pissed. I'm not the one who did that guy."

"No. You're the one who missed him and the old guy."

"Yeah, okay. Shit happens. It was dark; I was gonna unload on him when Blow opened up."

"He sure did—on both of them."

"I'm ready, though. I've got my piece under the table, just in case."

"For fuck's sake, don't do that—nothing's happening here. We're just three guys drinking free wine."

Pete shook his head in exasperation. "And... what the fuck was he talking about? *Evil, veil?* Man, I don't know. When he goes off like that, I almost wish he'd shoot me."

"Don't say that! Don't say that." Not normally given to superstition, Johnny was nonetheless spooked when anyone tempted fate. As a rule of thumb, he didn't want to be collateral damage when the grand piano fell from the sky.

"You know...I've hung with lots of short guys, but Clarence's way shorter than any of them. He's like a tall dwarf. With that blond little-boy haircut on that melon head...and those pouty lips. Man, the fucker's weird." Pete slapped his left hand on the table. "And those driving gloves—all girly-looking with the knuckles cut out." He shrugged in disgust. "I've never seen him take those things off—even though I've been doing all the driving. Seriously. What's that about?"

"I dunno. Maybe it's just his thing—like Italians wearing gold chains.

"Yeah, sure, whatever." Pete was on a roll. "Shit. Who names their kid Clarence?" For sarcastic effect, he gave extended play to the first syllable. "And Blow." He shook his head. "Add Clarence to Blow and in my opinion you get *blowjob*. That puppy's problems started right-the-fuck there." He jabbed an *aha* finger in the air and sneered. "Puppy's problems—now, Johnny, isn't that interesting?"

"Okay, enough, or I leave and let you explain."

At this point, both men were on edge. They spent the next few minutes in silence, listening to the insistent rumble and hum outside the office.

Clarence returned with a bottle and three fresh glasses. Holding the wine like a trophy, he announced, "It's a 2016 Burgundy—this will go down well." He put the glasses on the counter and opened the bottle, smiling as he sniffed the cork.

"I think you'll enjoy this." Actually, no, he didn't. He didn't think they enjoyed anything but beer—beer that arrived in large plastic jugs. Nonetheless, he cheerfully filled the glasses and sat back down at the table. Swirling the wine,

Clarence brought the glass to his nose, sniffed, and held it aloft. "Salut." Both men returned the toast, though Pete's face made it clear he had no idea why *saloo* was a toast.

"Ever wondered...?" Clarence said, holding his glass up to the fluorescent light, marvelling at the wine's colour.

Both men hated this part. It didn't matter what came next. They'd only known Clarence for a month or more, but they already recognized that questions beginning with "ever wondered?" were tests they were doomed to fail. And though he didn't look it, after the previous night in the forest, they knew Clarence Blow was unpredictable, someone not to piss off.

Waiting for him to continue, Johnny could feel his testicles rolling slowly up into the shelter of his pelvis. He tried to look attentive, but he also needed to look like he was enjoying the wine, which was difficult, because he had cotton mouth from the tension. He didn't look Pete's way, but he could feel Pete's dark vibes.

Johnny moved his left shoulder slightly, he hoped imperceptibly, to find the comfort of the weapon under his jacket. He knew Pete's right hand was still under the table, and he wondered if Blow would notice that a right-handed man was drinking wine with his left.

Clarence put his glass down and returned to his unfinished question. "Ever wondered about dogs?"

Neither man answered, each hoping the other would think of something to say. When Clarence looked from Pete to Johnny and back again, Pete spoke up, "You mean why dogs are man's best friend?"

Clarence shook his head slowly like he was actually considering Pete's answer. "Close, but no."

"You mean, why dogs and not cats?" Johnny offered doubtfully.

"Definitely not." Clarence poured another glass for himself and offered to pour two more. Both men declined. "Why are dogs loyal? Why do they so willingly put themselves in harm's way to protect a human? What are they thinking? *Do* they think?"

Pete raised his glass as a cover for not having an answer. Heart racing, he felt sweat beading on his forehead. He hoped it wasn't obvious. Johnny nodded as if he was thinking hard, weighing points of view to find the right one to express. Maybe Clarence would answer it himself.

"Take that dog tonight, covered in its master's blood. It must have known he was dead. And yet it didn't want to leave. Even when it was wounded, I thought it might come back." Clarence swirled the wine around, pondering his own questions. "In a forest black as ink, where was it running to?"

"Yeah… I think they think." Pete threw caution to the wind. "I had a dog, Randy. He knew all kinds of—"

Pete had never had a dog. He was just desperate enough to fake it. Clarence raised a hand. Pete didn't finish his sentence, which was probably for the best, as he knew squat about dogs.

"I know. I know." Clarence was peeved at how tedious a conversation with these two could be. "I'm sure Randy could fetch, open doors, catch and return a ball—maybe even wash your socks—but that's not what I'm talking about. That's called training, or conditioning—Pavlov's dog."

"Well, I wasn't—"

"No matter." Clarence cut him off. "I'm talking about what they think, how they think, and if they think at all."

Though he was still smiling, his voice had risen to something just shy of hysterical.

Pete was relieved. He didn't know who Pavlov was, but there was no way in God's blue beyond that he was going to ask. He wiped away a drop of sweat gliding down his nose.

Clarence noticed. "What's wrong with you, Peter? You're all flushed and sweaty." Blow didn't give him time to answer. "It's not hot in here; we're not sweating. I think you must have something on your mind."

"No . . . I'm okay."

"Is it something you ate, then?"

"No. Well, maybe. I don't know."

"Something you did that you want to talk about, perhaps?"

Pete shrugged, looking for support from Johnny. He got none and turned defensively back to Clarence. "Did? What did I do?"

Clarence's mouth morphed into a cruel grin. "I thought *you'd* know that, Peter. So — what's troubling you?"

Pete shook his head, his face now contorted in anger and frustration. "So what — what?" It was a juvenile taunt and he chuckled uncomfortably. His finger twitched on the trigger.

"I see." Clarence nodded, sipping his wine. "Okay. So the first *what* is: what's your right hand doing under the table?"

Johnny's jaw tightened. He set his glass down and leaned back in his chair, keeping his eyes on the heel of the shotgun.

"Okay. Sure. Why's that fucking piece pointed at me?" Spittle flew; Pete watched Clarence nod at the shotgun.

Clarence laughed and shook his head in disbelief. "You are seriously overwound, Peter. That shotgun isn't loaded. Remember? I unloaded it in the forest." He was so casual that he sounded utterly convincing. "Sorry. Look, no problem. Take it easy; I'll put it on the floor." He took another sip of wine and put the glass down—though he must have been distracted, because the foot of the glass was halfway off the table.

Pete started to say, "Watch out, your glass—"

The noise was deafening. Pete's head exploded as he and his chair shot back across the room, slamming against a metal cabinet. The Glock was still in Pete's hand when his body slid to the floor. Blood, bone, and brains covered the wall. Below, automotive paint binders and a collection of classic car models wept blood and grey matter.

Johnny was trying to say something but nothing emerged. His hands were raised in surrender when his bladder gave way.

Clarence looked over at him and barked, "Put your hands down, John—you've got nothing to fear." He took the bottle and refilled their two glasses. "We'll finish our wine, then give him a bath . . . after that, we'll clean this place up. No problem. I got out a mop, two bottles of cleaning solvent and about a hundred rags. There's also a can of white paint left over from the renovations, and some filler to deal with the holes. We'll be fine."

Johnny took several deep breaths and swallowed half the glass. Clarence rolled his eyes impatiently. Johnny kept exhaling in gasps. "*Phew*, man. Oh man, *phew . . . phew*."

"I know. It's a shock. But it'll pass."

"Man, I dunno. What the fuck was that?"

"Were you two friends?"

"What? No, we weren't friends; you hired us. I never met him before that."

"Peter was a liability and we have a lot of work to do."

Clarence moved his glass in tight circles, enjoying watching the burgundy swirl inside. "He'll be replaced by someone reliable tomorrow. Finish your wine, John, and we'll roll up our sleeves."

"Yeah, okay. Sure."

"To change the subject: do you remember what happened after those two men went down?"

For a moment, Johnny couldn't focus on anything but Pete's head, inside out on the floor. "Wait. Yeah, there was that great Jesus bird—musta bin an eagle or somethin'—came outta nowhere. Man, that was spooky—scared the shit outta Pete too. He took a shot at it."

"And missed, again..." Clarence hadn't paused out of respect; the corner of his mouth was tucked firmly into his right cheek. "Which, given its three- or four-foot wingspan, speaks volumes about Peter's marksmanship."

"Weird, it wasn't scared away by the shotgun..."

"Okay, let's get to it. Just before we do, though, tell me what happened here." Clarence's eyes narrowed as he studied John's face.

Johnny's throat was so constricted, he tilted the glass to his mouth, hoping the last drops would allow him to speak rather than squawk. "Pete pulled a gun; you defended yourself." Though only a whisper, he had delivered the correct answer.

"Just so. I think you'll find this interesting..." Clarence seemed to be studying the bottom of his now empty glass.

John's eyes were riveted on the blood and brain matter coursing down the wall. It was a race won by the large glob dropping like pigeon poop on a picnic table.

"Did you know that your tongue is the only muscle in

your body that's not completely anchored? One end of it floats. Peter should have done a better job of tethering his tongue instead of letting it flap."

Shivering from shock, Johnny couldn't manage a verbal response, so he nodded and kept on nodding. Until he worried that his nodding might set Clarence off—he stopped abruptly and cleared his throat.

Clarence, disappointed that his anatomical anecdote had failed to produce a proper response, pushed away from the table. "To work then." He retrieved two pairs of pink rubber gloves from the cleaning supply drawer and tossed a pair to John; they slapped comically against his cheek. He eased his own over his driving gloves.

THREE HOURS LATER they were sitting in the same chairs, having coffee. There was no sign of what had happened, owing in part to the office's metal and plastic finishes. The rags had already been incinerated, and short of a full-on forensic scan, the place was just as it appeared: an industrial park auto-body office with outstanding soundproofing.

"Well, then, let's call it a night." Clarence pushed his chair away from the table and stood. "I'll tell the boss we need to replace the sample books, that we had a leak and I tossed them in the incinerator. He'll understand." He patted John hard on the back. "Put this behind you. Peter was a bad hire; that's on me. And don't worry about pissing yourself, either. That was the least of what needed cleaning up."

"Thanks." Johnny's face flushed with embarrassment. "How'd you know he had that piece under the table? Was it him drinking the wine with his left hand, or the sweat?"

"No, no, I'm not that clever." That was insincere; Clarence was absolutely that clever. "The room's wired. I was listening from the wine cellar. The owner uses it when people come in with their expensive cars. They arrive with wives or brothers or lawyers or accountants; restoration work can easily run into six figures. So when he leaves to get the wine to seal the deal, he knows their negotiating strategy before he returns."

Johnny couldn't recall if he'd said anything to Pete that he needed to worry about, but just in case he had, he changed the subject. As he set the glasses on the counter, he asked, "So, are you married, Clarence?"

"I was. Tragically, though...she died." He raised a gloved hand to add a correction: "Though she died...tragically." Clarence pursed his mouth in satisfaction.

Johnny was pretty sure there was a difference, he just couldn't imagine what it was. "Cancer?"

"No, no...a gas explosion." Clarence opened the door and followed Johnny out of the office. Walking past the soda machine, he stopped and took hold of Johnny's arm. He yelled something and pointed toward the tank. John leaned in to hear him.

"I forgot. We have to put another forty pounds of soda in the bath." Clarence pointed to the ladder hooked to a horizontal rail at the top of the tank. "Drums are over there — grab one and I'll get the remote for the tank."

Clarence shut down the agitator, opened the tank's cover, and waited for Johnny. Though the exhaust fans continued to howl, communicating was a little easier with the agitator quiet. Johnny discarded the lid and carried the plastic container to the foot of the ladder.

"Be careful," Clarence hollered. "I'll hold the ladder, just get it to the top and pour it in from the last rung." Clarence laid the remote on the concrete floor and waited for John to start climbing. Holding the sides of the ladder, he could feel the man's fear shivering through the metal.

Johnny wasn't very confident, but having dumped three dead-weight bodies in the bath earlier, he felt he could manage the bucket. And, since he and Clarence were in this together, there was no refusing. Using one hand for support and the other for the container made climbing difficult. But he was determined not to fail; he'd seen Blow's response to failure.

Clarence stabilized the ladder with both hands. Above him, Johnny paused with his shins leaning against the tank's edge. He lifted the large bucket to his chest with both hands.

The moment he leaned forward to tip the bucket into the tank, Clarence hauled the bottom of the ladder off the floor. A teeter-totter second later, Johnny and the soda bucket disappeared.

There wasn't a sound, at least none Clarence could hear. He thought a yelp might break through the din, but no — Johnny's legs flew high in the air and out of sight without a peep. Clarence set the ladder down, picked up the remote, closed the tank, and turned the agitator back on.

[5]

ROOM 302 WAS TWO FLOORS ABOVE CAFÉ LAURENT, THE HOTEL'S jazz bar, MacNeice's nightly stop before turning in. He'd sit at the bar nursing a Calvados—an alternative to the unavailable grappa.

For the most part, the venue featured piano trios, though on this occasion the trio had added a vocalist—Dominique Dupuis. When D.D. hadn't appeared by 10:40 p.m., MacNeice wished the bartender bonne nuit and headed to the elevator.

Once in bed, he adjusted his pillow so he could hear the music seep into the room as perfume might. He closed his eyes to a sensual instrumental of "My Funny Valentine." The musicians were in no hurry; the piano player casually, expertly employed spaces between the notes. MacNeice was surprised that he could distinguish the heartbeat of the bass and the drummer's brushes as they swept lazily over the drumhead. Strangely, the tempo was timed precisely to his breathing.

Though smoking in bars had long been outlawed in Paris, it didn't surprise him that his room was smoky. Jazz was smoky. MacNeice could feel the weight of his body sinking deeper into the bedding; he smiled and drifted off toward sleep.

Through fading consciousness, he heard a sultry voice humming along with the piano before sliding into the lyrics. Her voice was soft, but not because of distance; it sounded like she was a breath away. MacNeice opened his eyes. She was in bed beside him.

It was Aziz, sounding hauntingly like Billie Holiday. Certain he must be dreaming, MacNeice opened his eyes wider. She was propped up on one elbow, leaning toward him. The sheet was draped across her breasts like a satin gown. She was incandescent as she sang and her voice was filled with longing.

He turned on his side; he wanted to touch her but felt she might vanish if he did. Her eyes smiled down at him. A small diamond hung around her neck, its facets catching the light like a tiny disco ball. But what light? The room was dark. Another sparkle drew his attention, glittering high on her cheekbone.

As if hearing it for the first time, he considered the lyrics. Was it a love song or one filled with longing and loss? What man wouldn't care for such a woman? He stopped, realizing that he was investigating a masterpiece. The sparkle slid slowly down her cheek and fell—blossomed—on the sheet.

He had been so preoccupied with Aziz's tears that he

hadn't heard the phone ring. When he finally noticed, he waited for it to stop, but the ringing persisted. Reluctantly, apologetically, he leaned over for the receiver and responded to the front desk: "Oui, qu'est-ce qu'il y a?"

[6]

"**M**ACNEICE? IS THAT YOU?"

In a panic, his eyes opened wide. He scanned the bedroom, shocked to find himself in his stone cottage in Dundurn. His heart was pounding; he was alone at home.

"Mac...is this a bad time to call? You were speaking rather horrid French."

It was a woman's voice. Completely disoriented, he cleared his throat. "Yes. I'm here...What time is it?"

"Just gone nine-thirty." Realizing he was still confused, she added, "Mac, it's Mary. Do you want to call me back?"

Embarrassed, he bolted upright. "No, Mary, no. What can I do for you?"

"Well, I've received an interesting call from a Detective Sergeant Steiner—he's currently with a veterinarian."

"A veteran...?" In a flash, his stomach tightened at the thought of pursuing another burnt-out warrior. It had taken a month in Paris to get over the last one.

"A *veterinarian*." Mary Richardson, Dundurn's chief pathologist, was as smart as anyone he'd ever met—and she had a very short fuse. "Again, shall I call back?" Mary hated wasting time.

"I'm sorry; just a bit lagged...Got in late last night."

"I'm aware. I was just speaking to DI Aziz; she assured me you'd be up, because of course you're six hours ahead."

"Tell me about the vet."

"Right. Steiner says a dog was found on the side of the highway. Its injuries were minor, but there's a considerable amount of blood and matter on its coat that appears to be human. He's asked me to investigate." She paused to let that sink in. "The vet's name is Christopher Redsell."

From the ambient sounds of traffic, she was already on the move. "Where are you now, Mary?"

"I'll arrive at his clinic in twelve minutes; Highway 8 on the Dundurn side of St. Davids. While it's too soon to declare a homicide, Redsell's description of blood and matter—well, I just thought you should be there. Unless of course you'd rather delegate it."

That stung. Mary's clipped accent only made it worse. He cast the sheets aside. "I'll be right behind you."

EIGHTEEN MINUTES LATER, MacNeice was manoeuvring the heavy Chevy down the mountain road, dodging potholes where he could, easing through them where he couldn't. With this daily ritual, he often imagined himself a cowboy, riding his horse down a steep and uneven slope. He'd lean back in the saddle, at one with his mount. The horse would grunt; its hips would shift with the gait, and so would his. Not much had changed, just the mode and horsepower.

Rather than thinking about Aziz singing to him in a Parisian bed, he decided to check in with Steiner. Over the radiophone, he greeted the dispatcher. "Patch me through to Detective Sergeant Steiner."

Moments passed, then a click. "Steiner, sir."

"Tell me what you know so far, Gerry."

"We're waiting for Richardson's analysis — she just arrived. I've got two cruisers out on Highway 8 where the dog was found. They've found a dried-up puddle of blood and bloody tracks along the westbound south shoulder. We don't know how far they go, but they're tracking and already five clicks from where they started. Haven't been able to reach Dr. Evan Moore, the dog's owner. I've sent a uniform to his house over at Jordan Harbour."

"Good, very good."

"Vet says the dog coulda been running all night... might've covered forty miles — or more. No idea where he began, but it appears he was heading home."

"I'll meet them on the road. Call in a K9 team."

"Yes, sir."

Paris, the clubs, the walking and watching — it all evaporated. This, exactly this, was his reality. Dundurn Homicide's Detective Superintendent MacNeice had spent a month away — breathing, borrowing another city's air, someone else's night — only to return to the psychic stain of violence, the familiar and unforgiving ache in his spirit. He drove on in silence.

Rounding a bend, MacNeice spotted the high-top lights of a patrol car and behind it, a cruiser had pulled off to the side, the constable directing traffic. MacNeice opened his window.

"DS MacNeice," he said, as the officer leaned in.

"Yes, sir. Constable Jensen Kendrik."

"Tell me, how far have you come?"

"There's a trail eight miles or so behind us, sir. And it goes on from here." Kendrik pointed in the direction of Dundurn. "The blood fell in regular intervals, so if he stuck to the highway, the path won't be hard to follow."

"There'll be a K9 team here soon. Get as far as you can, as fast as you can, but stop if the trail goes off the road." MacNeice put the car in gear. "Understood?"

"Yessir." Kendrik tapped the roof and stepped back as MacNeice pulled away.

[7]

RICHARDSON STOOD OVER THE DOG, PICKING PALE SPECKS FROM its coat with stainless-steel tweezers. The animal was groggy but conscious; the vet's soothing voice kept him calm.

Steiner was so intimidated by Richardson that he whispered his update at the door, certain the pathologist wanted total silence. He leaned closer to MacNeice. "I feel like I'm in grade six again. You know what I mean?"

"I do."

"The dog's been a prince."

Aware that MacNeice had entered the room, Mary Richardson swung around. "Mac. Thank you for coming after that rude awakening. If either of you care, whispering is always more disturbing than talking."

"Sorry, ma'am," Steiner said.

Returning to her task, she responded, "Detective Sergeant, I'm Doctor Richardson, C.P. Richardson, or simply Doctor. I am not, nor have I ever been, *ma'am*." She made a sound like a bleating lamb.

"MacNeice, come, we've much to discuss." As she waited, her gloved hand rested gently on the dog's rump. "This gorgeous creature comes bearing horrific gifts. Dr. Redsell has identified—correctly—that much of the blood is human. In addition, there are these fascinating fragments. I'll confirm my thesis back in the lab, but do you care to take an educated guess at what part of the anatomy they recently called home?" She moved the large circular lamp closer to the dog and stood back.

MacNeice stepped forward and studied the blood-matted fur. "A lot of thick and congealed blood mixed with dust and small fragments of bone? Though the colours differ...some are creamy, others almost pale brown."

"Splendid, as always." Richardson smiled warmly. "Your observation skills survived Paris."

She placed the tip of the tweezers next to the first of three particles on a tray. "White is rib." The next was cream-coloured. "Cartilage." Finally, she pointed to the light brown one. "Sternum." Richardson set the tweezers down. "That's a guess, but there's a bucketload of knowledge before you." Redsell smiled, enjoying the show. "Those tan bits are the key—they're not from an arm or leg."

"What can we assume about the person these belonged to, Mary?"

"Well, of course, nestled behind the sternum and rib-cage is the engine room. So, I believe he—and it *is* a he—is dead." Somewhere outside the room, a horse whinnied. "Ah, that will be Dr. Redsell's herniated patient. "We must vacate shortly." Richardson took a plastic comb from its sterile solution. "I'll remove what remains of the particles and be gone before that creature breaks down your door."

As MacNeice and Steiner left the room, followed by Redsell, the vet asked Steiner, "Have you given any thought to our conversation?"

"Yeah, but I don't have a solution for you."

"What's the concern?" MacNeice asked. For a moment he wasn't certain who was going to answer — Steiner had a sudden interest in the floor tiles. But Redsell stepped forward and explained that the issue was Jack. He needed someone to agree to take him in and care for him.

Steiner shrugged. "Dr. Redsell doesn't have room, sir. And the men that brought him in can't take him."

"Detective MacNeice, dogs — animals generally — have well-developed instincts. They know whether you're going to harm them or care for them. Presumably, it's only for a short while, until his family is located."

Without thinking, MacNeice said, "I'll take him, if he'll take me."

Redsell nodded. "Perfect. I'll have him cleaned up and ready to go in an hour. We'll walk you through his wound care and what kind of food would be best for now." He shook MacNeice's hand, "Have you ever had a dog, Detective?"

"When I was a boy, my family did, but not since then."

MacNeice wondered if he was making a serious mistake — one that he, and more importantly Jack, would soon regret. He also wondered what would happen if Jack refused to leave with him. But he'd offered and that was that. "One small caveat, Doctor. I've got to head out to meet with the K9 unit following Jack's tracks back to where he was injured."

"Okay . . . well, in that case, Carole, our receptionist, will keep him at the front desk for what, three or four hours?"

"I think I can make that work." MacNeice had no idea if it would work. He was still thinking about the gore on Jack's coat and about what he'd find at the end of the trail. The thought made his stomach tighten.

[8]

"**WELCOME HOME, BOSS. ARE YOU IN TODAY?**" **DETECTIVE** Inspector Vertesi asked cheerfully.

"Not for a while. I'm following a trail of blood." MacNeice smiled; it sounded like a line from a western.

"Hard-core, yeah. That's why I'm calling. Duty sergeant took a call from Evan Moore's neighbour; she's his bridge partner. They were supposed to play this morning at the club in Jordan Harbour."

"Okay . . ."

"Moose put her through to Missing Persons, but following a hunch about what's happening out there, they let us know. Neighbour said there was no answer at home or on his cell."

"Steiner's got a uniform headed there. Give him her coordinates."

"Will do."

"She knocked on his door?"

"No answer. Moore's dog barks whenever the doorbell rings, but not this time."

"That's because he's a witness to a killing."

"Figured as much when Richardson called in for you."

"Before I go, is Aziz there?"

"Yessir. Hang on..."

Seconds passed... "Bonjour, Mac."

"Fiza. Your wound has healed?"

"Four days ago. I've been slathering vitamin E cream on it ever since."

"Can you join me on this one?"

"Certainly. I'm done rearranging the pads and pencils on my desk. Where are you?"

"Highway 8, approaching Vineland. You can't miss us, we're in the Niagara-bound lane. Hitch a ride with a patrol car; I'm about to do something radical."

"Working on another suspension?"

"No, just a time saver."

Jensen Kendrik's car was leading K9's wide-body pickup with its red and blue flashing lights. In the back, the dogs stood in their crates, sniffing the air, excited to get to work. Nestled next to them was a fat-tired ATV. The small convoy appeared to be averaging fifteen miles or so per hour. MacNeice flashed his lights before coming to a stop on the side of the highway; Kendrik left his vehicle and came on the run.

"Everything okay, sir?"

"Yes, fine. Working on the assumption that the dog never left the highway, I'll go two miles ahead and check. If there are tracks, I'll radio back and go another two miles, and then another. Understood?"

"So we can hopscotch forward."

"Exactly." MacNeice eased the Chevy off the gravel and sped away.

Unbeckoned, his thoughts returned to Fiza. They were to meet in Paris, and when she hadn't arrived, he'd called her. The gunshot wound to her lower back had been healing well, but shortly after MacNeice left, it had begun to open. Her surgeon suggested it might have been caused by lack of bedrest, excessive exercise, stress, or a combination of all three. As the web of torn flesh worked to heal, she had spent most of her suspension on bedrest, receiving daily wound care — rather than strolling the streets of the Left Bank with him.

Four miles on, MacNeice stopped again. Jogging across the road, he studied the gravel. As with the other stops, the blood was coated by a grey film of road dust, but this time the drops were larger. What struck him, though, was the distance between them: they were farther apart. Out of desperation or fear, Jack had been running faster.

Farther on, at Lincoln Avenue and Highway 8, MacNeice got out of the car and crossed the road again. He was hunched over the soft shoulder when a cruiser came to a stop nearby. Aziz stepped out. MacNeice glanced back; the little caravan was almost on them.

He wanted to greet her with Parisian kisses on her cheeks, but opted for a strong handshake. "You look well, Fiza."

"Thank you; I am." She understood the urgency. "What are we looking for?"

"Blood tracks. The dog was running, and I assume at some point he left the road. That's why the K9 unit's here."

Aziz nodded and began walking slowly forward. Bending over, she said, "There's some, Mac; here, look." She was like a kid finding a starfish on the beach.

He squatted above the droplets. "That's Jack...," he pointed ahead, "but he's slower here, pacing himself."

"Jack's the dog?"

"Yes. You'll meet him soon." He smiled. "You look wonderful, Fiza. I mean healthy—wonderful."

"Two uniforms approaching, sir." Her smile was wide, but brief.

MacNeice introduced Aziz to Kendrik and the K9 unit sergeant, Paul Ryu, who studied the bloody tracks they'd found. "Sir, we can take it from here," Kendrik said.

[9]

HIS CLIENT SAT BEHIND A BLACK GRANITE DESK THAT FELT COLD TO the touch, no matter the season. Clarence felt that the windowless "maximum modern" office suited him. Its panelled dark grey walls felt like suede to the touch. The floor was polished black marble. The art—three square paintings—left Blow feeling that the artist could have put in a little more effort. They were lit so that not a sliver of light spilled beyond the frames.

Two enormous club chairs were positioned at a slight angle facing the desk. Clarence hated them; they made him feel even smaller than he was. Like a child, he sank into them, feeling as if he was being swallowed. As often as he could, he sat on the cushion's edge. For now he stood and scanned a book he'd pulled from a shelf—*International Finance and Tax Law.*

"What do you know about my business, Clarence?" His client's chair was dark green leather and looked like it belonged in the hall of a mountain king.

"In what sense, sir?"

"Well, my brother tells me you've been naughty with Riviera's dip-'n'-strip. I have a pretty good idea what that means and don't need to know more. But you've worked with me for what, a decade as an accountant, and six months on this file. What do you know about what I do—that goes beyond the ledger sheet."

The client's glasses reflected the light from a desk lamp, making it difficult to see his eyes. He lifted a cigarette to his mouth, and for an instant, when he exhaled, his head was obscured by a smoky fog, until a silent ventilation system made it disappear.

"Sir, I'm paid to do your cleaning. I'm a very good cleaner, and you pay me well." Clarence shut the book and slid it back onto the shelf. "I don't need to know anything more."

"Very good. Yes, very good . . . an interesting analogy." He snuffed his cigarette in an alabaster ashtray and studied Clarence. "Except on this occasion, sticking with your analogy, I gave you one suit to clean and you cleaned two."

"Correct." Clarence sat down.

"After which you cleaned two more. Does that sum it up, Clarence?"

"It does. I cleaned four."

"Am I missing anything?"

"A dog, sir. You're missing the dog."

"A dog?"

"The one that got away."

"I see. Can we live with that?" He allowed a brief, wry smile.

"Yes, sir ... I don't think the dog will talk."

[10]

APPROACHING SECORD, MACNEICE REALIZED HE HADN'T EATEN ANY-thing. Glancing hopefully at Aziz, he asked, "Are you hungry?"

"Peckish, but please don't say takeout."

The radiophone interrupted them. "Ryu, sir. Tracks continue west along Highway 8. Over."

"Understood, Sergeant. I'll be away from the vehicle, so use my cell number."

"Roger that."

Knowing a call could come at any moment, MacNeice suggested, "I have Chris and Marcello's frozen lasagna. I could microwave it?"

"Splendid — a brunch."

For several miles, neither of them spoke. Aziz looked out

at the passing subdivisions, some dating back to the fifties, others so recent the trees on the lawns were still saplings. As they approached their turn, MacNeice's cellphone rang.

"Ryu, sir. The dog left Highway 8; we're near the top of Highway 20, still stickin' to the shoulder."

"How wide apart are the blood splatters?"

"How wide . . . ah, I see; to determine his speed."

"Exactly."

"Wider than on Highway 8, but he was running downhill. I'll get back to you soon."

MacNeice eased the Chevy into his lane to avoid the loud scrape of its chassis on bedrock. A month away hadn't diminished his muscle memory, timing, and visual recall for the position of each pothole.

Once inside the cottage, he left Aziz in the living room and set about preparing the lasagna. He put a tray together with sparkling water, cutlery, glasses, and napkins before suggesting they have lunch on the patio.

"Again, perfect," Aziz said. "I recall having wine out there among the trees . . . it was lovely." Looking out the large window, she appeared relaxed and worry-free. He recalled Kate standing in the same spot, also lost in thought.

Outside, they sat listening to the sounds of birds. Aziz peered into the trees while MacNeice studied her hands. They were elegant and so unlike those of a cop. Her slender fingers gave no suggestion of their strength. He'd seen men's eyes widen in surprise when shaking her hand—which, he assumed, was the desired effect.

Kate protected her hands, which were strong from decades of playing violin. When greeting a male stranger, she'd lay hers on his, like a leaf falling on pavement.

Sensing his gaze, Aziz grinned. "You've hooked me on birds, Mac." Turning back to the forest: "On bedrest, I was fixated by them. When I was able to, I'd sit by the window and wait; I learned patience." She wiped the corners of her lips with a napkin and pushed the empty dish away. "I learned that from you. Birds, not patience."

"I really don't know much about them; being a spotter's my real strength. Kate's dad was an excellent birder. We made a good pair, me spotting, him identifying." MacNeice laughed. "He thought I anthropomorphized birds, and all creatures, too much."

"I've noticed that."

"To be fair, at his home in Suffolk, he'd speak to the robins that came to his door for treats. A blackbird he called 'Button' would take currants from his hand." MacNeice gave a tender shrug at the memory. "I'll make coffee. Macchiato for you?"

"Please."

Aziz sat watching the sparrows and chickadees coming and going across the patio; they were curious to see what was happening, and what might be in it for them.

When MacNeice returned, they sat together watching a particularly bold chickadee land on the opposite edge of the table. It turned its head sideways as if attached to a tiny pendulum. "You can see why the birds call this home."

"I can," Aziz said. She inhaled the aroma of her espresso.

The air was getting heavy with what wasn't being said, and the view helped keep it that way. The trees climbed slowly up the escarpment there, producing a deceptive perspective. The trunks in the distance appeared to levitate, their summer canopies merging with those in the

foreground and those higher up the mountain—building
a lush green wall to the sky.

A century earlier, the grand mansion on the mountain's
brow had been destroyed by fire. The stone cottage, which
had served as its gatehouse, was isolated. And yet, the city
had kept the lane leading up to it more or less intact, out of
habit or history, no one seemed to know.

"Tell me about Paris."

"Ahh . . . where to begin?" An ant—little more than a
speck—appeared on the table. MacNeice watched it doodle
around, looking for something to take away. "You probably know this, but Paris light is very special, so unlike
Dundurn; the city often seems set in amber. I took long
walks along the Seine, rain or shine. I wandered about,
went to cafés, museums. And the music—not just jazz—
there were classical concerts every day and night. And
I made a new discovery: rich and delicious hot chocolate
offered in paper espresso cups. By the end, I was ordering
a double."

"Sounds divine." She let her head fall back, and her throat
presented her chin like a trophy. She turned slightly, aware
that he was watching her. "You mentioned a mission before
you left."

"I met with Chanel Bourget and her partner. It was very
emotional for Chanel—when she left Dundurn, she was
catatonic, and the French Consul General had to physically
support her." MacNeice finished his coffee. "No longer. She
was radiant. It was also very clear she wanted me to like her
partner—and I did."

"Did you retrieve Venganza's portfolio?"

"It's in the evidence vault."

More silence. This time it was interrupted by a call from Kendrik.

"Sir, we're on the Lincoln Alexander Parkway. Ryu's on the ATV with the dogs riding shotgun in the back. So far, no matter the road, that dog ran in a straight line. Ryu says it's unusual. Dogs like to stop and sniff, do their business, wander where their noses take them. Not this guy."

"I guess he had a job to do."

"Yessir—stay tuned."

MacNeice put the phone down, took a deep breath and exhaled, letting his shoulders sink into their cradles. "You were missed in Paris, Fiza." He cleared his throat to cover the fact that he hadn't intended to say anything. "I'm sorry. I don't know—"

"You don't have to say anything, Mac. It was the intensity of the last case. We were both exhausted."

They sat quietly for another fifteen minutes, but the atmosphere remained charged between them. Fortunately, the chickadees provided a distraction.

MacNeice's cell rang. "Kendrik again. Sir, we're a couple of miles from the end of the Parkway. No sign of a change in direction. Up ahead, though, it's all residential development, so Ryu will probably go cross-country."

"But isn't there a large conservation area beyond the housing?"

"Several, and a golf course."

"Somewhere, if a shotgun went off in the night, you might not hear it?"

"Possibly…"

MacNeice stood up, "We're on our way. Stay in touch, Jensen."

[11]

BEFORE LEAVING THE OFFICE, CLARENCE PIVOTED TO FACE THE client. "Sir, tell me . . . how did your brother know?"

"He's had trouble with that incinerator when it runs for a long time. In this case, you programmed it for four hours; it shut down in three. Most of what was there was ash, aside from four sets of jawbones and teeth."

"Good to know." Clarence nodded to falsely suggest he'd forgotten. "That's funny, and I thought I was just being thorough."

"Also good to know is that the monitor for the underground bunker holding the used soda revealed it had a full tank added over the weekend . . . that and he was down two buckets of soda." The client's pen was poised to resume writing. "Finally, while you left a detailed note about the water damage in the office, he found traces of blood in the tires of his model Ferrari, and more in the corner near the cabinet." He eyed Clarence. "Do be more thorough. My brother doesn't enjoy cleaning up after your cleaning. And choose your subcontractors more wisely."

Driving away, Clarence was seething. Nothing made him feel smaller than being dressed down by a man who projected confidence better than he did. On the other hand, he was extremely well paid, and as Peter and John would have collected fifteen thousand each, he'd saved his client thirty thousand dollars.

It was true that the night had turned sour. The old man and his dog had stepped out of the dark... They'd gone into the forest to kill and bury a man, and before they'd started digging, it was all *woof woof* and what's what. Who walks a dog in a forest in the middle of the night?

He laughed out loud. It had taken only a few seconds for Clarence to realize he had no choice — the old man had it coming, just like the guy they'd planned to bury there. As for Peter and John, in a splash-'n'-flash they'd gone from assets to ashes.

He knew he'd have to be much smarter about disposal. As an accountant, he'd never been asked to make bodies disappear, even though he had made income vanish with great finesse. Presumably that's why he'd been chosen for the client's special projects.

Clarence Blow — unlike Peter and John, who wouldn't have known a personal goal from a slapshot — had a goal. He also had a budget. And while he wasn't quite at quitting time, he was getting closer.

He'd done the research. He'd fly to Polynesia, find a peaceful island where people wouldn't ask questions. He'd be in paradise, and for once he'd be different for reasons other than his height — like being reasonably attractive and reasonably wealthy and reasonably skilled. Moreover, everyone needs an accountant.

Placing an asset, or a liability, where no one would ever find it required a particular skill set. When doing Riviera's books, Clarence had moved seven-figure sums out of the country to avoid tax. In addition, he needed to avoid the scrutiny of a company audit and questions about how an autobody shop with ten employees could generate such enormous revenues. To protect himself, Clarence never asked; he just simplified the numbers. Riviera's tax return wasn't challenged even when its net revenue was pegged at $43,207.17. After all, it was an autobody shop.

Arriving at his west-end bungalow, Blow was uneasy. Once inside, he turned on the lights and paused for a moment, listening. Other than the air conditioner's hum, it was quiet. He sighed. "You've got a problem, Clarence Blow...a serious problem."

He went to pour a glass of cranberry juice and briefly considered how difficult it might be to recruit Russians, Jamaicans, Asians, or skinheads. He assumed that they all moved in gangs with their own codes and they'd ask too many questions: *What do we need the runt for? We do the dirty work. We don't need a manager. We don't want anybody watching us — especially someone we don't know. We just need to meet the man that bankrolls the little guy. Then we'll just blow Blow away.* In short, it would end with an extremely hostile takeover.

Peter and John had been freelancers. Clarence had a nagging suspicion that neither had ever killed anyone. After all, how was he supposed to check their references? It didn't help that Peter's first shot had landed three feet wide of the actual target, winging the old man, or that his attempt to shoot the giant bird hadn't even been close, though it was clear it wasn't impressed by firepower.

He realized he hadn't hired killers, just movers for the heavy lifting, while he'd been left to do the actual killing. Before Clarence had entered that forest, he'd only killed one person. And though it had been messy to the max, he hadn't been there. An undetectable minor tweak to a gas line and the house exploded with such fury that he'd convinced himself it was painless.

It had been tax time and Clarence was working late; as he was leaving the office to go home the cops called to say he had no home to go to. It wasn't until late morning of the following day that his wife's remains were found — pretty much everywhere. Months later, Blow sued the gas company, which in turn sued the installing subcontractor.

The case was settled out of court. A bereaved Clarence Blow had retrieved the framed wedding photograph from his office and held it to his chest for the cameras, tearfully asking for privacy while he put the pieces of his shattered life back together. There were sideways glances among the reporters, surprised by his use of dramatic irony. He knew what they were thinking and kept his wide smile tucked away to enjoy later.

Four men in one night; the thought of it left him exhausted. His mind drifted freely from the past to the future. To slow it down, he kicked off his shoes and stretched out on the sofa, exhaling a long sigh. He peeled off his driving gloves and stared up at the fan circling slowly overhead. He couldn't escape the big problem — he was now on his own.

[12]

MACNEICE'S PHONE RANG. "SIR, RYU'S LEFT THE PARKWAY. THE dogs are out heading along Golf Links Road. I've called in another traffic unit to lead us through, 'cause we're heading into a residential neighbourhood."

"We'll be there soon," MacNeice said.

The radiophone burped. "Steiner, sir. Just got word from Jordan Harbour. Uniform said there was no answer at Evan Moore's. But Betty Woodworth, his neighbour and bridge partner, says Jack and Moore are inseparable and Moore is a highly disciplined creature of habit. She was worried enough about the silence to call it in to Missing Persons. The only thing she knew was that he'd been on a field trip."

"Field trip?"

"Yes, sir. Apparently he's a birder. I thought that meant he hunts birds. She said that was true, but only with a camera. Every year he heads off to Point Pelee during migration."

"But that's not in August..."

"She said that too. He's got a network of fellow birders who spot this bird or that, and off he goes to see them. She made it clear that Evans never failed to call if he couldn't make it to bridge."

"Any family?"

"He's a widower. He has a marine biologist son, David Moore. He's in New Zealand studying—let me get this right—the impact of acidification on coral communities."

"Reachable?"

"Yes, sir. She corresponds with him—he checks up on his dad by talking to Betty. We have his cell number and email address."

"Did Woodworth notice anything unusual around Moore's house in the last few days? People or vehicles she's never seen before? Did she give us a description of Moore's vehicle?"

"Nothing unusual. It's a quiet neighbourhood, so she would have noticed. He drives a blue Subaru Forester, maybe eight or nine years old."

When the call ended, Aziz shook her head. "A birder. What are the chances?"

"A birder with a dog...how does that even work?" MacNeice remembered seeing duck hunters up north cruising by in shallow aluminum camo boats, dogs standing in the bows like figureheads on man-of-wars.

"Penny for your thoughts?" She turned in her seat and leaned against the door.

"Oh...just that we started following this trail where it ended, and now we're speeding toward the beginning. And considering Jack's wounds and loss of blood, his hours-long journey was Homeric." He took a deep breath and looked her way.

His cellphone rang again. "Kendrik, sir."

"Go ahead."

"We're almost at the dead end on Golf Links Road. Wilson Street and Jerseyville Road are on the other side of an island of houses to the right. Ryu thinks the dog probably stuck to the main roads. He's over there now."

"We're about five hundred yards behind you."

"Welcome back to the parade, sir. Ryu cut through some yards; just texted — *Got tracks on Jerseyville.* Follow my right turn, sir. Over."

Aziz shook her head. "I like your reference to Homer. It's difficult not to see this as an odyssey when you consider the distance."

"The distance — wounded and bleeding — and we're still not where he began." MacNeice checked the time on the dash: 2:34 p.m. He took out Redsell's card. "Fiza, can you dial this number and put it on speaker for me?"

She set the phone down as it rang. "Redsell Veterinary, can I help you?"

"Carole?"

"Yes, who's calling?"

"Detective Superintendent MacNeice, I'm —"

"Oh, I know, sir. Jack's asleep beside me."

"Well, you see, we're still following his tracks. And right now we're out by Ancaster, still not at the beginning of the trail."

"Oh my . . . the poor thing, eh? He musta been so frightened to run that far."

"It's hard to imagine. So—"

"I know, you're calling to say you'll be late."

"Yes..."

"No problem, dear, you just come when you can—long as you're here before six-thirty."

[13]

AHUNDRED YARDS SHY OF THE PADDY GREENE INTERSECTION, THE blood tracks left the highway and veered into a corn-field. Ryu was on the road squatting next to his dogs, while Kendrik and a traffic cop peered like tourists down rows of corn taller than they were.

The dogs strained at their leads; Ryu nodded toward the field. "Your dog came through there, sir."

"You think the trail takes us to that forest on the other side?"

"I do." He pointed to the intersection. "Power Line Road's at the end of Paddy Greene. According to the map, there's a trail entrance to the forest north on Power Line. Once the dogs have taken off, we can follow them on the tablet."

"On your command, Sergeant."

Ryu unsnapped the leads; the dogs leapt over the ditch and disappeared into a row. The sergeant leaned against his vehicle, watching the tablet as two red dots moved upwards on a bright beige field. The top of the screen was dark green.

As the dots raced through the corn, the screen adjusted; the beige field kept shrinking until the screen was entirely green. "They're in the forest, sir. I think it's time we hit that trail."

For a minute or two, Ryu, MacNeice, and Aziz watched the tablet in silence, until Ryu pointed to two stationary dots. "The boys have stopped. Now they'll wait."

"Meaning they've found something?" Aziz asked.

"The starting point of the trail."

When they'd relocated to the trail's entrance off Power Line, MacNeice studied the ground around them for tire tracks or foot or paw prints. There was no shortage of them, but all had been made when the ground was wet. Now it was bone-dry. "It hasn't rained in a while?"

"No, sir. Hot and dry for a few weeks."

"Right." He looked down the path. "Aziz will accompany me. Ryu will take us to the dogs—put your boot baggies on." He looked over at the traffic cop's name tag. "Constable Hernandez—thanks for running interference. You and Hendrik remain here and restrict access."

Entering the forest, they stayed off the path, stepping over branches and around small shrubs to avoid disturbing any fresh prints. Following the dots on the screen, Ryu said, "At the fork ahead, we go left." He added that the dogs hadn't moved but would soon pick up his scent.

As soon as Ryu turned onto the left fork, both dogs began calling. They were somewhere ahead.

"Does this trail have another exit?" MacNeice asked, ducking under a branch.

Ryu stopped to manoeuvre the map. "There's another entrance a few hundred yards or so beyond the one we took...and another that comes out near the community centre. It's called the Headwaters Trail and it wanders all through the forest." He returned to the position locator and added, "The boys are about ninety yards in front of us—it's just too dense to see them."

"That program you're using, has it recorded the entire route Jack took?" MacNeice didn't want to lose the entirety of what the dog had accomplished, in part because he was so impressed by it.

"From where I picked up—yes, sir. I'll provide it on a USB when we're done. Right now, we're off to the left of the path your dog took. He missed this trail altogether when he was shot and likely just bolted."

"Back on the road, could you estimate how fast he was running?"

"Not precisely, no. But just as you said, the distance between the blood drops got greater the closer we came to this place. I understand he's a Lab-whippet mix—so he probably lit out of here doing twenty-five, thirty miles an hour." Ryu stepped over a fallen tree. "Scared as hell...or just pissed off."

Somewhere in the canopy above came a rapid, high-pitched call, a sustained cackle. MacNeice stopped in his tracks and listened. Aziz, who was several yards ahead of him, turned back, "A blue jay?"

"A hawk—just letting us know that it knows we're here."

"A welcome greeting..."

"Likely not, but keep in mind Moore is a birdwatcher."

Hoarse barking replaced the bird call, followed by clear-throated yapping. "First one's Benny, the other one's Poirot—they want their treats." Ryu closed the tablet and followed the sound. "Not far, thirty yards or so."

With still no sight of the dogs, Aziz and Ryu focused on the ground, trying to avoid the rocks and stumps and clotted vegetation that might trip them up.

When they'd covered what they thought was half the distance to the dogs, MacNeice heard a low, muffled *phu-wumph...phu-wumph...phu-wumph* and looked up as a hawk flew over his head and arced swiftly toward Aziz, talons splayed.

"Aziz, duck!" he screamed.

She did better than that. Startled, she turned around, tripped, and fell. As she was falling, an immense shadow crossed her face. "Bloody hell!"

The hawk sliced the air, dodging trees and branches, before landing on a high limb, where it stopped to study them. Ryu laughed nervously. "Jesus—it was going for your head, like a frickin' gunship from *Star Wars*." He helped her to her feet. "Tip to tip, those wings musta been four feet across."

MacNeice focused on the bird as it nonchalantly began grooming the small feathers on its chest. "Too big for a Cooper's hawk...and way too aggressive."

"What the hell is it, and why'd it attack me?" Aziz was truly frightened. "I mean, I love birds."

"That's a raptor...a bird that rips apart the birds you love, Fiza. See all that fine grey banding on its chest? I'm pretty sure that's a northern goshawk—isn't it gorgeous?"

"Sorry, I'm just not ready for admiration."

"It would have planned that attack twenty or thirty yards away. They're so fast, it could get to you and disappear before you blinked. I think it's a female, just warning us…"

Instinctively, Ryu and Aziz crouched as they walked. MacNeice smiled at the absurdity of their posture but completely understood the reaction. He watched the hawk for a moment as it lifted its grey head, peered down at him, and returned to grooming—all as if nothing had happened. Under his breath, he said, "You've made your point."

It was his first sighting of a goshawk in Canada, and only the second time he'd ever seen one. The first had been in Suffolk. Long after that he had read a book by a woman whose father, and subsequently she, had raised and trained goshawks. That had interested him, because the woman was doing it as a way of dealing with the loss of her father. After reading it, he'd wondered—only for a moment—if that could help him recover from the loss of Kate. It was a romantic but absolutely impossible idea. He was too attached to the sparrows, songbirds, field mice, and rabbits that surrounded his cottage to invite a raptor into the mix.

Ryu approached the dogs—their paws dancing happily—sweeping his gaze over the area. "Good job. Good job." He gave them their treats—gristly sticks of dried meat—which they devoured enthusiastically.

MacNeice and Aziz scanned the area, trying to spot a body—or body parts. At first the afternoon sun raked the trees and covered the ground in bright dappled light that made the shadows appear darker. As their eyes adjusted, they could see the individual roughed-up dead leaves of the forest floor. MacNeice took a fallen twig and pierced a leaf that looked darker than the rest; as if he were checking a roasted marshmallow, he brought it closer.

The leaf was lacquered in blood. He held the stick out to Aziz, but she was already pointing to a large patch of blood-soaked leaves.

"Do you have a flashlight, Sergeant?"

"Yes, sir." Ryu handed it to MacNeice.

The clearing was small, which made the blinding effect of sunlight more dramatic. However, using the flashlight as a second sun, MacNeice reduced the shadows. What hadn't soaked into the muddle of ground cover lay in dried pools on dead leaves. Some were scuffed up—likely from a struggle, maybe the violent thrashing of a victim.

Ryu walked to the far side of the patch and crouched. "Sweet Jesus." He jumped up. "There's more than one, sir; lotsa blood over here." He pointed to another patch of leaves off to the side. "And a partial shoe print..."

MacNeice stepped around the bloodied ground cover to study the trunk of a paper birch. He found a cluster of small holes, too low and too identical for a woodpecker. More telling, though, each had stained the trunk's white satin paper with blood. He continued over to where Ryu was and found a second blast cluster, which had shredded the bark of a young maple.

"Shotgun. Two blasts. Two victims." Picking at one of the holes in the trunk, he retrieved a pellet. Rolling it in his hand, he couldn't tell the gauge. Forensics could.

"Another print here as well, Mac." Aziz was at the edge of the clearing. "Looks like they came and left through here..."

"The bodies appear to have been dragged out in bags or tarpaulins," Ryu said. "See the way the leaves have been ploughed heading back along this path? It's so worn in the middle you can't make it out, but you can over here."

MacNeice wondered why anyone would enter a forest at night, kill two people, then remove the bodies. "Let's spiral out from here. Perhaps they're buried nearby." While that didn't make any sense, he couldn't ignore the possibility. "Careful as we go; don't mess up any evidence. Look for pieces of clothing, roughed-up ground, heel marks where bodies were dragged, cigarette butts—anything that didn't grow in the forest."

"How wide a circle, sir?" Ryu was already moving.

"Fifty yards in diameter from this spot."

As he made his way deeper into the forest, MacNeice heard the goshawk's call. It sounded insistent, but whether it was a distress cry or just calling its mate, he didn't know. As long as it kept calling from a distance...

The dry vegetation crackled underfoot, releasing a musty but not unpleasant odour. It took him back to hot summers on Georgian Bay, where it had been so parched that the star moss was as crispy as the lichen clinging to rocks.

Something rustled in the nearby ground cover. "Keep your head down, friend, for your sake and mine."

"You say something, sir?"

"Just talking to myself, Sergeant."

Paris had drifted away overnight, like sun dots on water—here, then gone—lost altogether. The more he walked, the more he was convinced they wouldn't find the bodies there. Something about that bloody clearing suggested a botched execution, and the reaction was to remove the bodies and get out fast. But why? Even without Jack's trail back to this place, to anyone who might wander by, the evidence would suggest something awful must have happened.

He was about to turn around when he noticed a huge maple; its trunk had to be five feet wide. Stepping closer to admire it, he looked up at the great circular spread of its canopy. Beyond it, a white pine stood even taller, a hundred feet above the forest floor. Through its branches, he caught a glimpse of a large clot of twigs and leaves: the hawk's nest.

MacNeice froze and cast a cautious eye around the forest. Other than the hollow sound of a woodpecker working a dead tree, it was uncomfortably quiet.

He moved closer to the maple, thinking that a diving goshawk would have to negotiate a hard turn to avoid slamming into the trunk. That's when he saw camouflage netting draped over a large shrub hidden behind the tree.

MacNeice lifted the netting and stepped inside to find a small folding table and a chair. On the table was a Thermos, logbook, file folder, and pen, a narrow box of pencil crayons, night-vision goggles, field binoculars, and a 35mm Canon with a telephoto lens. MacNeice slipped on his latex gloves and opened the folder. He scrolled through dozens of photos printed twelve to a page: goshawk in flight; with its partner; nesting alone; feeding the nestlings through to adolescence . . . and quite a few of a happy Jack.

On the ground beside the table was a metal bowl of water and, beside it, a small plastic cooler. Positioned at the edge of the netting was a tripod. Its head mount was tilted almost vertically, waiting for the camera. He opened the logbook where a maple leaf served as a bookmark. It was gridded with dates, times, locations, and a wider section of comments followed by initials. Judging by the entries, there appeared to be two observers—E.M. and C.G.—working in eight-hour shifts. Six a.m. to two p.m. and eight p.m. to four a.m. E.M.'s final entry, at 2:45 a.m., read: *Last adolescent, hasn't returned—assume it won't. Female staying in or nearby nest...male not seen this shift.* On the left-hand page, there were pencil crayon sketches of the female: detailed drawings and notes about her colouring, the shape of her tail, the dark cap and white stripe on her head.

Though the drawings were naive, they'd been rendered with intelligence and care. They bore no resemblance to Venganza's park sketches from his last case, other than the recording of details—*because it was important to do so.*

He flipped back a few pages to C.G.'s entries, where the sketches were more refined and similarly annotated. C.G.'s last entry that day was: *At end of shift, only one adolescent returned to nest. Assume other two gone for good.*

MacNeice turned to the first page; the names Colin Gleadow and Evan Moore were printed in capital letters, followed by their telephone numbers. He punched Gleadow's into his phone but didn't press Call.

Inside the cooler was an empty plastic container of soup, a sandwich still neatly wrapped in wax paper, and zip-lock bags of kibble and dog treats. Moore's Thermos of tea was still warm.

He checked his watch, to determine when he needed to leave and collect Jack. Would the vet have a leash? He looked around the blind for a leash, and, seeing none, assumed Moore might have left it in the car. He took out his cell and called Kendrik.

"Yes, sir."

"Circle the forest; I think you'll find an older-model blue

Subaru Forester near the community centre. See if you can get it open. I'm looking for a dog leash and anything else of interest. Use your gloves, Jensen."

"For clarification, a B&E?"

"Enter without breaking, please."

"Understood."

MacNeice stepped out of the netting and gazed at the empty nest. He scanned the surrounding trees but saw no sign of the goshawk. Nor were there any calls to be heard, save for chickadees chattering from a sumac thicket in a shallow gully nearby.

Aziz was walking slowing through the forest. Between her posture and the nervous attention she was giving the tree canopy, it was clear her search of the ground had been compromised. As she approached, she appeared relieved to see MacNeice standing upright and smiling.

"Okay, yes. I don't want to be assaulted by an angry bird." She noticed the camouflage netting. "What have you got here?"

"Dr. Evan Moore's observation blind; his partner is Colin Gleadow. They worked in eight-hour shifts. Gleadow should have been here this morning." MacNeice looked up to the nest as his thoughts wandered.

"What do you make of it, Mac? Could he be a suspect?"

"No . . . if he was involved, he wouldn't have left this diary." He shrugged. "I think Dr. Moore and Jack walked into an unfolding crime scene."

"And the other victim?"

"Was the intended execution . . . It was late; they wouldn't have expected a birder."

"It would've been traumatic for the goshawk; maybe

that's why she attacked..." Aziz said, scanning the higher branches.

"It's possible. Moore's final posting suggests the adolescents may have left for good." He went over to examine a large clump of feathers under the white pine. In it were the remains of a cardinal's wing, plus the skull of a starling. Smaller grey feathers were everywhere, as if someone had shaken a torn pillow.

Aziz looked down in amazement. "Savage beasts, aren't they?"

"Incredibly efficient — a family of five to feed... She wasn't the savage in this forest last night." MacNeice stepped away, avoiding the open grave of feathers.

Aziz fell in behind. "I didn't see anything unusual on my walkabout. Nothing disturbed and, judging by what was left here, the killers didn't do a walkabout either."

Ryu was waiting for them. "You've found something?" MacNeice said.

"Yessir. I'll call him Victim One. He was bleeding before he reached that clearing — not badly. It mighta been a nosebleed. But there was enough that Benny and Poirot could track it back to the entrance." The dogs were nuzzling his legs for a treat. "We just came back to track Victim Two, but he didn't enter the forest with the others."

"No — his name is Dr. Evan Moore, a birdwatcher with a blind near that goshawk's nest. His gear is there, including a logbook."

"Your dog's human?" Ryu said, shaking his head.

"Had Moore stayed in the blind, he'd likely be here today."

MacNeice's cellphone rang. "Subaru's in the community

centre lot. Leash was inside. Nothing unusual. A blanket on the passenger seat; I guess Jack rode shotgun. Other than that, a change purse full of coins, some gardening tools in the trunk, a shovel, a bag of dog cookies, and a box of poop bags—" Kendrik stopped short. "Sir, we've got sirens heading our way. I'll get out there and direct traffic."

[14]

LEAVING AZIZ AT THE SCENE, MACNEICE EASED THE CHEVY PAST FIVE emergency vehicles already parked along Powerline. He was on his way to pick up Jack. At Jerseyville, he took the first deep breath he'd taken since they entered the forest.

How was Paris, Mac?

"Ah, it's you." He sighed and checked his rear-view mirror for no particular reason; "I followed shadows, Kate, just as I once followed yours."

Romantic shadows?

"No . . . just shadow-tracking to fill a void." MacNeice was cruising in the slow lane, mostly to let the day turn over in his head. "I was there to decompress, and I did."

Thought so, when you didn't reach out for me.

"Hmm. I met a man at the hotel's jazz bar; he was French

but spoke English fairly well. His wife didn't like jazz; she'd gone to bed. When the first set was over, I asked him where he was from and what he did. He said he'd just retired as chief of Homicide for a region in the southwest. They'd come to Paris to celebrate his retraite. Then he asked the same question of me."

Like soulmates . . . Just kidding.

"But you're right; we were both on our second Calvados when I told him. He immediately took my hand and gave it a solemn shake. Then I asked how many homicides he had to deal with in a year."

Just to compare notes — you weren't competing?

"No, just curious. He answered that in thirty-five years as regional head of Homicide, there had never been a homicide, not one."

My word . . . it must have been hard to justify that title. And did you share your numbers?

"I told him that Dundurn averages ten to fifteen homicides a year . . . He asked me how long I've been on that job. Twenty-nine years, I said. I could see him doing the math — counting bodies — after which he shook his head and under his breath said, 'Merde.'"

Was it a merde *of pity or envy?*

"Hard to say exactly. His eyebrows jumped around for a while, and after that, his toasts went from *santé* to *courage*."

MacNeice's cell rang. He pulled over to check the call display — DC Wallace. They hadn't spoken since his suspension. "Yes, sir?"

A long pause followed before Wallace spoke. "I see you're back at work, Mac. I have you down as returning tomorrow."

"An unusual case, sir. I'm on my way to pick up a material witness."

"Who's that?" Wallace bristled.

"His name's Jack." MacNeice was too tired to explain further.

"Got it. A call came in from Singapore; it was transferred here. Gloria took the number, said someone in DPD would call back."

"Last name Moore?"

"How'd you know?"

"A neighbour of Dr. Evan Moore told us; he's one of the victims. She said his son was working in New Zealand."

"David Moore." Wallace read out the phone number before asking, "You're going to deliver the bad news...?"

"Very bad. We haven't located the remains, but he probably bled out in a forest. The other body's missing too, no ID."

"Keep me posted. If you need more resources, just ask." He was about to hang up, then added, "I've approved another six months of your Sumner sessions." Wallace didn't wait for either a thank-you or a goodbye.

MacNeice placed a call to Colin Gleadow. In spite of what he'd said to Aziz, if he had even a scintilla of doubt about whether Gleadow was involved, MacNeice would have him picked up immediately. The phone rang several times before it was answered. "Who's calling?" The voice was weak and raspy.

"Detective Superintendent MacNeice, Dundurn Homicide. Is this Colin Gleadow?"

"I don't follow... Sorry, yes, I am."

"I believe you share an observation blind with Dr. Evan Moore?"

"Yes..." Followed by a deep, rolling cough.

"You're laid low, Mr. Gleadow?"

"Bronchitis, maybe pneumonia. Why are you calling? What's happened?"

"We believe Dr. Moore came to harm last night in the forest."

Gleadow struggled to suppress another cough. "But you're from Homicide... What are you actually saying?"

"There appear to be two victims, but we haven't located their remains. Dr. Moore's dog was wounded but escaped— his coat had traces of human blood. The incident took place roughly eighty or ninety yards from your blind. Moore's notes were updated; his last entry was in the middle of the night."

"No, this isn't true—it can't be." From the sounds of it, Gleadow was struggling to get up. "I'm coming. I'll be there—"

"Don't do that. The site is closed for our investigation. Police will collect everything from the blind; you've no need to be concerned about it."

Gleadow broke into a deep, ragged cough and dropped the receiver. When he picked it up, he was breathless. "Evan... can't be gone. He can't... What can I do, Detective?"

"For the moment I only have one question. After that, you can rest. Did Dr. Moore have concerns for his safety... or was there anyone that might have wanted to harm him?"

It took several seconds for Gleadow to answer, and when he did, his voice was clear. "Ev was loved—I mean, *loved*. He was my mentor... and not just mine." He gasped for air that wasn't there. "No... biologists don't attract vendettas." He couldn't keep his congestion or tears at bay any longer. He whispered, "I'm sorry..." before hanging up.

"TALK TO HIM. Softly or firmly—but keep talking to him." Carole had embraced the task of getting Jack ready. "In that bag, you've got an advanced starter kit. Kibble, treats, poop bags, a leash, antibiotics, ointment and bandages for the wound—basically, the works. Oh, and there's a squeaky toy too... though he may not play with it at first."

MacNeice was watching the dog watching him. He wondered if Jack could smell where he'd been. Turning back to Carole, he asked, "Where will he sleep?"

"Hard to say. You can fold up a blanket, keep it in the corner of your bedroom. He might sleep on that, or your sofa—or on your bed if you let him."

"I assume he'll be upset—I mean, mourning." He turned to Redsell, who'd just dropped a report on Carole's desk. "Do I try to comfort him?"

"He's not human, but in that respect, he might as well be. The answer is, do what you would with a human friend. Jack will let you know whether he wants more of whatever that is. Trust me, he's probably already figured you out."

[15]

THE CLANKING OF THE DOOR KNOCKER WOKE CLARENCE FROM a deep sleep. Four insistent clanks followed before he went to open a sliver of curtain. Once he saw the dark blue Mercedes idling nearby, he knew.

He took several deep breaths, slapped his cheeks a few times, and opened the door. "Hello, Father, I wasn't expecting you..."

Eugene Bernard Blow gave him a quick once-over. "Did I catch you at a bad time?"

"No, Father. I was just lying down after a long day."

The old man looked at him disapprovingly. He was smart enough not to ask about Clarence's day, having developed a robust distrust of anything his son said. "Your mother

thinks a family dinner is in order, next Friday. It's our fiftieth anniversary."

"Oh, a half-century. Impressive." Clarence's voice lacked
any hint of sincerity.

His father's smile — an empty Hallmark card — dissolved
in a flash. "Shall I mark you down as one guest or two?"

"Maybe just me."

"Right. Well, until Friday, then. Goodbye." His father
turned and walked briskly down the steps.

Clarence shut the door and smiled. He knew his father
hated ambiguity, perhaps because Clarence used it as a
weapon. Though certain that he was superior to Eugene
Blow, Clarence knew that as long as he drew breath, he'd
never measure up to his father's greatness. It was too bad,
Clarence thought, that he'd already used his free pass with
gas explosions.

Before heading to the shower, he grinned at the brown-
skinned woman emerging from frothy surf on the "Beaches
of Polynesia" poster. He read the advertising slogan yet
again, convinced it was a solemn promise: "Picture yourself under a blue azure sky, frolicking in a warm turquoise
sea."

"I am, I am. Soon . . . maybe two more disposals."
Clarence stripped and, walking tall into the shower, he set
out to sing "Some Enchanted Evening" in its entirety.

Covered in soap, he belted out the song's lyrics. Over the
shower and the show tune, Clarence heard his cellphone
ring. He swore, stepped out, stamped his feet on the mat,
and ran to the bedroom. "Yes, sir?"

"Mr. Blow, it took some time for you to answer . . ."

"Sorry, sir, I was in the shower. How can I help?" Clarence said, wiping the soap from his face.

"You've been quiet, Clarence."

"The day, sir. Just for a day."

"A day can be an eternity, Mr. Blow. As an accountant, you know that."

"I do. Do you have a disposal?"

"If I said yes, would you have the means?"

"Well, I—"

"No. I thought not."

"But I can—"

"No, I don't believe you *can*. That's the point of this call. We need secure practices, men we can trust with our disposals—men of absolute discretion. You'd be a fool and a very poor accountant not to realize that disposing of your disposal team is inefficient."

"I do understand—"

"Two replacements arrive early this evening. They have all the qualities I've mentioned. You'll meet them at seven p.m. in the McDonald's parking lot at Main and Dundurn. They'll be driving a black Lincoln Navigator, license plate LRV-6."

"LRV, Luxury Rental Vehicles—your brother's company."

"Exactly. But don't get too attached to that plate; it'll change soon."

"And the disposal?"

"The following day."

"Would you like to meet the men?"

"If I wanted to meet them, why would I need you?"

"Clearly. I'll be there at seven."

"Before you go, Clarence . . . you'd be wise to dispel any

lingering thoughts of dealing with these men as you dealt with the others. Were you to try, you just might find yourself in the dip-'n'-strip."

Clarence felt his face flush. He was a little boy again, being scolded for his bedwetting. Except now he was the little man being mocked for hiring incompetent thugs.

That self-pitying funk didn't last long. Within minutes he returned to his life-saving mantra: one more disposal — maybe two.

[16]

AS MACNEICE CAME TO A STOP NEAR THE FOREST TRAIL, JACK cowered in the back seat, shivering from cone to tail. Power Line Road was awash in cop cars and forensic vans. Before he had time to shut the engine down, he saw Aziz and Vertesi approaching. The truth was, MacNeice didn't have the stamina to go back to the sad and bloody little clearing. Worse, Jack was now whimpering so pitifully that he realized it had been a mistake to bring him. He left the engine running and rolled down the window.

"Good to see you, boss." Vertesi noticed the dog in the back seat. "See you've picked up a stray . . . he looks scared."

Aziz bent down and peered inside. "Jack was there—he has reason to be shaken." She looked at MacNeice and realized he had no intention of getting out. "Mac, you're done. Go home."

"Yeah," Vertesi said. "This place is bluer than a cop convention. They're going through at arm's-length. So far, no bodies." He added, "One of the uniforms took a hit on the back of the head from a bird; Fiza said it was a gosh hawk."

A flicker of a smile crossed Aziz's face. "Goshawk; one word."

"So now we got cops looking up as much as down."

"Steel pellets, Mac. Twelve-gauge," Aziz said. "Forensics confirmed two victims, said if they were chest shots at a range of ten to fifteen feet, they'd be fatal."

MacNeice shook his head. "And the nearby houses? Anyone hear or see anything?"

Vertesi glanced at his notes. "According to Christine and Brad Wingate in the first house, they thought the noise was a bird banger the corn farmer installed to protect his crops."

"In the middle of the night?"

"Apparently he hasn't worked the bugs out." Vertesi shrugged. "But they gave us their security camera footage — we've got a van passing by at 2:39 a.m. and leaving at 3:08 a.m. It's blurry; maybe Ryan can sharpen it."

"That's promising... Okay, Jack's had enough. We'll take the scenic route home."

He checked the rear-view at Jerseyville; the dog was in the middle of the back seat looking at him. The evening sun streamed through the rear window, turning the cone into a halo and Jack's eyes to dark pools. When MacNeice turned left, the light shifted, and Jack was just a dog with a bandaged leg and a wounded heart.

[17]

MACNEICE HAD BEEN AWAKE FOR AN HOUR WHEN THE CLOCK RADIO came to life. Jack was curled up on the carpet at the end of the bed. His chest rose and fell, and only his nose poked out of the cone.

When MacNeice came out of the shower, Jack wasn't in the bedroom. He listened for a moment and heard him lapping up water, his collar tag *ting-a-ling*ing against the edge of the bowl. MacNeice went to him and removed the cone; he wouldn't put it on again unless Jack disturbed the wound.

An hour later, Jack's tail was up for the first time. MacNeice lifted him onto the Chevy's front passenger seat, where he sat erect and ready to go. MacNeice tossed the bag containing kibble, bowls, treats, and the cone into the back seat. He descended the hill carefully and smiled as Jack leaned into the turns. Driving west along King, MacNeice noticed him looking straight ahead, not once glancing to see the dogs they passed along the way.

When MacNeice pulled over to punch in a call, Jack seemed momentarily curious. Dr. Sumner's voicemail recording listed several options, the last of which was "Finally, if you are experiencing extreme anxiety, a psychotic episode, or suicidal thoughts, please call 911 immediately — and don't forget your health card." A pause followed before the beep.

"Dr. Sumner, it's DS MacNeice... I'm back in town and would appreciate an appointment... Please leave me a message." When MacNeice hung up, Jack looked his way again, then turned back to the road like he understood.

"We're all wandering knights, Jack, looking for something to fight for and something to fight against." He rubbed the dog's shoulders. "Jaan Kaplinski, a poet, said that..." His cellphone rang; he didn't recognize the area code. "MacNeice."

A voice broke through the static. "Detective MacNeice. I've been given your number; my name is David Moore. I believe you've information concerning my father, Dr. Evan Moore?"

"Where are you calling from?"

"Singapore. I'm currently at a conference but leaving for New Zealand tomorrow — what's happened?"

"I can tell you what we know. You're aware of your father's birdwatching activity?"

"Yes, of course. But this sounds ominous..."

"I'm afraid it is. We haven't found your father, but we do have Jack. Jack's leg was injured, likely by shrapnel — but more than that, there was a considerable amount of human blood on his coat."

It sounded as if the oxygen had left David Moore. For several seconds the phone connection was swallowed by static. When he finally responded, his voice was clearer. "I don't understand. Are you saying my father is dead, but you haven't found his body?" Before MacNeice could answer, Moore continued, more urgently, "Are you sure the blood was his? How can you be certain?"

"We know two men were shot at close range. We know your father had just made an entry in his field notes corroborating the date and time. Nothing in the blind was disturbed; it was as if he'd just stepped away." He could hear Moore breathing again. "His Subaru was found where he'd left it, and he missed a bridge game, which his partner said never happens..."

"But there could be another explanation."

"I wish I could be more hopeful. If you said your father didn't have a strong bond with Jack..."

He heard a series of muted sobs, and seconds later Moore said, "They were inseparable."

"The evidence is that Jack ran all night, to Vineland, where he collapsed."

"Going home..."

"We think so." MacNeice waited a moment before adding, "We're speculating that someone else was led into the forest to be executed, and your father interrupted them — the scene isn't that far from his blind."

"Northern goshawks..." Moore offered wistfully. "But wait, isn't it possible he's in a hospital? He could—?" Realizing how unlikely that was, he ran out of steam and fell silent.

"Are you coming home, Dr. Moore?"

Moore didn't answer right away, and when he did, his decision surprised MacNeice. "This morning I secured further funding for our project, and I'm due back on site in two days...It takes two days to get there...What can I do if I come back? He's gone. You don't have his body; what would I do there?"

"Well, your blood work can positively identify if the blood found on Jack belonged to your father or rule that out."

"But I can *send* that to you. I'll do it here and send it off in a blood-bank cooler. It'll be there tomorrow."

"Very good. Yes, do that." MacNeice was relieved to hear Moore's suggestion. "And there's Jack. Are there any family members who might take him?"

Static again... "Not nearby. Where is he now? Can he stay there?"

"He's sitting next to me, on my way to work." MacNeice added, "I've agreed to take him for as long as necessary."

"Dad's brother, Bill, is out in BC. He and his wife are retired; I'll ask if they can take him."

"Thank you."

"Look...I'm sorry if not rushing home sounds callous. I just know I'm needed here—I mean, in New Zealand—and there's nothing constructive that I can accomplish in Dundurn...I hope you understand."

"We don't know each other, Mr. Moore—"

"Please call me David."

"David—don't concern yourself with what I think. Apart from that blood sample and calling your uncle, you're right that there's nothing you can do."

After the call, MacNeice smiled. "Well, you're a lucky

boy; it's take-your-dog-to-work day." He rubbed Jack's ear; the dog closed his eyes and leaned into MacNeice's fingers. "You'll be fine . . . we'll be okay."

WALKING THROUGH THE City Hall lobby toward the deputy chief's office, MacNeice and Jack drew stares, but no one stepped forward to stop them.

When MacNeice arrived at Wallace's door, the receptionist, Gloria, greeted him warmly. Looking down at Jack, she smiled broadly before theatrically gritting her teeth to suggest impending terror. "I'll just let him know you're here with a *friend*, Detective Superintendent."

She placed a quick call, and on replacing the receiver, she said, "He'll see you now, Mac."

As MacNeice led Jack into the inner office, Wallace looked up from whatever he was writing with a smile of greeting, but it quickly faded. "What's this?"

"A dog, sir. His name's Jack." MacNeice had wanted to keep it light but realized his timing was off.

"Don't be a smartass, Detective. What are you doing in my office with a fucking dog?"

"May we sit down, sir?"

"Sit."

MacNeice explained what had happened in the forest and the marathon run that Jack had endured. He made his final argument in a measured tone — as much for Jack's sake as his own — about the wounded animal being the sole witness and survivor . . .

Wallace interrupted. "Not. My. Fucking. Problem."

MacNeice continued. "I agree. But it is *my* problem. This

dog is a material witness to a double homicide and I believe he'll be important to our investigation."

He waited for blowback that didn't come, though Wallace's face had turned to what MacNeice's mother called "grave mauve" and his jaw was on lockdown.

MacNeice realized the meeting was effectively over and stood up. He nodded once, turned, and left the office. Jack's head was low; his tail was tucked firmly between his legs.

[18]

IN SPITE OF THE WAY IT BEGAN, JACK'S DAY AT THE OFFICE TURNED into an adventure, complete with treats. Word got out before MacNeice made it from City Hall to Division One. Leo "Moose" Stanitz, the desk sergeant, was first to appear — volunteering to watch Jack. An hour later, Sergeant Ryu, who wasn't stationed at Division One, arrived with his K9 report and memory stick. Seeing Jack, he immediately took a knee; Jack tilted his head and soon realized Ryu had dog treats in his pocket. Within minutes, Ryu and Jack had set out for a walk.

The desk phone rang. Ryan picked it up and managed to say "Division One" before turning to MacNeice. "Dr. Richardson, sir."

"MacNeice."

"Mac, I know it's not within my purview to comment or speculate on a crime scene, but if you'll permit me to go freestyle, I do have a thought."

"Of course."

"They entered the forest to kill and bury one victim. When by circumstance they killed two, they came up with an alternative plan." She paused for a moment. "How would you deal with two corpses? The bay? The lake?"

"Not if I didn't have that set up beforehand...and if I did, what was I doing in the forest?"

"Do you opt for another forest?"

"Middle of the night, two bodies bleeding out...wouldn't make sense to go looking. There had to be a solid Plan B."

"Perhaps it's my bias, but what about an unscrupulous funeral home?"

"Jesus, Mary. You might be ready for a career change."

"Not at all, Detective. I'm Type A. I want the whole meal—not just the gravy."

"Again! Jesus, Mary..."

"Such sacrilege!" Mary laughed heartily. "I do so admire your delicate spirit, MacNeice." She turned serious again. "Word has it you've taken on Dr. Moore's dog."

"Yes, though I don't know for how long. He's here in the office."

Her voice softened. "If you'd like to bring him..."

"You mean Jack?"

"Yes. If you and Jack would enjoy a day or an evening out at our farm, Donald—and our dog, Isadora—would welcome your company." To take the pressure off a response, she added, "It's an open invitation. I'll text the coordinates."

"Thank you. Give me a day or two to see how his recovery

goes. Before you hang up, Mary, there'll be a blood sample arriving tomorrow from Singapore. It's from Dr. Moore's son, to verify that the blood you collected from Jack is his father's. Can you have it picked up at Toronto International?"

"Certainly—Junior will take the van. That boy likes a field trip. Right then, ta-ta for now, and good hunting."

DRIVING HOME ALONG Main, his mind went back to the forest, and from there, to wondering where the bodies might be. A funeral home, however willing, wouldn't keep shotgunned corpses around. Even if the bodies had been stuffed into coffins, they'd need a bent cemetery . . . too complicated to pull together in the middle of the night. But a crematorium—and a friendly operator who didn't mind being woken up in the middle of the night—was unlikely but possible. Jack glanced over as if he were thinking the same thing.

It might be prejudicial, but he imagined that men with rough hands and overalls were more likely to have carried out this job than anyone who wore white gloves and a morning coat for a living.

[19]

CLARENCE BLOW PARKED SEVERAL CARS AWAY FROM THE BLACK
Lincoln, not because there wasn't a spot beside it—he
thought there'd be an advantage in appearing by surprise.
He would then set the pace and declare who was in charge
before they had time to shake hands. But, with the heavily
tinted windows, he couldn't tell if anyone was inside, even
though the taillights were on and the engine was running.

Just as he reached out to knock on the passenger window,
it slid down and he was greeted by the smell of fast food.
"Climb in, little man," a deep voice said. With the Lincoln's
interior lights disabled and Clarence standing in the sun, he
could only make out a large dark mass in the driver's seat.

The phrase "little man" had almost sounded affectionate, like "little brother." And the fact was that Clarence had

to climb onto the backseat. This thought went through his mind, followed by the reason he needed one or two more disposals. He'd already saved enough money to live on, if not lavishly, then at least comfortably.

He closed the door and was about to say something to the driver when a voice from the semi-reclined passenger seat startled him.

"We got you a Big Mac, fries, and a Coke." A large hand swung over the armrest with a bag.

Clarence took it, stifling an urge to make a clever remark about what was in a so-called Big Mac. "Very kind, gentlemen...but I've just eaten. I will, however, accept the Coke." While his eyes adjusted to the light, he smiled. "Anyone like another burger?"

"Don't you worry about that," said the voice from the driver's seat. "While we chow, you can tell us about yourself, Mr. Blow."

"Well..." Shifting into the middle seat, Clarence glanced over at the man in the passenger seat. He was white and wore a white polo shirt, and even sitting down, he looked athletic; his left hand made the burger seem small. "I'm an accountant by trade—"

"Stop right there." Polo Shirt wiped his mouth with a napkin. "Being a blacksmith's a trade. An accountant's a profession. Don't assume you have to simple-fuck this thing, Blow."

Was he using his last name to ridicule him, or just for emphasis? Whichever it was, Clarence decided he needed to seize control. "What are your names, please?"

Polo Shirt smiled and sucked his teeth. "No, thank you, Clar-ence."

"Look, I need to make myself—"

A large, shiny black head swung around from the driver's seat. "I'm One. That rangy fella, he's Two. You good with that, Mr. Blow? Because if you ain't, then I'm A and he's B." The man's eyes widened, sending waves of creases rippling up his forehead.

Clarence chose his words carefully. "Yes. I can deal with that, Mr. One."

The driver smiled broadly. "Not mister. You call me One. I ain't your mister—understood?"

"Understood." It wasn't that the atmosphere in the Lincoln was menacing—it felt much worse than that. Questions about who was in charge weren't important, especially if he kept Polynesia in mind. He decided on a new mantra—*keep your priorities straight*—and sipped Coke through the plastic straw. "You're both American...?"

There was a long silence, broken only by munching. The longer it continued, the more it seemed like Clarence's question would hang in the space until the mothership drifted away. Finally Two answered, several fries poised at his mouth: "Eastish, westish—we come from there." *Pop* went the fries; Two winked at Clarence and dug into the container for more.

On impulse, Clarence tried another tack. "You know... if your goal is to go east, there's always east to go." He nodded in satisfaction and took another sip of Coke.

The Lincoln fell silent again. Clarence recalled his client's comment about ending up in the bath. But if he wanted him dead, this was an elaborate and unnecessary way to do it. The air was thick with the smell of speed cuisine and his own affliction: fear.

Finally, One cleared his throat and turned to squint at Clarence. "So, my man. If you go east, you've always got east to go? I got that right?"

"Exactly...but really, it was just an amusing thought I didn't—"

One closed his eyes, then opened them slowly. "Then you're forever a cowboy, that right too?"

"Saddle up, Blow." Two was delighted and smacked his thigh with his free hand.

"I'm sorry, I don't follow..."

"No, you don't." One swung back around and emitted a loud carbonated burp.

Two was incredulous. "You kiddin' me, a fella as smart as you don't get it?" He shook his head in exasperation. "Look, if you're going east all the time—like you said—by definition you're always coming from the west...so you're a cowboy. The west, cowboys—got it?"

"Fella's a redneck. That can't be good," One added softly.

"Ah, yes. I see, of course. Clever." Clarence's heart was stuck so deep in his throat that his voice sounded an octave higher.

"No." One's head swung around again; he wasn't smiling. "It ain't clever. You were trying to be clever. I was just being logical—going and coming both lead you to the same place, eventually." He pursed his lips, waiting to see if Clarence had understood the message. Once it registered on Clarence's face, One continued. "Now, we can dance like this all night, but you and we get paid to do somethin' else, am I right, Clarence?"

"Quite so. Yes." He wished with all his might that he could just get out of the Lincoln, go home, grab his money, and be on the next flight to Samoa.

"Then how about we get down to what we're here for."
One waited for Clarence's nod. When Clarence offered it,
he added, "I don't know the name of your client—and don't
want to know. I understand that tomorrow we have what
you both call a disposal, so let me tell you where we've been
in this luxury rental vehicle. You okay with that?"

"I am. Yes." For the first time in the killing game,
Clarence felt owned. If this was what prison was like, he
had every reason to dread being apprehended.

"We've been in this worked-over town of yours for some
time..."

"Reminds us of Erie and Pittsburgh—shithole better-
days cities..." Two caught One's frown. "Sorry, One.
Continue..."

"I will. And, Two, please dial down the profanity—
you're better than that, and it leaves Mr. Blow with a poor
impression of us." He turned back to Clarence. "Since we've
been here, we been checkin' things out. At first sight, Two
thought it looked like Atlanta, without all us coloured
folks." He smiled at Clarence, whose face remained frozen.
"Anyway, whatever else it is, Dundurn is Lord Almighty
blessed with nature—the lake, the split-up bay, that ridge
over there—"

"We call it the Mountain."

"The what?" Two exclaimed, startling Clarence.

One looked Two's way. "Let folks call it what they like.
It don't matter a Tic Tac to us." He turned back to Clarence.
"And y'all seem to have forests everywhere. We were up
on...the Mountain and found a very pretty spot. So sweet it
coulda been set aside for the purpose."

"Would you like to see it?" Two asked.

"No, that's okay. I trust you."

"Now, why would you say that?" One squinted at him in disbelief. "You got no more reason to trust me than a gator has a snake."

Two picked up the bag and stuffed the garbage inside. Reaching for Clarence's Coke cup, he asked, "You done with that?"

"Yes. Thank you." Two crushed the cup and shoved it into the bag before getting out and slamming the door.

"Is Two okay?" Clarence kept his hand on the door handle, just in case.

"He's fine." One glanced at him in the rear-view mirror.

"Have you considered using the lake, One?" Clarence thought it best to turn the subject back to the job.

"No way."

Clarence was trying to breathe normally; he was also trying to avoid the eyes looking back at him in the mirror.

"Shall we take a little road trip, then?" One asked.

[20]

"**D**'YOU BELIEVE IN THE SOUL, MR. BLOW?" ONE'S EYES PEERED back at him in the rear-view.

"I'm not sure I do, no." It was getting close to morning, and Clarence just wanted to sleep.

"No, or you're not sure?" Two seized the point.

One looked back again. "Mmm, mmm. Well, that man on the Mountain had a soul. And even if you don't know it, you got one too."

Clarence could feel the blood rushing up his neck, but he didn't care. "Please tell me why we dumped him under those trees." He'd considered keeping quiet, but he was determined not to be cowed. "You said yesterday that you'd found the perfect place for him . . . Why there? I really want to know." As he spoke, Clarence's fear completely abandoned him; he was drifting toward hysteria.

Two snapped his head around. "Settle down. One knows what he's doing. That's all you gotta know."

"Okay, okay. But consider this: a day from now, that body's going to stink up the whole county. It'll be discovered; do you think that's what my client meant by disposal?"

One leaned into the space between the front seats but kept his eyes on the road, "Your client didn't care if he was found; he only needs to be missing for a day or two." With his voice rising like a pastor's call to prayer, One added, "Thereafter, he shall rise like Lazarus before the world... and unto the world he shall be known."

"Halle-fucking-lujah," Two said, with a modest fist pump.

"Two, we spoke about your language, about how you need to keep it down whenever someone new is around. For the last time now."

"You're right, I apologize."

Clarence didn't know if One was joking or whether he was going to lay a beating on his partner any second, so he made sure his voice was calm when he spoke. "You met my client?"

As the Lincoln tore through the night, One answered. "Didn't have to..."

Clarence's eyes widened as the suv wandered into the oncoming lane. "Please, One, watch the road."

One chuckled. "I surely will. D'you remember what you said after you were briefed, little man?"

"Not exactly, no." Clarence could feel the Polynesian beach fading like a teardrop on a hot stove.

"No. But, you see, I do. And Two, do you recall those words?"

"Well, yes, I do . . . When Clarence climbed himself onto that back seat, he said we didn't have to *disappear* this guy like he did the other two, we just had to *dispose* of him."

One nodded proudly. "See what a fine memory Two has? Now, does that sound familiar?"

"Vaguely, yes. Though, honestly, I just meant the manner of the disposal didn't need to be the same as for the other two."

"Mm-hmm . . . you mean the other four."

"Excuse me?"

"You also disposed of your own crew — that makes four — and all of 'em had souls." The Lincoln went quiet until One's eyes reappeared in the mirror. "Blow, you got a finer tongue-hold on words than either of us. Two and me, we'd be forgiven for faulty syntax, or poor accounting, but you . . . you should actually know better."

"Ya see, Clarence —" Two jumped in with his opinion. "It's like this: disposal's a two-part thing. First, there's the bang-bang. Second, we take out the trash. But we like to be more . . . what's that word again, One?"

"Considerate? Compassionate? Go with compassionate."

Hard to imagine how compassion worked for a man with two holes in his face and no back to his head, but Clarence kept quiet.

Two nodded thoughtfully. "Compassionate — like that field. We picked that spot because, well — who gets laid to rest in a place like that? The old tree, that cliff, a pretty view of the lake and all . . . I guess you also noticed that we delivered him to Lincoln — *in a Lincoln*."

One whistled through his teeth. "Solid-gold destiny right there; coulda been a Cadillac. And Mr. Blow, pick yourself

up off that back seat." He waited until Clarence was looking ahead through the windshield. "See that hood ornament
gliding through the night?"

"Yes, I see it."

"That's a cross, and that makes this a Christian luxury
vehicle."

"A case of double destiny." Two was tickled with his play
on words.

"That fella shuffled off this mortal coil; his soul's probably hovering over him like a dove."

Clarence recognized that One loved the sound of his own
voice. Thinking the threat had passed, he offered, "Shuffle
off this mortal coil...that's Shakespeare. *Hamlet*, I believe."
That last bit was insincere; he knew exactly the passage and
where it fell in the play.

No sooner had the words left his lips than he regretted
saying them. One and Two went quiet again but exchanged
quick glances. In that awful silence the only sound Clarence
could hear came from the engine, and the Lincoln's body
complaining about a poorly maintained highway. It didn't
last; of course it couldn't last.

One's eyes popped into the rear-view. "You see, Mr. Blow,
that's what I'm talking about. You can wrap that tongue
of yours around words that leave us...speechless. If you'd
asked me where'd I get 'shuffle off the mortal coil' from,
I woulda said from the air, like hay fever. It just floated by
one day and I caught it. Got it?"

"I got it...I was only..."

"You *was only* demonstrating, by example, the distance
between us. No harm in that..." One nodded slowly as if
he were running through the scene again. "Thing is, you

did get educated. You're a refined man. We're just two fellas who, well…we got another kind of education."

"True that, One." Two was looking out the side window. "Got our degrees, too."

One smiled broadly and nodded in agreement. "And yet here we are, together in the disposal business. Ain't that a revelation, Clarence?"

"Yes, I—"

One interrupted him by pointing his index finger at the Lincoln's luxurious ceiling upholstery—or to Heaven. "You best be smart not to correct me on Revelations, 'cause I will whup your little-boy ass with scriptures, psalm, and verse. So tread carefully…"

"Amen, brother." Two added reverently, letting out a happy snort.

Together, he and One fell into belly laughs, until eventually Clarence was laughing too. He laughed so hard he was crying, and through his tears he returned to the Polynesian beach, and a future in which he'd recount the moment.

They'd just passed Kenilworth on King when the laughter stopped. A sudden gust buffeted the Lincoln so hard that One had to take the steering wheel in both hands. Clarence was going to say something about it when a deluge slashed the driver's side and lightning illuminated the car's interior like daylight. One turned the wipers to max, but they couldn't keep up with the downpour. He slowed, put the four-way flashers on, and was easing over to the side of the road when lightning struck a nearby telephone pole, sending it sideways and flinging the wires it supported into the air. The car swerved back to the middle of the road as the wires hit a metal fence and did their electric dance.

The rain came in shearing car-wash waves as they drove through the downtown core. But by the time the Lincoln arrived at McDonald's, the storm was tearing off toward the big city. One stopped next to Clarence's car and shifted into park with a lurch.

"Well, that was biblical," Clarence said as he prepared to exit the car.

"But don't take it personally," One replied. "Good night, Mr. Blow."

"Good morning, One and Two."

ONCE HE WAS behind the wheel, Clarence took several deep breaths and whispered, "One, two, buckle my shoe; three, four, knock at the door…" He was happy and grateful to be alive, but he knew One and Two were waiting for their money to clear transfer the next day—which, given the time, was only hours away. "Five, six, pick up sticks…"

Epiphanies arrive like lightning—in a flash—and Clarence was having his.

The money.

If there was any problem with the transfer, it wasn't hard to imagine who One and Two would hold responsible. Clarence Blow suddenly understood how expendable he was, now that he wasn't calling all the shots. To make matters worse, if his client knew he was planning to disappear in the near future, the transfer would be stopped, and Clarence wouldn't know until One and Two came calling.

Clarence quickly ran another scenario, in which he gave up the client's name to save himself. But if One and Two already knew who the client was, they wouldn't need

Clarence. *Bang-bang*. This theory was supported by something the client had said when Clarence asked him about meeting the new hires: "If I wanted to meet them, then why would I need you?"

Clarence should have left for the beach. Instead, he asked himself why he'd accepted the role of disposal go-between in the first place. The answer, of course, was that he'd listened to his ego. The idea that someone believed in him, that he could be the gangster of gangsters and pay him exceedingly well for it—it had made him feel important. Maybe, he thought, that's what he and every scapegoat had in common.

He realized he had three choices:

1. Run like hell. Pack light—money and a toothbrush— and leave on the first flight for anywhere an ocean away.

2. Go to the police. Spill it all. Spend the rest of his life in prison. No Polynesia.

3. Continue as the gangster of gangsters until the client, or One and Two—the real gangsters—realized he was an added expense and a liability, and took steps to limit their exposure. *Bang-bang*.

"The little man in the front seat chooses...number one!"—The audience roars—"Smart choice...smart choice. Thank you...thank you." Not surprisingly, saying it out loud didn't make Clarence feel better; he started the engine and drove out of the parking lot. It wasn't until he pulled up in front of his house that he realized the wipers had been squawking over a dry windshield.

[21]

IT BEGAN WITH A TWO-ALARM FIRE. ACTUALLY, NO — IT BEGAN BEFORE that, with pissed-off-god thunder and lightning that ripped a path through the belly of Ohio before skidding across Lake Erie. When it hit landfall west of Woodstock, it tore along the landscape like an angry drunk in a pickup truck. Lightning bolts bounced off water towers and barns, split trees like a howitzer, and tore off shingles and shutters and anything else that wasn't bolted down. As it made its way toward the brow of Dundurn, it looked from below as if a terrible artillery battle was being waged on high, illuminating the trees that hugged the Mountain's edge until they appeared possessed and began dancing wildly.

On land cleared of an orchard, one tree remained — an oak that had broken ground centuries earlier. Over time that young oak had flourished; it was loved and adored by Jeremiah Stokes, a grenadier captain in John Graves Simcoe's Rangers. He'd been granted the five-hundred-acre plot atop the escarpment in 1811, and the tree was the property's centrepiece. Within its orbit, Stokes built his homestead, planted crops, kept cattle, horses, and fowls. It was said that he had a gift for farming. However, in 1813 retreating American soldiers torched the Stokes home and stole the livestock. When hostilities ceased, Jeremiah set about building another homestead — much larger than the first — and the oak remained a centrepiece.

Fire, however, was to become the tragic backstory for the Stokes family. After Jeremiah died in 1824, his home, and the homes built on the same property by generations of his descendants, were destroyed by fire four times in the 1800s, and the last in 1951.

Each time a house was lost, another was built elsewhere. Ironically, the family considered it bad luck to sleep on the ashes of the previous home. While relocating didn't prove the existence of good luck, there was another reason why they shifted like chess pieces across the landscape: the game board was shrinking.

As the family's fortunes declined, successive descendants sold parcels of land to clear their debts. By the beginning of the twentieth century, the original allotment had been reduced from 500 to 248 acres, and by the end of the century it was further reduced to 87 acres. A modest bungalow was erected next to the road, and behind it, all the way to the edge of the escarpment, stood the former orchard, a fallow field, and the one mighty oak.

The fruit orchard had been productive for decades until

one by one the trees had died of disease, neglect, or old age. In February 2020, the last surviving heirs — Abigail and Florence, ninety-six-year-old twins — sold the property to a lawyer from Toronto and moved to a retirement home in Grimsby. The only caveat to the sale was that the oak be protected from development in perpetuity. When asked why they had such an attachment to the old tree, neither could recall exactly; they just knew it was special. Abigail, the oldest by ten minutes, suggested it was because of initials carved on the trunk. "But over time, even those have disappeared..."

Four months after closing, their bungalow was flattened — notable as the first Stokes house not destroyed by fire — and the dead fruit trees were hoisted from the ground and stacked like cordwood in an enormous pile twenty feet from the oak. The owner's plan was to set a controlled fire, overseen by the local fire department. The burn, the developer believed, would provide nutrient-rich ash for a future vineyard he would respectfully call the Jeremiah Stokes Winery.

AS THE MARAUDING storm gained speed and approached the escarpment's edge, the updraft from below only intensified its ferocity. Sucked over the precipice, it then roared skyward before curling menacingly in on itself. Down the road, a neighbour rushed to close the shutters slapping against the masonry. It was 4:02 a.m. As he reached for them, he was blinded by an incandescent explosion.

The noble oak that Jeremiah and his descendants had protected had blown apart and was on fire. He secured the shutters and ran to the phone. In a panic, he answered the monotone 911 operator by shouting, "It's an inferno! My God, it's all on fire!"

THAT SAME BOLT of lightning caused Jack to whimper and MacNeice to wake up. While the trees swayed and the windows rattled, no rain fell. Falling back against his pillows, MacNeice closed his eyes. When lightning cracked again, followed by thunder, he spoke softly to Jack: "It's okay, boy...it's okay."

The storm hit the lower city with such speed that the neighbourhoods closest to the Mountain were spared; they stayed dry under the curl of a deluge that hammered everything from Main Street to the lake.

Because the storm had toppled trees and power lines from Ohio to southwest Ontario, the Department of Highways, expecting the worst, had stopped all traffic from crossing the Sky-High Bridge. Cars and trucks were backed up for miles on either side, forced to wait until the storm rolled on.

MacNeice was fast asleep when, at 5:51 a.m. on Tuesday, the telephone rang. It was Aziz. She was somewhere outdoors, the wind buffeting her phone. Disoriented, he sat up before saying, "What's happened, Fiza?"

"There's been a fire, Mac. Up on the Mountain in Lincoln."

"A fire?" MacNeice was worried that he was dreaming again.

"Regional Road 73, just off Spiece. A tree was hit by lightning; it set a huge pile of dead trees on fire. There's a body in the woodpile."

He felt his chest tighten, a familiar invisible weight. "We'll be right there." Realizing how ridiculous that sounded, he corrected himself: "I'll be right there." Jack was sitting up next to the bed, studying his face.

"And there's something else — firefighters are rigging some portable lighting now so we can make it out."

"On my way . . . Is there coffee?"

"Local detachment did a run, but be warned, it's the dreaded double-double."

[22]

THE SUN APPEARED AT 6:21 A.M. MACNEICE KNEW BECAUSE HE WAS there the moment it happened. The sky on the eastern horizon shifted from amber to peach, and finally, audaciously, to flaming orange. Before that, as he made his way to Lincoln, everything, whether simple or complex, had been reduced to a silhouette. Houses and chimneys and hip-roofed barns, tractors in fields shrouded at the axles by a ground mist, the trees along the way; the birds flying with purpose across the night-green sky looked like cutouts. And then, just as he approached the parked vehicles, the world regained its third dimension.

MacNeice lowered the windows and came to a stop behind a regional cruiser. On the other side of the road, a Vineland Fire Department pumper idled, its emergency lights stuttering nervously. Beyond it, in a halo of shockingly bright artificial light, a clutch of figures stood near a pile of steaming wood.

MacNeice stepped out of the Chevy and lifted Jack down to the road, where he looked off toward the sun. "Isn't it a sight, Jack? No wonder our ancestors—mine, and maybe yours—thought it was divine." Hearing his name, the dog looked up briefly before peeing against the Chevy's wheel. The climax was fast approaching—nature held its breath, waiting for the moment when the orange ball popped clear of the horizon. As they watched it happen, the VFD's portable light show seemed cheap and shabby.

And right on cue, a rooster crowed and a donkey brayed, and seconds later, a dog's bark echoed down the road. Jack noticed, but other than ear and nose twitches, he didn't respond.

"Not exactly a gentle re-entry for you, Mac." Aziz was picking her way through the large root divots. She seemed surprised at first to see Jack but smiled and greeted him with a head-scratch.

"What have we got?" MacNeice asked.

"Of course, the barbecue smell gives it away: a male corpse badly, but not entirely, burned." She pointed to an oak tree; half its crown had fallen onto what looked like a partially burned bonfire. The other half had toppled close to the escarpment's edge, heaving up the ancient root system embedded in an enormous clump of soil.

"Lightning struck the oak. The left side was on fire when it fell and hit that stack of old fruit trees, then the whole thing went up—even in the storm."

"Where was the body before the fire started?"

"Face up under the right side of the pile; two shots to the face."

"Head or feet pointed to the edge?"

"Shoes, actually. Expensive shoes."

"His body angled one way or the other, or ninety degrees from the edge?"

"Not angled, more or less at ninety degrees. What are you getting at, Mac?"

"I don't know. I just think it makes sense to consider... if you're going to kill someone and leave them here — why here, why like that?"

"A ritual or symbol?"

"A consideration." MacNeice lifted Jack back into the car and helped him settle. "Stay here, boy. I won't be long." When he turned back to Aziz, she was smiling.

Around them, firefighters were busy dismantling the auxiliary lighting and rolling up hoses. Turning to Aziz, MacNeice asked, "Wasn't there something else?"

"Yes, human remains entangled in the oak's roots, and a metal object that looks like a crescent moon embedded in one root."

"Let's go there first, give these people a chance to clear up." They stepped over and around the charred oak limbs. The leaves that remained identifiable disintegrated underfoot. When they stood at the divide of the trunk, MacNeice was taken aback. "This thing was massive — five feet or more in diameter? That hole goes down six or seven feet ... an incalculable loss."

"Crew chief from VFD said everyone in Vineland knows this tree. People come here for their wedding photos. He's a landscaper in his off time; says it's a white oak, more than three hundred years old."

"A noble tree cleaved by heaven..." MacNeice

whispered, laying his palm for a moment on the inside of the trunk, likely one of the first times its core had felt a human touch. "It fell toward the view . . ." He climbed the torn trunk and looked down to see an elegantly shaped metal smile emerging from a root. Partially caked with mud and ash, its form gave it away. "That's a gorget. Romans wore them to protect their necks in battle. But much later it was used to identify officers and offered no protection at all. Worse, for a sharpshooter, the gorget was an ideal target."

He brushed the metal clear and used his Maglite to illuminate the surface. "Come close. Can you see it?"

She climbed up beside him and held on to his shoulder for balance, "Not really."

He redirected the beam to rake across the metal. "How about now?"

"Yes," she said, excitedly. "But what is it?"

"A royal coat of arms." He tried to free the gorget, but the root held it fast. "Where are the remains?"

"Down to the left." Aziz climbed over the broken trunk and straddled the exposed trench. "Right there, between those two large roots; it's a jawbone."

MacNeice knelt on the split trunk. Emerging from the earth, with most of its teeth intact, was a lower jaw. He scanned the ground around it, but the skull and body, if there, remained hidden. MacNeice stepped off to the side and gazed out to Lake Ontario. The sun had found the port side of a lake freighter heading for Dundurn Bay; the curls of its wake were etched in sunlight.

"Judging by the teeth, the owner may have been fairly young," Aziz suggested.

"Probably . . . assuming that's his gorget, an almost full set of teeth is remarkable. Back then, dentistry relied on a set of iron pliers."

"A soldier, then? Buried by comrades or family. But a sniper would've taken the gorget as a trophy, no?"

"Yes. And he wouldn't have taken the time to bury him." MacNeice turned back to Aziz and smiled. "Not the worst place to greet eternity . . ." Looking down at the jaw, he added, "If it's from the early 1800s, Sheilagh Thomas, the professor from Brant University, should come in. She helped us a few years ago."

"That's the forensic anthropologist who took a shine to you . . ." Aziz said teasingly.

"Oh, really? I hadn't noticed." MacNeice shook his head and walked off through the maze of oak branches to the woodpile. The sweet-and-sour smell of burnt flesh, mixed with that of the still steaming and crackling tree, intensified with every step.

While the firefighters had removed the blackened trunks partially covering the body, the remainder served as a barricade a few feet away.

Hands folded peacefully over its stomach, the body was precisely perpendicular to the ridge. The details of the face were reduced to a black crust, the lipless mouth framed by exposed teeth the colour of nicotine. There were two entry wounds, one above the left eye, the other below. "The first round rendered the second unnecessary . . ."

While the clothing on the front of the body had disintegrated, under the hip bones, the legs, and the arms, a suit, shirt, and trousers remained intact. There the exposed flesh was seared salmon pink.

"The right shoe wasn't torched...its laces are as he tied them," Aziz said.

"Fiza, put your doctorate to work here—agree or disagree with my early morning, where's-my-coffee thesis."

"Ah, the coffee; you would've hated it. Right, I'm listening."

MacNeice smiled. "We're not dealing with crazed killers. While it would simplify things if this was the crew from the forest, the weapon is different, the body didn't vanish, it was laid out here to be discovered. The forest was amateurish; this is professional."

"Agreed on all points, but one." She turned to him. "We agree the other was botched; John Doe was likely the intended victim when the unfortunate Dr. Moore appeared. But the play could still be the same; the puppet master's simply using new puppets."

"Any thoughts about where the first two might be?"

"Not yet. But it's human nature: if you've made a total bollocks of your first effort, you go overboard with the second."

"Meaning?"

"Those first two bodies have vanished forever. It's the only way the puppet master saves face."

"We're making a lot of assumptions—it might have been a spur-of-the-moment decision—but then how would you entice someone into a forest in the middle of the night while carrying a shotgun?"

"Precisely; it was premeditated. Whether their strategy was poor or they hadn't done site research to be certain they wouldn't be interrupted, they had to adjust on the fly. In contrast, this was executed perfectly—laid out under the trees..." Aziz shrugged.

"Save for the lightning. And yet, after a day in this heat, the smell would definitely bring the cops." MacNeice drove his hands into his pockets. "Whoever did this knew he'd be found."

[23]

RICHARDSON STOOD IN THE ROAD IN HER DISTINCTIVE LINEN COAT. Hands on hips, she took a deep breath and exhaled. "Apart from that familiar pong, Detectives, this is divine." Swinging an arm slowly in front of her as if to claim the horizon, the chief pathologist continued. "And yet, even a splendid view can come to this..." With that, her reverie evaporated. "While Junior pulls our kit together, let's see what you've found."

MacNeice suggested they first check the older remains and pointed to the base of the fallen oak. Richardson was wearing sturdy oxfords and, despite being much older than him, she marched across the field, easily negotiating the heaved divots, her eyes remaining focused on the split trunk.

"They're on the far side, Mary; you'll have to climb over. Watch yourself."

"Hah. You mistake me for a city girl, Mac. This is heaven to me — my bones jump with a familiar joy." She climbed up the base of the trunk and dropped down to the other side. "Oh my . . . how lovely."

When they reached her, Richardson was already squatting beside the metal crescent. "Do you know what this beauty is, either of you?"

"A gorget?" Aziz answered, giving MacNeice a nudge.

Richardson swung around to her. "My, aren't you the dark horse, Aziz. Yes, you are correct." She turned back, leaned closer, and spit on the exposed crescent. Taking a tissue from her pocket, she began rubbing. "There. That's better."

"What do you have, Mary?"

"The regimental engraving — see here." She moved her hand away. "VII TH above that wreath, and below it, GREN — Seventh Grenadiers. The other side will have the regiment's name, though someone will need to be careful extricating it."

Aziz was amazed. "I'm surprised it's so shiny, like silver, now that you —"

"Spat on it, yes. But while like silver, this one is not. This is gilt brass . . . applied with mercury, a process called fire gilding. Appropriate, given the circumstance." She touched the piece affectionately. "Of course, that centrepiece is the coat of arms of George III . . ."

Richardson's English accent was educated but decidedly not posh. And while her manner could be brusque, MacNeice assumed that must be due to the accumulated weight of four decades as a pathologist. Her accent contrasted with Fiza's, which was softer, more lyrical. "Posh," she would say mockingly.

He refocused his attention on the task. "The jawbone's on the other side of the roots, to your left, but we haven't disturbed the ground to search for the rest of the remains."

Aziz wondered aloud as they climbed over the root, "Out of interest, Doctor Richardson, how did you know that was a gorget?"

"Ah, well, somewhere in the heap of stone where I grew up, we had one, and the corresponding sword, to boot. They belonged to my great — I always lose track — my paternal grandfather, nine or ten greats ago. He fought in the Napoleonic Wars. My father would let me put the gorget around my neck and go off to the barnyard to terrorize the chickens with my sword . . . While I've never had authority issues, our chickens certainly did." She manoeuvred around the exposed trench. "My brother has that farm now, but I doubt he's been in the attic in years."

She squatted down, this time with her gloves on. She picked up the jawbone and studied it carefully, turning it over, checking the remaining teeth to see if they were loose. "You see here?" She pointed to the narrow tips at either end of the jawbone. "These are the temporomandibular joints . . ." she put a free finger on her own jaw just under the ear, to indicate where they connect. "They're held in place by the masticatory muscles, elastic bands that allow you to —" she opened and closed her mouth " — jaw, jaw, jaw." Turning the bone on its side, she continued, "Now, the muscles are obviously lost, but what's interesting is that where the jaw rested, well, both ends are relatively clean . . . My hypothesis is that when this magnificent tree was destroyed, the mandible was wrenched from its resting place on the skull."

"Should Junior start digging?" Aziz asked.

"No..." Richardson laid the jawbone down and stood up. "Much as he'd enjoy that, we must remain in our millennium..." She turned to MacNeice. "You'll recall Dr. Thomas, the forensic anthropologist from Brant University?"

"I do, yes."

"This will make her very happy. I'll call if you like, or you could..."

"No, I think you'll be able to describe it best." MacNeice felt Aziz's eyes on him.

"I'll assume a patrol car will remain on site until she arrives. We can't have a coyote wandering off with that mandible, can we." Not waiting for an answer, Richardson continued. "For now, Junior will rig a tent over the upturned root ball. Luckily, there's no shortage of logs with which to secure it." Richardson looked out toward the lake and sighed. "Shall we press on?"

As they approached the woodpile, Junior appeared, garbed in a hazmat suit and carrying two large cases. MacNeice and Aziz stood back as Richardson took close-up photographs of the corpse, paying particular attention to the head wounds. When it came time to roll the body over onto a clean white plastic sheet, she suggested the detectives turn their attention back to the view.

Richardson provided reportage. "His trousers, what's left of them, have fallen away. There's one back pocket... empty but for a small piece of paper... if you have an evidence bag?"

"I'll get one from the car," Aziz said.

"No need. Junior will put it in one of ours." Together

they laid the upper torso down. As it sank, a wheezing sound escaped from the blackened mouth. "Internal gases at work...very unpleasant."

Handing the bagged slip of paper to MacNeice, Junior said, "Looks like a Wi-Fi access code."

"Dr. Richardson, could you remove the right shoe? It may be traceable." Aziz made the request without turning around. "If you could bag that as well, please."

They stood with their backs to the action. MacNeice watched Jack, his head on his front paws, which were draped over the Chevy's open window. Aziz looked off to the lake.

"Brioni; not cheap..." Junior said, bagging the shoe.

"No need to look, but I have his head in my hands," Richardson said. "Impossible to say which round came first. The entry above the eye exited through the parietal bone. The other, through his cheekbone, jettisoned the back of his skull. But those remains aren't present."

"He wasn't shot here..."

"Correct. Forensics will comb this field. If they're nearby, they'll find them. I believe the weapon was a high-calibre handgun with high-velocity rounds."

"His age, any other details?"

"Possibly midforties; could be younger. We'll learn more back at the lab. Junior, measure his height—he's Caucasian, roughly a hundred and seventy pounds, and fit."

"Five foot eleven, Chief." Junior pressed the button and the metal tape zipped noisily into its shell.

[24]

BY THE TIME CLARENCE WOKE UP AT 10:14 A.M., HE'D THOUGHT OF another way to handle the current situation.

The best way to survive was to make himself indispensable. That sounded simple enough, but it took him the rest of the morning to figure out how to go about doing so. Once he had, he immediately headed to the client's office.

Approaching the door, he walked with a distinct lift in his step. No question, meeting One and Two had been challenging. Within seconds their banter had overtaken his and he felt tiny in the back seat. Clarence had convinced himself that he was only a smartass around incompetent people, and he'd been surprised to discover that other men willing to kill for money weren't always stupid. After all, Clarence killed for money, and he wasn't. Even his father, who despised him, would have to admit he was clever. Useless, sure, but clever.

He stood at the door to the inner sanctum, took a deep breath — knocked twice — and entered the black room. Inside, he crossed swiftly to the desk and offered his hand to his client. "Sir, it went very well. What's next?"

The client tucked in his chin and studied Clarence; he was wiping his hands with a tissue. "You seem . . . a changed man, Mr. Blow. How do you account for that?"

"Thanks to you and your brother, sir, we have two professionals. So I'd like to propose that we expand the business." He sat down and gently slapped the arms of the chair to emphasize his point.

"I gather you haven't heard the news today?"

"What news?" The old fears began to surface; Clarence held them at bay with a smile.

"Lightning struck a tree out in Lincoln; that tree hit some other dead trees, and the whole thing went up."

Clarence felt the man's gaze burrowing a hole in his skull, but he remained calm, waiting for what was coming next.

"You see . . . they found a body under the burnt trees. It'd been shot twice and was burned, but not completely."

Clarence surrendered to an emotion rising in his stomach, something he knew would only get worse if he tried to stifle it. It came out as a chortle that might have been mistaken as gas, but in seconds he was laughing hysterically. Gaining control of himself, he took a deep breath, wiped the tears from his eyes, and pulled himself up in the chair. "What are the chances? That's as Canadian as a puck in the teeth."

"So you're not concerned?" The client leaned forward on

his elbows. "Clearly you find the situation hilarious, but you also see how it's unfortunate?"

"Unfortunate, sir?" His eyebrows shot up with incredulity. "Not at all. What they've found is a dead man with two holes in his head. He had no identification on him, and his features are probably gone. I think it's genius. When you call in a lightning strike to finish the job, that's divine intervention—but don't ask me to repeat it."

"Well, frankly, I'm impressed by your confidence. I'd assumed you'd be contrite, prostrate with failure...But I think I see why you're so ebullient, though I wouldn't have gotten there on my own."

"You're welcome, sir." He let the acknowledgement sink in before adding, "It's important that the money be in the accounts by three p.m. I'll take mine, assuming you have it ready?" He waited for the nod, and when it came, he continued, "Can we discuss how to expand our enterprise?"

"Frankly, I need a moment to adjust my opinion of you, Blow. The money has already been transferred, and yours is here." He sat back in his chair. "Tell me, Clarence, how you think our enterprise works."

Hearing his first name lowered Blow's heart rate but didn't slow his mind. "You have contacts. The contacts have problems that require solving. I provide the solutions. With our new hires, I can provide the solution to your satisfaction. Your contacts don't know I exist. Our new hires don't know you, I assume. And neither I nor our new hires know your contact. Finally, the target doesn't know any of us...though presumably they know why they were targeted."

"Succinctly and accurately put. Go on, son."

Being addressed as "son" disarmed him. Clarence turned

an emotional moment into thoughtful consideration about how to proceed. "Sir, a great accountant keeps the 'for your eyes only' information in his head—not on computer or in a file folder. There isn't and never will be a record of our transactions. With that assurance, you can expand your network with confidence."

Clarence paused for emphasis before he went on. "One thing we may want to consider is a two-tier offering: disposal versus disappearance." He smiled. "For example, last night was a disposal. The one in the forest, a disappearance. One is temporary—but difficult to trace; the other is eternal. Each priced accordingly: gold and platinum."

"You're a very thoughtful young man, Clarence, but have you considered the weakness inherent in that proposal?"

"Yes, I have." No, he hadn't, but he was quick to find one. "Each point of contact is a weakness. Waterboard the contact who paid for the disposal to make him give you up, and then you might give me up, and under gulag beatings, I might give up the two men who execute the disposal. And it might work the other way around... assuming there's torture, or a lavish incentive, to do so."

"Exactly. And how would you deal with that?"

"Each of us—everyone in the chain—must be accountable. Your contacts only know you; you know your contact and me. I know you and the new men I work with—I don't know and have no interest in knowing their names. The level of exposure, while it runs throughout, is limited."

"But nothing in life is guaranteed."

"Correct. Leaving aside that a breach of trust in this enterprise is a capital offence, there's now a high degree of professionalism throughout our chain of command. For example, I trust that you choose your clients, and they you, because of a mutual trust. I feel I can trust the men your brother provided, and when their fee is paid, they'll trust me as I do you."

"Therein is the risk."

"As with all things in life. My advice is to take it."

The client rose to indicate that the meeting was over. "I feel—for the first time since I've known you, Clarence—that I understand you. And you'll be pleased to know there'll soon be another assignment."

"Wonderful, sir. And will you give my proposal serious consideration?"

"Of course…" The client handed him a large gym bag with a happy-customer smile.

When Clarence reached the door, he turned for one last act of daring. "Sir, I hope you think of me as more than a middleman?" He kept it light but wanted the point to hit home.

"Ah, I see. Very clever. You refer to my comment the other day… No. You're critical to our collective success."

As Clarence got into his car and drove away, he let out a hoot. Glancing into the rear-view, he grinned. "Little man, you are brilliant."

[25]

MACNEICE HAD AVOIDED HIS BURGEONING INBOX UNTIL THE CLERK
added another report to the pile, which sent most of
them to the floor. A half-hour later he'd completed a topline
read, filed half, and discarded the rest. At the bottom of the
tray was a handwritten envelope: *DS MacNeice—Personal*.
No return address; postmarked Dundurn, five weeks earlier.

With Jack asleep under his desk and Aziz off to Missing
Persons with Richardson's description of the charred body,
MacNeice went outside to read the letter. He wanted fresh
air and birdcalls—in mid-August, that was mostly the per-
ennially cheerful and chatty sparrows.

He couldn't recall the last time he'd received a letter in
the mail and couldn't imagine who it was from. He tapped
the envelope on his knee, slid his finger along the flap, and

then looked up as a patrol car pulled in from Main Street and parked along the treeline. He unfolded the letter and was stunned by the first sentence. But then, no one anticipates a letter from the dead.

> DS MacNeice,
> Call it hypervigilance, but I can feel you coming for me. You and I will meet — of that, I'm certain. You've been closing fastm quietly, stalking me. I respect that.
>
> By the time you read this letter, I'll be dead. Not escaped. You're too savvy to let that happen. I'm done running.
>
> I've been studying you as well, but maybe you also sense that.
>
> I've only one project left to complete. Warning: don't be clumsy when you come. I know you've got some cowboys in Tactical.
>
> As I doubt we'll ever sit down and have this conversation, I'm going to imagine the one I think we should have had:
>
> V: Don't show me a man who says he's seen action without first observing how he holds a glass of wine.
>
> M: Why's that?
>
> V: Well, if he holds a glass of wine without its surface rippling from the tiny tremors inside him, I'll tell you his was a support role, far from the dying.
>
> M: Or not there at all...
>
> V: Precisely. The men who have been there choose Guinness, because the foam masks their trembling.
>
> M: Go on.
>
> V: Bravest man I ever knew was sent shivering and

stuttering from the room when his five-year-old learned how to pop a paper bag.

M: Are you executing innocent people to erase those moments of courage or rage?

V: No. That's impossible. I've met ancients who fought on the beaches of Dieppe and Normandy. We stood around as soldiers do, looking anywhere but into each other's eyes. My eyes stayed on their wineglasses. Every glass shook — just like mine — and not because they were frail. We won't be sharing a glass of wine together, MacNeice, but I'd bet all my service medals that you'd have tiny tremors when holding yours too.

M: I haven't checked.

V: Bullshit. Now's not the time for that; I'm already dead.

M: Okay, what now?

V: My last words on love and promises: you know what it means to command. When it takes getting drunk before we can say to a comrade, "I love you." It's the truth, but I've never said it sober.

M: Surely your men felt it, though.

V: I saw photos of you with your team, and everyone looked so real, so present — that came from you — you set the tone, the standard. It doesn't mean they won't get wounded or killed, but they follow your lead. Is that respect or love or regimented training? I think it's love.

M: I think it's trust, and it takes time.

V: DI Aziz has been wounded more than once; Vertesi, once; Swetsky, once, that I could find. Maracle — a vet — once. You've been wounded several times. It takes love, MacNeice. Nobody needs to do our work. We could all find something else to do.

M: *Carry on...*

V: *You promise to protect them. It's completely irrational because it's impossible. Still, you tell yourself you will. I'm certain you do it...*

M: *I do. And I hate myself every time.*

V: *For me it was the* IEDs, RPGs, *and Taliban fighters who were also farmers and the descendants of fighters and farmers. They knew the terrain like they knew the faces of their children. It was only the immense and occasionally indiscriminate firepower the coalition rained down on them that gave us an advantage. And, like Vietnam, every bombing that wipes out a family, a harvest, or a goat makes guerrillas of those who survive.*

M: *So your point is—?*

V: *It wasn't the combat that undid me. It was my failure to keep my promises. Art was the only way I could make sense of it. It included the way I would end my life.*

M: *Is that it?*

V: *I wanted a last chance to compare warfare to copfare.*

M: *Meaning how you function compared to how I do?*

V: *Yes. In warfare each side has maps, intel, and on-the-ground eyes. Each side can deploy personnel, ordnance, and TV dinners when and where they're needed. When there's anyone or anything we determine to be a target, there's a means to eliminate that target. Please keep that in mind when you come for me.*

M: *I will.*

V: *The various agencies of law enforcement are territorial. They consider intelligence to be privileged information.*

M: *Why do you think it's that way?*

V: *Because the number of dead cops is low. If it were high, they'd be keen to work together. As it is, they all play chess on separate boards, so only occasionally does a pawn fall off.*

M: *Are you a psychopath, and a cynic?*

V: *You may find it hard to believe, but I'm not cynical—I'm simply a burnt-out realist.*

M: *Does law enforcement have any advantage?*

V: *You mean beyond that low body count?*

M: *Yes.*

V: *I think so. There are pockets, individuals with intelligence. Not drone and satellite eavesdropping and such. It's people like you, with experience, street smarts, and intuition. You can be nimble and follow hunches. You can be quick to act. Armies—the military—can't be that quick, or that invisible.*

M: *These are your last words for me?*

V: *Yes. I'll end where I began. I wish we'd met under different circumstances, but I'm certain we'll meet. Whenever you pour a glass of wine and notice the ripples, you'll think of me. Get out while you can, MacNeice. Failing that, find something, or someone, to steady your hand when the tremors come.*

Remember, Detective: the scariest battleground is the one between your ears.

Farewell,

Venny

[26]

AS HE MOVED BETWEEN THE FIRST AND SECOND FLOOR, MACNEICE put the letter in his jacket pocket. While he didn't know why, he couldn't imagine what good would come of sharing it. It would join Venganza's Paris portfolio; date-stamped, given its own sealed plastic bag and catalogued as evidence; an item on a list. Getting it out of his head would take much longer.

When he entered the office, Jack stood up. MacNeice turned to Ryan. "He wants to take me for a walk; we won't be long."

Crossing the street at Jackson, they entered Whitehern's garden. MacNeice realized he was breathing easier; the letter was from a man he barely knew, but one he felt he knew well.

Jack sniffed every bush and tree; MacNeice was happy to let him dictate pace and direction. Outside the garden, the smell of heat rose off the pavement; inside, birds congregated under the cool, dense canopy. Up ahead, two young mothers were slowly pushing their strollers and talking. They'd stop to laugh, then start walking, only to burst into laughter and stop again. Both wore running shoes, black leggings, and loose T-shirts — one blue, the other grey. Since Jack didn't seem to mind, MacNeice carried on behind them, happy to be in range of their laughter. Jack, on the other hand, was just happy to follow his nose.

MacNeice's phone rang; the two women turned around. They'd been unaware of his presence, but seeing the dog, they smiled and went back to their conversation. He didn't look at the call display when he answered. "MacNeice..." He watched three pigeons, heads down, pecking around a nearby bin.

"It's David — David Moore."

"Hello, David." MacNeice was surprised to hear from him.

"Sorry for the connection; I'm calling from New Zealand to let you know my uncle and his wife are coming to Dundurn tomorrow. They'll stay at my father's for a week or two ... The good news is they'll take Jack back to BC. I guess you'll be relieved to hear that..."

"To be honest—"

"You've been very kind, Detective, and we're very grateful. My uncle's name is Bill Moore; he'll call when he arrives."

"I was happy I could help; I've enjoyed Jack's company."

"Is there any news about my father?"

"It's very early in our investigation, David. That shouldn't be mistaken for inaction; we'll find out what happened, I promise you." That word again. He had no way to back it up, and though it might provide temporary comfort to Moore, MacNeice already regretted it—just as Venganza had.

Through the static, David said, "Right...I understand. You can't find the answer until you do, same as my work. I'll break off now...call me if anything changes. Goodbye."

"Take care, Dav—" The line went dead. MacNeice sat down on a bench; Jack stood before him for a moment, then lay down in the shade. A feeling of loss swept over MacNeice and his eyes filled with tears. He wiped them away and took a deep breath.

You're coming face to face with another loss, Mac.

"Jesus, Kate...a month away and I'm in worse shape than when I left."

Though actually you're not. I've been watching you. You're more reflective; your spirit's calmer.

"Phew...I don't know. I'm on a bench in the middle of the day in tears."

Yes, you are. You're not consumed by anguish.

"I used to love it when you'd get all..."

Cosmic was the word you used.

"Yeah, you remember."

Jack had been looking up at him from the moment MacNeice answered the call from David Moore, his tail slapping the stone walkway. He took the dog's head in both hands. "You are a beauty, Jack. But it appears you aren't meant to be my beauty." They left the garden and ambled back toward Division One, Jack sniffing and anointing the same hydrants, poles, and hedges he'd peed on earlier.

[27]

I T WAS A WARM AND BALMY EVENING; THE SOUNDS OF PASSING TRAF-
fic competed with swallows, crickets, and cicadas, all eager to
announce that the sun was about to set. The sky presented its
daily bruises—of contrails, smoke, and smog—to the night.

"You know... in every life, there's a pistachio you just
can't open."

Minutes passed, but One's eyes stayed closed. Clarence
thought he might have fallen asleep; that or he was lost in
thought. He correctly assumed that One was speaking to
him, but without a context for the comment, Clarence knew
better than to respond.

One was lying on a blue nylon recliner. Next to him, in
an upright chair, Two was drinking a beer and staring up
at a willow swaying gently in the breeze.

Sitting at the picnic table, Clarence was determined to wait it out. In front of him sat an American beer—the colour of pale piss—that he'd been nursing.

Finally, One continued. "You see, Mister Blow"—he gave Clarence the side-eye—"not long ago, we had this contract for a disposal. I think Two would agree that our execution of the plan was flawless..."

"It was that," Two said softly, without looking away from the tree.

"Fella never saw us coming...the man had no peripheral vision whatsoever. It was gonna be smooth." One closed his eyes again, as if the story ended there.

Though he tried to resist, Clarence was hooked. "So, what happened?"

One side-eyed him again, reminding Clarence of those nature programs where a whale's eye comes close to a diver, and for a moment that enormous creature studies the diver as some vaguely interesting but crudely designed object. "The man was on his cellphone, those pretty little white things hooked into his ears. He stepped off the curb..."

"Splat," Two said, smiling Clarence's way.

"Loaded garbage truck, heading to the dump."

Two shook his head from side to side at the memory. "You might say it was poetic justice. We were there to dispose—and he got disposed."

"And yet, he was our pistachio," One said.

"But you got paid...I mean, your contract was fulfilled."

"True. Professionally, we did feel robbed by the truck—but damn straight, we expected to be paid."

What followed was another long pause. Two turned his

attention back to the tree, lazily moving his head in synch with its canopy.

One pursed his lips, relaxed, and took a deep breath, "So we took on another disposal, one we wouldn't be paid for..." he said on the exhale.

Two tilted his head and looked at Clarence. "Can you guess who that was, little man?"

"The person who hired you."

"He's clever, One. That's a fact."

"Correct... Now, Mr. Blow, seeing as how you're so smart, can you guess why I told you about our pistachio?"

"A cautionary tale?" Clarence watched the two men exchange smiles. He had no intention of being another pistachio—plus, they'd been paid. They were already expecting their next assignment. He was the leader and no longer felt threatened by them—at least not every second. He'd established a simple framework for success. Though he'd yet to inform his client, Clarence had decided. From now on, everyone would disappear.

To shift the conversation, Clarence grinned. "That garbage truck was an act of God."

One looked his way and nodded. "Musta been."

"And sweet, too...disposed of by a disposal truck," Clarence said, echoing Two's quip.

"True..." One now sounded like he was really falling asleep.

"Except God didn't get paid either." Clarence took a sip of his beer.

"Tread softly, Blow...very softly." Though his voice was a whisper, One's message was loud and clear.

Clarence watched the muscles in One's jaw flicker

vise-tight. Henceforward there'd be no wisecracks involving religion. He considered apologizing, saying he'd only meant it as a clever joke about robbing God of His creation—but realized that would be a mistake. Instead, he squinted through another sip of beer.

One tilted his head as Clarence pulled off his signature driving gloves and stuffed them into the empty beer case. He flexed his fingers, enjoying the freedom, and smiled sheepishly as One's face relaxed, like he was at the beach on a warm and balmy evening.

[28]

RYAN HAD DONE ALL HE COULD TO ENHANCE THE VAN SHOT FROM Power Line Road. As the final image loaded on the screen, MacNeice and Vertesi stood waiting.

It appeared to be an older-model, dark-coloured van. "Print it out for the whiteboard—stick it next to the forest crime scene photos. Check for any highlights: a damaged bumper, fender, rust around the wheel wells, the name of a company..."

When it was on the board, Ryan looked at it again before returning to his computer. He began enlarging the image until it took up the entire screen, until it looked like a late-night television channel after all the programs had ended— a wall of grey snow.

MacNeice left Ryan alone to figure it out and went to

study the photos from Lincoln. The charred victim, a shoe, fabric from the pant leg, and a small piece of paper that might be a Wi-Fi password.

"Did you get anywhere with that slip of paper?"

Ryan answered over his shoulder. "It's a bit like a needle looking for its haystack, sir. I might get lucky, but my odds are worse than winning the lottery if I never buy a ticket."

"So that's a no?" MacNeice was still focused on the slip of paper. "Let's not give up on it just yet. Tell me the likely scenarios where a man might be handed something like that."

"Restaurants and bars give them out..." Ryan offered. "Hotels, I guess..."

"Used to be a book of matches from a nightclub in a dead guy's pocket...but maybe that was just the movies..." Vertesi said from his desk. "Cool names like the Black Cat Club, a place with a huge galooch guarding the door..."

MacNeice was going to let it slide, but asked, "*Galooch*... is that Italian?"

"You'd think. I know I did. Growing up, the guys I knew used it to describe a big, clumsy guy. I asked my dad; he said it wasn't Italian." Vertesi chuckled. "Then I asked my uncle...he punched me hard on the shoulder and said, 'Hey, wait, yeah. It means a guy like you, Mikey.'"

"*Gaa-looch*...I like the sound. Mind if I use it?" MacNeice smiled.

"I've got something, sir." Ryan moved his chair aside; with a stylus, he drew a large circle around an area of TV snow. MacNeice and Vertesi couldn't see anything.

"A half-pie curve at the bottom. The straight part runs from eleven to five o'clock."

Ryan sketched on a notepad what he alone could see.

"See how everything is snow — consistent snow — but here, you've got random dark bits that run down? They're not random. I'll try and enhance it again . . . looks like a dent to me."

"I want to see what you see, Ryan," MacNeice said.

"I'll do my best, sir . . ."

"Before you do, print it out for the whiteboard." MacNeice studied the security camera capture and time code. "The van arrived shortly after Moore's last logbook entry."

"That's the sound of progress . . ." Aziz said, from the corridor. When she appeared, she looked at the whiteboard, then back to MacNeice. "What is it?"

"The van . . . from Power Line," MacNeice said.

"Right . . ."

Vertesi added, "Ryan sees a dent; he's trying to adjust the image so we can see it too."

"Oh yes . . . a faint happy-face thing down at the bottom there?"

Ryan swung around on his chair, beaming. "You can see it?"

"I think so . . . a half-circle?"

"Can you put your finger on it?" MacNeice asked.

"Here." With her finger on the printout, she moved so Ryan could see.

"Impressive, but it's still lost on me." MacNeice returned to his desk. "Anything from Missing Persons?"

Aziz draped her jacket over her chair. "Nothing yet. They'll scan missing persons records and send any that fit our profile."

"Can I offer you a coffee?"

"Yes, please . . . they use the coffee from Missing Persons to dissolve concrete." She leaned down to rub Jack's ear.

"I'll come. Macchiato, if you please." Jack fell in line behind them.

MacNeice's hands were gliding through the ritual of making espresso when Aziz asked, "What's next?"

"Crematoriums, and industrial or farm incinerators. How many, and how close are they to the city?"

"Oh my, we're descending to nasty." She smiled as he added a tiny foamed-milk cap to her cup.

As they walked back to their desks, MacNeice said, "Jack's gone from being an orphan to having an uncle — Dr. Moore's brother, from BC."

She paused at the stairwell. "Sorry . . . I imagine that's a very mixed blessing for you."

"Yes . . ."

"I've seen how he watches you, Mac. You filled a hole in his life too — I'm sorry, that sounded like Jack was filling one in yours."

"Well, it's true; he has."

Sensing the conversation was heading in a direction that wouldn't do either of them any good, Aziz nodded sharply. "Right then, I'll start researching . . ." She sipped her coffee. "Again, who attempts to bury someone in the woods if they've got access to a crematorium or an incinerator?"

"Mary first planted the idea of an unscrupulous undertaker. As to why that wasn't their first choice . . . I don't know."

Back in the cubicles, MacNeice noticed that Ryan had moved on to studying the paper slip in the evidence bag. He shrugged in defeat, handing it to Aziz. "Probably a Wi-Fi code, but for what? Basically, this kind of Wi-Fi is an added incentive: free internet for a limited time and range. If it was a restaurant, they'd put it on the menu or something, and hotels usually print it on cards or key covers."

"What about an airline lounge, for business travellers?" MacNeice asked.

"Absolutely—it's used for convenience; the range is limited to the lounge—and it's temporary because whoever is using it is leaving on a plane."

[29]

"LET'S JUST SAY THEY COME FROM NEAR AND NOT VERY FAR away." The client sat quietly in his big chair awaiting the second act of Clarence's business strategy. The desk clock switched over to 8:05 a.m.

Clarence told him he was still considering the most efficient and safest process of killing. "Similar to the work I do as your accountant, it comes down to cost savings, risk mitigation, and enhanced security. Therefore, I now believe that every disposal must also be a disappearance, not merely a body waiting to be discovered. That's the 'what' of it. If you agree, I'll work on the 'how.'"

No one had ever accused Clarence of having a quiet mind, but at that precise moment, it was Zen-level quiet. He studied the client's face and felt no pressure to fill the void with something pithy. He believed his silence projected strength, prudence, and intelligence. And, apart from his right index finger tapping lightly on the armrest, he was at ease.

The client cleared his throat before commenting on the business proposal. "With regard to the disappearance of our subjects, I've no issue with it in principle, unless the customer wants a body to be discovered. We don't need to go into the reasons, though it might be obvious."

"I see..."

Glancing at the empty wall, he continued, "The customer delivers the subject in a nondescript van that would go unnoticed in any city. The drivers take the subject to Riviera — its rear parking lot is hidden from view — and leave as quickly as they arrived."

"Yes, and we transfer the subject to a Riviera van." Clarence understood the process.

"Correct. But, as you know, my brother didn't appreciate the way that was handled last time. He wants less exposure, particularly with regards to his stripping bath and incinerator. I'm sure you understand..."

"I do."

"The next subject — let's call him Lincoln — went smoothly. He arrived drugged and bound and your men put him in the SUV — albeit from my brother's livery, when he had been told it would only be used for scouting. And, were it not for that lightning strike, the body might still be under those trees."

Clarence raised his hand; he didn't want a conversation about innovation devolving into an accounting of his failures. "Sir, that makes a strong case for disappearance..."

"It does... and your next contract might sound prescient

in that regard, as it takes place today—the subject is local and must disappear. I'll be in touch within the next hour." Seeing Clarence's nod, he smiled. "You surprise me, Blow; you're somewhat of an enigma, but this is a happy surprise."

Leaving the office, Clarence was once again struck by how fast he'd changed his fortunes. The terror—that urgent need to flee—had evaporated. The only thing that mattered now was for it all to go without incident, apart from the actual killing. There could be no pistachios.

[30]

THE SUN SLID THROUGH AN OPENING IN THE SHEERS AND CAUGHT Dr. Sumner's cheek as she looked up from her notes. "I took a call from your commanding officer this morning," she said. "DC Wallace mentioned that you had returned from your suspension and arrived at his office with a dog."

"His name is Jack." MacNeice smiled, and immediately wished he hadn't.

"Would you care to explain, Detective?"

"It was a spontaneous decision, one I felt was right given the circumstances."

She referred to her notes again. "Because the dog was witness to a homicide?"

"Correct. And I'm Jack's surrogate human until a family member arrives."

"Should they decide they don't want him, do have you a backup plan?"

"I'll adopt him. To be honest, I haven't thought that far ahead." MacNeice stopped short of mentioning the half-baked lineup strategy he'd been mulling over.

Sumner registered his hesitation. "There's something else about that?"

He watched the pen in her hand for any sudden movement toward the page. "Well...Jack witnessed a double homicide. I'm convinced that if he was put in a room with the suspects, he'd recognize them and react."

"Are you suggesting that his reaction could be submitted as evidence?"

MacNeice's face brightened. "It would certainly be dramatic and very telling. Even if it wasn't possible to enter the dog's reaction in court, it would reveal something to me, to our investigators."

"Have you ever had a dog, Detective?"

"Funny, the vet asked the same question. Not exactly, no. My parents did."

"Tell me more."

He wondered at the relevance, but didn't ask. "I was ten when my father brought a puppy home, but it wasn't till I was twelve or thirteen that I thought of Silver as my best friend. My mother would say we were inseparable; I suppose that was true."

Sumner put down her pen, "Given how close you were, why haven't you had your own as an adult?"

"I don't know...I guess life and work took over."

"And a human relationship..."

"Of course."

"Does your relationship with Kate continue as before?"

MacNeice's eyes wandered to the window; the sun had slipped behind a cloud and the low hum of air conditioning had replaced birdsong. "I talk to her...though not during my month in Paris. Interesting, isn't it?"

"Is it? As you weren't investigating a homicide, perhaps you didn't need her there. And being in the city where you met, she was all around you in the sights and sounds."

That had changed when he'd returned to Dundurn. No, that wasn't true. It had changed when he fell asleep on the return flight from Paris. He was overtaken by an idyllic dream of Kate—at least that's how it began. He felt relieved to have the opportunity to tell Sumner about it and fixed his eyes on her hands.

"There's a clearing in the forest across the road from the cottage, with a limestone flat, like a table, that heats up with the sun. We'd often have picnics there. It was as if we were far away from everything, surrounded by the forest, birds in the trees; on the ground, the occasional rabbit or fox. I don't know why, but on that rock, we always spoke in hushed tones. Only fifty yards from our door, but it was sacred in some way...In my dream, Kate was on her stomach, lying on a sunflower-yellow beach blanket, reading a book. I approached quietly, careful not to break a twig or make a sound, not to frighten or surprise her—she hated surprises—but just to observe her more closely. Buttressed by her elbows, shoulder blades together, her muscles were emphasized."

He'd study those small, tight muscles whenever he could. If she practised in a tank top, they'd dance across her upper back. Sax players, drummers, and pianists develop muscles, but a violinist's upper body is a watchmaker's masterpiece, subtle, refined, and captivating, at least to him.

"She'd tied up her hair with a pencil through the knot. She'd often do that when making notes about the music she was practising." He lifted his eyes to see if Sumner was still listening. She waved her hand for him to continue. "She was wearing a sky-blue bikini. The dream was so vivid I could hear chickadees chatting above her. I noticed a young fox lying off to the side of the clearing, its head resting on its front paws, watching her as if she was the most enchanting thing it had ever seen." MacNeice smiled at Sumner, embarrassed and no longer sure that telling her about the dream made any sense. "I'm sorry, Doctor. I realize I'm rambling with no apparent end in sight."

"But there was an end to the dream. Tell me about that."

He nodded. "It ended with a wake-up call: *We're going through an area of turbulence. Return to your seats and fasten your seatbelts.*"

That was a lie. The end had been quite different.

In the dream, Kate had heard him coming and whispered, "You can't creep up on a fiddler's ears." He crouched beside her and laid his cool hands on her warm back. She let her head fall. He unsnapped the bikini top to apply sunblock.

When he'd finished putting the lotion on her shoulders, he turned his attention to the muscles supporting her lower back. As he applied the cream, he noticed the birds weren't singing. He looked for them in the canopy; they were huddled quietly on a branch, as if holding their breath. The fox had slipped away. Looking down at Kate's back, he recoiled in horror. The flesh was pale grey, not hot pink from the sun. She was emaciated. Her spine and ribs—just a bone cage. The intricate Swiss-watch muscles had atrophied. Her almost transparent flesh moved like crêpe under his touch; her breathing was intermittent and reduced to a reedy wheeze.

Wide-eyed, frightened, and seized by panic, MacNeice bolted upright, startling his seatmate. The dream was over, and he was strapped into 12A, heading back to reality.

Sumner's eyes narrowed. "Where were you just now, Detective?"

"Sorry, Doctor. I don't know. A bit of jet lag; it creeps up on you."

Sumner wrote something on her pad: *somnum exterreri*. Reading it upside down, he couldn't make sense of it, knew he wasn't supposed to. She peered over her glasses at him. "Well, let's leave that for the time being..."

The session lasted another ten minutes. MacNeice was dodging bullets and she knew it. He registered the change in Sumner's face, a slight tightening around the eyes. When the session ended, she stood and glanced at her calendar. "I want to see you again, Detective. This week if possible. Bring Jack; I'd like to meet him."

"Thank you. If I still have him, I will."

Sumner leaned against the windowsill and crossed her arms. "You know, MacNeice, our work is more productive when you don't edit your thoughts." She wasn't waiting for a response.

IN THE CAR, he googled the translation of *somnum exterreri*. She'd seen through the dream for what it had become—a *nightmare*.

That was a mistake, Mac.

"I know. I wasn't ready to talk about it."

Clearly. And crêpe? Was my skin that bad? No, it couldn't have been.

"The cream wasn't for the sun, Kate. It was for bedsores. Your skin was always soft, but in that dream..."

Don't say any more; I prefer the beginning, in my bikini. And, though I probably never said it at the time, I always loved your hands on me. In fact, I loved the way you saw me... Do you recall what I was reading that day?

"I didn't notice the book... my attention was elsewhere."

Cheeky boy; it was Federico Garcia Lorca. Just at the moment you unfastened my top, I read, "To see you naked is to remember the Earth."

"God, I wish I'd whispered that in your ear."

You gave me so much more than a line from a poem, Mac.

[31]

"**B**OSS, YOU'VE GOT EVAN MOORE'S BROTHER AND HIS WIFE IN THE interview room," Vertesi's voice rose at the end, as if it was a concern.

Aziz added, "Jack's with them, Mac."

"Ah, I see." He nodded and draped his jacket over his chair. "Anything else?"

"A potential break from Missing Persons," Aziz said. "I'll pull it together. Do you want a coffee?"

"Maybe later."

He approached the door slowly so he could briefly observe the couple through the narrow window. Jack was enjoying an ear rub from Bill Moore — the grin on the man's face made MacNeice smile. Seeing they had mugs of tea or coffee, MacNeice decided to make a coffee—fuel for saying goodbye to Jack.

As it streamed into his cup, he had what he'd later tell Sumner was a breakthrough. By sublimating the need for a human relationship into the companionship of a dog, he was avoiding the dilemma between a dead Kate and a very alive Fiza Aziz. He realized how much life he was missing by choosing pain over joy. Comforted by that insight, he took the cup and walked away from his thoughts.

When he opened the door, Jack looked up and wagged his tail but stayed beside Moore, perhaps hoping the ear rub would continue. Bill Moore was bald, and what remained of his hair barely made it above his ears. The dome was pink from living under a hat, but the rest of his face was tanned. MacNeice had read in the file that he and Evan had been born two years apart; their narrow faces were both worn by nature, and Bill shared his brother's sparkling eyes. As he and his wife stood to greet MacNeice, their faces returned to reflecting the gravity of the moment.

Bill and Dorothy were environmental engineers who'd retired from city life to Salt Spring Island to continue the fight for Canada's old-growth forests, funded by a three-year grant to study the age and health of the trees along British Columbia's coastlines.

When the subject turned to Evan, Dorothy teared up. Bill didn't try to stop the tears streaming down his cheeks; he wiped them away and asked, "How close are you to finding Evan?" They were consumed by shock and disbelief but still clinging to hope. "Isn't it possible Ev's somewhere, incapacitated but alive?"

MacNeice reminded them that Evan Moore's DNA had been found at the scene and that it was very early in the investigation. He then turned the conversation to Jack. "Are you heading back to BC right away?"

"We're staying at Ev's for the moment, but yes, we'll go back soon, probably next weekend." Bill sensed MacNeice's concern. "If there's a problem with our leaving, Detective, Dot can go back for our work—I'll leave whenever I can."

"There's no problem. I was only thinking that once we have a suspect, or suspects, I'd be interested in having Jack appear before a lineup. I feel certain he'll tell us if we're on the right path."

"You can do that?" Dorothy asked in amazement.

"If you're asking whether we can use Jack's reaction in a court case, the answer's probably not. But I'm certain if Jack identifies someone, it will have an impact on the suspect and help us narrow our investigation."

"My lord, what an idea." Bill tousled Jack's head. "If you need Jack and me, we'll be here. Dorothy's the real brains of our team; I basically do what I'm told."

"Of course you do, sweetheart." Dorothy rolled her eyes.

"I'd appreciate it." MacNeice noticed Jack was looking up at him. "Did anyone tell you about Jack's injuries?"

"Yes, Detective Inspector Aziz. She also said how you and Jack have become friends, and for that, we're grateful. It's impossible to know the depth of his grief...the measure of his loss."

When the meeting ended, MacNeice retrieved the bag with the leash, kibble, treats, and Jack's squeaky toy. He met them at the elevator; Jack's tail was wagging as he shoved his snout into the bag. MacNeice knelt down, taking Jack's head in his hands. He placed his forehead on the dog's fore-head and whispered something before standing to shake Bill and Dorothy's hands.

"I'll keep you informed. And if you have any questions, don't hesitate to call me or DI Aziz."

FIZA LOOKED UP when he entered the cubicle. "We've heard from Missing Persons. Two men have been reported missing—one for three days, the other for two." She refreshed her computer for the details.

Two photographs of the same man appeared. One was a portrait, the kind you'd use for a business announcement, the other a full-length photo of him standing next to a beautiful woman at a black-tie event. "Rodney James Conroy. Thirty-four, from Montreal. Reported missing by his wife. He's a venture capitalist and investment manager—no children—apparently disappeared on a fishing trip."

"What made her report him?" MacNeice asked.

"She got worried when one of the friends he was supposed to be away with called to see if Rodney was up for a foursome of golf. She couldn't reach him by phone, and the next morning she called all his friends; it turned out no one had gone fishing."

"An affair?" Vertesi asked with a shrug.

"Possibly. However, Conroy's height and weight match the body in Lincoln." Aziz referred to her notebook. "When asked to describe her husband, the wife said he was a sharp dresser; he had to be for work. But then this—he left home in a dark suit, white dress shirt, tie, and—wait for it—black Brioni shoes."

"Definitely didn't go fishing," MacNeice said.

Aziz flipped a page in her notebook. "He told his wife he had a business dinner first, so he packed his fishing gear and clothes in a Canadiens hockey bag."

"Is he with a firm in Quebec or on his own?" MacNeice asked.

"He's a partner in Sarlat, Dixon, Conroy — SDC — a small firm referred to variously as up-and-coming, aggressive and ambitious, and, my personal favourite, Bitcoin's best friend — though that one is a few years old."

"And the second missing person?"

"Possibly for the forest." She tapped the keyboard to reveal front, side, and back photos of an obese man in a Metallica tank top, baggy shorts, and hightops. The tattoos on his shoulders, arms, chest, and neck extended to his jawline, suggesting that the ink would eventually overtake his face. His head was topped by a yellow mane that rolled down his back. On his right shoulder — more fat than muscle — was a tattoo that read "Bitch Buster" above women's faces bouncing off a spiked-knuckle fist.

"Let me guess — assault charges?"

"Exactly. Neil 'Big Cookie' Sloan is from Sudbury. He assaulted a prostitute for refusing to have sex with him. Broke her jaw, blinded her in one eye, and injured two cops who attempted to arrest him. It took four more cops to subdue him. That netted him two years plus a day; he was released six weeks ago."

"Does he have family?"

"No. Since his release, he's been living in a renovated garage and working at a sawmill. Landlord went to see him about the rent, found the door open and a pot of stew burning on the hotplate. There were signs of a brawl."

MacNeice turned to Vertesi and pointed at the screen, seeking clarification. "He's a galooch, correct?" Vertesi pursed his lips and nodded affirmatively. Of Aziz, MacNeice asked, "Hell's Angels, any biker connection?"

"No. Cookie suffers from vertigo."

Vertesi snorted. MacNeice smiled and sighed. "Let it out, Michael, so we can move on."

"Sorry, boss. Won't happen again."

MacNeice nodded. "Did they take DNA samples from him, try to tie him to any other crimes?"

"No."

MacNeice studied Big Cookie, then turned to look at the whiteboard and asked Ryan to print out the venture capitalist headshot and tape it beside the Lincoln victim.

"And the other one?"

"Big Cookie's not our forest John Doe. He's someone you'd shoot from a distance, on the street, or in a bar before he gets a chance to stand up. And if you had to disappear that body, you wouldn't walk him into the forest to shoot him, then drag his dead weight back out. He's someone else's problem. But if I were with the Sudbury OPP detachment, I'd be checking friends, known associates, and relatives of the prostitute. It's easy to imagine that someone thought two years wasn't enough for the loss of an eye."

"I'll have the Lincoln DNA sent to Montreal for a match." Aziz turned to her computer.

MacNeice studied the picture of the corpse. "We'll need cooperation from the Montreal police to find out about his business. Was it solvent, were there any questionable deals, did he do business in Dundurn, and if so, with whom?" He turned around. "Michael, what's the investigation status on that house-fire fatality?"

"It's in the fire marshal's hands, boss. Her best guess is four or five weeks to determine whether it was foul play, misadventure, or accidental death."

MacNeice looked back to the whiteboard. "In that case, you're working with us."

Vertesi leaned back in his chair and fist-pumped the air.

The phone rang; Ryan listened for a moment, then hung up and swung around. "Sir, Dr. Richardson called to say she has something interesting... when you have a moment."

[32]

BACK IN THE BUNGALOW, CLARENCE'S THOUGHTS RETURNED TO THE meeting —and how struck he was by receiving his client's respect and even affection, which was in stark contrast to his father's revulsion for his only son. Over a glass of cranberry juice, he surveyed the trail of his childhood for clues that might reveal why he was so despised. Clarence had achieved slightly above-average grades all through school, but not because he couldn't have done better; he found school, the entire whoop-de-do experience of it, intensely boring.

Once it became evident their son wasn't destined to be at the top of any class, he overheard his mother ask his father, "Our boy's bookish; that's good, isn't it?" Recalling that conversation, Clarence smiled. She may as well have said, "Well at least he's not a complete failure; he can read." That much was true; reading was his means of escape.

There had been a period in his early teens — just a moment in the arc of his life — when he'd flirted with delinquency. Dwelling on the details of those transgressions brought his former partner in crime into focus for the first time in decades. Tommy Cameron, his cousin of the same age on his mother's side, was a dedicated wild child. If his parents had known half of what he'd gotten up to in his teens, they'd have dropped him off at the juvenile detention centre themselves.

Clarence had been a sucker for Tommy's antics, and they'd made a bizarre pair — Tom at fourteen was already over six feet tall, while Clarence had yet to — and never would — rise above five-two. While arson, theft, and premeditated vandalism had been Tommy's true passions, he also had a spur-of-the-moment penchant for tossing rocks through shop windows. He didn't do it to make a statement about the insanity of runaway consumerism — no, as he told his cousin, he just loved the sound of shattering glass. But it didn't stop there.

When, on a lark, Tommy tried out for the junior football team and didn't make it, he'd set fire to the stands at Woodlands Park, where the team practised. And, since Clarence was with him, they had both been charged with arson.

Clarence laughed at the memory; it was the only time he'd ever seen his father in a purple rage. Thereafter the old man — he'd been born old — slid into a cold chrome indifference toward his son, from which he never emerged.

Standing side by side in the dock, Tom and Clarence had waited for the judge's decision. Clarence kept his head down.

His knees were shaking; he was too frightened to look cool. But Tommy seemed to be daring the judge. He smiled and stared him down like he really didn't care what happened. He was sentenced to the detention centre for six months and Clarence was sent home for three months of community work, for his role as the lookout. He chose to do his time working in a food bank, and just to show how undaunted and unmoved he was by the verdict, every day he'd slip granola bars into his knapsack only to throw them away later.

He was jotting down options for future "disappearances" when he recalled a past conversation with his mother. "Tommy's finally settled down; he's working in a crematorium." At the time Clarence had replied, "That's brilliant; he turned arson into a profession."

Lightning strikes twice! Clarence opened his laptop to hunt for any mention of Thomas Cameron. Five minutes later, he shut it down in frustration.

Reluctantly Clarence reached for his cellphone, put on a happy face, and dialed. "Hello, Mother...You're well? Yes, me too. Yes, I'm coming for dinner. Mom, I'm a bit pressed for time but thought I'd ask—do you have Tommy Cameron's number? No...Do you know the name of the crematorium where he works? Yes? Wonderful...Yes, I have a pen." He cradled the phone with his shoulder and took down the number. "Oh, I have to run, see you on Friday... Okay, bye now."

His adrenaline spiked as he entered the number. "Hello, Thomas? It's Clarence Blow...Yeah, a long time. I hear you're doing well." Clarence tried to sound serious, which was appropriate, given the proposition he wanted to make.

When they said goodbye a short while later, he was

tempted to take a victory lap around the living room. But Tom had only agreed to talk—about an opportunity that hadn't been revealed.

While Tom's voice was still a smooth baritone, he'd spoken in a very businesslike and professional manner, without all the expletives he'd preferred as a teen. Maybe the reform school and subsequent run-ins with the law had knocked the profanity out of him. There was no telling how he'd react to the idea of occasionally incinerating strangers for a cousin who'd been scared straight in the wake of the attempted torching in Woodlands Park.

Still, Tom had agreed to meet him in an hour at Mino's Beanstalk, a coffee bar and roasting facility near Clappison Corners. Tom's business, Clappison Crematorium, fronted an industrial park so far away from any other building it might have been in a park of its own. "What could be better than an out-of-the-way cremation?" Clarence muttered, studying the Google map for directions.

To kill time until the meeting, Clarence began searching the internet for information on crematoriums: whether an oversight body monitored output; the salary for someone who managed the operation; what time of day or night was best for cremations... It was a frustrating search that bore little fruit and left Clarence feeling unprepared as he left the bungalow. Estimating the drive would be twenty minutes, he spent that time thinking about how to pitch someone he hadn't really spoken to in years about a partnership in an off-the-book venture.

Cruising along the 403, Clarence began an accounting exercise. Regarding the cost, he considered whether it was best to begin with an offer. There was nothing in his brief scan that had addressed the profit/loss aspects of managing a crematorium. And he didn't want to make his offer in response to a perceived sense of Tom's needs. So what, then? *Round numbers*, he thought. *That's the ticket. Forty thousand per cremation. Start there.*

[33]

JUNIOR WAS ALONE IN THE LAB, AS RICHARDSON HAD BEEN CALLED to the CEO's office. "Pretty sure it's about funding... could be good news, probably isn't." He stood over a body on the autopsy table. Fortunately for MacNeice, it was covered. "You wanna see where we are on the barbecue boy... looks like lead poisoning."

"Actually, I'll just wait in Mary's office." MacNeice noted Junior's brief sly smile. They both recognized the truth — that making MacNeice uncomfortable gave him satisfaction.

Feigning disinterest, Junior shrugged. "Sure. Hopefully she won't be long." He moved the table aside and began hosing down the ceramic floor tiles, calling out, "Tea cosy is over the pot, if you're interested in a cup."

MacNeice waved without turning and sat down to take

in the details of Mary's office. Twelve large casebound books filled a shelf on the wall opposite her desk. Judging by the staining on the spines — he hoped it was residue from hand cream — three were most often consulted. A large X-ray was clipped onto the lightbox; he resisted the urge to turn it on, as he wouldn't know what to make of it.

Next to her desktop computer was a milk bottle doubling as a vase for five blue cornflowers, and near the phone was a silver-framed photo of Donald, her handsome, white-bearded husband. He was wearing a heavy cable-knit sweater, looking like the photograph Karsh had taken of Hemingway — the one that cemented the image of the Old Man and the Sea.

"Sorry to keep you waiting, Detective."

"I just got here ... Good meeting?"

"Yes, indeed." She hung her suit jacket on a hanger and switched to her lab coat. "Approval for an adjustable pedestal autopsy table to replace our ancient clunker." She took a small beaker of milk from the bar fridge and poured some into two mugs. "No sugar, if I recall?"

"Correct, thanks."

Pouring the tea, she said, "I only have McVitie's today — do they tempt you?"

"No, just the tea, thanks."

She sat at her desk and studied his face. "You appear rested and weary at the same time, Mac."

He smiled but didn't respond.

"Right..." Richardson reached behind her and turned on the lightbox. The X-ray looked like a jumble of dark matter.

"The stomach contents of your young man from Lincoln..." Using her cup, she gestured at the image.

"I thought you'd want to know about his last supper. It featured wine—red and lots of it— and bread—sourdough, we believe." She took a foot-long wooden ruler and pointed to the middle of the X-ray. "That dark lump and those smaller ones are caribou meat."

MacNeice's eyebrows shot up. She smiled. "Exactly, but it gets better. These mushy, pale pudding-like things surrounding the meat are duck foie gras." She put the ruler down and peered at him over her cup.

"Are you suggesting it was a dish featuring both?"

"Yes." She swapped her cup for the ruler. "But these chunks of meat suggest something else. Can you imagine what that is, Mac?"

He shook his head, trying to come up with an answer. "Well, 'chunks' suggests he didn't chew his food properly."

"Brilliant. I admit you had the clue, but nonetheless, well done. He wasn't chewing his meat—and caribou isn't hamburger—it requires chewing."

"Are you saying he was—in some distress?"

"Not my field... but, yes, I'd say very much so." She turned off the lightbox and returned to her tea. "In every other way, this man was fit. I'd suggest he managed his diet and weight like an athlete... and he wouldn't have been if he was accustomed to wolfing down caribou and foie gras." Mary finished her tea. "More tea, MacNeice?"

"No, thank you."

"Well then... I don't know where this man came from, but his final meal is telling us something." Richardson slid a photocopy of the X-ray across the desk. "Two final things to consider." She put another photocopy on top of the first. "This is his right hand and wrist. The left was so severely burned, the details were lost . . . but here" —she pointed to a dark line around the wrist—"he'd been bound, but wasn't when he was found."

"So along with the missing contents of his skull, this adds to the likelihood that he was killed elsewhere, then laid out in Lincoln with some care."

"The narrow contusion suggests a plastic tie, not rope or handcuffs." She drew his attention to the fingertips. "Note the fingernails . . ." Richardson gave him a marble-handled magnifying glass.

MacNeice enlarged the index and middle fingers. Then he looked at the ring and baby fingers. The nails were perfectly trimmed.

Mary nodded and smiled. "You see it, don't you . . ." she said. "Either he was fastidious about his own nail care or he'd recently had a manicure."

"Who does that, Mary?"

"Ha. Well, judging by your hands, not you. Like my husband, you're a pinch-clipper man. I'd say someone whose hands are in the spotlight—a politician, priest, or dentist, a moneyman . . . a pianist?"

"You've given this some thought." He shook his head in admiration. "Our missing person is a moneyman."

"Voila."

FROM THE CAR, he called Division One. "Ryan, is Aziz there? Okay, how about Michael?" He put the phone on speaker and looked at his own fingernails—short, and admittedly clipped that way.

"What've you got, boss?"

"We need to find a restaurant in Montreal that serves a caribou and foie gras dish."

"Jesus. That's rich enough to kill someone."

"Except our man, to quote Junior, died of 'lead poisoning.' When you find the restaurant, ask if that Wi-Fi number is theirs — and if the restaurant or its entrance is covered by cameras."

"Anything else?"

"Where's Aziz?"

"Back at Missing Persons, going over the latest postings to see if there's a blood match for the second guy from the forest. Last thing: Swets and Montile are back tomorrow. Their case is with the Crown prosecutor."

[34]

U P AT CLAPPISON CORNERS, CLARENCE WAS STEPPING FROM HIS car when he received a text that terrified him. He read it again before considering his options. There were only two: One, comply. Or two, a quick stop at the bungalow, then off to the airport for a flight to anywhere.

Clarence focused on the opportunity. "This one's going to be extra...a whole lot extra." He was about to text his client with a figure, then decided to wait until the job was done. He tapped his reply: Yes sir.

Blow opened Google Maps to study the house at 79 Undermount for access, or as he preferred to call it, "ingress-egress." He sent a series of texts to One:

Pick up next subject at 79 Undermount in exactly 2.5 hours. I'll send him home with a call at 2 p.m.

He drives a late model Volvo station wagon; will be in a hurry. You need to be waiting inside the house. Leave the Lincoln around the corner. Put the keys on front driver's side wheel for me.

Caution: subject's wife may be at home. Disable — don't dispose. Don't dispose of the subject either. Put him in the Volvo and follow me. I recognize this is different from what we discussed; there will be significant additional compensation! Delete this message.

He went up the two wooden steps to the porch and opened the screen door. A saloon in a dusty town drifted into his mind, and under his breath he sang, "I got spurs that jingle jangle jingle . . ."

He'd arrived at Mino's Beanstalk ten minutes early because he had a serious pitch to make — now more serious, given the change of plans for his next disposal. Clarence knew his first impression would be most important — and that meant not being late.

Clarence counted eleven customers. A staff of three were behind the bar; one stepped out to greet him. "Giacomo Pezi," he said. "Welcome to Mino's Beanstalk." Smiling broadly, he led Clarence to a small table in the corner.

"Thomas told me to expect you, Mr. Blow. This is the table he prefers; he'll be here soon." He pulled out a chair and Clarence sat down.

"How do you know Tom?"

"Thomas and I were in the same — what he calls 'the Glorious Reformius' — a reform school. When we were sixteen, we were asked what we'd most like to do. I said, 'Work in my father's coffee business in Trieste.' Tom said, 'Start fires.'" Giacomo clearly enjoyed the irony of that statement. "Today he's my partner."

Hearing the screen door open, Clarence turned to see a tall man silhouetted against the daylight, filling the entrance for a moment. The door slapped shut behind him as he approached. Clarence stood up and offered his hand, "Good to see you, Tom."

Tom Cameron wore a smart charcoal suit with a white shirt and dusty blue tie. His shoes were black and polished. He stood so close that Clarence had to look straight up when they shook hands. He giggled. "Same old Tom. It's been a long—"

"Very long, and I'm not the same old Tom." He smiled enigmatically. "Sit down, Clarence."

Giacomo nodded formally and went off to make coffee, his leaving only increasing the intensity of the awkward moment between the two estranged cousins. Normally Clarence would start blathering about this or that, using arcane metaphors or snippets of presumed wisdom from books he'd read for the sole purpose of giving him something to say in just such a moment.

Of course, Tom knew that, so Clarence kept quiet. When they were teenagers and Clarence went off about something he'd read, Tom would cover his ears and chant, "Fuckaduck-fuckaduck-fuckaduck," until his cousin shut up.

Giacomo returned and broke the silence. "Here you are...caffè corto, fresh-roasted Rwandan Arabica beans." He put the cups down and, with his baby finger, drew Clarence's attention to the thick, creamy surface of the brew. "Here you see the crema, thick and defined by tiger-striping. Feel the side of the cup, Mr. Blow."

Dutifully, Clarence felt the side of the cup. He smiled

sheepishly, like a schoolboy learning a lesson he wasn't the least bit interested in.

"You see, the coffee has not been overheated — or burnt — so it's not bitter."

"Amazing. Thank you, Giacomo . . . By the way, who's Mino?"

"I'm Mino, the nickname for Giacomo." He put two glasses of water on the table and left them alone.

Now Clarence had something to look at, to taste and comment on. Knowing that Tom thought enough of Giacomo's coffee to have invested in the business put some pressure on the first sip. He lifted the cup to his nose and inhaled. "Gorgeous smell." Tom smiled modestly; he'd already consumed half the cup before Clarence had tasted his.

After a short sip, Clarence set the small cup back on its saucer and shook his head. He turned to Giacomo, who was leaning on the bar, waiting for his response. "It is a revelation, Mino. And —" As a message to Tom that he was in the loop, he added, "Glorious indeed."

Tom almost coughed up his water and took a small napkin to wipe his mouth. "I see" — turning to Mino — "our origin story."

Giacomo shrugged and smiled. "We're proud of that story, no?"

"Yes . . . yes, we are."

That had the effect of breaking the ice between them. Tom asked Clarence if he'd arrived early by plan or whether he'd misjudged the traffic.

"The former. I didn't want to be late." Clarence finished his espresso and reached for the water. "How much time do you have now?"

"I set aside the hour."

Clarence nodded and began listing a series of questions about the crematorium business. How many people did the actual cremation, how did the government or municipality regulate the number of cremations per day, where did his business come from—these questions and many more were wrapped, Clarence hoped, in a conversational blanket that would suggest he was just supernaturally curious about the process.

Tom Cameron's early life had made him wary of being played, so he sat with his back erect and his face disengaged. His gaze shifted from Clarence's hands, which were gesticulating and making points, to his eyes—the latter, frequently. He knew it made his cousin uncomfortable.

Clarence's mouth began to twitch. He was finding it difficult to remember all the things he wanted to ask about the business, mostly because of his client's text rather than Tom's demeanour. He smiled nervously. "I know I've asked a lot of questions. I'm just aware of the time we have."

"No problem. First, we're not at capacity. On an average day we do one or two cremations—our business plan projects as many as ten to make a decent profit. Right now, I do the cremations. I've got a part-time office assistant who handles our website and marketing. She also makes people comfortable when they arrive for the processing of a loved one. I do the books.

"As for oversight, we have no limitations, in part because we're located out here. We're inspected once a quarter, but that's to determine if our process is harmful to the environment, which it isn't. The only thing coming out of our stack is steam.

"Our combustion reaches twenty-one hundred degrees; most others burn at eight to fifteen hundred. The effect of that higher temperature is fourfold: First, it's a shorter firing time — thirty minutes as opposed to an hour or more. Second, it cuts our fuel consumption by fifty percent or more — and further ensures that what finally goes up our stack has no impact on the surrounding air quality. Third, what's left after a twenty-one-hundred burn is a much finer ash, and that in turn eliminates the need for a cremulator, a device similar in function" — he nodded at the bar — "to that espresso grinder over there. If our process was any less efficient, we'd need a cremulator to pulverize the remaining fragments of bones and teeth." Tom held up four fingers and wiggled the last one. "Four, lower burn time, lower fuel consumption means the body-to-ash cycle — all in one process — has a positive impact on the bottom line by dramatically increasing our capacity for more cremations."

Tom tapped the top of his empty water glass and the waitress came to fill it. She smiled at Clarence and topped his up too before going back to the bar.

"Am I answering your questions?" Tom asked, putting the glass to his mouth.

"You are. Please continue." Clarence tried not to sound smug or sarcastic.

"The gases and odours that exit the body during firing are kept in a separate chamber from the smoke, and from there they go through a large stainless-pipe network — like steel intestines. That's the reason there are no noxious smells leaching into the environment. The quickest firing occurs when the body is cremated in a cardboard box. Conversely, the longest occurs when we're dealing with an ornate hard-wood coffin. Adding to that, the metal from those coffins needs to be sorted from the ash. All crematoriums deal with material that has to be sorted—artificial hips, knees, coffin hinges, screws, and nails. Things like breast implants and pacemakers are removed prior to the cremation; the former because they gum up the chamber, the latter because they contain a battery that'll explode. The final product from our higher temperature is a substance similar in texture to finely ground espresso."

He looked to see if Clarence was still listening.

"I'm with you. Go on."

"We pick up fifty percent of our cremations from the overflow of crematoria in the area. The ash is sealed in a plastic bag and our customer provides an urn. Some urns are very ornate and expensive; others are indistinguishable from a garden-variety vase. At the bottom end, the ashes are put in plastic-capped poster tubes."

Tom sipped his water. "Our basic cremation currently costs six to twelve hundred dollars, the difference between them depending on whether the body's delivered or not, or if it's going to burn in an oak or cardboard coffin. A full-service cremation funeral can run up to five or six thou-sand, depending on what the family wants. For example, a minister-delivered service with extras like writing and pub-lishing the obituary, body viewing, flowers, a light lunch for mourners outside the chapel, media notices, and so on. To date we've done three of those, all local.

"Our largest opportunity for growth is in burning vol-ume. If we burn for eight to twelve hours—charging the same amount per burn as the others charge, but doing so in half the time—we can process twice as many cremations and quadruple our net revenue. And because I have two primary chambers—well, if a couple died in a car crash, they could both be cremated at the same time." Cameron exhaled in conclusion. "That's pretty much it."

Clarence was surprised when Cameron asked if he wanted more coffee. Clarence said yes, though in truth he didn't want one; he was trying to create a mental record of what he'd heard, one that would enable him to recap it for his client and One and Two.

Tom raised his hand to get Giacomo's attention. "Two more coffees, Mino. Grazie mille."

When the coffees arrived, Tom checked his watch and picked up his cup. "Why are you here, cousin? I don't think you're interested in opening a crematorium and you haven't stayed in touch... You've got twenty-two minutes for your pitch."

"Still married, Tom, with children...?"

"Not what I expected, but yes. Happily married for eighteen years. Two girls—sixteen and eighteen. We live in Waterdown; my wife's a high school teacher."

"That's wonderful." Clarence was buying time when he didn't have any. He wasn't sure how best to make the proposition he'd come to deliver when it seemed that Tom Cameron had straightened out his life.

Tom seemed to enjoy how uncomfortable Clarence was. "You know, Clare... you were always a manipulator, trying to manoeuvre around what you wanted to do or say. Just tell me: Why. Are. You. Here?" He smiled warmly.

Clarence pulled his chair in closer and leaned across the table. He spoke softly. "I'm an accountant. A while ago, a client asked me to take care of something, so I did. I've been taking care of things for a while now...but we suddenly have a disposal problem."

Tom was no longer smiling. "I'm listening."

"This client has a client—or clients—I don't know which and don't want to know. There are people—men, so far—who've crossed them or betrayed them or stolen from them—again, I don't want the stories. My client needs those people disposed of—permanently. I have two associates who handle that work; they operate under aliases. Afterwards, it's my job to guarantee the bodies disappear. Forever."

"Christ, Clarence. You're serious?"

Clarence nodded.

Tom took a deep breath. "You're a very twisted and devious man."

"I am, I know. But here's the thing: this is very lucrative work, and I have an exit plan."

"You must realize that I've turned my life around. You do recognize that?"

"Oh, absolutely. That's very clear." Clarence was sincere. "But in this you wouldn't have contact with anyone but me—and two men with no names. You'd receive a body and, just like the master roaster who receives beans, you'd roast that body. The ashes...well, is there DNA in ashes?"

"Traceable human DNA goes up in smoke."

"So it's a simple transaction. You'd be paid handsomely for doing just what you do, except this work would be off-book."

"When you say handsomely, what do you mean?"

"Thirty thousand." Clarence had no difficulty doing the

switch from forty thousand, a simple negotiating tactic—go low and make an extra ten thousand in profit.

"Per cremation?" Tom's eyes opened wide.

"Per cremation." Clarence did some rapid calculations in his head. "If your net profit for a basic cremation is currently three hundred or thereabouts, thirty thousand would provide a tidy profit."

"Don't be a smartass. How soon and how many?"

"Sorry, Tom. One very soon—later today. As for how many, I can't say; I wait for the call."

"I'm not saying yes, Clarence, but if I did, you'd have to store today's for a few days. I'm upgrading the lining of the primary chambers. It's the one downside to high temperatures. They're almost there—just three days away."

Clarence could feel the colour draining from his face. He already knew he was picking up someone local. Worse, the plan called for Clarence to terrify him into running so he could be kidnapped. "Tom, I don't have anywhere to store him. That's my problem."

"Thirty K in advance?"

"If need be."

"Cousin, I wouldn't have a clue how to deal with that amount of money. So that alone might scare me off."

"Tom, I'm an accountant. That's what I do...I mean besides this."

"I need to walk a bit, get my thoughts together. You can wait here...I just need to think."

Clarence watched him leave. Tom stood on the shop's porch for a moment before turning left and disappearing from sight. Clarence suddenly felt a shiver of panic that he might call the police. He convinced himself that he wouldn't do that because they were family, but that didn't help. Since when had anyone in his family taken care of one another? Never, was the answer; that's how he and Tom had gotten fucked up in the first place.

[35]

CLARENCE FELT HE WAS BEING WATCHED; HIS CHEST TIGHTENED with fear as he scanned the other tables. Everyone was engaged in their own conversations; to his left, the waitress was leaning on the bar, smiling at him. He smiled back, and she asked if he needed anything. Relieved, he said yes. With a pirouette, she swung around the bar. "What can I do for you?"

Hers was an ambiguous question, but he answered it straight. "Do you have biscotti or a cookie? I've had two espressos on an empty stomach and—"

"Say no more, I'll grab both. On the house."

When Tom returned, he made a beeline for the table and sat down.

Clarence washed down a bite of biscotti with some water.

"Sorry, the coffee was going to my gut." He noted Tom watching Clarence.

"Before I say yes, I want some things understood." Tom tried to quiet a tic at the corner of his mouth.

Clarence moved the plate aside. His cousin's demeanour had brightened so much that if they had to go up to forty thousand, he wouldn't hesitate.

Tom raised a hand. "To be clear, I'm not saying yes — not yet." His questions ranged widely, even to wondering out loud just how Clarence's wife had died. "Did you do it?"

"I was never charged with her death; it was a gas explosion."

"I know it was. I read that in the *Standard*. But that wasn't my question."

Clarence took a sip of water, glanced at Tom, then looked over at the waitress arranging muffins on a platter.

Tom realized his cousin had no intention of answering, so he moved on to his next question. "How can you be certain the victims are guilty of something that would justify their execution?"

"I can't. And I don't try to be. Look, I can't help making assumptions, Tom. I assume these are all underworld figures and — in an age of CCTV cameras, cellphone cameras, and video recorders — disappearing people has become difficult."

"Have you personally killed anyone?"

"Honestly, Tom, the less you know, the better. As your financial advisor, I recommend you treat this as a simple — well, not simple, but basic — cash-for-ash transaction."

"What's your exit plan?"

"Why do you ask?"

"Why?" Tom was mystified. "Because I didn't come all

this way from the Glorious Reformius to end up back in prison."

"Just know I have one, and you should too. Who bank-rolls your business?"

"My father. I completed my apprenticeship and a few years later I was running a large crematorium. I thought I could improve on the basics of the business and Dad agreed. I've been paying him off...slowly."

"And you'll continue to do it...slowly. We'll put your earnings in an offshore account." Clarence glanced at his watch. "Now, Tom, we're well past the hour you allotted, and to be honest, I have to deal with this disposal..."

"I have an idea for that. You know C.C. has his pas-sions. He's the polar opposite of his brother-in-law — your dad always seemed so careful, while mine got caught up in schemes destined to fail...But some didn't; he's filthy rich, after all. And there's one passion that might interest you."

Clarence brightened, happy the questions were over and relieved he hadn't revealed anything he'd later regret.

As Tom told his father's story, there was no hint of bitter-ness. It might have been the story of a stranger, one devoid of judgment and scorn; he was as detached in his recounting as if he were reading from a novel.

It turned out that one of Charles "C.C." Cameron's pas-sions was horse racing. Not just going to the track and betting but owning a world-class facility to produce the thor-oughbreds that win the races. "To put C.C. in the limelight, and, of course, increase his wealth."

"Where is it?"

"Where *was* it. The sign's still there —"C.C. Rider Thoroughbreds"— a hundred and fifty acres, a half-hour from Mount Hope at Hall and Trimble Road. The farm's name comes from an old blues song. But, as with many of C.C.'s big ideas, there were fatal flaws that torpedoed the plan. First among them was hiring a bent breeder—anyway, the point is that the farm shuttered three years ago. He could have kept it going out of pride, but that would have left him open to further ridicule. C.C. sold off the horses, gave generous bonuses to the staff—that's the backstory."

"Interesting...why are you telling me this?"

"Because I have the keys. The barn is high and dry. The breeder's quarters are locked; I don't have those keys. There's a twelve-foot fence around the entire property, with evergreen trees around most of it; the barn is pretty much out of sight, behind a berm."

"What's his plan for the property?"

"Development. He's in no hurry to sell, not until the market demands it. After that, he'll make a fortune."

"How'd you come by the keys?"

"He thought the girls would love it up there, and they did, until the horses were gone." Tom smiled. "A key for the barn and a code for the main gate: 1066BOH." When he heard the code, Clarence looked up. "1066, the Battle of Hastings. C.C. loves English history."

"And the individual stalls?"

"Concrete exterior walls with a high barred window at the back of each stall; sturdy wooden divider walls with a gate low enough that the horses could stick their heads out and feel less like prisoners."

Clarence checked his watch again. "Tom, I have to go. Simple yes or no, are you in?" He pushed his chair back but waited for an answer.

Tom reached into his pocket. "I pulled this from my glovebox." He slid the C.C. Rider key fob across the table. Yeah, I'm in—in three days. Use your nav app to get there."

[36]

MACNEICE PARKED THE CHEVY AT THE TREELINE TO WATCH A STAR-ling groom its wing. The bird would stop, look around, make a couple of half-hearted calls, and then go back to preening.

His mind drifted to the body of the businessman found in Lincoln. Why had it been placed, not dumped, in that former orchard? From his recollection, Montreal had more than twice the homicides. Between the St. Lawrence River and plentiful deepwater lakes — why was a Montrealer left on the Niagara Escarpment?

He was startled when his cellphone rang; so was the star-ling. It stopped grooming, tilted its head left and right before flying off.

"MacNeice."

"Mac, I'm on Province Street with Sergeant Evanson from Missing Persons. I think we've got something. It might not have anything to do with Moore and the John Doe, but an eighty-four-year-old grandmother called in as I was going through files."

"Top line?" He took the key from the ignition and left the car.

"She spoke to her grandson last Saturday. He accepted an invitation for Sunday dinner but never came."

"And that was unusual...?"

"Highly. The one thing he would always accept was a roast chicken dinner. That was the draw— otherwise, she'd never see him." The squeak of the Division door echoed on the line and Aziz paused. "She said her grandson had been...in a few scrapes with the law, and was worried that something had happened. I asked her to define scrapes. She said that he'd gone away for three years for assault with a weapon."

"Name?"

"Peter Allen Raymond, twenty-six. No fixed address. She doesn't know if he has a job, though he was a housepainter for a time."

"Family, beyond the grandmother?"

"None. Divorced parents; mother died of pneumonia, father of an overdose. If he has a girlfriend, he's never mentioned her. When I asked for a description, she produced two photos. One's recent; one from before he went inside. He looks sketchy in both...When I asked about his personality or demeanour, she pursed her lips and asked where I was from."

"Was that an innocent question?"

"Hard to tell...I said I'm from Dundurn Homicide, Division One. That probably wasn't the answer she was looking for, but what the hell...my skin's a lot tougher than it looks."

"Thicker, you mean," he said playfully. "Mentioning Homicide must have surprised her."

"Correction noted. And it did shock her. Anyway, to my surprise, she said Peter is the son of an angry man and that all the ugly traits of the father seem worse in the son. She did say he was never violent with her."

"Any DNA?"

"He left a gym bag with a comb and hairbrush, a sweater, ball cap, socks, and running shoes—and a hefty pong suggesting he never washed any of it. I would assume there's enough there. Evanson's taking it for analysis."

"Is that it?"

"For the moment...Based on the photos, I wonder which end of the gun Raymond was on."

"Let's check the department's database. Hopefully it'll include known associates."

"Before you hang up, I've got information on the incinerators and crematoriums in Greater Dundurn. There are nineteen of the former, seven of the latter."

[37]

CINDY MORROW ARRIVED AT PROFESSOR ARNIE GARRICK'S OFFICE five minutes before her appointment, only to find the door closed. No problem; there were two straight-back wooden chairs outside every office. Cindy sat next to the door, relieved that she could hear Garrick inside on the telephone. At first he spoke softly, but as the call continued, his voice grew louder and more intense. He'd pause here and there; after each, he became more agitated.

Looking at the time on her cellphone—four minutes past the hour—she considered knocking. Instead she began mentally cataloguing the phrases that made it through the heavy door. "You can't... But I will go... Look, I don't need this... Yes, I told you... I need a little more time... Aw, fuck you, there's always more time. Be reasonable... I'm not afraid of... Where? Right now? Outside my house? My wife has nothing... Nothing to do... She doesn't even know I'm—"

Cindy heard the receiver slam onto its cradle and what sounded like documents slapping onto the desk. Garrick was mumbling and swearing. And then everything went quiet. Cindy realized that whatever was going on, it wasn't conducive to discussing her master's thesis. She got out of the chair as quietly as she could and reached down for her bag and briefcase. The door opened suddenly, and as she swung about, Garrick knocked her sideways, sending the contents of her briefcase across the floor.

"Shit. I'm so sorry!" He grabbed her arm to keep her from falling. He didn't let go; her face contorted in shock and from the pain of his grip. "I can't meet... I mean I can't stay. I'll get in touch; just talk to David Yeung." He released her arm and ran the length of the corridor; she heard him pounding down the two flights of stairs.

Cindy stepped over her papers to reach the window— Garrick was racing across the lawn to the faculty parking lot. While reassembling her notes, she heard a car squeal out of the lot, thumping heavily over the speed bumps.

When everything was back in her briefcase, she looked through the doorway at Professor Garrick's office. There were papers and documents scattered about as if a sudden breeze had sent them flying. Out of respect, she closed the door.

It was August and Brant University's campus was quiet. As far as she knew, she was the only person on the floor. She was shaking as she made her way outside, where she took several deep breaths. Looking up and down the tree-lined boulevard, she recognized no one. All she saw was proud parents with their freshman kids, wandering around like fascinated tourists — gawking and referring to maps.

Stepping into the administration building, she looked for a receptionist, but no one was there except a security guard, who was preoccupied with his cellphone. Cindy waited at the desk, thinking someone would arrive soon. To pass the time, she wrote down what she'd heard.

She imagined there'd be a man who took his job in security seriously; he'd look across the empty desk before putting a statement in the form of a question. He'd ask, *So, were you eavesdropping on Dr. Garrick, Ms. Morrow?* She'd explain that wasn't what had happened, that it was impossible not to hear him, that the professor seemed terrified...

Pulling the ballpoint from his pocket-protector, he would squint suspiciously. *Is that* your *assessment, Ms. Morrow, or did he say he was terrified?*

He knocked me over; he was freaking out, she'd explain. *He grabbed my arm. Look, see the bruises?*

She ran through enough scenarios to convince herself there was nothing tangible to report — especially to a security guard. She convinced herself that whatever had happened was none of her business. Leaving the admin building, she reassured herself it had probably been about home renovations — a heated exchange with a contractor. She'd pretty much settled on that until she recalled something else: *Garrick really was shit-scared.*

On the bus heading home, she thought about her relationship with the professor. Garrick had become a leader in the field of financial risk management after developing algorithms that could dramatically shrink tons of data to predict the future of a financial risk. That his engine missed predicting the timing and magnitude of the 2008 global melt-down had damaged his otherwise stellar reputation, but to his credit, he had accurately predicted the recovery.

Cindy wanted to work with him, not because his risk engine was perfect, but because it wasn't. Almost finished with her master's degree in machine learning, she was determined to move on to a doctorate by matching her discipline with Garrick's data-crunching technology.

It helped that he realized the importance of machine learning. Historically, the entire narrative of risk management had depended on ever faster, ever more robust super-computers to reduce ever greater amounts of information down to something an economist at a tier-one bank could use.

Machine learning was a nimbler and more lively discipline—like an AI robot, the computer learned and adapted, adapted and modelled, modelled and predicted. And, while she wasn't satisfied with her thesis title, it was accurate enough: "Modelling with Machine Learning to Accurately Predict the Future of Financial Risk."

A month earlier, she'd been far enough into her research to believe the best way to test it was in Garrick's lab. The scheduled meeting had been meant to establish how they could work together. That he would suggest she speak to David Yeung—another Master's student of Garrick's who was a year further into the program—was disappointing.

In the past when she'd attempted to explain machine learning, Yeung's eyes had glazed over, and sometimes they'd close altogether when she hypothesized about the impact it could have on predictive analytics.

Suddenly Cindy recalled a quip Yeung had made about

Professor Garrick and machine learning: "Arnie probably wants to use it to perfect his gambling."

"Does he have a problem?" she'd asked.

"Only when he loses." Yeung had laughed. "When he wins, he's obsessed. When he loses, he's addicted. I think he loses…a lot."

Cindy couldn't shake the feeling that she had to tell someone about what she'd heard. But who? Yeung would probably shrug it off.

Three hours later, back at her shared apartment, Cindy picked up her phone.

[38]

SPEEDING THROUGH BRANT UNIVERSITY'S CAMPUS, ARNIE GARRICK swerved to avoid hitting the wandering clutches of incoming students. Year after year they appeared, embarrassed, wishing Mom and Dad had simply dropped them off and gone home.

Garrick turned east on Main and floored the accelerator, weaving between vehicles, forcing drivers to swerve away or hit the brakes to avoid colliding with the maniac in the red Volvo. Arnie was oblivious to the havoc; he ignored the chorus of horns and screeching brakes that followed in his wake. He was deafened by panic and waves of sickening, horrific what-ifs. What if they'd already taken Elaine? What if they torched the house with Elaine inside? What if? What if?

Speeding into a hard right on Dundurn, the Volvo lurched, throwing Arnie against the door and his phone to the floor. Dread had overtaken him and he was struggling to breathe. Pedestrians were screaming at him, but the only noise he heard was inside his head.

Arnie glanced down; the phone lay between the gas and brake pedals. He didn't attempt to retrieve it. He used the steering wheel controls to call Elaine; it rang, once, twice, three times—*click*—"Hi...sorry I missed your call. Leave a message; I'll get back to you." *Beep.*

"Elaine, if you're home—pick up now. Call me. It's urgent." His breathing came in short, shallow bursts from the top of his throat. His mind was suddenly inventing reasons for why she hadn't answered the call—all of them bad. He pushed redial and waited..."Come on. Come on. For fuck's sake, Elaine, pick up the phone...*pick up the phone.*"

"Hi, honey, what's up?" Dr. Elaine Garrick's voice, like her general personality, was positive.

"Are you at home?"

"No, why?"

"I've fucked up. Don't go home." He swung east on Aberdeen, narrowly missing a teenager on a bike; the kid swore as Arnie passed.

"What? Honey, I'm almost there—"

"Elaine. Don't. I told you—*don't go home!*"

"Arnie, what's going on? Where am I supposed to go?" Her voice was incredulous.

"I don't know...Go to your parents'. Go there. Stay there."

"You're joking. Go to Oakville? You're seriously telling me to go to—" No more sunny disposition.

"Yes. Go there now."

"Arnie — what have you done?"

"Like I said: I fucked up."

Elaine was frightened. "How bad? It can't be so bad that—"

"Really bad—I'm so sorry." Ahead of Arnie, a UPS truck had stopped. Before jumping out with a parcel, the driver turned on the four-way flashers to alert traffic that his vehicle was taking up most of the lane. In between Arnie and the large van was a man in a motorized wheelchair; a Canadian flag danced atop a wire aerial. With no apparent concern for his safety, he swung the wheelchair into the oncoming lane, forcing a silver sedan onto the sidewalk and Arnie to slam on the brakes to avoid hitting them both. As Arnie eased by the sedan, he looked briefly at its driver; the woman's jaw dropped. She hit the horn for several seconds in protest.

"What's all that noise?"

"I can't talk, Elaine. I'm going home to get some things— I'll call you."

"Well then, I'll meet you there. Like I said, I'm almost—"

"No! Stay away."

"Arnie, you're scaring me. Just let me call the police."

"No. Fuck no. Go to your mother's." As he was barking commands he felt a wave of nausea and shame overtake him. "I love you . . . I'm so deeply sorry . . . forgive me."

"For what?"

Arnie Garrick ended the call.

Elaine called back several times, but he didn't answer. There was so much to say, and there was nothing more he could say.

Over the past week he had tried to reach the man he was

indebted to, without success. Admittedly, he'd ignored the three warning calls, even as the threats left on his cellphone had increased.

Of course, the problem was much larger than he'd recognized. Lately he'd funded his betting habit from monies raised for his lab. They were provided by Germany's Neurozietech, for the development of game-changing components that would—as all innovations in digital technology promised—provide more data, faster and more reliably, than ever before. The money came with an iron-clad stipulation of repayment coming due in October—roughly two months away—when the truth would come out. Not surprisingly, Arnie's response to the impending deadline had been a desperate gamble on a very large win, which he had lost.

Turning onto Undermount Avenue, he looked to see if anyone was waiting outside his house, but the street was quiet. It was always quiet—that was its charm. That and the handsome homes set on well-cared-for lawns surrounded by trees and landscaping. The neighbours, most of them working professionals, weren't home during the day unless they were down with the flu; judging by the absence of cars today, everyone was healthy.

He drove slowly, praying he wouldn't see Elaine's Prius approaching from the other direction. He reversed the Volvo into the driveway and waited with the engine running for something to happen; when nothing did, he turned the engine off and hurried inside.

Locking the side door behind him, he listened for any movement in the house. Hearing nothing, Arnie went upstairs to his office. He quickly retrieved his and Elaine's passports and twenty-two hundred-dollar bills from the safe.

He looked about the office like someone who knew he'd never return, and swung around to leave.

He might have believed it was a trick of the eye, that somehow the door's shadow had moved without the door shifting...if he'd had time to think. It was so swift—something large, hard, and dark struck him squarely on the nose. Arnie's head snapped back and he dropped in an instant, as if gravity had grown claws.

Before his torso had even touched the floor, Arnie was picked up, whisked downstairs, carried out the side door, and shoved into the back of his Volvo station wagon. Because it was a weekday and the neighbourhood was deserted, no one noticed the two men driving Arnie Garrick's car away, or the Lincoln Navigator that trailed behind.

[39]

HIS HANDS WERE TETHERED TO A LARGE METAL RING INSIDE A STALL. A blindfold covered his forehead and eyes. Clarence assumed from the snot, crusted blood, and bruising that his nose was broken. Professor Garrick had been deposited in stall number three, previous home to a thoroughbred named Wild Honey.

The man's breathing sounded like someone sucking through a clogged straw. Clarence feared he'd suffocate if they didn't remove the duct tape over his mouth. It wasn't a question of whether he'd die — that had been decided. And if he did die from suffocation in three days, it wouldn't matter — *just not now.*

One and Two stood at the entrance of the stall. Two was swinging on the stable door, his forearms resting on the crossbar and his chin propped up on his hands. "That man's got no idea what just happened. Take that duct tape off, and the first thing outta his mouth will be, 'This is an awful mistake.'"

"Nice house, wife's a doctor, living the good life — till now." One was sympathetic, but Clarence wasn't swayed. It was, after all, One who'd flattened the man's nose.

"I'm going to remove the tape so he can breathe. We can't have him dying here; he needs to stay alive for three more days."

"Golf ball in a sweat sock..." One took the sock from his pocket. "Give him a drink, Blow, tell him to flush out that nose — then put the sock in." One no longer seemed sympathetic. "Out here, his screaming will sound like a wounded animal, and that gate won't keep folks from pokin' around." With that and a nod, One and Two left the barn to smoke in the sunshine.

Clarence was angry about the process, even though he had enjoyed playing the heavy on the phone, bolstered by the professor's panicked responses.

Garrick didn't know what he'd done, or why he'd soon be dead. The dilemma for Clarence was that he enjoyed collecting or inventing stories. *But not this kind of story.*

Garrick shifted his hips and a dark plume spread from his crotch over his tan trousers. Shaking his head in disgust, Clarence kicked the man's right foot. "Come on, wake up."

Awake, Garrick moved his head from side to side and shoved his shoulders into the wall in an effort to sit up. Clarence observed these contortions, musing that it must be how animals feel when arriving at an abattoir. He kicked the man's foot again. "I'll give you some water. Make any noise and the gag goes on. Nod if you understand."

Garrick nodded. Clarence ripped off the tape. Immediately the man began pleading, "Please, mister. We can work this out. Please, I beg you. Listen—"

"New rule: I don't care about your story. Persist, and the gag goes on. Clear?"

"Clear—but—"

"No buts; no stories."

"I recognize your voice—you called me." Garrick shut up when he felt the sock touch his cheek.

"No talking."

"Just two questions: Is my wife okay? Where am I?"

"Yes, she is, and you're in purgatory." Clarence opened the water bottle and shoved it in the man's mouth. He gulped at first and coughed up what he'd taken. Clarence waited until he'd stopped before trying again.

When the man had moved his mouth away, Clarence told him to snort out the snot and blood clogging his nose. The first snort seemed painful, and it took several more wincing attempts. By the time Garrick had finished, he was able to breathe through his nose. Clarence put the sock-and-ball gag in his mouth and tied it tightly around his head.

OUTSIDE, ONE AND Two were enjoying the sun, sitting with their backs against the barn wall. Two's eyes were closed, his jaw slack; he was asleep.

One's eyes were also closed, but as Clarence approached, he opened his right eye and whispered, "Purgatory . . . that was good. Don't go bonding with that fella, Blow. He's dead already. Don't be givin' him reason to hope for some other outcome."

"Truly I tell you, you will not get out until you have paid the last penny," Clarence said, sliding down beside him.

One dropped his head, swivelling it slowly toward Clarence. "Matthew 5:26. Now, tell me...how'd a sinner like you come to know the Bible?"

Clarence was going to say something about it being a great work of fiction, but he wisely decided not to. "As you've noted, I'm not religious. But I've always been a reader, and that was one of the books in my house — though I'm the only one who ever picked it up. I thought it was a good but complicated story."

"Story..." One turned his head away and closed his eyes. "Mr. Blow, cast a glance beyond me to the right...Beyond that grassy hill there's a row of trees...you see them?"

Clarence followed the berm to the end. At a right angle from it, there was a wall of five trees. "I see them."

"Now, between the second and third tree from the left, look closely...There's a man sitting on a tractor. It's hard to see him for the shadows, but the tractor's red."

Clarence was hit by a sudden ripple of terror; he could just make out the silhouette of a man's head and torso. His shoulders were square; he was as still as a statue, looking back at them. "Jesus."

"Still just a story, Mr. Blow?"

"What do we do?"

"Nothin' yet. He wasn't there when we came. Probably workin' his field, noticed the Lincoln. Maybe he's just curious. In a minute we'll walk along casual-like in his direction. You'll say hello, ya' know, *howdy-do*. He's gonna ask what we're doin'; you'll say we're working for what's-his-name to check on the property . . . then we carry on checkin' the property." One noticed that the colour had drained from Clarence's face. "Man's just having a tea break, Blow, like folks up here likely do . . ."

Clarence ran through what had happened in the past two hours, worried that word was out about the torched Volvo on an old tractor path at a long-abandoned farm, miles from where they were sitting now. "The plates on the Lincoln, are they still the livery's?"

"No, sir. Ghost plates." One leaned forward into a squat and with little effort he was on his feet, stretching. "Let's take a walk, Clarence. Two, if you're listening, stay where you are."

Two didn't give any indication that he was listening, so they walked off toward the tree line. One kept bringing Clarence's attention to features in the landscape that weren't there, acting the part of a big-picture man spending an afternoon in the country. Clarence picked up on it quickly and laughed and nodded like it was all very fascinating.

Using his arms to suggest a vast expanse, One said, "He's still there, so he doesn't feel threatened . . ." He pointed back to the stables and Clarence swung around and appeared to be agreeing with whatever the gesture suggested.

As they drew closer, One whispered, "Okay . . . in ten steps you'll look up, spot the man, and smile. Greet him warmly and we'll continue on, unless he engages us. If he does, it's showtime. But keep it short."

As they approached the turn, Clarence noticed the man was drinking from a Thermos and eating a biscuit. A peaked cap shaded his eyes; he was watching them. His hair was silver and poked out beneath the cap.

"How you doin' over there?" Clarence called. "Hot enough for you?"

"Doing just fine. This is growing weather, so I'm happy."

"Oh yeah? What do you grow?"

"Corn, mostly; some soybeans. Say, what're you boys doing over there?"

"Ah, right, probably been a while since you've seen anyone." Clarence put his hands in his pockets and let his hips swing forward slightly, thinking that's what country folk did when they wanted to chew the fat. He heard One chuckle. "Mr. Cameron—C.C.—asked us to check on the property."

"Gonna sell it to developers, is he?" The farmer finished drinking and was screwing the cup onto the Thermos. "Heard that, anyways."

"Oh really...well, we have no idea. We've just been walking and talking about how this would make a terrific farm..."

"Farm for what?"

"Well...as you've probably guessed, we're not farmers, but what about hemp or cannabis? There's a big market for that now, eh?"

"Maybe." The man stuffed the Thermos into a small vinyl bag. "Maybe in a few years we'll all stop growing food and switch to dope."

"Or condominiums..." Clarence quipped.

"Might be right...Okay, boys, I'll get back to the beans; they ain't gonna grow themselves."

"But they do...don't they?" Clarence said.

"Back off, little man," One said under his breath.

"Son...every little thing on earth needs help growing. Without it, they grow up all twisted and such." The farmer pulled the brim of his hat down. "You fellas have a good day now." He started the tractor and rolled off out of sight.

"A lesson, Blow. Not from the scriptures but from life. You gave that farmer something to think about..."

"That's not a bad thing, is it?"

"Your job—our job—is to be forgettable. You gave that old man something to be vexed by; that makes you, and us, unforgettable. You don't want that farmer thinking about you, 'cause he'll be hooked. You see, little man...our fates are entwined."

As he started walking again, he took hold of Blow's shoulder and squeezed hard. From a distance it would appear an affectionate gesture between pals, but Clarence's body curled forward from the numbing pain. When his knees began to buckle, One let go.

"You've got an education, Clarence. But underneath the show-off remarks and class clownery is the angry, unsettled punk you've always been." One returned to pointing out features in the landscape that weren't there.

"I think..." Clarence didn't know what to say next; he just needed to say something.

One stopped and turned on him. "Point is—you don't *think*. You react." He squatted down and pulled out a tall weed with a small yellow flower. "My ancestors were princes and kings, not just cotton-picking slaves, sharecroppers, and train porters. That's recent history—it doesn't shape my conduct." He tossed the weed. "I know the risks we take and I will not allow your smart ass to jeopardize Two and me." He turned his gaze on Clarence. "Now...you got it?"

Clarence's shoulder was throbbing, but he managed to say—he hoped sincerely—"Yes...I got it."

"Then dig this: there won't be a second lesson." One laughed briefly from his gut. "But that isn't saying there won't be *other* lessons, 'cause you're one twisty little fish."

They continued in silence, passing the boarded-up house and aluminum bleachers with a skirt of weeds swallowing the bottom row. The training field had probably been sod when the centre was active, but now it looked like the farmer's seeds and passing birds had colluded — there were patches of bright green plants scattered in no discernable pattern.

As they approached the stables, Two was busy scuffing the dust from his boots. The windows of the Lincoln were down to let what little breeze there was cool the interior. Two had the look of a man ready for a beer.

"How's our friend inside?" One asked.

"Well . . . his nose is broken. He's pissed himself, he's scared as hell. Probably would make any deal he could just to go home." Two's tone wasn't sympathetic. "Gag's on, rope's secure, he ain't going anywhere."

"Give him some more water, Blow; there's another bottle in the Lincoln. Then we'll leave him — but make sure the gag is on tight."

Clarence agreed, then added, "He recognized my voice from the phone call."

One stopped, put his head down and nodded slowly. "In a few days that won't matter. But . . . once again, this wasn't part of our deal."

"I know. I'll talk to the client."

"No doubt . . . but the thing of it is, we could have snatched him anywhere — and that way he wouldn't have had time for phone calls. The moment you hung up, that man panicked; he probably called someone. The police, his wife, his preacher? That call increased our risk; by how much depends on who he called." One massaged his jaw. "We know he didn't call from the university — 'cause we're still here. If you hadn't thrown his cellphone into that burning car, we mighta checked those calls. Point is, you best be clear-headed when talking to your client."

Clarence didn't have an answer. He took a water bottle from the Lincoln and, as he stepped toward the barn, One added, "Don't talk to him. Not a word."

[40]

"YOU'RE SITTING NEXT TO ME, MAC, BUT YOU SEEM FAR AWAY... where are you?" Aziz spoke under her breath, looking up from her notes.

MacNeice smiled. "In the middle of a city on the edge of the world." He shook his head to lose the thought. "Sorry, that sounded cryptic."

"Cryptic, or mystic."

MacNeice's laugh was loud enough that Ryan turned around, shoved his headphones off his ears, and asked, "Sir?"

"Sorry to interrupt what you were doing... actually, what are you doing?"

"Researching the restrictions on industrial incinerators and crematoriums."

Impressed, MacNeice responded, "And?"

"Here's a few factoids: Incinerator operators must maintain a manifest of what they burn based on the limitations of their equipment to comply with environmental regulations. They're checked quarterly. Crematoriums have restrictions too, mostly for the operating time, based on location. Both industries also have to comply with government maintenance standards."

"Sounds like an honour situation rather than actual oversight..." Aziz said.

"Have you found any cases where the operator was caught cheating?" MacNeice asked.

"Yes, sir, but so far, the only one I've found is that incinerator homicide a few years ago. Nothing on crematoriums."

Ryan was putting his headphones back on when two phone lines rang. Picking up the first, he listened and then turned to Aziz, "Sergeant Evanson for you." The second call was from Colin Gleadow.

MacNeice picked it up. "How are you?"

"Not a hundred percent...but better." He sounded breathy. "The fog's lifting."

"That's good news."

"A week ago on Power Line Road, I saw two men leave the forest. I'd parked there because the community centre lot was full. I was getting ready to go in when they came out."

"What about them?"

"They didn't look like the day hikers or the cross-country cyclists you see up there. They were smoking and kept looking back along the path as if they were waiting for someone. Then one of them went back in while the other lit another cigarette. Basically, it didn't look like they were there to enjoy nature. I sat in my car until I saw them leave in a van."

MacNeice felt the hair on the back of his neck stand up. "Describe the van."

"Dark grey, long body, no windows apart from the driver and passenger doors. It looked old; I don't know the make. No company name..." He growled to clear his throat. "Anyway, they just seemed out of place."

"What do you think they were up to?" As he took notes, Aziz reached over and added an exclamation mark on the corner of his page. He looked over to her as she tapped a pad where she'd written: *Another MP. Local. Professor. Wife frightened.*

Gleadow coughed and took a deep breath. "They looked a bit rough. I thought maybe they were dumping some-thing...you know, garbage or construction waste. I was worried they'd found our blind. We don't leave anything valuable on site, just the folding table, chair, and netting... but still, I was concerned."

MacNeice asked if he'd noted the licence number. Gleadow had missed it. Any significant damage? A dent or scrape, a folded bumper? None that he'd noticed.

At that point Gleadow was wheezing so badly that MacNeice ended the call and turned to Aziz.

She laid the receiver softly in its cradle. "Brant University Professor Arnold Garrick called his wife on his way home from work, told her to go to her parents' in Oakville; wife said he was panicking. As soon as she got to Oakville, she called DPD—though he'd explicitly told her not to. It was patched into Missing Persons."

"Home is where?"

"Seventy-nine Undermount. Evanson's on his way there;

says he's got a bad feeling and wants us to meet him. He asked if we should bring the cavalry?"

MacNeice was already out of his chair, pulling on his jacket. "Call it in to Tactical. I'll bring the car around."

[41]

MACNEICE FLASHED HIS LIGHTS AND CAME TO A STOP BEHIND Evanson, who was parked several houses to the west of 79 Undermount. The sergeant got out of his car and climbed into the back seat. "I've been here five minutes or so. Nothing suspicious; looks as peaceful as any of these houses. Garrick drives a red Volvo wagon; his wife is Dr. Elaine Garrick—a GP—she doesn't know his plate number, thinks the car's five or six years old."

"Did he give any reason for his panic?" MacNeice asked.

"Kept saying he was sorry, that he'd fucked up. She was on her way home when he called."

MacNeice scanned the opposite side of the street for signs of life: someone gardening, washing their car, reading on the porch, walking the dog, pushing a pram...but there was nothing. Only two cars were in their driveways, and one of them was covered by a tarp.

Through his rear-view, he saw the armoured vehicle from Dundurn's Tactical Unit arrive; it seemed so out of place on the idyllic street. The rear doors opened to eight black-clad city soldiers putting on helmets. A large man with a familiar face stepped out of the front passenger door and turned their way. Seeing who was driving the Chevy, he smiled.

"You know him, sir?" Evanson asked.

"I do. We do." MacNeice stepped out and Sergeant Washburn took his hand, adding a shoulder pump for good measure.

"They're friends?" Evanson asked.

Vertesi explained. "That guy saved some lives at our last get-together."

"Oh yeah, that army vet holed up in a farmhouse..."

No one responded.

After MacNeice's briefing, Washburn offered his take. "Street's crickets, Mac. Doesn't mean that house is...but with no sign of the Volvo it may be quiet because it's empty. You thinking we go in hot?"

"Your call, Wash, but I'd say no. Do as little damage as possible...We'll wait here. If it's all clear, call us."

Washburn offered a deep bass chuckle. "Different from our last call...Okay, stand by."

With that he drew a circle in the air, and his team— four men, three women—disembarked and ran behind him toward the house. Three split off, heading for the back garden; two squatted on either side of the front bay window. Washburn and two others approached the front door—one carried a door ram. All but Washburn had assault weapons; his sidearm was on his thigh, strapped in its holster.

From what MacNeice could see and hear, opening the door proved easy. When they disappeared through, he held his breath, dreading the sound of gunfire.

Eight minutes passed. One of the team out front kept popping his head up to see what was happening through the bay window. After each look, he shook his head: *negative*. Washburn soon emerged and waved them over. MacNeice took another look around the neighbourhood; no one had stepped out to see what was unfolding at number 79.

"I won't say too much, sir, other than something happened here. I'd guess an abduction outside the second-floor office...definitely wasn't a robbery."

MacNeice studied the door; there were no signs that it had been forced. "How'd you gain entry?"

Washburn grinned and jiggled a brass key on a small ring. "Hidden from view, top left of the door frame. Classic."

Donning latex gloves, MacNeice stepped inside. Apart from his breathing and the low hum of the AC, the house was silent. To his left, the kitchen, white and modern, with no sign of breakfast—and no broken dishes, blood, or mayhem. So, too, the living room—lived-in traditional furniture, magazines and books stacked here and there—nothing disturbed. He looked over to the second-floor stairs, a print of coloured oblong blocks was tilted, its left side dropped by an inch or so, as if someone had brushed against it on their way down.

MacNeice scanned the living room again: big books on low shelves, a vase of flowers on a glass-topped table, framed photographs on the fireplace mantle—the place was too

neat to allow for an off-kilter painting. Out back, a stone ter-
race led down to a garden bordered by two maples. There
were four cushioned chairs around a table; it all screamed
comfortable living, nothing to see here.

He climbed the stairs to a small landing and noticed a
black scuff mark on the otherwise immaculate wood base-
board. Four more steps across the landing was a bathroom.
On the second floor, MacNeice's attention was immediately
drawn to the sight of two passports and a lot of cash scattered on the floor outside an office. He opened one of the
passports: Elaine Garrick. He picked up the other. "Hello,
Professor Garrick." MacNeice photographed the money and
passports before moving into the office.

A small safe was set in a niche — with its door ajar —
nothing inside. The desk was cluttered with file folders and
complex graphs, but otherwise the walls showcased framed
awards and distinctions, and a dozen or so images of Garrick
with groups of smiling people. MacNeice took more photos.

He counted the money: twenty-two hundred, in one-
hundred-dollar bills. MacNeice asked himself what someone would want from Garrick that didn't begin with this
cash. The professor had been running, had been holding
the bills and passports when he was abducted. So why had
they left the money?

When MacNeice turned to leave, the light caught a thin
slash of blood on the lower panel of the door. No wider
than a thread, it could easily have been overlooked on the
dark grey paint. He took photos of it and looked around for
more — but there wasn't any. The streak was roughly three
inches long, angling down forty-five degrees, and ended in
a teardrop of dried blood.

Garrick had been struck standing up. But an exploded lip or nose would have produced more blood—unless he'd collapsed and bled on himself. MacNeice returned to the landing, glancing into the master suite on his way—the bed was made, no blood, no clutter. More happy photos, more abstract art. A plush off-white carpet; again, no blood. Moving downstairs, he studied each step for signs suggesting a struggle, but, apart from the scuff mark and the tilted print, there was nothing.

Before leaving, he checked the digital security screen; there was nothing unusual. Garrick must have disarmed it when he got home. Or it didn't work, and his abductors were already waiting inside. The effectiveness of the system—like many in Dundurn—could have relied completely on the security stickers.

Washburn approached with the key. "Alarm probably wasn't armed... about as effective as the key stashed on the door frame." He shook MacNeice's hand, ending with a fist bump that MacNeice attempted awkwardly to return, causing them both to smile. "Thanks for the call, Mac."

"Before you go, give me your take on what you saw inside."

"The passports and money, the blood on the door, the scuff mark on the stairs—he was tapped unconscious, probably not to kill him. Might've been lifted for a ransom? Does a professor earn enough to make that profitable?" Washburn shrugged. "Gotta go, sir. Keep your head up." MacNeice watched him jog back to the armoured tank.

Aziz beckoned. "Mac, you'll want to hear this..."

Evanson was just ending a call. "Dundurn Fire was called to a blaze up on the Mountain, on an unmaintained road—a red Volvo wagon. No human remains; just a melted cellphone on the back seat. Car had been torched from the inside."

"Get back to Missing Persons, Sergeant. Use the provincial alert system to announce Brant University professor Arnold Garrick as missing, assumed kidnapped. Anyone seeing the professor is requested to call this number immediately . . . Give his description, and a description of his car. Use your number, not Homicide's. Clear?"

"Yes, sir; understood." MacNeice watched him run to his car and speed away.

"Washburn told us about the passports and cash, boss . . ." Vertesi said. "You think Garrick's still alive?"

"I don't know, but the alerts are for those who took him—I want them to know that the entire province, not just law enforcement, is looking for Garrick." He turned to Aziz. "Fiza . . . what kind of criminal would leave behind twenty-two hundred dollars?"

She shrugged. "Someone who thought it wasn't worth picking up. Or money wasn't the reason they were here."

"You mean, like, it was pocket change for rich hit men?" Vertesi asked doubtfully.

"Well-paid hitmen—or women." She smiled. "Okay, that last bit was cheeky. Speaking generally, women are too reasonable to be hitwomen."

MacNeice and Vertesi didn't argue the point.

Aziz continued. "One possibility, and it's a stretch, is that whoever took Garrick has ethics. Stealing wasn't the assignment; it didn't matter that it was easy money."

"I look forward to meeting someone like that." MacNeice turned his attention to the neighbourhood. "Notice anything unusual about this street?" he asked.

"You mean the Sleepy Hollowness?" Vertesi said.

"No, Michael." MacNeice shook his head. "I see lovely houses on a quiet street. But when a tactical van rolls in with all its huffing and puffing, spilling out cops in combat gear with assault rifles who rush to 79 like there are terrorists inside—not a soul appears. Name any other street where that would be the case. Knock on the doors, Michael; find someone. Aziz and I will be back at Division."

Minutes later, MacNeice was turning east on Main when his radiophone rang. He reached over and switched it to speaker. "MacNeice."

"Evanson sir; that alert goes live in ninety seconds. That's not why I'm calling, though. There's a student of Garrick's on the line; can I patch her through? I think it's important."

After several clicks, the call was live. "DS MacNeice, who's calling?"

"Oh, hi. My name's Cindy Morrow...I'm one of Professor Garrick's master's students."

"Yes, Cindy. With me is Detective Aziz; what can you tell us?"

"Well, like I told the sergeant...I was supposed to meet with the professor today. I showed up a few minutes early and sat outside his office..." Cindy was well into a speedy recounting of what had happened when the provincial alert blared through her cellphone—and the phones of everyone else in Ontario.

When it was over, there was a pause, and Cindy asked breathlessly, "Oh my God...what's happening?"

"As of yet, we don't know. Can you make it down to Division One so we can take your full statement? As that alert makes clear, this is an urgent matter."

"Okay, sure. I can be there in a half-hour."

Aziz turned to face him. "You're not on the edge of the world anymore, are you?"

"No . . . I'm not." He smiled. "Get Forensics into Garrick's office before people clean it up."

They were turning into the division parking lot when Vertesi called. MacNeice pulled to a stop along the treeline. "Michael, you've got someone at home on Undermount?"

"Not yet, but we've got the Montreal restaurant that serves a caribou and foie gras dish. Cheval Fou — Crazy Horse — it's on Plateau-Mont-Royal."

"How'd you find it so quickly?"

"My cousin Alessandro's a chef in Montreal; I thought I'd see if he knew, and bingo. It's called Cheval Fou for a reason: every dish is a dare. To give me an idea of how crazy their food is, he told me to go as far from a Mediterranean diet as you can — then turn right and just keep going till you drop."

"The Wi-Fi number?"

"Haven't gotten anyone on the line, sir. I've left messages, but for now, I don't want to involve the local cops."

AT 7:23 P.M., Garrick's student was following Sergeant Stanitz up the stairs to the interview room.

Cindy Morrow stood up when Aziz came in and introduced herself with two cups of tea, sugar packets and stir sticks tucked into the breast pocket of her jacket. "I've taken the liberty of pouring tea with milk. If you like, I have sugar as well."

"Oh, no sugar, thank you." She was nervous but composed.

Morrow spoke about the phone call and the professor running away from the building. "After he left, I went to report it, but there was no one there, so I went home."

"What were you and the professor working on? If it's really technical, imagine you're speaking to your grade five teacher."

"Grade five, that's funny . . . Okay, so the professor's pretty famous for developing a computer program that collects and analyzes financial data for tier-one banks . . . a predictive tool. It's robust and fast—and speed is good."

"And it works?"

"Yes, but not always. He missed the '08 crash by a country mile . . . but then he accurately predicted the recovery."

"And what do you bring to this?"

"Machine learning. It's fairly new."

"Is that intended to be literal—learning machines?"

"Okay, so how can I put it?" Morrow's brow furrowed. "It's not just that machine learning can crunch more data faster, though it can do that. It's that it simultaneously finds patterns in the data—that's its genius. Like Usain Bolt running a marathon at the same speed that he runs a hundred metres. And as if, while he's running, he's also solving a Rubik's Cube—meaning machine learning is fast and super intelligent. But the best part is, once it's accomplished one task, it'll be faster and smarter the next time." She smiled. "How was that?"

"Good. Why is Garrick interested in machine learning?"

"I probably shouldn't say this, but another Master's student told me Arnie would probably use it for gambling. I don't know if that's true." Aziz raised an eyebrow.

When the interview was over, Aziz saw Morrow off in the elevator and turned to see Ryan running toward her. "Duty sergeant called; Garrick's wife is here for MacNeice."

"And?"

"He was called to the Deputy Chief's office."

"Thanks. Ask Stanitz to take her to an interview room."

Aziz smiled as she watched Ryan jog back to the cubicle, but her thoughts were with MacNeice. She assumed Wallace was going to tear into him for improper use of the provincial alert. Had it been rash or reckless? Both, probably.

Aziz went to make more tea. When she arrived at the interview room, Elaine Garrick was mid-pace, clutching a balled-up tissue. Before they could introduce themselves, Dr. Garrick blurted, "Can you tell me anything?" Aziz offered a hand and was about to respond, when she added, "And why am I in the homicide department?"

"I'm Detective Inspector Fiza Aziz. There's no suggestion that your husband's been murdered, but you're here because there have been three recent homicides in Greater Dundurn, and we're ruling out all possibilities. We're doing all we can to ensure that Professor Garrick is found quickly."

"Was that the reason for the alert?"

"Precisely." Aziz sat at the table and motioned for Dr. Garrick to sit as well. "It's English breakfast tea, with milk. If you'd like sugar, Dr. Garrick, I've a packet in my pocket."

Garrick shook her head in frustration and sat down. "Are you certain he was taken? How can you be certain?"

"Your husband's car was found burnt out on the Mountain and there's evidence that he was taken from the house." Aziz calmly delivered the facts. "He was also overheard at the university taking a call that sounded threatening."

"Christ . . . what's he done?" It was a rhetorical question. "The house? What did you find?"

"Do you mind if I call you Elaine?"

"No...please do."

"I can appreciate that this is terrifying for you, Elaine, but I trust you'll understand when I say let me ask the questions. I promise that I'll answer yours in time, but every second counts here."

Elaine nodded and managed to apologize before her tears began falling. Aziz waited. As Elaine picked up her cup, Aziz said, "Your husband called you from the car..."

"Yes."

"To the best of your recollection, tell me about that call. Don't leave anything out, including your thoughts about what might be happening and his state of mind. With your permission, I'll record the interview to ensure that I don't miss anything." Rather than using the department's tape recorder, Aziz placed her cell on the table between them. "DI Aziz, Division One, interview with Dr. Elaine Garrick... From the beginning, Elaine?"

"Arnie said—" Her eyes flooded with tears, and she tightened her jaw before continuing. "He said he was sorry..." She buried her face in her hands and began sobbing.

Aziz reached over to the credenza for a box of tissues. Moments later, Elaine took out several tissues, wiped her face, and blew her nose. Straightening up in the chair, she continued. "I was just heading home from the clinic when he called..."

[42]

CLARENCE WAS IN HIS CAR, BEHIND THE LINCOLN; ONE WAS JUST pulling away when the alert's sustained blaring began. Instinctively One hit the brakes and the Lincoln lurched to an ungainly stop. In his car, an already rattled Clarence dropped his keys underfoot. On the sidewalks about him, pedestrians had stopped in their tracks to stare at their cellphones.

Clarence saw the Lincoln shift into Park and assumed that One was about to deliver his next lesson, but the door didn't open. Instead, seconds later, the Lincoln pulled away. With a racing heart, Clarence picked up his keys, put his own car in Drive, and moved into traffic, trying his best to be invisible.

He should have expected it, but he was still startled when

his phone rang. "Clarence, we need to talk. When can you be here?"

Obviously the client had heard the alert. Clarence did his best to sound confident, "Best guess, thirty minutes."

"Make it fifteen minutes." The call disconnected.

Clarence didn't like being summoned. It was something his father had always done, and Clarence had always resisted. He would either pick up a book or move in slow motion. Pulling over again, he shifted into Park, opened the windows, and turned off the ignition. Adding to his defiance now was his conviction that however botched the abduction was, the responsibility belonged with the one who'd detailed how it should be done: namely, the client.

Looking out at the street, it occurred to Clarence that many of the shops or banks would have CCTV cameras that might have recorded him leaving the car on his way to pick up the Lincoln. Or they might have recorded him following Garrick's Volvo—none of which would have happened if they'd stuck to their normal delivery system.

He realized he needed to build a defence. Breaking from the norm had caused chaos. A daylight kidnapping was not the quiet transfer of a subject for disposal. Why had it been so time-sensitive? Sending a subject racing through the city, and with the ability to make calls along the way, was amateurish.

Clarence would say that the call he'd made—as instructed—had been so effective that the professor was too petrified to call the cops, for fear his wife would be killed. Had Garrick called them, the whole operation would have ended on Undermount.

The snatch had been impeccable and discreet. Not even

Garrick's wife would suspect anything...that is, until she got upstairs. And no one calls Missing Persons when someone's been out of touch for just a few hours—which meant Garrick had spoken to her. An imperfect plan had been executed to perfection; the text from his client with the additional instructions was the original sin.

Then there was the matter of the additional cost for the operation. A twenty-five percent surcharge sounded reasonable—or it might be too much. Clarence dropped it to twenty. That made him angry at himself, so he moved it back up, to thirty percent. Thirty left negotiating room...

His phone rang; it was a 905 area code. "Hello..."

"Clarence, it's Tom. Was that what I think it was?"

He considered lying and saying it wasn't their disposal, but decided to tell the truth. "Yes."

"Are we cool?"

"All the way." Trying to sound as confident as possible, Clarence added, "Has there been any change at your end? I mean, regarding our delivery timing?"

"We're still on the original schedule."

"Fine. Thanks for calling. Sorry, I'm just going into a meeting." He waited for Tom to hang up before starting the engine.

THE MEETING WAS over in less than five minutes. As he was leaving, Clarence Blow stood tall and walked with confidence to his car.

Clarence had begun his offensive before he reached the client's desk; so as not to offend, he maintained a humble air of certainty—that there couldn't be any more mistakes going forward. He smiled an authentic smile, but in truth, his certainty had wavered.

"It's a compelling argument... You have my word this won't happen again."

Clarence thanked the client and moved on to discussing compensation. Before he could make his case for the additional percentage, his client raised a hand. Clarence pursed his lips mid-sentence and tried to relax.

"I've already set aside a twenty-five percent increase for you and your colleagues; it will be paid when the disposal is confirmed." He waved nonchalantly in the direction of the door.

Clarence thanked him again and asked if he had any questions. The client said, "That alert was, well, shocking." He raised his eyes toward the ceiling, as if a better word was hanging like a bat, before addressing Clarence again. "We—and I'm certain that includes you and your colleagues—would prefer there be no public profile... and while this does nothing to expose our partnership, it is nonetheless disconcerting, and I've been left to downplay its importance to my client. Do you get my meaning?"

"I get it, yes." Clarence could see that his clipped answer made the client uneasy, but it was the truth—or the best truth he could come up with in the moment.

"And we're certain the disposal will go smoothly?"

"Absolutely." Clarence nodded; this time, he was definitive.

"Well then, very good. I don't mind saying that I was alarmed by that alert... very alarmed."

Clarence smiled but said nothing. It wouldn't help his case to admit that the alert had also scared him. Putting on his best professional face, he asked, "And when is our next disposal?"

"I'll let you know...but soon." The client picked up a file folder. "I'm sure you have more important things to do. Goodbye, Clarence."

[43]

"**I HEARD YOU SHOOK THE BUSHES." DS JOHN SWETSKY'S VOICE**, anchored somewhere below his spleen, was gruff but upbeat.

"Ah, the alert..." MacNeice could hear an orchestra of accordions in the background of the call. He was on his way home, having left a lengthy briefing with Wallace and his public relations assistant. They'd spend the rest of the evening distilling what he'd given them into a concise media briefing. "Somewhat, yes. I'm told you and Montile are joining us tomorrow."

"Yep... So tell me, you took a shot to the jaw from Wallace or from the province?"

"Wallace may have taken a shot, but he never passed it on to me."

"Did the alert have the desired effect?"

"I'm certain it had an impact. The people we're dealing with have enjoyed the shade too long. And since there's no escaping those alerts, whoever hired them heard it too. I'm assuming it's the same team, or a mutation of it, as the one from the forest and orchard killings — though this iteration is wildly off-script."

"A whole lot of assuming, Mac..."

"Garrick was likely taken from his home on Undermount. He made it there from his Brant U office in a red Volvo. I want to know which route he took."

"To see if he was picked up on security cameras..."

"That, yes. But since his car was found burnt out back on the Mountain, whoever took it there had another vehicle to drive away. If we chart the shortest distance between the house and the ditched Volvo, we might get lucky and spot that second vehicle."

"A good hunch. A big job."

"Here's another — Aziz has put together a list of farm and industrial incinerators and crematoriums."

"With no budget for site visits?"

"Correct."

"I'll call Division Two. DS McMillan owes us, Mac. Trust me, I won't be subtle."

"I'm sure you won't." Unsubtle was a Swetsky specialty. "Before I let you go — what are you watching?"

"International polka competition finals, from Warsaw. Wife loves it; therefore, so do I."

DRIVING UP THE mountain lane, MacNeice noticed yellow-green lights blinking sporadically throughout the woods. Once inside his cottage, he dropped his keys on the hall table, slipped off his shoes, and went to the living room to look out at the forest.

The night was young but alight with fireflies, more than he'd ever seen. And though he'd intended to heat something up for dinner right away, he instead poured a glass of Sassicaia grappa and sat by the window.

A few minutes later, he reached for his binoculars to search for anything that might also be watching the fireflies. He imagined that a coyote would have the right disposition; after all, they had no natural predators and no problem finding meals of voles, moles, rabbits, or rats. It was reasonable, as sentient creatures, that they might pause for a moment of joy, of observation — how could they not?

Jack had taught him that much in such a short time; that dog had studied life. He was curious about everything, using his nose as a guide, signalling his interest with twitchy nostrils. If Jack were beside him now, MacNeice was certain they'd both be tilting their heads back and forth, enjoying the wonder together.

Adjusting the weathered field glasses he'd inherited from Kate's father, MacNeice slowed his breathing and peered down the colonnade of trees to the jagged last storeys of the ancient wall — above which there was only sky. Within minutes, hidden in shadow, a pair of yellow eyes appeared. Holding his breath, he adjusted the focus. Coyote. Moments after the image sharpened, the eyes turned away and the shadow moved. MacNeice tracked it for another ten feet as it loped along the dark rampart.

But in that moment when the animal's eyes were mingling with the yellow-green fireflies, it seemed to MacNeice that nothing—not even Paris—could be more beautiful or romantic, even if no one was there to share it with him.

It had been different in Paris. There he was alone among millions of people and, barring a long-legged shadow with dancing hair, or a violin concerto that might suddenly, like a full moon clearing a cloud bank, throw his thoughts back to Kate—barring all that, he felt free of the burden of memory and had moved through the city as invisible as a spy.

Here at the window, he was gripped by the absence of human touch. Emptying the glass, he closed his eyes to the forest and went off to bed.

THE NEXT MORNING, he made a double espresso and stood before the same window. The fireflies were long gone to bed, but several chickadees were hopping from the branches to the patio table and down to the ground. Venganza's comment came back to him; he held his mug as still as he could and looked down to see if there were tremors. There they were, like ripples from fallen tears—as if they'd carry on forever. MacNeice tried to put the shaking down to fatigue, but he finally accepted Vennie's point.

He called Dr. Sumner and left a message asking for an appointment. At the end of his message, he added, "Doctor... I dodged your question last session. I know you wrote down *somnum exterreri*. You were right...it was a nightmare." He glanced over at the kitchen clock—5:12 a.m.

[44]

WHEN MORNING CAME FOR CLARENCE, IT ARRIVED WITH THE EASY rise and fall of his breathing. He couldn't recall a time when he'd had such a deep sleep, and he was in no hurry to open his eyes to a new day. Not that he was dreading it — which was odd, because he had many reasons to feel dread. He was instead overwhelmed by a sense of well-being, happy to let his eyes open when they wanted to — and when they did, he was gazing at a ceiling streaked by sunshine.

"Time to wake up, Mr. Blow."

Clarence shrieked and bolted upright so quickly that he fell out of bed, his legs caught in the duvet. In an instant, his high-pitched scream was replaced by unhinged fury. "Fuck! Fuck!" Wrestling himself free of the bedding, he stood up and straightened his pajamas. With his heart pounding, he struggled for breath. "For fuck's sake . . . What're you doing here . . .? How did you get in . . .? *You can't do this.*"

"You done?" One sat, his body relaxed and his legs out-stretched, in a chair festooned with pink roses.

Clarence wasn't done. Not by a long shot. His fury raged. The only response he could summon was snarled through clenched teeth: "I'm done. I'm fucking done." For further emphasis, he threw the duvet on the bed and sat on the edge to catch his breath.

"Good morning, sunshine." Two appeared in the door-way, a glass of cranberry juice in hand. "I almost dropped the glass when you freaked out, little man. Sheesh, that was scary."

One leaned forward. "I'll ask again—you done?"

"Okay . . . get out of my room." His voice was justifiably sharp. "Go on. I'll take a shower, then we can talk."

One tilted his head toward Two. "Smack him hard enough to wake him up. Blow's dreaming he's in control of the situation."

Two set the glass of juice on the dresser and came around the bed. Before he could reach him, Clarence scrambled across to the other side; furious, he discarded caution. With his fists clenched and full of fool's courage, he snapped, "I am not a child. I don't need to be disciplined. Stop this right now."

One let his head fall back against the chair and closed his eyes.

Two stomped onto the bed and lunged for Clarence, who ducked his grasp and scurried into the bathroom, locking the door behind him. "Stop this, One. We can talk it over—whatever it is."

"Come out, little man," Two said, tapping on the door with his fingernails.

"One, I'm a grown man. I have my dignity. I'll come—"

The door flew open, caught Clarence on the forehead, and knocked him down between the sink and the toilet. Two stepped in and hoisted him to his feet. Dragging him back into the bedroom, he shoved him hard onto the bed. Keeping hold of Clarence's nightshirt collar, he said, "Time to get spanked."

"But I don't—" The blow came swift across his left cheek, slamming him against the headboard. Clarence was stunned, his face burning and ear screaming. He checked for blood; he wanted to cry but didn't dare.

Two went back to his cranberry juice as if nothing had happened; he sipped it and winked at Clarence.

"Now, Mr. Blow, on to today's lesson. You'll want to pay attention... we're professionals; you aspire to be one. More plainly, you're a poser who wants it to come easy. We worked hard to get where we are; you have not. We work hard to get paid, but we work our hardest to not get caught. Got it, little man?"

Clarence couldn't bring himself to agree with such a low estimation of his ability, but he surrendered the point with a sulking nod.

"We've got a disposal right now breathing air and soiling himself. He's thirsty and scared. He's waiting for death but hoping something will happen to stave it off, that someone will appear to save him. He's got another two days layin' trussed up in that stable." One nodded as if he was considering those points over again. "That's torture, Blow. We didn't sign on for torture."

"I understand, but—"

"Maybe you do... You see, when you were tucked all comfy in your bed with that itty-bitty smile on your face, I could easily have snapped a round into your head. And other than a millisecond of searing pain, you'd be dead. That's what we do. That's what I mean when I say our targets never know what hits them."

"But I spoke to the client. There'll be no more texts, no more rushing around, and no more lack of planning. He completely agreed to that."

"Uh-huh. Well, the moment that alert went off, you were four seconds away from being dead. Keep that in mind when you promise something won't happen."

Clarence shook his head; it felt like parts of it had come loose inside, and he grimaced in pain.

"We'll come back for you after we visit the professor."

"What? Why?"

"You'll take us to meet your friend. Not to worry, Blow; we're all about being thorough."

"You don't need to... he's my cousin. You can trust him."

"Well, well, well. In that case, we do need to meet him. I also need to know the distance between those stables and his final destination. And that's not all..."

"But I can give you the distance."

"I'm sure you can. You see, though, I work by feel. I need to *feel* the distance—that's how I learn. And he may be your cousin... but I want to meet the man you're trusting. I need to see how this works. For example, there's the question of whether we dispatch the professor at the barn or somewhere else."

"Why do you need to meet him?"

"'Cause maybe he won't back out at the last minute—but then again, what if he does? If that happens, and I know how to light that oven, how to flick whatever switch needs flicking—it's like we're boy scouts, Clarence. We need to be prepared."

"But that wasn't the deal I made." It most definitely *was* the deal he'd made with Tom. He was just worried that One and Two would scare him off.

"He's family. He'll adjust to the new deal, don't you fret about that."

"I'd much rather you trust me."

One pursed his lips. "You know, when that alert came over our phones and radio, we were caught off guard. I have to admit we didn't know about that local feature. But, in truth, you never told us about it, either." Clarence flinched as One slapped his hands on the arms of the chair like an exclamation mark. "Now here we are, safe and sound. But don't mistake my words, Mr. Blow; you're beginning to look like a pistachio."

"No. No. I'm not a pistachio. You'll get paid—paid extra—and it won't happen again. I promise you, I've never heard an alert like that. As for him being up there for two more days—this is the only time. It's all immediate after this one."

"Uh-huh. Well, we'll head out to check on the professor, give him some water an' flush out his stall as best we can..." One pulled himself out of the chair and ran his paw across the dresser as he headed to the door. "We're in a white Escalade with Quebec plates—the Lincoln's been retired." He smiled and followed Two out of the bedroom.

Seconds later, Clarence heard the front door close. He

sagged onto his bed and began crying. When he'd pulled himself together, he took a hot shower. By the time he was sitting down to dry toast and marmalade, he realized those tears had contained more humiliation than fear. If One really wanted him dead, he would never have woken up.

He was desperate for a plan, because now it was obvious that when the disposal had been paid for, he'd be the last loose end for his client.

He stared at the Polynesia poster, feeling a fool for thinking that escape was a possibility. He wondered if One or Two had questioned why that poster had such pride of place in his house. If they poked about, they'd have found travel brochures and books with titles like *A History of Polynesia* and *James Cook's First Voyage*. Put that together with the volume of cash, and anyone possessing a dollop of suspicion would have realized Clarence had an exit strategy.

Clarence realized he couldn't afford a Plan B; he'd focus all his energy on Plan A: see the disposal through and then, without warning, leave. "I'll go on my own terms, to a place where no one will find me." He smiled at the suntanned poster girl. "There will never be a repeat of this morning." Clarence rummaged through his closet and pulled on a linen jacket, one that allowed him to carry his handgun undetected, before getting on with his day.

[45]

EMERGING FROM THE STAIRWELL AT DIVISION ONE, MACNEICE MET DI Charlie Maracle. They shook hands and, for a moment, regarded each other the way people do after surviving something awful.

MacNeice smiled. "You made it through your suspension okay?"

"Yeah, it wasn't so bad." Maracle laughed. "Gave me a chance to heal the ankle, go back to Six Nations, be with my people."

"Good to have you back, Charlie."

"Good to be here, sir. I also brought Detective Sergeant Lise Bichet with me. She spent seven years in the drug trenches of Toronto, got here a month ago ... Coffee, sir?"

"No thanks, I'm coffee'd out."

When MacNeice entered the cubicle, Aziz said, "There's a lineup for your time, Mac. Evanson's got something." She smiled. "Before that, though, we have a new team member."

"Lise Bichet, sir. I'm new to Dundurn, but I'm a quick learner." She couldn't have been more than five feet tall, but there was a toughness to her. Her hair was short and spiky; she looked like she spent thirty seconds in front of a mirror in the mornings.

Her sleeves were rolled up to the elbows; there was a small blue tattoo of a star on the webbing between her right thumb and forefinger. She wore black service fatigues, a black cowboy shirt—with pearl buttons—and a black nylon side holster high on her hip. Her shoes, also black, were more like hiking boots. Bichet's torso appeared solid, like a gymnast's; her wrists were thick and her forearm muscles well defined. Her handshake would end any questions about her size.

"Are you a boxer, Detective Sergeant?"

She leaned back as if avoiding a right hook. "Whoa, sir... is it that obvious?"

"You'll get used to it," Aziz said with smile.

"Yes, sir—since I was first in undercover. It came in handy once or twice. Do you box?" Her eyes widened, expecting to meet a fellow traveller.

"No, not at all." MacNeice shook his head. "I try to avoid the need to... Welcome to Division One, Sergeant."

MacNeice turned to Evanson, who was waiting nearby. "Okay, Sergeant, take it away."

"Yes, sir. The alert results came through..." He'd taped the responses and two maps to the whiteboard. "We had fifty-four calls yesterday; forty-one were people who remembered how fast the Volvo was going. One was a sixty-four-year-old who uses a motor scooter who thought the Volvo driver wanted to kill him."

With his pen, he pointed to the first map. "The sightings start here at Main on the edge of the Brant U campus; there were a dozen more before Dundurn. Then a bunch along Aberdeen...and two on Mountain Avenue. There were no more sightings...until later." He smiled and moved to the second map, which bore six red dots.

"A caller spotted the Volvo heading up the Jolley Cut; another reported it going east on Inverness. But our final caller"—he drew an X over the sixth dot—"was behind a red Volvo wagon that stopped at the Mohawk traffic light. It was trailing a black SUV—which ran the light. Our caller, a retired teacher, was upset there weren't any cops around to catch it and he went on a good rant about the end of civility."

"He connected the two vehicles?" MacNeice asked.

Evanson nodded. "The SUV moved off to the side of the road, where it stopped. When the light changed, it pulled back into traffic, ahead of the Volvo."

"Connected."

"The caller watched them drive off 'like a small convoy,' he said."

"Plate number or make of the SUV?" Swetsky asked.

"Negative. Closest he could get to a description was that it was large and had tinted windows like the cars that go to the airport." Evanson picked up his briefcase. "I should get back, sir."

"Thank you, Sergeant—great work."

MacNeice studied both maps. "There'll be CCTV captures along Upper James and..." He let his pencil travel to where the Volvo's trip had ended. "Michael and Charlie, check all the businesses along both sides of Upper James. Assuming there are cameras, we want to get to them before they're wiped."

Vertesi nodded. "On it, sir."

Maracle was peering at the map. "Strange that they'd take the Jolley Cut, not James Mountain Road. It's closer to Undermount and runs directly into Upper James."

"Everybody loves the Jolley Cut," Vertesi said. "It's more fun to drive and you still come out on top..."

"Gives you an idea of what Rocky does for kicks, Lise," DI Montile Williams quipped.

MacNeice examined the route. "You're less likely to get spotted on the Cut, but more exposed getting over to James." He tapped the map. "Ryan, find out if Traffic has speed cameras on James Mountain..."

MacNeice scribbled in his notebook: *They don't know the city. Because they're not from Dundurn.* "Okay, Michael, you're up."

"I spoke to Daniel Marchand, maître d' at Cheval Fou. That Wi-Fi handout is theirs. Rodney Conroy's a regular customer. Marchand remembers the last night he saw him— two days before he was found in Lincoln. It was apparently a client meeting: Conroy, with three other men." Vertesi read from his notes. "It wasn't a pleasant dinner; there were 'very tense, low voices.' I asked if everyone spoke. He said no, just an older man. He kept leaning into Rodney, seemed to be scolding him, 'like he'd been a naughty boy.'"

"How did it end?" MacNeice glanced at the photo of Conroy's body.

"Rodney paid and they all left. The older man walked by

Marchand without acknowledging him, and Conroy followed between the other two. When he slowed to shake Marchand's hand, one of the men shoved him forward. Marchand called Conroy later to see if everything was okay...but there was no answer, so he left a message."

"Conroy's last supper," Williams said. "Never break bread with a homicidally inclined client..."

"Any further details about those men? English, French-speaking, racial backgrounds?" MacNeice asked.

"Waiter said they were white. They ordered their meals in English, but with eastern European accents.

"Has Montreal confirmed his DNA?"

"Confirmed. Conroy's our victim."

[46]

CLARENCE WAS OUTSIDE HIS BUNGALOW, LEANING ON HIS CAR, when One and Two returned from the barn. At the sight of them, he pulled out his keys.

One swung the suv around and rolled down his window. "Nope. We'll go in the Es-ca-lade so I'll remember how to get there." He was smiling. "B'sides, you'll be able to tell us about your cousin the cremator."

"I call him Tom," Clarence said, reaching for the suv's back door.

"Nope again. Ride shotgun with me; it's easier to guide me up front."

As they drove away, Clarence asked, "How's the disposal?"

One tilted his head slightly. "His name's Professor Garrick. You down with that?"

"Yes. How's Professor Garrick?"

"Well, he hasn't fouled himself further."

"And we're mighty happy about that, Clarence," Two said, leaning into the gap between the two front seats.

"Man's hungry and scared. Two gave him water, but soon as that gag was off, he was begging, explaining himself... It was pitiful."

"I would've given him more if he'd shut up, but he couldn't— *'cause he's scared shitless.*"

They drove east on the 403 from Dundurn. Both men eyed Cootes Paradise, where the light made the shallow silt-bottom of Cootes look blue. "Pretty country, One..." Two said wistfully.

"Sure is. You'd never know by looking there what it's like on the other side, that big ol' waterfront..."

"Like to go boating here, if we had time..."

"We don't." One said. "What's that up there in the woods?"

"Yeah," Two said. "Strange place for a church..."

"The Sisters of St. Joseph convent, but it closed years ago."

"Appears St. Joseph had a lot of sisters," Two said to no one in particular.

Clarence tried to focus. "One, will you dispose of him at the farm or the crematorium? I should let—"

"Undecided. May even be on the way... with a plastic bag."

Clarence's stomach turned. "Sounds like torture "

"A bag? Naw... do it right and it's over pretty quick. Sure, there's a lot of buckin'-'n'-thrashin', but that just makes it quicker." Two was thinking out loud. "Then again, nothing beats a bullet to the brain for speed... though it's messy."

[47]

MACNEICE SAT DOWN AT HIS DESK AND ASKED AZIZ, "TELL ME about your meeting with Dr. Garrick...?"

She opened her notepad. "Our interview was just under an hour... Elaine was distraught and didn't understand anything from her husband's phone call. She said, 'Arnie was incoherent and terrified; he kept saying he was sorry and flipped out when I said I was almost home.' But the best way to hear that interview is unfiltered."

Aziz opened the file on her cellphone. As they listened, it was clear that Elaine Garrick couldn't imagine anyone wanting to harm her husband. "He can be irascible at work, but that just shows how serious he is about risk. Our personal finances are separate, but the university's commercialization office has just awarded Arnie a commission to purchase and develop more advanced technology for his lab."

"Has that been purchased?" Aziz asked.

"I don't know if it has..."

On the recording, Aziz went straight to the point. "Cindy Morrow, one of your husband's master's students, was told he had a gambling problem; were you aware of that?"

"People always tear Arnie down. When he didn't predict the 2008 collapse, they conveniently forget that he correctly predicted the recovery."

"I'll take that as a no. And yet, if your finances are separate, how can you be certain he wasn't in financial difficulty?" Aziz asked.

"Why are you asking that? I'm here to help find my husband—I don't know why—" Elaine was getting increasingly exasperated.

Aziz remained steadfast in her response. "Two reasons. Money issues are often the root cause of kidnappings, and because Arnie told you he was sorry for making a mistake—that he fucked up."

Garrick's voice faltered. "I trust my husband. I trust him. Do you understand that, Detective?"

It wasn't a question that sought an answer, so Aziz continued. "Outside your husband's home office, we found two passports—yours and his   and cash totalling twenty-two one-hundred-dollar bills. The safe was open. Did you have the combination for that safe, Elaine?"

"No...I believe Arnie keeps his patents in there."

"Did you know about the cash?"

"No..." She paused. "It's likely his idea of rainy-day money, but I wasn't aware of it."

"Do you believe your husband is faithful, Elaine?"

After a long sigh, Elaine said, "Sure, there were flirtations with grad students, but that was a long time ago...so the answer is, yes. I believe Arnie is a faithful, loving, supportive husband."

Aziz turned the recording off. "She said Arnie never used drugs, and given her work, she'd know if he had. Nor could she recall any mention of threats or enemies—beyond those typical of academia. I called the university's commercialization office earlier. A decision on whether they'll provide confidential information about Garrick's commission is being made before noon. I told them that if it's declined, I'll come with a court order."

"Very good," MacNeice said. "Garrick wouldn't be the first husband to have a secret life, and if it's not women or drugs, it could be gambling. Missing a market collapse, predicting a market correction—his skills revolve around money and risk."

With a meaty paw on both chair backs, Swetsky leaned over them. "What's next for me, Mac?"

"Incinerators and crematoriums in Metropolitan Dundurn, with Aziz."

Later, as Swetsky and Aziz were packing up to leave, Ryan took a call. He turned to Aziz. "Evanson, for you."

She picked up and began writing furiously on her pad. "Is that it? Okay. Thank you, Sergeant." Hanging up, she smiled. "While Evanson was here, Missing Persons had a call about a thirty-four-year-old white male from Dundurn who's just been reported missing. John Steadman hasn't been heard from in three days. His ex-wife called it in because he didn't pick up their four-year-old son yesterday. That has never happened before."

"Siblings, parents, known associates?"

"Brother helps run the father's tomato farm out near Leamington. They haven't heard from John in years; apparently he had some issues with the family. He also spent ten months of an eighteen-month sentence in jail for auto theft, and was renting the basement of a duplex on Kenilworth." She looked up from her notes. "Evanson sent a team to the apartment: cheap furniture, beer, photos of him with his son, not much in the fridge..."

"Photo coming?"

"Momentarily. And no known associates."

Ryan swung around and interjected, "No traffic cameras on any of the Mountain access roads, sir."

"Thanks, Ryan." MacNeice returned to the whiteboard. "Before we head out, let's review without Garrick. We have a deceased birdwatcher and an unknown male in the forest. We've got a dead Montreal investor. We've got John Steadman, who missed picking up his son, and Peter Raymond, who didn't show up for dinner."

MacNeice circled the names and continued. "Peter—no fixed address, no immediate family, a police record, missed chicken dinner with grandma." He drew an arrow linking him to Steadman. "John lives in a basement, is estranged from his family, has a police record, is divorced, and missed picking up his son." These were, he believed, the kind of men you might find hunched over a pitcher of beer in the middle of the day. "Montile and Lise, it's time for a show-and-tell. For starters, take the photos of Raymond and Steadman and start with the bars and beer halls on Barton Street."

[48]

ARRIVING AT CLAPPISON CREMATORIUM, ONE EASED THE ESCALADE past the arched oak doors of the entrance and down the driveway to the parking lot, where he shifted into Park. Though there was no music playing, One's head moved up and down as if there were — slow music. He lowered his window and scanned the scene, taking in the distance to the neighbouring buildings, the tree cover that would absorb sounds, the concrete ramp that led to the basement, and a dirt path barely wide enough for a car that cut through to the next street and the industrial district beyond.

He listened for nearby traffic sounds. He heard Harleys and tractor-trailers, gearing up or down on the hill. There was enough noise to make it difficult to talk, but it came in waves and wouldn't be loud enough to cover a gunshot.

"Two, you bring the silencer?"

"No . . . You think we'll need it?"

"No problem." One dropped the suv into Drive and circled about, coming to a stop just shy of the building's main entrance. He shut the engine down and looked over at Clarence. "Okay, Blow, let's go meet your cousin."

Stepping into the incandescent lobby, Clarence, One, and Two stopped to look around. It was a large pentagon, and each angle housed a pair of double oak doors framed with elaborate trim. Above them, a horizontal line of plaster moulding raced around the space. Above it were ornate columns with arches — the place had a bit of a holy feel.

Thomas Cameron entered the lobby with a smile. "Gentlemen."

"What's goin' on up there, boss?" One asked, taking Tom's outstretched hand and nodding to the ceiling.

Cameron glanced upwards. "Well . . . that's open to interpretation. It could be designed to lift your eyes to the heavens, or just a reference to a classical form of architecture known as a loggia . . ."

"Uh-huh . . . maybe the latter, but nope to the former. My heaven doesn't have a grid of nickel-rimmed LED potlights. Are they s'posed to be stars?"

Tom ignored the question in favour of an introduction. "I'm Thomas — Tom — Cameron. And you are?"

"I'm Two, he's One. Good to meet you, Tom." Two's smile was sincere — he really was impressed with the decor. "What's behind all these doors, if you don't mind my asking?"

Tom shot a look at Clarence, who was studying the stone floor, before shifting character to something between a showroom salesman and crematorium tour guide. With a wave of his left hand, he ushered Two over to the first set of doors and swung them open. Inside was a small chapel with twenty-four chairs, twelve per side. "Mr. Two—"

Two raised a hand. "Just Two, no mister."

"Okay … Well, this is one of three chapels — where family and loved ones view a coffin or hold a small service." He stepped inside; Two didn't follow. One was still studying the loggia, and Clarence was trying to thaw a frozen smile.

"What's the fourth room for?" Two asked.

"An elevator to the lower level, and sample coffins and urns." Tom stepped out of the chapel, adding as a postscript, "The adjoining wall can open so the chapel's twice the size for larger parties."

"Parties. Who'd want to have a party in this place?"

"Sorry, I meant 'parties' in the sense of 'Smith family, party of six.'" Cameron added a head waiter's flourish, but that only made Two squint more.

"You're havin' a bit of fun at my expense, Tommy." Two's mouth tightened as he studied Cameron.

"Not at all. It was merely a joke offered in good humour."

"Lesson number one," One interjected, massaging his neck from the strain of looking up. "I do feel, Thomas, in a very real way, that I am in the house of the Lord. Now, God does have a sense of humour — the duck-billed platypus and that loggia up there exist — but when it comes to the release of the spirit, I'm pretty certain He takes a dim view of comedy — as do I."

"Again, I meant no offence."

Tilting his head from one side to the other to relieve his neck, One asked, "Are you a pastor, Thomas?"

"Ah, no. I own and operate Clappison Crematorium. I have, of course, men and women of faith I occasionally call upon to conduct a funeral or memorial service, but by and large it's just the family and friends of the deceased." Clearly wondering what he'd gotten himself into, Tom managed to keep his smile. "Why don't we continue this conversation in my office?" Without waiting for agreement, he walked off. Clarence grinned nervously, trying to lift the tension for himself if no one else.

While the lobby was cream-coloured, presumably to project calm, Cameron's office walls were deep burgundy. Bookending the exterior wall were two tall, slim stained-glass windows. The segments looked like broken coloured glass assembled at random. It was cheerful, and sunlight showered the room with a riot of colour.

Regardless of its celestial lighting, this was an office for quiet conversation and financial decisions made under heart-breaking conditions. To that point, on the left side were two leather chairs, and matching sofa with a glass-top coffee table in between. Cameron's desk anchored the opposite wall, with two more chairs. Compassion and empathy were present in the pewter boxes of tissues on the desk and table. There were also two bottles of hand sanitizer.

"Because ya don't know where a cremator's hands have been..." Two said while giving his hands a squirt.

There were two imposing leather-bound books on the coffee table, and a small dish of wrapped mints. Two was about to reach for one when Tom lifted a chair from the couch ensemble, put it with the others and invited them to sit down.

Behind his desk to the right, a tall rosewood armoire

loomed like a butler waiting to serve. Hanging on the wall on the other side were two framed diplomas, and next to those was a door that Cameron said led to the elevator.

Clarence and One sat down, but Two decided to wander around and study everything. He went first to one of the windows, holding his arms out to see the colour patterns change as he moved them about. He let out a chuckle and turned around to see his shadow surrounded by colour patches. He glanced over to One, who nodded his head like a father watching his son play. Two laughed, then moved on to the shelving unit centred between the windows.

Cameron draped his jacket on the back of his chair. Sitting down, he smiled at One. "I assume you have questions?" He folded his hands together on the desk, professionally relaxed. "I have a few of my own."

Through his apprehension, Clarence listened with satisfaction as One asked the same basic questions he had previously. Tom appeared to relax his guard and slipped into the familiar territory of cremation techniques and equipment, gesturing to but not opening another set of leather-bound books off to the side of his desk. One didn't need to see the coffins, urns, and name plaques ranging from engraved bronze to photocopied paper labels.

For his part, Two seemed to enjoy exploring the office of a cremator. Several times, Clarence heard him whistle through his teeth or whisper phrases like, "No way . . . Wow, man . . . Totally holy."

Standing with his back to them, Two studied the artifacts on the shelf unit — one was made of polished metal, very precise but complicated. Clarence was certain he heard Two exclaim, "Shut the trucking gate." And then, a moment later, Two was holding something aloft. "Tom, what's this?"

"A relatively new knee joint from one of our recent cremations. I keep it there as a reminder to ask if the deceased has any implants, pacemakers, and so on. Something good to know prior to cremation."

"That makes sense..." Two went to the sofa and sat down. With his arms behind his head, he closed his eyes and inhaled deeply. Truth was, he was dog-tired. He could hear Cameron talking about temperatures and the benefits of his burner over others, as if One were there to buy the damn thing.

He swung his body around, draping his legs over the arm so his sneakers wouldn't scuff the leather, and lay down. He heard Cameron pause and One chuckle, but after that, he was gone. Asleep, he dreamed about going home to Topeka, but in an instant the destination changed—as happens in dreams—to one just outside Hays, Kansas, where his girlfriend, Dolores, still lived.

In his dream, he imagined a future. They'd walk through a meadow in the clean Kansas air, sweet at any time of the year. Factually true, if you were far from the city and clear of cattle, sheep, pigs, oil and gas patches, fracking... Two's brow furrowed, because most of that was within sight of Dolores's back door.

Two thought of the smells he liked second-best. The first was Dolores's kitchen, no matter what was on the stove; the other was the smell of fresh laundry from the line... but no, that might've been his mom's clothesline in Topeka.

Half-asleep, he smiled—dreams were the ultimate prison break.

When Blow and One had gone off walking, Two was considering buying a horse for Dolores. There was a barn on her property, though it would need a lot of work to make it a home for any animal, especially a horse. Even then, where would she ride? The answer: nowhere is where.

The rest of the land had been sold off for fracking long before Dolores rented the farmhouse. When they'd hooked up, he'd asked if she wanted to buy it all back—because maybe he'd do that for her. She'd looked at him with her dark eyes and said that the name Dolores in Spanish and Hebrew—and likely every other language—suggests "sorrowful." Two took that to mean no. Dolores was never too specific about anything, except how she liked to be loved.

But with this road trip on the back of the last one, he could afford to buy a decent farm, far away from fumes— maybe out in the foothills of the Rockies.

He recalled the hunting trip he'd taken with One to Alberta. Their contract had been with a rancher diagnosed with stage 4 brain cancer. He'd wanted to be surprised— executed from a distance out on his range—so the insurance company wouldn't think he'd committed suicide and deny his wife the payout. When One told him that was often an urban myth, that it depended on the policy, the rancher snapped back, "Out here ain't urban and sure as shit they'll refuse to pay."

Days before that contract was fulfilled, Two's jaw had dropped when they scouted the property. It was roughly a thousand acres of rolling hills, with a hazy wall of mountains in the distance. He told One, "This would be a damn hard place to leave."

The rancher lived a hundred yards from a two-lane

blacktop road, in a sprawling western-style home of stone and wood buttressed by a huge chimney constructed with boulders from the mountains. Clustered around the house were three barns, two silos, and a bunkhouse. Nearby, six horses were housed in a large paddock. As they drove by in their rented Buick, one horse was on its back doing the rhumba, sending up a cloud of dust. The others walked about, slowly munching the sparse grass without a care in the world. Two watched as gusts from the foothill thermals lifted their manes and tails. In that moment, he thought, *I can picture myself here . . . with Dolores.*

That image came to him now, when he wasn't entirely sure if he was asleep or just daydreaming he was somewhere else.

"Buddy — buddy." One shook his shoulder. "Rise and shine, brother . . ."

Two opened his eyes to see the three men looking down at him, all scene-of-the-crime-like. His smile was so wide that the corners of his mouth tucked into his cheeks, revealing dimples that only Dolores Díaz of Hays, Kansas, ever saw. He swung his legs around, slapped his thighs, and stood. "What'd I miss?"

"We're going down to see how this thing works." When Tom and Clarence had disappeared through the door, One asked quietly, "You all right, brother?"

"Yeah. But I'm getting itchy for the road . . . Bin dreamin' I'm not here."

"Very soon you won't be."

[49]

"I 'VE GOT A DI VERTESI FOR YOU, SIR."

"Maracle's on speaker with me, boss; we've got something. For the first mile or so, it's all residential—then we hit gold. There are banks, and all of them have security cameras covering the entrances. We'll send the footage back to Ryan."

"There are two shots of the suspects' vehicle, both a bit obstructed..." Maracle paused for the punchline. "The taillight bar makes it definite—a late-model Lincoln Navigator. The Volvo is trailing, but we don't have any clear shots, just the front fender."

Vertesi cleared his throat and continued. "We're about to review the Drug Mart's camera—it's mounted on the corner of the building with a partial view of the intersection.

So far, the plates are obstructed by vehicles or the camera angle."

"Keep going. And check to see if the suv returns the same way."

MacNeice closed his eyes to organize his thoughts. What would they have done with Garrick? If he was in the Volvo, he was probably transferred to the suv and ferried to another site. But if the objective was to kill him, why go for a ride at all?

Second to Garrick's home, the abandoned farm near the Volvo's discovery site was the ideal spot for an execution. He picked up his cellphone and punched in Aziz's number; it went to voicemail. "Fiza, a question about the Volvo: how thorough was that search at the farm?"

He ended the message and swung around to see Ryan taping glory shots of Lincoln Navigators to the whiteboard; they looked like Central Casting's idea of a mob vehicle or an airport limousine. "Ryan, put together a police bulletin using the Lincoln's front, side, and rear views, with the same views of Garrick's red Volvo. Send them to DPD Comm for immediate posting: 'Anyone who has seen these two vehicles travelling together is to call Dundurn Police Immediately.'"

"Will do, sir."

MacNeice was taking a closer look at the Lincoln when his phone rang. "Yes, Fiza."

"I wouldn't say it was a thorough search—there's acres of weedy fields and a rundown boarded-up house. The police searched the house, barn, shed, and the land immediately surrounding it all. They sent up a drone to complete a grid over the entire property, looking for ground that might have been recently disturbed—nothing came up." Aziz was speaking over the noise of traffic. "Do you think we need a closer look up there?"

"Not necessarily. Was there any indication of someone being dragged away?"

"Hard to say what was there before the DFD pumper arrived, but when we got there, the scene was awash with hoses, foam, firefighters, and cops." She waited for what sounded like a truck to pass. "I forgot to mention earlier, there was nothing retrievable from that cellphone in the Volvo."

"Left there to distract us," MacNeice said with a chuckle.

"Or to let us know we're not pursuing dolts. We're no longer dealing with the amateurs of the forest."

"But you also feel they're somehow connected?"

"Yes—but criminologists prefer facts to feelings," she said over the traffic.

"How are your interviews going?"

"The first three incinerators were washouts. One was the size of an oil drum and used primarily for plywood offcuts, parquet flooring—waste, basically. Its temperature limit was set accordingly, but due to shoddy maintenance, it could barely reach hot enough to slow-cook a steak. The other two were in factories with twenty-four-hour shifts over the period when the bodies would have arrived. There'd be eyes on, even on lunch breaks, and fifteen to twenty employees would have to be complicit." MacNeice heard her car door beep. "I'm stuck on something the foreman said while explaining the exhaust requirements for burning wood products, though: 'You couldn't incinerate a dead animal here because it would smell like an abattoir outside.'"

He heard Aziz close her car door. "That point alone

kills the theory. Anyway, non-animal-waste incinerators are being phased out because companies have found ways to monetize sawdust, wood shavings, and the like for particleboard and wood pulp, even kitty litter."

"So we focus on animal parts disposal."

"Correct," she said. "But those facilities are incinerating cattle or pigs. They'd have to be twisted to consider—late at night and on the spur of the moment—incinerating two dead men. Also, they're more highly regulated, though it's conceivable that if the perpetrators had easy access..."

"But then, why go into the forest?"

"Checkmate. Onto the crematoriums."

[50]

EXACTLY AN HOUR AFTER THE BULLETIN WENT LIVE, EVANSON
called. "Sir, there's a Larry Nichols on the line; he's a
computer technician who works out of the second floor of
his house. You'll want to hear what he saw from his window.
Can I patch him through?"

MacNeice was sitting beside Ryan; together they were
reviewing the Upper James video clips of a 2019 Lincoln
Navigator.

"Uh, hello?" The caller sounded confused, as might anyone who found themselves in the deep end of a world they
hardly knew existed.

"Mr. Nichols, it's Detective Superintendent MacNeice —
Dundurn Homicide. I understand you responded to the
police bulletin?"

"Yeah, that's right."

"Let's begin with some background, Larry . . ."

"Well, I repair high-end computers—security upgrades, virus removal, data retrievals, rebuilding, adding hard drives—stuff like that. My workshop's on my second floor, in what was originally the master bedroom."

"And where's home?"

"Eighteen Mountain Avenue . . . my workbench runs the length of the street-side windows. I was working on a hard drive when I noticed a black Lincoln pull up. I thought to myself, who's taking a trip now? But its door didn't open and none of my neighbours came out with their bags. Musta bin ten minutes or so, then the driver's door swings open and a big fella gets out. A second later the passenger door opens and another guy—he was big too, but less muscular—he gets out and looks around. So now I'm curious . . ."

"Facial features, clothes, shoes or boots, hair?"

"First one was a Black guy. Black suit, probably XXL, and a baggy white T-shirt. Oh yeah, and black shoes. Second one was a lean but solid white guy in a tan Eisenhower jacket—a windbreaker kinda thing—dark blue jeans, white basketball shoes, and another white T-shirt."

"You've got an excellent memory. How do you account for that?"

"That's funny, but not true. It's because I don't have a great memory that I write things down—all kinds of things, mostly to do with work. That's where it really helps."

"What made you write down what you saw on this occasion?"

"Well, anything that catches my eye, I make notes. I want

to write screenplays, and someone once told me that it all comes down to details and research."

"What else did you note?"

"Yeah, okay. They were both wearing shades. The Black guy's were black with black frames; the white guy was wearing aviators, silver like a mirror...though technically, I guess, a mirror isn't silver."

"Anything else?" MacNeice was also making notes.

"Sure, well, they didn't move for a while, so I thought they're waiting for someone to come out...but no." Nichols took a sip of something before continuing. "The Black fella took his car keys and put them on top of the wheel on the driver's side...and off they went."

"Which direction?"

"Toward South Street. They weren't in a hurry...just two guys out for a stroll. Oh yeah—their hair. The Black guy, short; the other guy longer and wavy. They were well groomed."

"Did someone come to retrieve the suv?"

"Oh...that's the icing on the cake."

"Why is that?"

"As big as those two were, the white guy that came for the keys was really short."

"Can you estimate how tall? Or did the angle from your window make that difficult?"

"It did, but when he opened the driver's door, he really had to climb up to get in."

"Five foot and change?"

"Not much change. Anyway, he got in and, a minute later, headed toward South Street."

"Was he wearing a suit?"

"No. He had a jacket, but I didn't write the details down. I think it was light coloured, dark trousers."

"How soon after the other two left did the last man arrive?"

"Twenty minutes, maybe..."

MacNeice invited Larry Nichols to Division One to record a formal statement and to work on facial composites of all three men.

"Wow, yeah, I'll be right there."

MacNeice hung up. "What have you got, Ryan?"

"Just printing out the CCTV shots. While you were on that call, Vertesi sent a text; they're on their way back. No video of the Navigator returning the same way."

"Smart...using the same route would've been a rookie mistake." MacNeice wondered if they'd just dumped the body and kept driving around the Great Lakes to Manitoba, or into the US. "Okay, what else?"

"I got something, though it's a bit fuzzy." Ryan handed the copy to MacNeice. "It's the Drug Mart camera; I cropped a shot of the Volvo."

Sunlight glared off the windshield, all but obscuring whatever was inside. But MacNeice knew that sitting patiently by the water on a sunny day might reveal a perch gliding through the weeds, and so he waited for something to appear beneath the surface. On the left side, among the reflected fragments of trees, shrubs, and a light standard, he could make out a mouth, a nose, and the seductive curve of mirrored aviators. To the right, behind a sun flare, two hands gripped the steering wheel. They were large enough to mask the driver's face—except for a sliver of black sunglasses.

[51]

"**A**NYTHING LATE-BREAKING THAT I CAN PUT OUT THERE?" WALLACE asked.

"You can say that we have some promising leads." From the corner of his eye, MacNeice saw Ryan wave. "We've identified the vehicle involved—a black 2019 Lincoln Navigator."

"How certain?"

"Conservatively, eighty percent."

"I'll take it; stay in touch." Wallace hung up.

"Sir, Montile's on the other line."

MacNeice picked it up. "Talk to me . . ."

"We're down near Sherman on Barton, at a bar called Bloody Well Right. Do you know it?"

"Beer pub, the north side?"

"Yeah, you've been here?"

"No...What have you got?"

"Wally Fudge. No joke—I have his driver's licence. He's missing an incisor and he's halfway through a jug of beer, probably not the first. But when we put the photos down—right away, he tapped Peter Raymond. 'That's Pete. He's a good buddy of mine...'"

"And the second photo?"

"Yeah, well...Wally's mind wanders. He puts back half a glass, smiles at Lise, and says, 'You're pretty...you got a boyfriend?'"

"I get the picture."

"He doesn't know Steadman, but he did see them together at the pub—with a little guy. I asked him to describe the little guy and all he said was that he looked like a dentist. But, judging by Fudge's teeth, his memory of what a dentist looks like is probably shaky. Anyway, when Fudge walked over to join their table, Peter shoved him away and said he didn't know him. Wally assumed he was working on a score, so he backed off."

"How long ago was that?"

"His best guess is six, maybe eight weeks."

"How does he know Raymond?"

"They're unofficial partners in a house-painting business. No surprise—business is slow."

"Is he in shape to give you a detailed description of the little guy?"

"Psshhh...if we dry him out. He's over in the corner right now working hard to convince Lise to be his girlfriend. Keeps talking about how he makes the best spaghetti and meatballs in Dundurn and wants to cook for her. He's drunk, but not disorderly."

"I imagine she can handle it."

"Yeah, probably; he's big, but he's soft. Anyway, we'll bring him in and let Swets fill him with coffee."

"Before you leave the pub, ask if he can describe the third man—anything he can recall—including shoe size."

"Will do. So far we've hit three hotels and four bars on Barton. I don't know anything about Steadman or the little guy, but Wally says Bloody Well Right's only one of his and Pete's hangouts. Apparently pubs are good for getting painting jobs. I'll ask for a list."

"Understood, though—" MacNeice was interrupted by glass smashing, furniture crashing, and people yelling. "He went for it?"

"Drop the dishes!" Williams barked. "Yeah, I guess he did. I only turned away for a second and now Wally's face-planted on the floor. Lise's knee is on his back and the cuffs are out."

"Call me back." MacNeice looked up to see that Vertesi and Maracle were hovering nearby, so he decided to fill them in. "Seems Lise had a go with the local talent, but she has it in hand." He pointed to the picture of the Volvo windshield. "Great work up there . . ."

"Yeah, it's a drag we didn't get anything better," Vertesi said, looking closely at the printout. "A cube van was blocking our view, so we didn't get the same shot of the Navigator's windshield."

"And no plate shots either," Maracle added. "But it seems sloppy, like they didn't care about the cameras."

"Or it's a set-up. They want us to check those cameras because they've already ditched the Lincoln," MacNeice said.

"So, they're *not* amateurs—that's good to know."

"That's the way to think of them." MacNeice's cellphone rang. "Williams — what's happening?"

"Wally leaned over like he had something confidential to say, made a play for her upper thigh — like that's the way to a policewoman's heart. A Mohawk College kid was at the next table and saw it happen; said Lise delivered a short right jab so fast he almost missed it. Wally's head snapped back — and so did his chair. His knees went up along with the table, beer jug and glasses, and my notebook and keys. Wally's sitting up now with a shattered nose; Lise is applying pressure. We've called an ambulance to take him to DGH... Lise wants to know if we call in the SIU?"

"Is Wally claiming he was assaulted?"

"He's not saying much of anything right now. Hold on, I'll ask." Williams held the phone up. "Mr. Fudge...Wally, I have a question. Nod your head if you're able to answer." There was some groaning and a bit of gargling. "I'll take that as yes...Mr. Fudge, do you know why the Detective Sergeant struck you?" Seconds passed before he answered, and when he did, it was so garbled that Williams had to repeat it back to him for confirmation.

"You said, and I quote, 'I didn't take any offence...It's just the beer talking.' Is that right, Mr. Fudge?" A few seconds later, Williams said to MacNeice, "He understands. I think he's digging the attention she's giving him. The guy's seriously round...The bartender's our second witness, so we're covered."

"Put Lise on the line..."

"Yessir." Seconds passed, then the sound of a hand grazing over the speaker.

"Sir?"

"How are you, Lise?"

"Me? I'm okay; no problem, sir."

"Will you press charges for assault?"

"Naw...no way. He tickled the bee and got stung."

MacNeice's eyebrows shot up. "You're a fan of Muhammad Ali?"

"Yeah...I'm sorry, sir; I didn't want my first day to start off like this. He made several remarks, kept touching my leg. I warned him and shoved him away, and warned him again. Then he went for my crotch—"

"No need to explain further. I'm sure he'll think twice before doing that again."

"Well...he sure didn't see it coming."

"I assume that was the idea."

[52]

LEAVING THE ELEVATOR, ONE NOTED, "A LONG RIDE FOR ONE FLOOR…"
Tom smiled. "We've descended two and a half floors. The space between is where all the filters are — I can take you back there if you'd like…"

"I would," One said as they walked into a large porcelain-walled room with a polished floor .

"These are KDH-8000 cremators from Denmark." Tom pointed to two large black metal sections in the wall. Off to one side stood two stainless-steel flatbed gurneys and two long metal poles, each fitted with a wide scraper at one end.

One was studying a microwave-sized black glass rectangle to the right of the door. "What's this for?"

Tom teased, "Touch it."

One did, and a monitor lit up with a colour graph and

several buttons—the screen seemed to be registering metrics such as fuel availability and consumption and temperature.

"We haven't done our tests to confirm the curing of the new chamber walls; that's the reason for the delay." Tom looked over at Clarence, who nodded. "So I can't do that now, but I can do a brief test fire. Interested?"

"Thank you, yes." One put his hands behind his back and leaned forward.

"Absolutely," Two added. He'd arrived late and was scanning the room, noting a wall-mounted telephone marked with emergency numbers, a glass cabinet showcasing assorted urns, a chair and small desk—nothing on it—and a laminated KDH-8000 poster that illustrated the burn-rate scale an operator could use to lengthen the burn or shorten it.

Ten minutes later, Tom stepped aside and said, "Okay, One. Show me what you've learned—fire it up on your own." He smiled brightly, like he expected One to decline. Instead, One cracked his knuckles and got to work.

By the time One had finished—without a misstep—Tom's jaw was slack. He shook his head. "You know... when I first saw this machine in Denmark, it took me three attempts to do what you did the first time. I really wasn't expecting you to ace it."

"I'm a good student with mechanical things... Now let's see where the smoke goes."

Clarence peeked into the fire chamber, expecting to be more impressed. The magic, he'd assumed, was just the fire. The entire rig looked like a high-end pizza oven, and he didn't understand why One found it so fascinating. While the other three headed to the pipe room, he stayed behind

to check his emails. One was from the client with a mysteri-
ous subject line — *RE: Bulletin* — but no message.

When Tom, One, and Two emerged from the pipe room,
all three were laughing. Clarence stood off to the side, pre-
tending to check his voice mail. He waited a few seconds
before tucking his phone away. "We've finished the tour?"

"We have." Tom said with a smile.

One nodded. "I'm mightily impressed, and, though the
tour is over, we're not done here."

Clarence and Tom both looked confused. Clarence drove
his hands into his pockets and asked, "Really? What else is
there to discuss?"

"Tom has some questions…"

"Right — I did say that. But actually, my concerns have
been answered… except for knowing what time you'll arrive
on the day of…" Tom wasn't sure whether to address the
question to One or Clarence, so he spoke to the floor.

One answered. "Ten in the p.m. We'll drive down the
ramp out back and ring the buzzer."

Tom slipped into something approximating a professional demeanour. "In that case, we're done for today. I'll
get back to testing those fire walls and see you tomorrow
evening."

Two gently mocked Tom's tone. "Thank you, Mr. Cameron,
for the introduction to the fascinating world of cremation." He
shook Tom's hand a little too vigorously, but departed with his
trademark charming smile.

One shook his head in embarrassment. "We're grateful
for your time, Tom."

[53]

BY 7:41 P.M., MARCELLO'S PIZZAS WERE BEING CONSUMED AT DESKS, over laptops, or in the case of Swetsky, while standing. When Aziz appeared carrying a plate, knife, and fork, a ripple of ridicule erupted. MacNeice was too deep in thought to stop; he asked that a slice of something be left for him.

Holding his interest on the whiteboard was the artist's rendering of suspect number three, sketched from Larry Nichols's recollection. "What one thing?" MacNeice murmured. That man's composite included a full-length portrait with a scale indicating that he was between five foot one and five foot three, whereas the other two were each six feet or more. Being tall wasn't a psychopathic prerequisite—Joseph Goebbels had accomplished that at five feet four inches—but the range of heights would make this trio stand out in public.

Being short wasn't the only thing setting the third suspect apart; his clothes and hair were different. He appeared neat, even fastidious. MacNeice could easily believe he was a math teacher or a dentist, as Wally Fudge had assumed. You couldn't say that of his colleagues.

An hour earlier, Bichet had returned with a bandaged-up Fudge. They seemed like old friends. Wally didn't have a concussion, and while no one would mistake him for being as sober as a judge, he was sober enough to recognize the third man's composite on sight. "That's the guy alright, 'cept when I saw him, he was wearing penny loafers."

MacNeice was always amazed at the odd things people recalled, especially in passing situations. Wally was curious about the mirror and asked if it was two-way. MacNeice confirmed that it was, then steered Fudge to scan the sketches of the short man's colleagues. He didn't recognize either of them.

"Tell me about your friend, Wally," MacNeice asked. "Is Peter clever . . . honest . . . peaceful . . . a drinker . . . given to violence? How would you describe him?"

Fudge scratched his cheek and smiled nervously. "Well . . . Pete's just a regular guy, ya know, like we all drink a bit . . ." He took MacNeice's lack of response for dissatisfaction, so he dropped his smile and added, "Pete can be nasty, eh? Like one minute he's buddy-buddy and the next, he's ticked off. Scary."

"Example?"

"Yeah . . . well, okay. We did this paint job for a friend of a friend of mine; nice house out in the west end, eh?" Wally seemed to be looking for agreement.

"Right, a nice house."

"Yeah. Was it ever...Anyways, we finish the job and the owner comes by, says he's not happy; he's going to dock our pay. Pete flips out. Shoves him against the wall, and he's like two inches from the guy's face—like he's gonna kiss him or chew his nose off — anyways, the guy paid us. But, yeah, Pete's a bit scary." Having shared all his wisdom on the subject, Fudge signed his statement about the incident at the pub and left the division to head back to the Bloody Well Right, where MacNeice was certain he'd hold court.

MacNeice released the composites for immediate posting on the DPD website and social and print media. He then continued to study the photos of Raymond and Steadman. Intuitively, he was convinced they were dead—killed or replaced by the two men in the Volvo. Finding a role for Fudge's little dentist presented a challenge, though.

Theories about the missing bodies—theories of cremation and its cousin, incineration—came with a glitch. Why wasn't Rodney Conroy cremated? And if Garrick was meant to be murdered, why not just incinerate him in the Volvo?

MacNeice swung around. "Fiza, slide over. I've got some questions for you and Swets about crematoriums."

Aziz scooted across the cubicle, managing a chair pirouette along the way, while Swetsky folded a pepperoni slice in his paw and leaned against the whiteboard's frame.

"Swets, you were told by Dundurn Cemetery and Crematorium that there are new crematoriums unaffiliated with cemeteries that might—What was the language they used?"

Swetsky wiped his mouth with the heel of his free hand. "Might be more flexible about who they cremate, 'cause they need to build business. The established facilities are in cemeteries, so no problem—they have plenty of customers. They also have more staff, more eyes on what's happening." He was talking with his pizza hand, waving it around to make his point. "You can put Grandpa under a headstone in the cemetery or in a vault called a columbarium." Nowadays, Swetsky recounted, people throw ashes over waterfalls, over gardens, mountaintops, golf courses—anywhere. "But the majority still want a service, and a place they can come back to visit any time."

Aziz rolled her chair back as Swetsky's gestures grew more enthusiastic. "John, could you please eat that or put it down?" She waited as Swetsky stuffed what remained into his mouth, before continuing. "The two I visited basically said the same thing about the independents. I asked if they were just slagging off the competition—the answer by one surprised me." She glanced at her notes and read aloud: "'Ours is a growth industry. The boomers—the largest and wealthiest generation in history—are aging fast. We can't handle that demand, so we use the independents. The ashes come back to us, we put on a proper funeral and offer a final resting place in a well-treed, visually appealing landscape, or in a columbarium, for contemplation. Independents don't have that—they're the best at doing one thing."

Swetsky nodded. "Yeah, a couple of those use state-of-the-art equipment. Cemeteries have older furnaces that aren't as efficient. The independents are faster, cleaner, and cheaper."

Aziz nodded back. "If a homicide detective arrives after a cremation, there's nothing left to identify the body. But there's an exception—if the deceased had a joint replacement, the device needs to be removed before the cremation and can be traced through its serial number. Otherwise —"

"It's a perfect crime," Swets finished.

MacNeice felt a chill run through his body. "The organization or network behind this is likely much larger, comprised of contractors and subcontractors. So far we've been chasing subcontractors." He pointed at the composite sketches. "We need to consider what happens when this is an enterprise."

MacNeice turned to include the whole team. "Our composites will be in every patrol car within the hour, and soon after across all media. First thing tomorrow, we'll make unannounced visits to the independent crematoriums. Let's find out all we can about the owners, and plan to arrive on their doorsteps starting at eight a.m."

BY 8:54 P.M., Aziz and MacNeice had found very little on the Secord Crematorium, as it had opened only the previous fall. By contrast, Bichet and Williams had made printouts of the Clappison Crematorium brochure, as well as supplementary literature on the operation's Danish 2100-degree equipment. As Williams read up on the cremation process, Bichet was digging up information about the owner and funeral director, Thomas Cameron. Retrieving the printout, she slid it across to him.

It took him all of ten seconds before he turned to MacNeice. "Sir, Lise has found something about Clappison that makes me think you and Fiz should go there."

"Mob connections?" Aziz asked.

"Coffee connections. Clappison's owner is a partner in Mino's Beanstalk, an Italian espresso bar not far from the crematorium. You love espresso, sir. It's close by . . . I thought you could check it out; says here they do their own roasting and sell the beans."

"Done. You and Lise take Secord — it's new and there's very little known about it."

[54]

BLACK AS NIGHT EVERY DAY; STEWING IN MY OWN JUICES.
Arnie's mind had slowed to the point where he couldn't form sentences for his thoughts. Of the senses that remained intact, his most valuable was sound. The sound of nightbirds and mosquitoes. Flies.

His head was wrapped in a blindfold secured with duct tape; his mouth was gagged. Both arms were tethered above him, as if testing his weight like a steer for slaughter; his outstretched legs, bound at the knees and ankles, ensured he couldn't move. The combination had introduced Arnie to pain on a scale he'd never experienced and couldn't have imagined.

The mouth gag had left his throat so desiccated that he couldn't make a sound. Worse was the memory of the last water he'd been given, which had swept down his throat like a wire brush on a sunburn.

On his first night in captivity, while shifting his torso to reduce a lower back spasm, the plastic ties around his wrists had cut into the flesh. He only realized this when blood streamed down his arms and pooled at his collarbone. To prevent them from cutting deeper, he had shifted his weight again—and managed to dislocate his right shoulder.

During the hours that followed, the parietal lobe, responsible for measuring pain in Garrick's brain, had adapted by shutting down. But in time the pain returned, and it took many forms.

Salty tears, burning eyes, searing cheek to chin.

Forced into shallow breathing by sour sweat and the ammonia reek of urine, the stink of feces hardened to paste beneath him that invaded his nostrils. What fluid remained trickled out like acid.

It was August, with daytime temperatures reaching the mid-thirties; with darkness they fell to the high twenties. Bat screeches sounded the arrival of his second night; that was when Arnie realized he was going to die—not from a bullet or knife but by leakage. He felt his kidneys collapsing, squeezing the life out of him.

During the night, something crawled on him, though he could barely feel it. Whatever it was scratched at his pants—he heard it. He tried shaking it off but, because his movements were so limited, it responded by climbing up onto his belly. Arnie thrust out his stomach, but in the effort he slammed his head hard against the wall, and knocked himself out.

Best thing is... it's best not to know.

He awoke with a violent headache; when that faded, he started considering the what-ifs of how he'd ended up blind-folded, gagged, and bound to a wall. Of course, he knew why he was where he was; he could even accept that he deserved to be there. But the where and why of how it had all begun proved more elusive — like trying to imagine one's brain as it tries to imagine itself.

I'm sorry, Elaine...

Arnie waited for the sound of an automobile and the inevitable footsteps that would follow.

Life came easy. I gambled until I stole money to gamble, until I couldn't bet my way out...

A salty crust of tears had sealed his eyes shut. Fresh tears had nowhere to go; they just shored up the foundation and burned his eyeballs. Arnie slowed his breathing further, thinking somehow that he was conserving oxygen, but within seconds and without notice, he was unconscious, and mercifully unaware of the rat's return.

[55]

THE CLIENT CALLED AT SEVEN A.M. HE DIDN'T RESPOND TO Clarence's greeting.

"There's an unflattering likeness of you in today's *Standard*. You're with, I assume, your colleagues. Have you seen it?"

"Ah, not yet." Clarence had been up until 4:35 a.m. Unable to sleep, he'd decided to use the time to put his cash into Saran Wrapped bricks — fifty thousand per brick. He'd retrieved the largest suitcase from the basement and stacked them side by side until the case was full.

"I must say I was shocked. We have until now been able to conduct our business offstage, and I —"

"Sir, I'll read the article and call you back in ten minutes."

"You can also turn on your television, if that's more

convenient. It's everywhere, Blow. And it will have an impact—not just on our relationship, but on my relationship with my client. Call me when you have a solution."

Clarence double-locked the suitcase and shoved it into his closet before leaving the bedroom. As he approached his front door, he could see Two stepping up to ring the bell. Clarence opened it and used a pre-emptive ploy. "Good morning. I assume you've seen the news?"

"Well, you see, sport..." Two handed him the morning paper. "The renderings of a Black man and white man are pretty Everyman, though for sure we gotta lose the sunglasses, and we won't be walking around together. But the one of you is pretty damn close, even your height—though they mighta gifted you an inch."

"I haven't seen the news yet; the client just called to tell me about the photos." Clarence stepped aside as Two passed by. Instinctively he scanned the street for anyone watching. Noticing the silver Toyota, he asked, "Is that your car out front?"

"It is, though I don't know what 'Yaris' means..."

Clarence walked into the kitchen. "Likely it means nothing, literally nothing." He turned on the coffee machine, pulled a tin from the cupboard, and began spooning coffee into a filter. "All set for tonight? Do you want coffee?"

"Yes. And no."

As the machine wheezed and poured, Clarence watched the cup as if it might overflow; he didn't want to read the article with Two standing there. Instead he asked, "Do we have a meeting that I've forgotten about?"

Two pursed his lips and shook his head in disappointment. "Mr. Blow, you know we don't have a meeting—you're the one who calls the meetings. No...One sent me by to talk about our future."

"Our future? Okay, well, tonight we dispose of the professor. We get paid, then we wait for our next disposal." He took a sip of the fresh coffee, peering at Two over the mug's rim.

Clarence had expected that in One's absence, Two would be a lighter touch, but that was not to be.

"We told you we don't do torture. You recall that?"

"I do."

"So this *cocka-fucking-mamie* plan, with that sorry fucker stashed in a stable—that sure as fuck qualifies as torture."

There was no sense trying to deny or defend or explain the situation. Clarence knew that Two was aware of the situation; he also knew that Two knew it was a one-time event. That going forward they'd already sorted out how to dispose of as many bodies as necessary.

"That was quite a portmanteau." Clarence was about to realize that he'd chosen the wrong way to respond.

"What'd you say?" Two snapped.

"Just that *cocka-fucking-mamie* is a grouping of two words into a new one. Though yours may never have been used in the entire history of the English language."

"You're mocking me, you little cuntfuck?"

"No...no, Two. Honestly, I'm not." Whether it was nerves or that he found Two hilariously funny, Clarence steeled himself to keep from collapsing into giggles. "Really I'm not. Though *cuntfuck* is another, you know"—he shrugged, he hoped, innocently—"portmanteau." He stepped back to give himself a little more space from Two. "I know this is a conflict for you and One, but it'll never happen again." Clarence watched the man's hands for any hint of movement. "I do admire your ability to swear a blue streak with me while restraining yourself around One. That takes discipline."

"No, it doesn't. It takes priorities. I owe my life to One and he'd say the same about me. It pains him to hear my foul tongue because he sees in me someone better than the person I see in the mirror."

Clarence felt a slight ease in the tension, and, while he was tempted to ask more about how One and Two had met, how they'd gotten into their line of work, he only had one question. "Are we good for tonight, then?"

"Yeah. We're good. But this time we'll go in three vehicles. Me in the Yaris, One in the Escalade, and you in your car. Tomorrow I'll return the Caddy and we'll be in cheaper wheels from now on."

"Okay."

"And One and I've split up. We'll stay in touch by phone. I'll pick up the professor and meet you and One at Tom's— ten p.m. If you got questions, or more surprises, you're best to text One; I'll get the message. Clear?"

"Very. Now I need to call the client. If he has another disposal, can I commit us?"

"That's a One question." Two headed toward the front door. "Read that paper, Blow." He looked back over his shoulder like he'd just thought of something. "You know, when we got here, I thought this was a sleepy town—I don't anymore."

The front door closed with a slap and Clarence picked up the *Standard*. The bulletin was front page, above the fold. Seconds after he'd finished reading it, his phone rang, and he answered without checking the caller. "I was just about to—"

"Son...it's your father."

"Hullo, Father." The disdain in Clarence's voice wasn't lost on his father.

The old man spoke quickly, having no interest in phony pleasantries. "I'm calling to remind you of our fiftieth anniversary dinner tonight. Your mother's looking forward to seeing you."

Another call was coming in—it was the client. "I'm sorry; I can't make it. I have clients arriving in town. That's one of them phoning now—say congrats to Mother. Cheery-bye." He knew his father would be apoplectic, and that gave Clarence a sense of power.

He accepted the call. "Apologies, sir, a colleague arrived unannounced."

"I see..." The client fumed silently for a moment. "You're familiar with the investment term risk and reward?"

"Of course."

"We are now—you and I, and your colleagues—in a position where the risk is far greater than the reward. Wouldn't you agree? And if you don't, please do enlighten me as to why not."

"I don't agree. We travel separately; the Lincoln cited in that bulletin was retired two days ago. And while disposal has been an issue—"

"Somewhat of an understatement..."

"Admittedly. At any rate, that's no longer a problem. All future disposals will occur immediately."

"The future...What we do in the future, if anything, will be done from a distance. We won't be meeting again."

"That's fine, as long as there's no delay in the compensation." Clarence's tone was curt but not impolite. Nonetheless, he was itching for an opportunity to place the responsibility for the artist sketches and Navigator photos where it belonged—with his client. A second later, that moment arrived.

"Mr. Blow, are there any amendments to the status quo that you or your people want to table?"

Amendments, table—as if this were a meeting of a board of executives and not an execution squad. Clarence smiled. "Yes, sir. Not to belabour the point, but this wouldn't be in the news if we'd been able to handle things our way. None of us want a repetition of this contract..." Clarence trailed off, determined not to fill the void that followed. As it lengthened, his smile widened.

At last the client spoke. "Please tell me that our disposal has occurred?"

"Tonight at ten, sir. Ashes to ashes..."

[56]

"BUON GIORNO, WELCOME." A MAN GREETED MACNEICE AND AZIZ with a generous smile as they stepped through the door. "You're in time for the first roast of the day." He kept his smile alive even as his eyes betrayed an instant wariness.

"You're Mino?" Aziz asked.

"Mino, si, Giacomo Pezi... And you, signorina?"

It wasn't unusual for an Italian man to address them in Italian, but MacNeice wondered if it was a reaction to a perceived threat.

"Detective Inspector Aziz. This is Detective Superintendent MacNeice."

Mino waved with his right hand. "So, you were just passing by and stopped for coffee?"

MacNeice smiled. "Yes... a double espresso macchiato, please."

Aziz was studying the pastry dish. "I'll have a cappuccino and—is that a blueberry muffin?"

"Si, though not Italian, it's made locally." He asked if they'd like their coffee at the bar or a table. "Inside or out, no matter."

"I'll have the muffin, and we'll sit at the table by the window," Aziz said.

When Mino arrived with a tray, he set the coffees down, then two short glasses of water, napkins, the muffin, and a small cluster of blueberries to dress the plate. He then informed them, the way a fine waiter does, that the beans were Arabica, from a small producer in Ghana.

Aziz leaned over the cup. "It smells lovely, Mino." She smiled warmly. "Before you go, could you look at a few sketches—people of interest—for a case we're working on?"

"Si... of course." He reached into the apron's chest-pocket for a pair of glasses and slid them low on his nose.

He studied the first one—a Black man with dark sunglasses—his height, weight, clothing, etc. He shrugged and put it down on the folder and repeated the same study of the white man wearing mirrored aviators. When he looked at the third picture, he paused and reread the descriptions of the other two. "This one's short, eh?" Mino looked at Aziz and back to the image before putting it face down on the other two. "No... I don't think so."

MacNeice had been studying Mino's reactions. As he lifted his cup, he asked casually, "You seemed to hesitate with that last composite. Perhaps if you see it again?" He flipped the photocopy over.

Giacomo looked at the image, shaking his head. "Sorry, I don't know him."

"Thank you. Your coffee's wonderful. But we're also here to learn more about crematoriums," Aziz said.

"Your partner owns Clappison Crematorium...?" MacNeice asked.

"Si, Thomas Cameron. He was here"—Giacomo shrugged—"maybe twenty minutes ago." He bowed slightly. "I'll let you enjoy your coffee..." With a smile, he returned to the bar.

Aziz bit into a piece of muffin and swooned at MacNeice. "Can I tempt you?" And then more quietly, "You think he recognized number three."

MacNeice had been enjoying his coffee the way whisky lovers sip Scotch. "No to the muffin. But yes to the second question—almost certainly." He stood and went over to the bar, where Giacomo was reviewing receipts.

Giacomo looked up. "Yes? What do you think? It's good, no?"

"Well beyond good. It's extraordinary." He looked over Mino's shoulder to watch another man pouring a large bag of beans into the roasting chamber. "Can I assume that you sell beans?"

"Si... that's the main part of our business—roasting, selling."

"And the Ghana?"

"No, that's private stock for an importer in Toronto."

"Too bad. Well, which would you recommend?"

"Go with the Kenyan AA."

"Done. I'll take two pounds; add the coffees and muffin to the tab." MacNeice reached for his wallet. "And

Mino—you recognized the short man, no need to deny it."

"Mi scusi?" Though he was reaching for the bags, it was clear Mino had heard the comment. His brow creased, he put the coffee in a cotton sack and tapped the amount into the machine before handing it to MacNeice for payment.

MacNeice tapped his credit card and waited quietly. When Mino handed him the receipt and the sack, MacNeice said, "I'll be back again, Giacomo." Mino's eyes widened. "I think you recognized that third man. Your coffee's special; I'd be disappointed not to have it again because you didn't speak up when given the opportunity to do so."

Aziz had finished her muffin and stood next to the table. Her right hand rested on her belt—close to but not exposing her service weapon.

When they were settled in the car, she noticed MacNeice hadn't put the key in the ignition. "Everything okay, Mac?"

He nodded. "I'll be right back…" He stepped out of the car, leaving the door open.

He was gone for a minute or two, then returned and started the engine. Dropping the car into reverse, he turned to look over his shoulder and noticed the look on Aziz's face. "Just following a hunch…"

"And?"

"Mino was on his cellphone with his back to the door. When he spotted me, he put it in his apron. I left my card."

[57]

THOMAS CAMERON APPEARED AT THE DOOR WEARING A PLASTIC apron and long rubber gloves. He removed the right glove and held it in his left, where it flopped like a dead mallard. "Can I help you?"

"I'm Detective Inspector Aziz; with me is Detective Superintendent MacNeice. We're here—"

"To learn about crematoriums. Yes, my partner called. Come in." They shook hands as he let them through. Locking the door behind them, he asked, "Shall we go to my office?"

"A couple of questions first," MacNeice said. "Why would Giacomo call you about our visit?"

"Because he's a good partner. We're both small business owners; he may have been concerned that two detectives were coming for a visit."

"Does he have a reason to be concerned?"

"No. But I imagine that's a common reaction whenever Dundurn detectives come calling."

"You have a point." MacNeice smiled. "Especially homicide detectives."

Cameron tilted his head and his somewhat boyish face tightened. "I don't believe you mentioned that to Mino, Detective."

"An oversight perhaps, though it's clear on the card I left him. To your office, then?"

"Yes, but you had another question…" Thomas returned the smile, leading the way.

"When did you develop such a refined taste for coffee?" That wasn't the question, but it would do for now.

"A long time ago… Giacomo's from Trieste. Coffee's in his blood, probably quite literally." When they reached his office, Thomas gestured to the chairs opposite the desk, then removed his protective gear and stacked it on a nearby shelf. "I'd offer coffee, but you've already had the best—"

"Correct. Giacomo probably mentioned our composite sketches… Tell me, do you call him Mino or Giacomo?" Aziz asked.

"Either… as the spirit moves." Cameron was relaxed and engaging. Tall and very slender, it was easy to imagine how comforting he'd be for bereaved families arriving for the cremation of a loved one.

They exchanged business cards, but as the conversation turned to Cameron's business, MacNeice was increasingly aware that the light in the room was changing—dramatically. He swung around to study the source. Two tall stained-glass windows illuminated the room with a jumble of colours that flickered and moved as though animated. MacNeice smiled in wonder.

"Magic hour—happens on days like this and shifts with the seasons. In winter, the sun almost misses them entirely, but in July and August, this is what early morning looks like. They'll calm down soon."

"One might assume that such a spirited display is the point," MacNeice said.

"It would be, but for the fact that it happens so early—and in here, not in one of the chapels." Cameron cleared away a stack of papers, opened a leather-clad notebook, and positioned his pen on top. "That said, I never quarrel with celestial timing." He waited.

Over the next half-hour, the detectives listened to an overview of Cameron's business model. This was followed by a review of the ledger—presented willingly and without hesitation—covering the last six months of operation. While there'd been an overall increase in the business, the source was the area's established funeral homes and cemeteries.

"Ours is not a get-rich proposition. But we provide a necessary and efficient service." Thomas shrugged his coat-hanger shoulders to suggest that was good enough for him.

Aziz asked, "When we arrived, you were wearing an apron. Have you just completed a cremation?"

"No. I was scrubbing the fire chamber; its walls have just been rebuilt, and I didn't want the brick-and-mortar dust to mingle with—"

"We'd be grateful for a tour, Thomas. But first, we have several composites—pictures of people of interest—that we'd like to show you."

Cameron pushed his notepad aside and waited, still

smiling, though less so. He seemed aware of MacNeice's intense focus on him. Aziz took the printouts from the folder and flipped them over one by one.

Thomas's hands floated above the first composite. "May I?" MacNeice nodded. Cameron looked closely at the white man wearing silver sunglasses. He set it down and reached for the sketch of the Black man wearing dark sunglasses. He studied them side by side before taking the third. He spent more time with this composite, carefully reading the details noted off to the side, before placing it beside the other two.

"I don't recognize them. Of course, the sunglasses make it difficult." He stacked them in the order they'd been given to him and handed them back to Aziz. "Can you tell me why you'd bring them here?"

"Yours isn't the only crematorium we're visiting, Thomas; that's all we can say." MacNeice noticed a slight narrowing of Thomas Cameron's eyes.

"I understand...Well, to our tour, then." He led them into the coffin room. "This is where we keep the sample coffins and urns..." He opened the elevator doors and ushered them inside.

WEAVING THROUGH TRAFFIC, MacNeice asked Aziz to call Wallace for a tap on Cameron's phone. When the call ended, she turned in her seat. "It'll be on within the hour. He said it's highly irregular and only temporary, till he has the judge's signature. He's using 'life in imminent danger' as his rationale."

"What did you make of Cameron?" MacNeice asked. He merged with the 403 traffic.

"Smooth...maybe too smooth. Since I have no experience with his world, I was somewhat persuaded by his sleek demeanour—he seemed authentic." She looked out at Cootes Paradise. "I was struck by the attention he gave the composites."

"Working hard to convince us that he didn't know them, perhaps..."

"It was faultless." She seemed lost in thought.

They'd just crested the hip of Main Street, where the road dropped down to City Hall and Division One. MacNeice felt the weight of her silence, and rather than wonder what was causing it or whether he was projecting, he asked, "Something on your mind, Fiz?"

She pushed herself upright. "Kate was cremated...Did you watch it happen?"

Her question was unexpected. He swallowed uneasily and smiled uncomfortably. "No..." The bottom fell out of his voice. "She didn't want me to...Worried that would dominate my memory of her...of us."

Aziz remained quiet and turned her attention to the cyclists enjoying the downhill ride, pumping away on racing bikes, wearing candy-coloured Lycra and helmets that looked like the shiny shells of exotic beetles.

[58]

"**E**VERY MAN SHOULD HAVE PASSIONS THAT LINGER RATHER THAN fester." It was the kind of pronouncement that would make most listeners recoil. "I've had my share, and I've followed every one of them." Charles Cameron put the Range Rover into Park and went to open the gate. "Just be a sec..."

Returning, he picked up his narrative. "This was one of those passions. It didn't work out...but it was a helluva ride." He drove through, turned off the engine, and walked over to close the gate. His passengers exited the Range Rover and waited for him next to the vehicle.

Fists on his hips, Charles continued. "We'll do a tour around the track and look at the buildings — though I know you don't give a shit about houses, stables, and such."

Both men said that wasn't true, but it was — and Charles

Cameron knew it. Irving Kelber and Gary Cuttlesworth were property developers; as far as they were concerned, passions like this place were hobbies or distractions, and C.C. was a dabbler who'd occasionally gotten lucky.

Charles drew a horizontal line in the air. "One hundred and fifty acres of environmentally sound land — farmland before I came along. Now it's got city water and services." The men nodded approvingly but without conviction.

"Before we do a look-see, I need to get something straight. This ain't the Marrakesh Express; I've got a number in my head. If you accept it, we'll have a deal; you wanna haggle, this'll be a short stroll and we'll go back to town. You good with that?"

Kelber, a compact man in his fifties, smiled. "Whether we turn around or not depends entirely on the figure that's in your head. I'm not sure why you dragged us out here before sharing the amount, to be honest."

"Look, Kelber-Cuttlesworth builds high-end homes. But you're not the only ones, and I have time. Dundurn's coming to me, and there's nothing else like this property by a long shot."

"So tell us the number before we get too excited and take this on as a passion project." Kelber smiled at the absurdity of his own statement.

"Three million."

Pursing his lips, Kelber nodded and turned to Cuttlesworth. Whatever crossed the space between them was lost on Charles; he was busy admiring the landscape as if he'd created it.

Kelber got his attention. "Charles, I don't know what to make of your reference to Marrakesh, as I've never been there."

"'Marrakesh Express.' Crosby, Stills, and Nash—no?" Cameron shrugged. "I like the phrase—love the song."

Cuttlesworth spoke up for the first time. "It's like that sign out there—C.C. Rider—that's an old song too."

"Exactly. Music's one of my passions."

"Clearly," Cuttlesworth said. "If Irv hasn't told you, he's the big-picture partner. I'm the details man."

"Good for you." Charles couldn't feign interest in their corporate structure.

Cuttlesworth nodded. "Let's do that look-see."

Not being taken seriously wasn't new to Charles Cameron. He'd had no idea why Cuttlesworth had joined them—and now he knew. Charles pointed left to the field and its modest viewing stand, and then to the right, to the stables. "If you'd like to know more about raising thoroughbreds..."

"Unnecessary—but seeing this up close does suggest a spectacular failure." Cuttlesworth rolled up his sleeves and glanced admiringly at Cameron. "This would've crushed most men."

"I wasn't crushed...my net wealth practically doubled within two years of folding this place. Now, to the clubhouse or the stables?"

"The stables..." Cuttlesworth set off at an ambling pace.

Kelber's tie caught a morning breeze and flipped up to his chin. Tucking it into his shirt, he turned to Cameron. "Charles...you've never worked as a developer, correct?"

"No."

"I thought not. You stated a number; I don't how you arrived there. As we go, I'll outline the considerations that would determine whether we'll consider three million."

"I'm listening…" Charles shoved his hands deep in the pockets of his linen trousers and walked with his head down, as if it helped him listen.

Kelber was also looking down, but at the fine dust collecting on his shiny black shoes. "To take on a hundred-and-fifty-acre housing development, we'd immediately allocate twenty acres for green space and another ten for roads… leaving a hundred and twenty acres. For argument's sake, let's say we put up four hundred and eighty homes at three to four thousand square feet each on quarter-acre lots."

"Sounds good. I might even buy one for my son's family."

"I'd expect no less of you." Kelber patted the much-taller Cameron on the shoulder. "And, analogous to your offer to buy your son a home, you'd want to know the true value of that investment—whatever the selling price might be. Is it worth it?"

"Don't dumb it down on my account, Irv."

"I'm doing that assessment with your three-million asking price. You see, we have hard costs and soft costs. Hard are things like—what the hell is that smell?"

They were just coming up to the stables, and with every quiver of breeze their nostrils registered something foul and sour. Cuttlesworth was twenty feet ahead of them when he turned back, covering his mouth and nose.

"I don't know what that is," Charles said. "The stables have been closed up for a long time… must be the neighbour spreading fertilizer."

"In August? I don't think so." Cuttlesworth spoke with authority, whether real or imagined.

Kelber pulled out his tie to cover his nostrils. They kept walking until they were near the barn's open door. "That

should've been locked; must've been the groundskeeper."
Standing on the track, Charles said, "Maybe something died
inside. Stay here . . . I'll go check."

"No, I'll come along," Cuttlesworth said, his face buried
in his elbow. "You sure you didn't leave one of those thoroughbreds behind?"

"More likely a dead raccoon, no big deal . . ."

AS HE EXITED the barn, Cuttlesworth passed out, gashing
his forehead on the door frame. Fifty minutes later, with
his head in a feed pail, he shook and heaved as a paramedic
tried to dodge the vomit to clean and bandage the wound.

Upwind and some distance away from each other, Irving
and Charles sat on dusty plastic chairs. Both men appeared
to be in shock.

Charles was mindlessly flipping the lid of a silver Zippo
that bore his initials; an unlit cigarette dangled from his
lip. Four police vehicles — two regional, and two OPP —
were parked bumper-to-bumper along the property's access
road. The cops stood in a clutch, some of them laughing.
They weren't being disrespectful, at least, not intentionally.
They were just accustomed to arriving on the scene to much
greater tragedies than a severely dehydrated man tied to a
stable wall, reeking of piss and shit.

[59]

MACNEICE, AZIZ, AND SWETSKY WERE IN THE CHEVY SPEEDING along behind Vertesi, who was following Sergeant Evanson. The lights on all three vehicles were flashing and Evanson was running his *whoop-whoop* siren to clear the road. With less than a car's length between them, they sped through the intersection of Upper James and Mohawk.

MacNeice wondered why Vertesi was driving alone. "John, where's Maracle?"

"He's following up with one of the incinerator contacts, about something that didn't make sense."

"Okay." He felt a flicker of unease but put it aside. "What do we know about where we're headed?" MacNeice glanced at him through the rear-view.

Swetsky straddled the driveshaft and rested his enormous

arms on the shoulders of the front seats. "Not much. The owner was showing the property to some developers, and they found a guy they thought was dead in a stable."

"They're sure it's him?"

"Yeah, he still had his wallet. Williams and Bichet were just coming back from Secord, so I told them to head over to St. Joe's. The ambulance is there now . . . paramedic wouldn't speculate on his chances. Cop on the scene was willing to, though . . ."

"And?"

"Minus to plus zero."

A cruiser sped toward them, leading an ambulance — together, they slalomed through traffic. One by one, the three unmarked Dundurn PD vehicles pulled to the right to let them scream by, then they veered back onto the road, speeding toward the farm.

"Shall I call Elaine Garrick?" Aziz asked, cellphone in hand.

"Yes. You can't say much, just that her husband's alive and heading to St. Joe's."

Swetsky lowered his voice. "Mac, it's like we're dealing with a gang that can't shoot straight. You grab someone, rough him up, leave two grand on the floor, torch his car, don't ask for a ransom, don't finish him off — then leave him in a stable with his wallet. That's not how this is supposed to work."

"No, it isn't." MacNeice kept his concentration on the road.

Aziz raised her hand for quiet. "Dr. Garrick, hello. It's DI Aziz . . . I only have a moment . . ." She listened for the obvious question. "Yes, we do — your husband is alive. He'll arrive at St. Joseph's in approximately ten minutes."

Garrick's wife let out a shriek that burst out of the phone's tiny speaker. She began sobbing, but Aziz cut off any further questions. "Elaine. Go and be with your husband. Two of our detectives will meet you at the ICU ... but you need to leave now ... Yes, a team effort. No, we haven't arrested anyone."

"Skin in the game ..." Swetsky said to no one in particular.

[60]

AS THEY APPROACHED THE FARM'S GATE, TWO OPP CRUISERS WERE pulling out. The drivers — one male, one female — nodded in that cool, minimal-effort, fighter-pilot way. The three unmarked cars moved slowly along the road and parked on the grass.

A regional cop came forward and introduced himself as patrolman Les Richards. He was sporting a grey mesh summer Stetson that left a grid of sun and shadow on his face. Speaking with a slight Caribbean accent, he said, "I'll be leaving too, sir. I know you've been looking for this guy; everything was catalogued before he was cut down. I sent the photographs to Missing Persons, for the record."

"Thank you. Before you go, who are the men on the grass, and the one bent over behind the second ambulance?"

Richards took the notebook from his breast pocket and nodded in the direction of the ambulance. "Gary Cuttlesworth — developer from Burlington — went into the stable with the owner; came out and passed out. Appears he's got a weak stomach." He nodded toward the two on the grass. "One on the left is Irving Kelber — Cuttlesworth's partner — also from Burlington. He had the good sense not to go inside." Richards eased his index finger from the notebook and pointed to the right, at a man dwarfing a plastic chair. "That other fella with the dart hanging from his mouth? He's the owner of this place; his name is..." He looked down again. "Charles Cameron — nickname C.C. Local rich blowhard; has a son who runs a local crematorium."

Aziz and MacNeice's eyebrows shot up.

"That's his shiny new Rah-Rah out near the gate." Richards put the notebook back in his pocket. "C.C.'s fixing to sell this property; that's the extent of what we found out, sir. Good luck — I hope the guy makes it." He put his right-hand index and second fingers up to the brim of his Stetson in a casual salute and walked smartly back to his cruiser.

Evanson was on his cellphone, pacing back and forth some distance away; Swetsky and the others were more than twenty yards from the barn's entrance. They'd been taking turns going inside, but no one could stay for long. As MacNeice and Aziz drew closer, she cupped her nose and nodded for him to go in; she went to join the others.

MacNeice took a deep breath before stepping inside. The cops had left a plastic pyramid to indicate the stall — though the smell alone would have led him there. MacNeice looked down at the concrete floor and wondered what, if anything, would prove useful to Forensics. Standing in front of the open gate, he read the plaque on the door: "Wild Honey". Judging by the state of the door's wooden rail, there was evidence that at one point Honey had tried to chew her way out.

In the stall, a nylon rope was tethered to an iron ring; shreds of duct tape and the remains of zip ties lay scattered about. The source of the stench was a large dark patch on the floor—at its centre, a Rorschach smear of feces. Waiting to be bagged was a soiled sweat sock, a golf ball, and a black towel wrapped with duct tape in the shape of a man's head.

MacNeice took shallow breaths but soon felt light-headed. When his cellphone buzzed, he took the opportunity to leave. Outside, he took a deep breath, only to realize he needed to step much farther away.

Walking along the track, he saw that he had a message from Missing Persons. He turned to see Evanson, Vertesi, Swetsky, and Aziz all staring at their phones. Aziz looked his way and nodded in the direction of the far fence.

In the distance, MacNeice saw a tractor parked outside the property and a man standing at the fence.

"Michael, jog over there." He pointed to the man, who in turn waved back. "Find out who that is and what he's seen . . ." Like a football coach sending a player onto the field, MacNeice slapped Vertesi on the back, and off he went.

"Aziz, it's time we met Charles Cameron." He looked over to the others. "John, Charlie, you go find out what Cuttlesworth and Kelber know."

Evanson looked like a kid who hadn't been chosen for a baseball team—except that he also seemed relieved. "Sir, there's been a lot of personnel on site—they're gonna talk. I suggest we get ahead of it before the media take over."

"Good point. Call DC Wallace from your car. He'll want

a download before it's released to the media. If he sets up an in-person media briefing and invites you, consider it an order." As the sergeant walked off, MacNeice turned to Aziz. "I think we're approaching the moment when Jack will be invited to review a lineup."

"You're still serious about that?"

"Very. Evan Moore and his son deserve that." He looked back to watch Evanson drive away. "Okay. Let's get to know C.C."

Charles Cameron seemed lost in a mental fog and didn't notice them approaching.

"By the way, Forensics will be here within the hour."

"Good. Take the lead here; I want to know if he's in shock because of what he saw in the barn or if it's because his son may be involved."

"Garrick wasn't cremated," Aziz speculated, "because Thomas Cameron was rebuilding the oven linings."

"Exactly. This could have been the professor's holding cell."

"Judging by those photographs, it's doubtful Garrick would have made it to his cremation alive."

"Not unusual; people don't usually arrive—" MacNeice stopped when he realized she was joking. "Are the composites still in the car?"

Aziz nodded. "I'll get them."

MacNeice studied Cameron flipping the lighter lid with his thumb.

Kelber and Cuttlesworth—the latter done with his vomiting and sporting a freshly bandaged forehead—had been moved away from each other and C.C., who was sitting at the apex of a large triangle. Kelber sat stone-faced with his arms and legs crossed, the picture of a brooding man. It was easy to see that he wished he'd never set foot in C.C's Range Rover, let alone on the grounds of a vanity project that forever more would be referred to as "the place where they found the professor..."

[61]

THEY WERE FIVE FEET IN FRONT OF CHARLES CAMERON, BUT HE STILL hadn't noticed them. When he did, the cigarette that had been hanging from his mouth dropped to the ground. He made no move to retrieve it. He glanced from Aziz to MacNeice and back again before nodding.

"Sir, I'm DI Aziz; with me is DS MacNeice. Please provide us with the names of anyone with access to this property."

Cameron wheezed and fell into a smoker's cough. When it subsided, he said, "Ah, well, there's me...my grounds-keeper, my son...I'm pretty sure that's all."

"Names?"

"Yeah. Groundskeeper is Harry Ellis. Tom Cameron's my son."

Aziz smiled. "Can I call you Charles?"

"Charles, C.C.—either one."

"I understand your groundskeeper having a key—though it appears he hasn't been groundskeeping recently. But why would your son have one? Is he a business partner, perhaps?"

"No, he's not a partner; he's my son. We kept quarter horses to pace the thoroughbreds. His girls would ride them around the field..."

"Have you any idea how that man ended up in your stable?"

"No. I didn't know he was here. When we went in, I thought he was dead...smelled like he was."

"Any signs of a break-in that you've noticed? A damaged lock? A breach in the fencing?"

"The lock was fine. Look, I came out of that barn and called 911. Cuttlesworth fainted. He was bleeding, I woke him up, he started puking. I didn't walk around checking the fences." C.C. reached down for the cigarette, then added, "Must have been ten minutes later"—he waved like he was feeding chickens—"when this circus rolled in...Safe bet I've lost the sale to those two."

"Do you know the man in the stable?"

"No. I only found out who he was after the cops came."

"Are you an investor in your son's businesses, Mr. Cameron?" MacNeice asked.

"What?" C.C.'s head shot up. "The cremation thing? Yes. If you mean that coffee shop, no."

Aziz looked up from her notes. "How did your son and Giacomo Pezi meet?"

C.C.'s back straightened. He studied them for the first time. "What's my son got to do with this?"

"Just a coincidence, perhaps. We met with Thomas earlier about another matter."

"Where are you from? What's going on here?" Cameron stood up so abruptly that his chair cartwheeled away behind him.

"If you mean which division, Division One. If which department, Homicide," MacNeice said.

"Mr. Cameron." Aziz waited for him to look at her. "We've met with several independent crematoriums."

"And what—Giacomo and Tom are murdering people? This is bullshit." Though it was misshapen and damp from the ground and his sweaty palm, Cameron put the cigarette between his teeth, lit it, and then inhaled and exhaled through his nostrils like an angry bull.

"Returning to DI Aziz's question, how did Tom and Giacomo meet?"

Cameron was losing his patience. "Do you know who you're talking to?"

"The sign says 'C.C. Rider Thoroughbreds.' You introduced yourself as Charles, or C.C., Cameron." Aziz answered flatly. She removed the composites from the folder. "Sir, please look at these sketches and tell us if you recognize any of these men." She passed the printouts to Charles. "Take your time."

"I'm out of time." He flipped through the first two, looking at them briefly. "No and no." The last one, MacNeice expected, would get the same short shrift, but it didn't. For a few seconds Cameron hesitated before returning all three. "No. We done here?"

"You didn't recognize the last one?" Aziz held it up again.

"That does it, we're done. My lawyer is Barry Kessler;

if you want to discuss this further, look him up." Cameron ground the barely smoked cigarette into the grass and turned to the other two men. "Irv! Gary! Your ride's leaving." He stomped off through the long grass, smashing fuzzy white dandelion pappi and sending clouds of parachute seeds off on the breeze.

Watching Cameron, Aziz noted, "He hasn't done his groundskeeper any favours by marching off in such a snit."

"Looks like Tommy's about to get an earful," MacNeice said, reaching for his cellphone. He punched in a number and waited. "Montile, how's Garrick?"

"Not good. They're putting him into an induced coma to get him stabilized. The ICU doc only gave us a few seconds. I asked him about his chances."

"And?" MacNeice asked.

"Optimistically, sixty-forty — against. His wife's upped that to fifty-fifty because he's healthy and athletic..." Williams waited for a hospital announcement to finish. "When she'd gone off to be with him, the doc said if Garrick hadn't been found when he was, he would have been dead before dinner."

MacNeice's phone buzzed. It was Vertesi calling from the shadows obscuring the fence, so he ended the call with Williams to answer Michael. "What have you got?"

"Boss, you and Fiza should hear this."

AFTER HE WAS introduced, MacNeice asked about the farm — Jan Vanderkooy said he grew cash crops of soya beans and corn, while his wife grew garden vegetables for sale at the Dundurn Farmers' Market.

"Do you know anything about the sale of this property?" MacNeice asked.

Vanderkooy nodded and smiled, sending fans of thin wrinkles into his temples. "You know, farmers are humanity's eternal optimists... but we must also be realists. D'ya understand?"

"If you mean that development is inevitable... yes."

"Maybe I don't..." Jan tilted his head back in consideration. "My family came here in 1951; three years later, we bought a farm. It was in ruins and owned by the bank. My father worked at Firestone, mother was a nurse—and we all worked here. *Inevitable* is a big word. It has a relationship with time... yeah?"

"It does."

Vanderkooy tugged his cap, perhaps as a signal that he was about to get down to business. "Development is bound to happen—yes. My wife, Hannah, and I accept that. But until that time comes, we are optimistic farmers. My father rode this same tractor until he was ninety-three. We're happy doing what we do. Can you say that for yourself, Detective?"

"That's a simple question without a simple answer."

"If you say so..." Vanderkooy clearly wasn't baiting MacNeice; he smiled genuinely and changed the subject. "Maybe I should shut up now and tell you what I saw."

"Please." MacNeice glanced over his shoulder and noted the forensic van's arrival.

Vanderkooy recounted his tea break two days earlier: how he'd noticed a big black suv parked by the barn, and how two men—one short and white, one tall and Black— had been walking slowly around the property. There had been a third man sitting against the barn; Jan hadn't seen him as clearly as the others but thought he was white.

As he began offering more detailed descriptions of the men he'd met, Aziz pulled out the composites and held them up. "Do these sketches help?"

Vanderkooy pulled a worn case from his pocket, put on his glasses, and peered at the images. "Yeah, close, eh? I spoke to this one." He pointed at the short man.

"About?"

"What you call chit-chat—waste-of-time talk." He put his glasses away. "He's a smart aleck, that one; I don't think his friend liked that. Short fella said they were hired to check on the property—like security. I could believe that of the other fella, but not both, and that made me doubt them."

[62]

HUMILIATED BY HIS FATHER FROM THE DAY HE WAS BORN, CLARENCE was now being summoned to his client's office like a schoolboy answering for something he hadn't done.

But the summons wasn't the first insult of the day for Clarence Blow; that distinction went to Tom Cameron and the four consecutive texts he'd sent earlier.

> 10:00 a.m. TWO DETECTIVES WERE HERE DOING RESEARCH —
> they had artist sketches of the three of you!
> 11:03 a.m. WTF! THEY FOUND YOUR GUY — SERIOUSLY, WTF!
> 11:05 a.m. COUSIN — What have you gotten me into?
> 11:58 a.m. WE NEED TO TALK — not over phone!

Thirty-four minutes after the last text, Clarence heard the reason for Tom's panic over the radio. At first it was just breaking news to announce that the missing professor had been found alive. But by the top of the hour, further announcements included the details that Garrick had been found in a stable near Binbrook and his condition was listed as critical.

Clarence was furious. He jammed a holstered weapon into his belt so violently that its clip grabbed his flesh. He let out a yelp and checked for blood—but there was only a magenta welt. Clarence moved the holster further back on his hip and slipped a madras sport jacket over his lime-green polo.

He made a mental note of those he feared—fear being a relatively new feeling for him—and there was no shortage. One and Two; the client's brother, who'd no doubt use his stripping bath and incinerator to clean things up if need be. Tom Cameron had a record, and though he looked and acted civilized—well, he had a record. For that matter, Tom's father probably knew a guy who knew a guy. Not once did Clarence consider that he should be afraid of the cops.

It was odd and somewhat comforting that, with everything unravelling around him, he'd managed to convince himself that he wasn't afraid for long. Even his roily fury was tempered by the belief that he could still leave for Samoa at any moment.

Clarence stood transfixed before the Polynesian beauty on his wall. Only a week or so earlier he'd counted the water droplets on her shoulders—twelve on the right, fourteen on the left. He was daydreaming about the warmth of the water when he heard a car arrive.

From the window he saw the Yaris. Two emerged from it wearing a blue cotton suit, a white T-shirt, blue sunglasses, and blindingly white Stan Smith shoes. He glanced casually around for any eyes. As he reached for the knocker, Clarence opened the door and quipped, "You've had quite the makeover..."

Two peered over the frames of his glasses, tightened his lips, and walked past Clarence into the house. "Close the door, Blow." He went to the kitchen and opened the refrigerator. "No cranberry juice?"

Clarence offered to make coffee.

"No, sir. Let's just sit and watch the traffic out your picture window."

Once they were settled side by side on the sofa, Clarence asked, "What are we discussing on this impromptu mano-a-mano visit?"

Two shook his head. "You never miss an opportunity to use that slicker-than-shit tongue of yours..." He smiled. "Thing is, I'm pretty sure you know why I'm here. You're just being—what's the word I'm looking for?—coy?"

"If you mean evasive...possibly." Clarence let his arms relax beside him, feeling the comfort of the weapon at his side. "I'm aware that Professor Garrick was found and taken to hospital—"

"There you go, little man—you knew all along. Now, why would that bring me here?"

Clarence was about to respond when Two raised a hand. "What comes next is important; it'll tell me if you've been listening over our time together." As Clarence opened his mouth to respond, Two pointed at his stomach. "But first, take care of that. Your piece has sprung a leak."

Clarence leapt up with a mix of shock and embarrassment. He pulled up his lime polo—now sporting a large raspberry stain from his earlier run-in with the holster—and darted into the kitchen to put a paper towel on the wound.

"You'll need somethin' better than that. I'll get your first-aid kit?"

"I'll do it."

"Lemme take that jacket...I didn't know they were still making *mad-ras*. I'll take your pistola too, so you don't stain that pretty leather holster..." He placed the weapon on the counter, then sat down on a stool.

Clarence disappeared into the bathroom. Over the water running, Two called out, "It's for exactly that reason I don't wear my weapon on my hip. You pinch that flesh, it hurts like hell, then it takes forever to heal 'cause you're always wearing a belt. I might have a spare shoulder holster if you want it."

Five minutes later, Clarence emerged looking sheepish, now dressed in an orange polo shirt. Two watched him put on the jacket, leaving his gun on the counter. "Now, back to my question...any thoughts?"

"Pistachio," Clarence said. He felt defeated—in stark contrast to only a few minutes earlier.

"So you have been listening. One said you were, but I wasn't sure. Pistachio's the correct answer." He smiled admiringly at Clarence. "Is pistachio why you're back to packing your bags again?"

"Again?"

"Yeah, you were packing the other day, but I guess you're making sure we get paid first."

"I am...It's not as clear-cut as the example One used, but we'll get paid."

"Not as clear-cut? How fucking not?"

"Well, the client set this whole thing up to fail—that's on him."

"If that's how you see it..."

"And I brought in Tom, and he gave us the barn. It should have worked but the timing was against us—so our disposal couldn't be disposed of."

"That it?" Two's elbows were on the counter, his hands folded together like a knuckle club.

"Well, that's what happened."

"From where you stand, Clarence." Two removed the sunglasses and set them on the bar. "Okay, listen up. Here's what happened: We don't know your client—*you are our client*." He raised an index finger when Clarence attempted to interrupt. "You came up with the cremator and using the barn. You're the contractor; we're your subcontractors. We work for you; you make sure we get paid. You keeping up so far?"

"I am, but—"

"No buts. I'm your gentle reminder. Timing wasn't against *us*—it was against *you*. So don't be a smartass pistachio."

"I won't be. I'm responsible for you being paid."

"Paid with—Wait, what was the word One used?" Two scratched his head. "Oh, I remember—with *alacrity*. *Fuckingfast* would be my word, but One was sure you'd know what *alacrity* means."

"I do. Though...there may be another disposal for us, so—"

"Nope. You're on your own there. Once we're paid"— he pointed at an unseen horizon just below the range hood—"we're one-two-zip-a-dee-doo-dah gone." Standing to leave, he said, "Oh, and One wants to make a final visit to the crematorium. For business purposes."

"You mean tonight, as scheduled—go out there together, tonight?" Clarence's eyes widened in disbelief. The police would likely visit Tommy's crematorium again, but Tom would do okay because nothing had happened yet. You can't arrest someone for something they haven't done. He convinced himself there was nothing to worry about.

Two seemed to enjoy the outward signs of Blow's internal conversation. He wanted to be flexible. "Tomorrow's fine. And remember—separate cars. I'm the only one at this point who blends in with the scenery, with you being short and One being Black, so best we go alone."

As Two reached the door, he turned back. "One last thing." He swung both sides of his jacket open to reveal two shoulder holsters. "I love the old westerns, Clarence, so I trained myself to draw with both hands. Ya wanna see?"

Despite his dropped jaw, Clarence managed to utter, "No . . . no, thank you."

"Just go with what you're comfortable gripping. Nickel-plated thirty-eights work for me. If that little guy on the bar fits your hand, then that's the right one for you." He closed the jacket and nodded. "See you later, Clarence."

[63]

MACNEICE AND AZIZ STOOD AT THE INTERVIEW ROOM DOOR. HE looked through the sidelight and saw Thomas Cameron, his fingers nervously tapping the table's edge, while his lawyer, Leonard Green, tapped his cellphone. Both had paper cups in front of them.

"I'm for an espresso. Do you want one?" MacNeice asked.

"Not for the moment." Aziz tucked a file folder under her arm and opened the door.

"Thomas, thank you for coming in for this interview." Aziz held out her hand, and while Tom seemed reluctant, he took it. "And you're Mr. Cameron's counsel?"

"Leonard Green, QC . . . and yourself?" Green opened a thin silver case and retrieved a business card.

"Dr. Fiza Aziz, Detective Inspector, Dundurn Homicide."

They shook hands. As she sat down, she added, "Detective Superintendent MacNeice will join us shortly."

Green couldn't resist. "Doctor of...?"

"Criminology." She allowed herself a brief smile.

Seconds later, MacNeice stepped in; he could feel the tension in the room as he offered a hand to Cameron. "If you'd like coffee, we have Mino's beans."

Neither man responded. They were dressed for business: Cameron wore a double-breasted dark grey suit, crisp white shirt, and burgundy tie, while Green wore navy blue with a shiny blue tie. Green was momentarily preoccupied with his soft leather briefcase; he smiled and handed MacNeice a card before retrieving a Montblanc pen and yellow legal pad. He then placed the briefcase against the wall, where it sagged from sheer elegance.

Aziz noticed that the colour had drained from Cameron's cheeks. "Mr. Green, do you have any questions before we begin?"

"Only one. Can I have an espresso?"

"Certainly. I'll make it," MacNeice said. "Thomas, last chance."

"No, thank you."

MacNeice finished his cup and left the room. He walked back to the cubicle, where Lise Bichet was bent over her computer, her fingers flying across the keyboard. He smiled and tapped Williams on the shoulder. "Find anything in records about Thomas Cameron?"

"Two juvenile charges. The first for an attempt to burn down the stands at Woodlands Park. The second also involved arson; he firebombed a shop on King Street and was caught next door, throwing a brick through another window. Convicted in both cases; the latter carried a two-year sentence."

"Was he alone?"

"Not for the first; yes for the second. The Woodlands case also involved Cameron's cousin, Clarence Blow, who received three months of community service." Williams went over to the printer and handed MacNeice the documents.

MacNeice fanned through the six pages. "Impressive. When did this come in?"

"About five minutes ago. They come with a proviso that the first charge, given their age, won't be cited as a police record. Also, Vertesi called; the groundskeeper for C.C. Rider has been out in Cape Breton, working on his father's boat, for the past three weeks — said you'd know what that meant."

"Thanks, Montile." MacNeice went to make Green's coffee. While it was pouring, he scanned the pages. The police description of Cameron at fourteen noted that he was six foot three, while his cousin was closing in on five feet. "An odd couple . . ." MacNeice leaned over a cubicle and called out, "Montile . . ."

"Yessir." Williams's head popped up above the office landscape.

"Find out why the name Clarence Blow is familiar to me. What does he do, where does he live, work, et cetera. Get photos."

"Lise is already on it, sir."

MACNEICE RE-ENTERED THE small interview room where, judging by their faces, Cameron and Green were anxious to get going. Aziz waited for the room to settle. "I'll just give DS MacNeice an update on what he missed . . ."

No one interrupted her rapid account of the past ten minutes. Cameron had admitted to having a key to C.C. Rider Thoroughbreds and he'd spoken about how happy his daughters had been to ride the quarter horses there. Glancing at MacNeice, Aziz continued, "Why he kept the key after the horses were long gone was still unanswered when you walked in, sir."

"Well, Thomas, where's that key now?"

Cameron brought his hands to the edge of the table, suggesting that a prayer might follow, "It's true, there'd be no need for me to go back there, and I haven't. As for the key, I assume it's in a drawer somewhere, but I've no idea where. Where do keys go when they're no longer needed?"

"Are you saying you may have lost or discarded it?" Aziz asked.

"Maybe. Don't you have keys that you've lost track of because they're no longer useful?"

Green jumped in to help. "What's the relevance of this to my client?"

"A key was used in the commission of an indictable offence at C.C. Rider Thoroughbreds," MacNeice said. "Ruling out Charles Cameron, who was clearly surprised to find Professor Garrick on the property, and his groundskeeper, who's in Cape Breton, that leaves your client."

Green objected. "The groundskeeper could have given his key to someone, or duplicated it for several—"

MacNeice sensed Green was just warming up, so he stopped him. "What area of the law do you specialize in, Mr. Green?"

"Commercial litigation, corporate law. But this is an interview—"

"So it is." MacNeice turned back to Cameron. "You're aware that this is a homicide unit? You may wonder why we're involved if the person found isn't dead."

Thomas shrugged as if he didn't need to consider the question—or he may have been questioning his choice of counsel. Either way, he was composed; it was clear this wasn't the first time he'd been interviewed by cops.

"Leaving aside that Professor Garrick may yet succumb to his injuries, our ongoing investigation involves the murder of as many as three others." MacNeice let that sink in before adding, "You're on track, Thomas, to being charged as an accessory in an attempted homicide and being linked to those four other deaths."

Green slapped his Montblanc down on the legal pad. "I think that's highly unlikely. All you have is a missing key, and you're leaping to these wild conclusions."

MacNeice smiled wearily. "DI Aziz, give Thomas another opportunity to review those composites."

Cameron studied the images before him and, just as before, shook his head. "I wish I could help, but I don't know them."

MacNeice reached for Montile's printouts. He turned over Cameron's profile—the one created following his first juvenile offence.

Thomas snapped back in his chair and stared at MacNeice. "I...I can't believe this." He shoved it away as if its proximity alone might cast a spell. "I was fourteen. I was angry. I paid for that. Why are you—"

"And this?" He turned over the profile of Clarence Blow. "Your cousin..."

Cameron's composure slipped; the flush on his neck reached his chin. "He had very little to do with it."

Green was trying to find an entry point to defend his client. "Why are you conflating a rebellious teenager's mistake with a capital crime?"

MacNeice nodded Green's way to let him know he'd heard him, then laid the police composite of the third suspect next to the image of the teenage Clarence Blow. The muscles that kept Cameron's mouth shut flickered, but he remained silent.

Aziz was also surprised to see the image—and the name attached to it. She tapped Blow's photograph. "It bears an uncanny resemblance to the rendering, does it not—even down to his height."

Cameron shrugged but said nothing.

"Isn't it possible, Mr. Cameron, that you gave your key to Mr. Blow and forgot that you'd done so?" Aziz sounded almost motherly.

"It's absurd to connect my cousin to the farm—as I said, I don't where that key is." Cameron dropped his hands into his lap.

"I think we're done for today," MacNeice said, abruptly terminating the interview.

Both men left the room looking confused. They filed past Swetsky, who was making his way along the corridor.

Aziz turned off the recorder. "I suspect Cameron's relieved to be walking—was that your idea?"

"Partly... though he's too smart not to know what happened here." MacNeice looked at the gangly teenager in the photocopy. "Thomas is in an extremely precarious position..."

Swetsky filled the interview room door. "Five and Dime at Big Mac. Best stay seated for this one."

[64]

"**TAYLOR BARROW DAINTRY, THIRTY-SIX, AND LESTER ALLEN**
Wright, forty-one—cellmates at the Oklahoma State
Penitentiary in McAlester. Guards gave 'em the nickname
'Five and Dime.' Daintry was doing five years for assault;
he overlapped with Wright, who was doing ten for assault
and battery. The nickname stuck because they were always
together—buddies, not sweethearts. Got those composites
handy?"

Fiza pulled them from the folder. Swetsky set the one
of Clarence Blow aside and tapped the Black man's sketch.
"Lester Wright." He laid a wanted poster beside it. "Lester's
a lay preacher. Before he was arrested, he was a high school
English teacher." Swetsky then slid Daintry's poster next
to Wright's. "This guy's another story . . . former bull rider,

cowhand, carpenter, and handyman. Dropped out of high school in grade nine to join the rodeo circuit. Our composites weren't perfect, but they were close enough for these two to be identified stateside."

"Professionals," MacNeice said under his breath.

"Their Big Mac release dates happened within a month or so of each other. They were listed as wanted because they skipped parole twenty-two months ago." Swetsky grinned, enjoying the moment.

"A pastor and a bull rider came to Dundurn . . ." MacNeice read the bulletins aloud. "Lester Wright's a wide load — six feet. Daintry's six-two; as it turns out, he's built like a bull rider. What does Clarence Blow bring to the party?"

"The source of the work?" Aziz suggested.

"Little big man . . . Phil Spector . . ." Swetsky mused.

"Bosses aren't usually present for the dirty work, but Blow was." MacNeice felt like they were still missing something. "John, what are those Russian dolls that contain ever smaller dolls?"

"Matryoshka — or babushka — dolls. I always thought they were creepy . . ." he answered with a shrug.

"What if these three" — MacNeice moved his hand over the images of Blow, Daintry, and White — "are the dolls on the outside, for show?"

"Based on what?" John asked.

"On Cheval Fou — Rodney Conroy's dinner that led to him being found in Lincoln. He's closer to the heart of our babushka."

"So it's a network?" Aziz asked.

"Exactly. We have three confirmed dead: Rodney James Conroy, Dr. Evan Moore, and the John Doe. Add to that John and Peter are still missing, and Garrick would've been dead if Thomas Cameron's fire chambers weren't being redone." On the back of Clarence Blow's profile, MacNeice began drawing a diagram, but the more he drew, the less it looked like a Russian doll. "Actually, it's more like an octopus — we don't know how many legs it has, but in the end, the requests come from the head and the action's fulfilled by the legs." He paused. "The same as it ever was, I guess."

"I understand the high-roller Montrealer, maybe even the professor, but those local boys — the house painter and the other guy — if they're dead, who would pay to hit them?" Swetsky said dismissively.

"Maybe someone needed them silenced. And we don't know who died next to Moore in that forest," Aziz offered.

[65]

"**W**ELCOME TO DUNDURN'S STARGATE HOTEL, SIR. DO YOU HAVE a reservation?"

"No... I hope that's not necessary, Denise." He turned his eyes from her name tag to her face.

"Let me see what I can do..." She tapped a few keys and smiled in return. "I have a junior suite on the seventeenth floor with a wonderful view of Dundurn Bay. Will that do?"

"Splendid. My name is Stephen John, CEO of SAI—Superior Accounting, Incorporated. Please put the room on my business account..." He handed her a platinum card.

"Certainly, Mr. John. How many nights will you be staying?"

"Four, possibly five..." He looked around the lobby. "Slow at the hotel these days?"

"Oh, we're down a bit, but no...we're doing okay." *Tap-tap-tap-tap*... "Will that be one key or two, and do you require underground parking?"

"One key's fine, and yes to underground parking."

He set his suitcase, heavy duffle bag, and briefcase on a rolling luggage cart and walked off to the elevator. As he approached the seventeenth floor, his phone rang. When he saw "Kelly Travel" on the small screen, he answered. "Yes... Thank you...An open-ended first-class ticket. Qantas is perfect...I won't need a return ticket just yet...Oh, I didn't know...Well, book me a return ticket for three months from departure. Thank you. Toodle-oo to you."

DRIVING AWAY FROM the Stargate, Clarence Blow was filled with pride that his nom de guerre had been accepted so easily. And happier still that Stephen John's replacement passport would arrive at the hotel's front desk by the following morning at the latest.

His exit secured, Clarence turned his attention to being paid in full for the Garrick debacle. That was non-negotiable. When the client called, Clarence had been busy tearing up the Polyncsia poster and related brochures and putting them in the garbage bin on the parking level. "Clarence. I'll see you in my office—immediately."

Clarence wasn't in the mood to be barked at or to grovel, and he wasn't about to apologize for failing to dispose of Garrick. He had an accountant's ability to remember many things beyond numbers, and he was more than ready to recite the chronology of his client's failures. And, following Two's earlier visit, he had all the incentive required to demand the entire fee.

CLARENCE WALKED OFF the elevator outside the client's office, certain it would be an ugly meeting. He felt for his pistol, surprised to find that its weight gave him no comfort.

While waiting to enter that dark room, Clarence recalled another, long-ago bout of rage — perhaps with prescient finality, his wife's response that he was "an unhinged and pathetic little man," and his response to her: "I'll be late tonight, darling. Don't wait up." He had delighted in the sly smile that crept over his face back then and how he'd continued smiling as he shut the door on his wife for the last time.

Clarence realized he was wearing that smile again.

[66]

"**S**IR, YOU MIGHT REMEMBER HEARING ABOUT CLARENCE BLOW seven years ago. He and his wife, Tilly, lived on Binkley Road, in the west end." Bichet pointed to a press photo of the site on her computer.

"The penny drops..." Aziz said, watching MacNeice.

Bichet referred to her notes. "Blow is, or was, an accountant. He was at his office when a gas explosion demolished the house, killing Tilly. He was investigated but not charged. Forensics and the fire marshal believed the explosion was caused by a nicked gas line, following work recently completed at the house."

"Where is he now, Sergeant?"

"Well, that's the thing, sir. He kept his office in the Pigott Building for another four years. During that time, he rented an apartment on Herkimer Street. Since then, I haven't found any trace of him, as a practising accountant, an apartment renter, or a homeowner . . . and he doesn't appear to be filing personal or corporate taxes in Ontario."

"Cellphone?"

"No, sir. At least, not under his name."

"Family?"

"Yes, sir. Parents; father's still a practising chartered accountant."

"Photographs from the time of the incident?"

"Affirmative." She handed the printouts to MacNeice.

MacNeice taped up Blow's juvenile mugshot and a press photo taken the day of the explosion next to the photos of Wright and Daintry. He studied them quietly before turning back to Williams, Aziz, and Bichet.

"Lise and Montile—get on the parents. We need to confirm that Clarence Blow is alive and hasn't left the province. Before you go, Montile, get an update on Garrick's condition."

"Yes, sir," said Williams.

"Ryan, put the latest photo of Blow into the DPD system and get it out to the media. Label him as a person of interest."

Swetsky was smiling. "You're fucking with their heads . . ."

"A bit." MacNeice realized that the computer tech, Larry Nichol, had spotted Blow near Garrick's house, and it was Blow who had engaged Vanderkooy in conversation. He'd probably spoken to Giacomo too.

"Think Blow might strike a deal to save himself?" Aziz asked.

"That's the dream scenario, yes."

Ryan swung around. "Sir, Vertesi's on his way back, DI Maracle's on the line . . ."

With a catch in his chest, MacNeice realized Maracle had been out of the pocket for some time. "Charlie?"

"Sir, I know you've got a crematorium on the go, but there's something about industrial incinerators that's been bugging me..."

"In what sense?"

"Dave DiLillo from Erie Prefab called. They build garages, sunroom additions, that kind of thing. I was there yesterday asking about their incinerator—it's one of the small ones. Everything they're using it for seemed legit."

"And now it doesn't?"

"No—they are legit. DiLillo called to tell me that he mentioned my visit to the incinerator company rep when they were playing golf. The rep remembered that he'd delivered another unit exactly like DiLillo's to an autobody shop on Arvin near Green Road. They rebuild antique and luxury cars."

"I don't understand..."

"That's the point, sir. Neither did the guy who sold it to them. And DiLillo couldn't stop wondering why a garage needed an incinerator."

"I assume you have an answer?"

"Well...So I picked up my brother's '57 Thunderbird and drove it over to Riviera Automobile Restoration. I met the owner, a guy named Ronald 'Ronnie' Slater. I wanted to get a rough estimate for restoring the 'Bird to mint condition."

"And...?" MacNeice felt uneasy that Maracle had gone hunting alone. He recalled him saying that his favourite position on patrol in Afghanistan had been point, and that a close second was being a scout.

"It took Slater thirty minutes to cough up an estimate.

When I asked him why it was so expensive, he gave me the old *If you have to ask, you can't afford it*. He took me into the shop—it was noisy as hell, guys working on a '49 Hudson Hornet and an Alfa Romeo Spider. They've got this huge tank—Slater called it a dip-'n'-strip—that strips metal clean. And beside it was the incinerator, exactly like DiLillo's. It's used to burn wooden skids and other wood products."

"Charlie—please tell me you're not there now?"

"No, I'm a few blocks away. Anyway, Slater could see I was impressed by his operation, and I hadn't rejected his high five, low six ballpark for Donny's 'Bird. I guess he was convinced I could afford it, so he showed me the back lot."

"Okay . . .?"

"A Ferrari under a car cover, a '59 Mark IX Jag, and two Caddies, one from the forties, the other all fins and chrome. A gullwing Mercedes without an engine . . . and a dark grey Econoline van—no lettering."

MacNeice swallowed hard. "Please tell me you didn't ask about it?"

"Paid no attention to it, sir," Maracle said. "Last thing: he's got six SUVs—all fairly new. I asked what they were in for—it's his livery service for customers like me when their vehicles are being restored."

"A Lincoln Navigator?"

"Yep. I played disinterested—said they looked like prom boats to me."

The call ended and MacNeice went to the white-board, where he wrote: *Ronald Slater, Riviera Automobile Restoration—Arvin Road and Green Road. Grey van, incinerator/stripping bath, Lincoln Navigator.*

[67]

MACNEICE TURNED TO SWETSKY. "JOHN, CALL FORENSICS. WE NEED a large team ready to go within the hour. When I get the nod from Wallace, take Vertesi and the warrant to Riviera. I want to know what's been dissolving in that stripping bath besides rust and paint."

"And Cameron's crematorium, Mac?" Aziz tapped her notes from the interview.

Swetsky turned to her. "You think he'll do a runner?"

"Not at all. He and his counsel know what we have is circumstantial... Cameron might decide to fight, or flip, or just wait us out." Aziz added, "Plus, I expect his father will show up with a big-fee defence lawyer."

MacNeice nodded. "I'll request twenty-four-hour surveillance on the crematorium." He walked down to the parking lot and punched in a number. Waiting for the connection, he scanned the trees lining the lot—nothing in flight. The heat was stifling; the breeze passed lackadaisically through the trees, reaching him without a hint of cool... "How are you, Bill?"

Bill Moore was alone with Jack at Evan's house, his wife having returned to BC. When MacNeice asked how Jack was doing, he laughed ruefully. "To be honest, it was hard going for him in the beginning, understandably, with Ev's things around him—the smells and all. Even the doorbell ring sends him bounding off to see if Ev's home. Mostly it's the lady next door."

"He's recovering well, I assume?"

"Pretty much. We go walking on the beach or out to the Niagara Parkway where the trees are thick and it's not hot. Anyway, has something happened, Detective?"

"Almost. Not there yet, but we're much closer."

"Anything to do with that professor they found alive?"

"Yes—we may need to borrow Jack soon."

"You want him to identify somebody?"

"Exactly. And we'd all like to see him before he heads out west for good."

Moore asked, "Can I tell Evan's son that we're getting close?"

"If he calls you... tell him the case is developing very quickly."

Moore was relieved. "Thank goodness. It's been very hard on David... Well, on all of us." He cleared his throat. "Jack and I can be there within an hour—anytime, day or night."

HAVING STEPPED OUTSIDE to clear his head, MacNeice sat down on the parking lot bench and leaned back. In the heat he could smell engine oil and lubricant, the hot rubber of cruiser tires. He called Wallace.

The Deputy Chief congratulated him on Garrick's rescue. MacNeice deflected the credit, but the DC was having none of it.

"So, Detective, what do you need now?"

"A search warrant and a robust team from Forensics, sir. And, separately, twenty-four-hour surveillance on a crematorium."

It took all of six minutes, a long conversation by Wallace's standards. He whistled through his teeth, making the sound of a bomb falling— then, "You've got it" — and hung up.

Across the lot and farther down the line of trees, MacNeice heard a robin calling. Not the melodic, cheery song of morning or evening, but a short, rapid warning to a mate or offspring.

MacNeice stood up to scan the trees and fence. "There you are." He spotted a grey-and-white cat prowling slowly along the fence, pausing every few steps to check the canopy for movement. In the upper branches of a young maple, the robin darted frantically from limb to limb—and the sparrows that had a ringside seat had stopped talking.

His phone rang. He checked the display—*Dr. A. Sumner.* Focusing on the unfolding drama before him, he answered. "MacNeice."

"While it's not the reason for my call, on hearing the news about Professor Garrick, I couldn't help but assume you were involved."

"Not in his discovery or rescue, but in the wider and related investigation...Do you know him?"

"I don't, but his wife, Elaine, did a practicum with me at Brant years ago. She's a fine physician. At the time, I thought she'd choose psychiatry." MacNeice heard her open a door, followed by the familiar squeak of Sumner's task chair as she sat down at her desk. "Right...Well, to the reason for my call. DC Wallace mentioned you today; he said you were, and I quote, up to your eyeballs. If that's accurate, I thought it best to let you know I'm available should you feel the need to talk."

A session with Sumner would certainly clear out what he'd recently stored in his mental closet, but MacNeice was currently running so smoothly on adrenalin and caffeine that he knew an hour in her office would dull his edge — and right now, he needed to be sharp. "Thank you, Doctor. I appreciate the offer. I can't now, but will when I can..."

The robin had finally had enough. It dropped swiftly toward the cat, which cowered to avoid the attack — claws and beak. The bird landed one strike, then banked and landed on a nearby branch, where its scolding continued. Hunkered down, tail flicking nervously, the cat slipped between the fence pickets and disappeared.

Vindicated, the robin flew the length of the parking lot and swung right toward Main Street. The scene so distracted MacNeice that he didn't hear Sumner's goodbye.

[68]

IF THE THOUGHT HAD CROSSED HIS MIND – EVEN FOR A SECOND – before he opened the door, he would have fled and never looked back. Unfortunately, that possibility only flashed before him the moment Clarence stepped into the room.

His client was at the desk—arms crossed like an angry father. One, sitting opposite, gave a perfunctory nod to Clarence; Two seemed to be enjoying the abstract art on the black wall. Hearing the door open, he turned, smiled briefly, and returned to the painting.

Clarence's heart pounded and he felt faint; he leaned back against the closed door and let out an involuntary sigh.

"Sit down, Mr. Blow," One said, patting the arm of the empty chair.

Why was One giving orders now? Clarence looked to

the client for a reaction, but the man remained stone-faced, focused on his pen as if it might levitate.

"What's going on here, sir?" Clarence snapped. He made his way to the open chair. Sitting on the edge so his shoes remained on the floor, he turned to One. "This is *my client — my job*. You don't belong here. You'll get your money, now get—"

The strike was loud, and came so fast that Clarence's head snapped sideways. The client's arms flew up and he blurted something like "Wha-hah!"

Clarence thought his jaw was broken. His cheek stung and there was a high-frequency hiss in his right ear. He'd lived his whole life without being struck, and now it had happened twice in a matter of days. He looked to the client, hoping for some degree of compassion, but his attention had returned to his pen.

Clarence turned to One to speak in his own defence. "I—"

"Best be quiet now, little man. No one needs to hear how you've got things under control." One didn't appear angry; rather, he seemed empathetic.

A part of Clarence wanted to curl up and have a good cry, but a larger part wanted him to spray the room with his sidearm. With his head feeling like a shaken snow globe, he decided to answer, "Got it..."

"Good choice. Now, before you arrived, we were about to hear *your client*—Mr. Jeremy Slater here—explain why the contract on the professor won't be honoured. So, Clarence, this is good timing on your part."

Clearly rattled by the unexpected violence, Slater began moving things around on his desk. His face was flushed, he cleared his throat. "Well . . . Yes, I acknowledge that I changed the plan with regards to this disposal—we all answer to our clients, and I'm no exception. Nonetheless, Mr. Blow did, on several occasions, assure me that the contract would be fulfilled. Had it been, we all would have been compensated . . ."

"Uh-huh . . ." One was listening intently.

Two had settled on the corner of Slater's desk and was letting his Stan Smiths glide back and forth above the oak flooring.

While the invasion of his personal space unnerved him, Slater soldiered on. "However, upon hearing of the professor's release, my client feels justified in refusing to pay for a contract that remains unfulfilled—it's that simple. Now, I can promise that another contract is imminent, and I'm happy to engage you all, but I'm afraid we must move on from this one without compensation. So, regrettably and without blame—I'm not blaming anyone . . ."

The client had run out of steam, perhaps because Two was twirling the point of Slater's onyx-handled stiletto letter opener slowly around the tip of his left index finger.

"That it, boss?" One asked, shifting his upper torso forward so his arms were resting on the desk.

Slater laid his hands flat to suggest some degree of finality. "Well . . . yes I'm sure you understand my position . . . I don't know if Mr. Blow has led you to believe otherwise—"

Suddenly Two stuck the letter opener into Slater's left hand, pinning it to the desk. "Hold up there, buckaroo." He leaned over, bringing his face close to Slater's. "You're trying to throw *our* client, Mr. Blow, under the stagecoach?"

Pain and fear registered on Slater's face. "Stop—I'm just

saying—I'm not privy—to what he may have told you—about our contract conditions—" he stuttered.

Two withdrew the letter opener from Slater's hand and returned to twirling it on his finger. With a belated yelp, Slater pressed his other hand over the wound.

Two shook his head and turned to his partner. "One, what's that word in hardware stores, the one they use when they know they're gonna lose money on a wrench but win on a drill?"

One chuckled; Blow and Slater looked confused. "A loss leader. Two's suggesting that you treat the professor's contract as a loss leader."

"That's exactly right," Two said. "So, who's givin' away that wrench—and we don't care who, or even if you split it."

Clarence felt a line had just been crossed. He sat up and pointed a finger at Slater. "It won't be split. I promised that you'll settle the debt. This was *your* loss leader; *you* put this plan in motion. *You* agreed to pay the surcharge." Clarence glanced over at Two, who smiled and gave him an *attaboy* wink.

What followed was a heavy silence. One started nodding—slowly—like he had a tune going on in his head, then sat back, pursed his lips, and thrust out his lower jaw.

Two grinned as he pointed the onyx handle in One's direction. "That, boys, is not good. That's a look you don't wanna see." He studied Slater and Blow to make sure they understood. "So, chief, now that Clarence has had his say, it's time to clear your tab. And just so you both know, we're down to seconds, not minutes, before this gloomy room gets painted red."

[69]

WILLIAMS AND BICHET APPROACHED THE ABERDEEN MANSION slowly on foot. A dark blue Mercedes was idling outside; its driver stood waiting for his passenger. Seeing them approach, he made no attempt to hide his suspicion and contempt.

"Here's trouble..." Bichet said.

"Naw... Probably thinks we're Jehovah Witnesses."

As they walked up the driveway heading for the house, the driver stepped away from the vehicle to block them. "Can I help you?"

Both detectives flashed their badges and kept walking. As they approached the door, it swung open. An elderly man stood before them — he seemed surprised, somewhat peeved; he was very short. His brow crumpled with concern, as if their arrival meant he'd be late for something important.

"Who are you? Why are you here?" While they were legitimate questions, something in Eugene Blow's eyes suggested he'd been expecting them.

Williams gave the reason and the man sagged into his suit. With a wave of his hand, he dismissed his chauffeur and stepped back. "Inside..."

He explained that his wife had taken to her bed, refusing to believe that she'd seen Clarence's likeness in the *Standard*, insisting there must be some mistake.

"And you, sir—do you refuse to believe it?" Bichet asked.

"No...no. While I certainly don't understand everything, I can't say it's unbelievable. So far as I'm concerned, Clarence is a chartered accountant." He grappled for a better word than *secretive* and settled on *private*. "Clarence is extremely private; I've no idea where his office is, or whether he even has one. He speaks about clients coming in from out of town but has never—not once—mentioned who they are, or talked about his practice on their behalf."

"Tell us about your relationship with your son, Mr. Blow," Bichet asked.

"I think you've gotten a sense of it. At any rate, it's difficult...non-existent. Put bluntly, my son and I don't trust each other. However, he's still his mother's little boy, so for her sake, I hope this is all a ghastly mistake."

"Have you any recent photographs of him, sir?" Williams asked.

Blow shook his head as if the question was absurd. "No. Barely a few from his adolescence, and Clarence avoids us like the plague. He's never liked being photographed."

"Why is that?" Bichet asked.

"Clarence was undone by his height. Where you and I might use that to excel in our endeavours, he became ... ever smaller." He raised his hand as if to silence himself. "I'm sorry I don't sound like a loving father — Clarence would never accuse me of being one — but what else can I say?"

"Do you know any of his friends or associates?" Williams asked.

"Of the former, he's too calculating to have friends. Of the latter, no."

"Do you have his current address?"

"Yes, 7 Southview Place. It's a small home on a cul-de-sac in the west end."

TWO HOURS LATER, MacNeice and Aziz met Williams and Bichet on the stoop of a nondescript ranch-style bungalow. The curtains were drawn and the garden needed tending, but other than that, there was nothing to set it apart from the neighbouring houses.

"When we arrived," Williams said, "the next-door neighbour came out. Lise asked her if she knew Clarence Blow."

Bichet picked up the narrative. "She said no, that this house belongs to someone named Stephen John. When I asked her to describe him, the first thing she said was that he's about my height, lives alone, and never seems to have visitors — except for recently, when two men started coming to see him."

"One white, the other Black?" Aziz said.

"Correct. And an old man came in a chauffeur-driven car a couple of days ago — he didn't stay long."

"That was Eugene Blow, Clarence's father, Williams added.

"Interesting...Anything else?"

Williams shook his head. "Not much, sir. The back garden's on the edge of a shallow ravine; there's a swing set back there that looks like it hasn't been used in years. The lawn's merged with the weeds from the forest, and there's a rusted-out barbecue on the back stoop that hasn't seen burgers in a long time. All the windows have closed curtains or blinds."

"Doors secure?" MacNeice asked, adding that he'd brought a search warrant.

"Pretty much, but we could knock out a window."

"No need," Bichet said, pulling a leather kit from the thigh pocket of her fatigues. "With your permission, sir?"

MacNeice smiled. "You have it... And check the door before you open it—just in case this place is wired to explode."

Williams shot a look at Aziz before turning to MacNeice. "Why don't we step off the porch, just in case?"

Bichet knelt, a thin metal tool poised before the lock. Less than a minute later she nodded at the others, opened the door slightly, and deployed a dentist's mirror on the end of a telescoping rod. Slipping it through the narrow gap between door and frame, she slid it slowly from the base up, until she'd reached the limit of her height.

Stepping onto the bottom stair, Williams said, "Wait, I'm coming—"

"Stay where you are; I got this," Bichet interrupted. She took a vertical leap up onto the iron railing and tipped forward to support herself on the door frame. Sliding the mirror along the remaining gap, she surveyed the rest of the door. Satisfied there wasn't a tripwire, Bichet dropped down to the stoop, gave one swift kick, and the door flew open.

[70]

THE MOMENT THE TRANSACTION WAS CONFIRMED, SLATER OPENED his mouth to say something—just as Two drove the letter opener so deep into his ear that only the onyx handle remained visible. Slater's head slammed onto the leather desk pad, where it remained more or less still—even as his body was seized by spasms.

Two hustled a wide-eyed Clarence out of the building and into the Yaris.

Unable to speak, the fear that Clarence had kept at bay broke free. There were questions—four-alarm questions—but he didn't dare ask them. He didn't even protest when Two hustled him into his rental and drove away, leaving Blow's car parked outside Slater's building.

Driving under the speed limit, Two kept to his lane,

determined to be unremarkable. Clarence tried to swallow, but everything was dry, even his teeth, and he wished Two would just leave him at the side of the road. When he realized where they were headed, he was seized by another wave of panic, this one feeding a fear that Clarence had felt from the outset: he knew absolutely nothing about One and Two except how swiftly death occurred around them. And the weight of his holster brought him no comfort.

"You would have liked my grandpa," Two said, glancing over at Clarence. "Before the war, he fought in Spain, got shot in the foot—that gave him a limp. When the real war kicked off in '39, he joined the Merchant Navy in Nova Scotia, met my grandma there—I'm actually part Canadian."

Clarence managed to squeak, "Really...? What's One doing?"

"Yeah, not bad for a ranch hand who'd never been off dry land. Anyway...he told me once about a convoy in '41. They were on their way to England, weighed down with heavy stuff like grain, tanks, probably bombs..." Satisfied that Clarence seemed to be listening, he continued. "Around midnight two of the ships near his blew up, one after the other; the one closest was blown clear out of the water."

"Jesus Christ."

"That's probably what he said—he also said it was like shootin' fish in a barrel. Anyway, two things about his story of that night stuck with me ever since he told me about it."

"What were they?" Clarence wanted the lesson—he was desperate to know why they'd left One behind.

"Gramps said the radio operator came out of his shack when that first ship blew, holding a frying pan with eggs he'd been cookin'—they were still runny and slid off the pan onto his pants and boots, but the man took no notice. He just kept screamin' over and over, "We're all gonna die! We're all gonna die!" Two nodded for emphasis. "Scary shit, but that's only the first part..."

"About the radio op—"

"Hell, no. About an Anglican priest. After the second ship exploded, he was in the mess hall with some nurses and wives—young women who were scared like him. The priest didn't offer any comfort, didn't recite nothin' from the scriptures—he pasted himself to the bulkhead, singing 'Give me land, lotsa land, under starry skies above...' He sang that in fine choral fettle pretty much till dawn. When he realized they'd made it through the night, he disappeared into his cabin and didn't come out until they docked in England."

Two smiled at the story while Clarence waited for a moral that didn't come. He looked out the window and realized they were already halfway to Clappison Corners.

Two noticed him checking the side mirror. "One's coming...just had some housekeeping to do."

"Why are we going to Tom's?"

"We've got a business idea."

"Do you need me there?"

Two smiled. "Why, you got somewhere else to go?"

[71]

"TELL ME SOMETHING..."

About what?

"About anything. Tell me something about anything."

You're looking for a story?

"Yes. No. I'm looking for closeness. I need to escape my head—just for a while."

Mac, I'm only alive in your thoughts. You brought me here.

"Sir. Down here..." Williams called from Blow's bungalow basement.

Lit by fluorescents—some tubes flickering, one burnt out—the basement appeared neglected and forgotten, except for the laundry machines.

Williams stood near the stacked units. "See that electrical panel on the far wall?" MacNeice looked over at the grey metal cabinet. "That's the unit for the house...but there's also this one, maybe installed before the house was rewired. It's empty except for this plywood panel; you can see where its edges have scraped the sides of the metal box." Centred near the bottom of the panel was a small hole. Williams put his finger in it and pulled hard. It squawked but came free to reveal a short-barrelled shotgun resting diagonally in the cavity. "Fired recently. Hasn't been cleaned."

"Shells?"

Williams smiled. "You can always tell when someone's been fussing with acoustic ceiling panels. Fingerprints, for one..." He walked to the end of the basement and pointed to the floor. "Gypsum powder."

He removed the panel above and tilted it, sending a box skidding into his hand. "Twelve-gauge, six shells missing. Two in the chamber of that piece—that leaves three unaccounted for..."

"Well, well, well, back to the forest—" MacNeice's cellphone rang, interrupting him.

"Mac, get down to Riviera, quick as you can."

"What have you got, Swets?"

"Best you see for yourself."

"I'll be right there." MacNeice turned to Williams. "Get Forensics in. I'll take Aziz; you and Lise keep going here till they arrive. Great work."

He punched in another call and waited. "Bill, it's not exactly a lineup, but it's the next best thing. Can I borrow Jack in two hours?" Bill confirmed they'd make it, and MacNeice ended the call.

Aziz asked, "You're going to do what I think you are—?"

"Most likely." He lit up the blue dome light and swung

the Chevy out of the cul-de-sac, driving quickly along Main, heading to the north end. Once he'd turned east on Burlington Street, his cellphone rang again. "MacNeice."

"It's me, sir." Williams was using speakerphone. "Lise was out front a few minutes ago, I'll let her tell you..."

"That neighbour came out again. She remembers Stephen John saying that he heads an industrial waste company—that he moved to Dundurn from Vancouver some time ago."

"When will Forensics arrive?"

"They're tied up at Riviera; nearest they could give me is two hours."

"Good. Don't let them on site until we get back. We're bringing Jack..."

[72]

SEVERAL COPS STOOD AT THE ROADSIDE BLOCKING THE ENTRANCE, while Swetsky was under the Riviera sign, hands in pockets, beefy forearms bare to the elbows. He kept shifting his weight from one foot to the other, as if he was waiting for the referee's whistle to start a game.

MacNeice said under his breath, "John's got something big..."

Aziz quipped back, "Oh, I thought he needed to visit the loo."

As they approached, Swetsky spoke in a hurry. "Before we go in... there's a lot here. The office, the garage, an incinerator, the stripping tank. The smell and ventilation noise are something fierce; there are masks if you want 'em. The yard out back is where they store cars and trucks and the LRV vanity plate SUVs from their leasing business."

"The owner's here?"

"Ronald—Ronnie—Slater. He's in the office waiting for his lawyer; a uniform's with him. The five guys working on cars were interviewed and sent home."

"Has Forensics searched the office?"

"Not yet—it'll be the last they do. Let's head to the back-yard first."

Walking down the driveway, MacNeice craned his head to study the large chimney and its metal top hat. "Is that the exhaust for the incinerator or the stripping bath?"

"Both. The HVAC system is Ford-plant big, and this is a small operation." Swetsky led them past the black forensics van and into the yard. He pointed to a large metal plate in the ground and said, "That's where the used sodium hydrox-ide goes. It gets sucked out usually once a month. Supposed to be empty now."

"And then where does it go?" Aziz asked.

"Dunno. Ronnie's response was that it's not like nuclear waste—it's all legit."

"Comforting," Aziz said sardonically.

There was no need to ask where to go next. The two for-ensics teams in hazmat suits offered a clear destination: a grey Econoline van was getting stem-to-stern attention. Aziz knew what she was looking for and walked off to examine the panelling near the driver's door.

She closed her eyes and ran her hands over the external panelling several times. Each time, she shortened the path until, opening her eyes, she was certain she was looking at the crescent-shaped dent. Turning to a member of the for-ensics team, she asked if it was okay to mark something on the van with a Sharpie. When he confirmed that it was, she asked for one.

"What colour?"

"Black."

Moments later she returned the marker, pausing to look inside the van. "Have you found anything?"

"Oh yeah...they cleaned it pretty good, but we've got eight BBs in an evidence bag."

"BBs?"

"Sorry, that's slang for buckshot. Twelve-gauge; they're in that rolling lab. We've also got biological evidence." He drew her attention to the floor of the van. "Traces of blood got caught in this metal joint."

Aziz looked down at the joints. "So BBs are tiny metal marbles. Assuming the van was speeding, they'd roll about and get caught in these joints, or in the corners?" She noticed his eyes widen. "That's where you found them?"

"Yeah, two in the brace joint on your left, the rest in the same joint on the right. We're about to examine the chassis, wheel wells, and tires to see if there's soil from the forest or Power Line Road."

MacNeice approached Aziz. "What'd you find?"

"A match to our video: a crescent-moon dent on the driver's door. And blood and shotgun pellets inside...You?"

"Navigator's clean. We might get lucky if Clarence Blow's prints from the house match any inside the Lincoln. Oklahoma's sending prints for the other two so...we'll see." He seemed lost in thought.

"Mac, what's on your mind? We're almost overwhelmed with evidence here, and we haven't even stepped inside the building yet."

"No doubt, and it's all solid."

"Did you tell John about the shotgun in the cabinet?"

"Not yet." MacNeice was watching a small plastic bag as it skipped across the lot; it came to rest on the taillight of an old Cadillac. Turning to Aziz, he said, "I can't actually recall a case where evidence has mounted so quickly..."

"My thoughts exactly." She shrugged. "So?"

"It's a poverty of riches, Fiza. We're close to finding these three, and inching closer to figuring out who gave them orders..." The plastic bag was back on the move again, ricocheting off a wheel and fender to the end of the lot, where it slapped into the chain-link fence. "But what's Rodney Conway's connection to Dundurn?"

"You're convinced we're chasing the octopus's legs, not the head?"

"I am. And if we catch the leg, it'll just grow another one..." He shrugged. "If it's a smart octopus, these three men have no idea where the head is." MacNeice watched as the metal fence exhaled, releasing the deflated bag and letting it slide slowly to the ground.

Behind them, Riviera's metal door swung open with a bang. Vertesi emerged in a full-face respirator that made him look like a firefighter from the neck up, in contrast with his shirt, suit pants, and cross trainers. As he approached them he was saying something, but he sounded like Colonel Kurtz or Darth Vader. MacNeice motioned for him to take off the mask.

Vertesi tucked it under his arm. "It's not so bad inside now. Slater's still in the office, about to blow a gasket—that's an automotive term for your benefit, Fiz. Forensics are in that stripping tank and they're talking about a strange scum.

And they haven't even started with the incinerator." Vertesi scratched his head. "Something else, though, boss...I can smell fresh paint in that office, like they've been redecorating. But nothing's really spruced up...it's just the smell of paint. Can we get Ronnie out of there so we can check it out?"

"No problem. I'll move him downtown," Swetsky said, coming over from the forensics van. "Got a match—blood in the van is Evan Moore's."

ONCE SLATER HAD been taken away, MacNeice scanned the office before zeroing in on one wall. He turned on his cell's flashlight, rested his left cheek against the wall, and swung the beam slowly across the surface...searching. Switching it off, he ran a palm over the wall above the credenza as if reading a Braille message, pausing frequently.

Moments later, he swung about and smiled at Aziz and Vertesi. "There are patches...small ones, scattered roughly in a circle. Good catch, Michael. See if you can borrow someone from Forensics."

"Be right back," Vertesi said as he left.

Slipping on his gloves, MacNeice turned to Aziz. "Help me move this unit...nice and steady so we don't damage the toy cars."

After they'd slid the credenza away from the wall, MacNeice picked up a red Ferrari convertible. He was impressed with its weight. "Steel, and the tires are rubber, not plastic."

"I've never understood it—I mean, the actual Ferrari. Is it the romance of the open road or the promise of romance?" Aziz gave a gentle shrug.

"Both." MacNeice turned on his flashlight again and examined the model's working doors and the tiny replica of Enzo's legendary engine under the hood. With everything open, he rotated the car slowly, the way a jeweller would a diamond. "A microscope is going to light up with this one."

"You can see blood?"

"I see something that shouldn't be on a model inspected and approved by Enzo Ferrari; I'd expect it to be speck- and stain-free."

"These binders, Mac—finishes, parts, and so on. They're all brand new," said Aziz. "You'd think—well, I'd think that in an autobody shop, they'd be a bit greasy."

The door opened with a wheeze and Vertesi walked in, along with woman in a hazmat suit, carrying a polished aluminum case. She removed her respirator. "How can I help?"

"For starters," MacNeice said, "there's spot filler on this wall. We want to know if it was meant to cover a twelve-gauge shotgun blast. Secondly, those miniature cars may have biological material on them. Otherwise, I want this room swept."

Leaving the office, MacNeice asked, "Michael, what else can you tell us?"

"Well, there's a basement with a wine cellar. And here's the thing—the office is wired. There's a mic in the overhead light, another in the telephone's chassis." Vertesi continued, "I think I know why. Slater presents an estimate, then goes down to select a wine to share with his customers—but he's listening to their conversation. We found the equipment."

"To gain an advantage in his negotiations," Aziz said, shaking her head.

They left the office and headed over to the stripping bath. A member of the forensics team emerged from the tank and climbed down the ladder, holding something in one hand. Removing his respirator and goggles, he turned toward them.

"Should we also be wearing respirators?" Aziz asked.

"Not unless you're going inside." He nodded at the tank. "It has its own freakin' climate, and it's bad weather..."

"What've you found?" MacNeice was curious about his samples.

Lifting two plastic bags, the technician said, "Swabs from the wall above the caustic soda line and the underside of that roof."

Vertesi asked, "What do you think it is?"

The technician pointed at the tank's retractable cover. "When that thing closes and they turn it on, it's like boiling a chicken in a pot."

"A ring of fat collects...?" MacNeice speculated.

"That's the idea...we suspect whatever it is didn't come from an automobile."

Back outside, the forensics team leader gave them an update on the vehicles. So far, the Econoline van had produced traces of Dr. Moore's blood and that of an unidentified subject. They'd recovered eight twelve-gauge pellets and soil possibly linked to Power Line Road. The black LRV Lincoln had provided diverse fingerprints for analysis. "Now we'll dismantle the incinerator and investigate that underground storage tank."

"That last one sounds dangerous..." MacNeice said.

[73]

"**S**IT TALL, CLARENCE. LOOK AT ME LIKE WE'RE JUST TWO GUYS yakking. Don't turn away until I tell you.""

Clarence knew enough to do what he was told.

Instead of pulling into the crematorium's circular drive behind Tom's car, or taking the driveway through to the parking lot, Two continued past the entrance, frequently checking his rear and side mirrors. After two hundred yards he turned left into the industrial park, and then left again at the first intersection. In seconds his attention shifted to the trees dividing the crematorium parking lot from the street of brightly coloured corrugated buildings.

When he seemed convinced they weren't being followed, Two eased the Yaris onto the walking path. He glanced at Clarence. "Keep your elbows in..."

Pine needles and branches whisked both sides of the car as the accountant in Clarence considered the cost of a new paint job for the Yaris. From the ramp leading down to the crematorium's basement, One flashed the Escalade's high beams. Two swung the car wide and backed in off to one side of the ramp, positioned for a quick exit.

"Good thing you noticed that unmarked sedan..." One said as they walked together down to the basement door.

"Duty cop puttin' in time. But hey, I was surprised you got here first..."

One pushed the doorbell. "Only took a few seconds to tidy up."

"Please explain what happened back there?" Clarence asked wearily. "And why we're here?"

One pressed the button again. "We're about done, since there'll be no more contracts—"

Clarence suppressed a laugh. "Right—that was pretty clear when Two shoved a letter opener into my client's brain. You both got your money—but for the record, I didn't." Clarence was careful not to make it sound like more than a simple fact.

"The difference between us, Mr. Blow, is that you're the loss leader on this one." One turned to Clarence and added, "This is no time to be sly. Your bags are packed and you're in a hotel ready to leave town, just like we are."

A humiliating blush climbed up Clarence's neck. "That's true. But then again, why are we here?"

With a couple of mechanical clicks, the interior locks disengaged and the door swung open. Tom stared briefly at One, then glared at Clarence.

One reached out and laid a hand on Tom's shoulder.

Calmly and unthreateningly, he said, "We're here to get another briefing on that cremator, and maybe take a brochure and the manufacturer's card. Think this might be a good business opportunity for Two and me."

"Down the road a bit, in another time zone," Two added. "You're too good to compete with, Tommy." He looked up like he was imagining their future signage. "We wanna be one of a kind wherever we open shop."

Clarence took Two's bit of showmanship to suggest that they really were thinking about running a fancy crematorium, probably somewhere far away. But he assumed this visit was also about tidying things up.

[74]

JACK TOURED THE DIVISION, WHERE HE WAS GREETED WITH BACK rubs, haunch scratches, and dog cookies from Moose. Afterwards, Bill Moore accepted Sergeant Stanitz's invitation to walk over to the Dundurn Art Gallery's coffee bar and trade war stories, leaving Jack to do his work.

MacNeice and Aziz left for Southview Place with Jack sitting upright in the back seat, his head swivelling to take in both sides of the road, seemingly happy to listen to familiar voices. MacNeice was sharing what he'd learned about a dog's sense of smell. The more he spoke about it, the more animated he became. Frequently glancing Fiza's way, he noticed her wide smile — until, embarrassed, she cleared her throat and stopped smiling.

"I'm boring you . . ." he said.

"Absolutely not."

"Okay, then . . ." MacNeice continued. "In a packed stadium Jack would be able to detect Evan Moore's scent — from the other end of the field in the top row of seats — even though everyone in the stadium has their own scent." He checked the rear-view. Jack was watching him; he seemed intrigued, as if in agreement.

They drove the rest of the way in companionable silence, with Jack rubbernecking all the dogs they passed.

Bichet was sitting on the steps of Clarence Blow's house when MacNeice and Aziz arrived, having parked half a block away. Williams got out of his unmarked car to watch them approach. Within seconds, Jack began tugging at his leash. Williams crouched, ready for the face licking that would follow.

But Jack was no longer pulling the leash. His tail was between his legs; his ears were pinned back — he was wary.

Aziz's eyes widened. "He knows, Mac. He bloody well knows. He's frightened by the house . . ." She realized she was witnessing a theory come to life.

By the time the three of them reached Williams and Bichet, Jack was so distracted he might have been alone. The hackles on his back were raised, he was crouching low — more cat than dog.

"Open the door, Montile — and step aside." As MacNeice waited on the sidewalk, Jack drew the leash tight; straining forward to the point where he was coughing. Before they reached the door, he was practically crawling; the fur on his back stood straight from neck to tail.

On entering the house, a rumbling growl began in Jack's throat; it continued until they entered Clarence Blow's bedroom. Williams and Bichet had laid out some of Blow's clothing; the shotgun was resting on the floor at the foot of the bed.

For a second Jack fell silent, his nose twitching wildly. An instant later he was barking, snarling, and snapping. First he lunged for the bed and then he sniffed the end of the barrel, stomped on the weapon's stock before twisting wildly on the leash.

Having confirmed his theory, MacNeice struggled to remove Jack from the room, resisting the dog's attempts to stay and fight. Reaching the door, he was knocked off-balance and slammed Aziz into the door frame. "Go. Go, I'm fine," she assured him over the noise.

Jack snarled and strained against the leash. His legs were stiff and they got entangled in a scatter rug as MacNeice pulled him across the floor. Frothing at the mouth, Jack used all his strength to try to return to the bedroom. Even as the lead choked him, he wouldn't stop straining. Aziz ran to open the door ahead of them — then woman, man, and dog spilled furiously from the house.

Williams and Bichet were so startled that they both backed onto the lawn. The next-door neighbour stood at her window — no longer surreptitiously behind the curtain, her mouth agape, probably wondering what on earth a rabid dog had to do with poor Stephen John.

Still dragging Jack, MacNeice looked over his shoulder at Williams. "Seal it up for Forensics — we're done."

MacNeice considered picking up Jack and making a dash for the car, but then he considered the dog's weight and strength and thought it best to keep pulling him forward. As the collar dug into his throat, Jack continued coughing, but each time MacNeice relaxed the leash, Jack would turn and lunge back toward the house. So pulling it was.

Whatever MacNeice thought he might accomplish by taking Jack into that house, he could see only the raging animal before him. He knelt in front of Jack and began whispering over the dog's wheezing growl, consumed by guilt and shame for having exposed him to such trauma.

Time stopped—with MacNeice kneeling on the sidewalk and Aziz standing a respectful distance away—before Jack's fur settled into place and his heaving subsided. When it did, he sat down on his haunches and shook his head as if emerging from a nightmare. When he stood, he shook himself all over, and went to a tree to pee.

MacNeice and Aziz didn't talk on the way back to Division One. In the back seat, Jack's eyes were closed and his head rested on his outstretched legs.

[75]

AS THE CONVERSATION UNFOLDED BETWEEN TOM, ONE, AND TWO, Clarence thought he'd mistaken the look Cameron had given him at the door. Here he was, calmly leading a crematorium master class, and appeared contented to be doing so.

Clarence stood off to one side. He watched as Tom smiled, cajoled, instructed, corrected, and complimented both men as they took the equipment through its cycles. He imagined they were like old friends at a casino, happy to tap the buttons to make things happen — things like a full burn.

Clarence felt for his weapon; he was still filled with dread. He knew Two had two guns — much larger ones — and he could draw them fast, like a cowboy. And what One might have under his jacket, Clarence didn't want to know.

Once again he asked himself why he hadn't just gone

to the airport...why he'd gone to the client's office at all. Money was the answer—and now he was stuck with One and Two as they tidied up.

Clarence snapped to attention when he saw both men shake Tom's hand; the master class was over. "Are we done?"

One and Two swung around as if he'd interrupted them; One raised his eyebrows and Two shook his head in dismay. Clarence tried to repair the damage. "I just meant if we're done, I'd like to get back to the city."

"We know what you meant, Clarence," One said, turning back to Cameron. "You'll have to excuse your cousin, Tom."

"I was simply saying that—"

"We know; we all know," One said without taking his eyes off Tom Cameron. "You mentioned you have some brochures in your office, Tom—why don't I come and get those, and then we'll be on our way."

[76]

MACNEICE AND AZIZ BROUGHT BILL MOORE IN TO RECOUNT HOW Jack had effectively confirmed Blow's guilt. Bill and Jack left the division shortly after, and MacNeice was relieved to see the dog's tail held high as they waved them off.

They were going up the back stairs when Maracle met them coming down. "Call came in, sir. There's been a killing in an office — sounds professional."

"Got a name?"

"Jeremy Slater, a wealthy businessman. Wife came to meet him at his office and found him with a letter opener in his ear and two holes in his forehead."

"Slater . . . You're certain?" Aziz asked.

"Yep. Same name as the guy who's sitting in the interview room. Some coincidence, huh?"

"Okay . . . anything else?"

"Soon as Swets got off that call, the patrolman doing surveillance out by Thomas Cameron's crematorium called. Two passenger vehicles went by and turned into the industrial subdivision. It might not be anything, but since Williams and Bichet were on their way back from the west end, John told them to check it out but not engage — they're on their way there."

"Why did the cop consider the vehicles suspicious?" Aziz asked.

"All he'd seen going in there were pickup trucks, commercial vans, Harleys, and tractor-trailers. Then along comes an Escalade and, five minutes later, a Toyota."

"Occupants?"

"Tinted windows on the Caddy, but there were two males in the Toyota."

"Who's left upstairs?"

"Swetsky is coming down; he's letting Dr. Richardson know. Vertesi's hanging back for you."

"Good call. Is Slater's lawyer up there?"

"Yes, sir. Both of them are steaming."

MacNeice smiled. "If it's the same crew, I don't expect you'll find much in the way of prints or casings, and if you do — it's probably a mug's game. They know we know who they are — Jeremy Slater may have ordered the killings, so look for a paper trail, a computer, phone history, a hidden safe somewhere, or large amounts of cash . . ."

Seconds later, Swetsky thundered into the stairwell. "Mac, can I take Aziz? I think Slater's wife would appreciate speaking to her . . ."

[77]

A CREMATION BUSINESS WOULD LET TWO FINALLY REALIZE THE dream of an honest living. Hell, the last time he'd made one was early in his circuit days, before taking a fall for money became an option. That proved to be a short-term strategy, one he never should have signed on his body for. Now the idea of getting ready for work, walking out with a sandwich and a kiss, of being home at six to sit on the porch with Dolores... Well, hell, who wouldn't prefer that to what he was doing now?

Dolores knew little about what he'd done to end up in prison—and even less about what he'd been doing since. He thought that might be why she hung back whenever he brought up their future together.

It's true that, during a beer-fuelled interlude with One on

Burlington Beach, they had both agreed a crematorium business would make a perfect cover for their contract work, but in the last couple of days, going legit had become the what-if scenario that dominated their thoughts and conversations.

One had hit on it first—he decided he could be the pastor and Two the technician, and together they could run a straight-up compassionate end-of-life service. The idea rang honest and real—even though they hadn't always been able to live up to it, their intention had been to execute with compassion—their no-torture rule.

One and Tom were upstairs, covering off the last few details, while Two ran through the notes he'd taken from Tom's practice drills; he studied the sleek black computer screen to confirm he'd gotten them right. If they went legit, he didn't want to be the one to screw it up. Two was determined to succeed; he wanted that for both of them.

When their fake passports hadn't been challenged at the border, he'd been filled with a sense of freedom. And just a day earlier, with the lazy blue lake lapping at their feet, he'd told One, "An honest living's the ultimate way to disappear." Looking down at his notes now, he felt happier than ever...excluding the times he'd woken up next to Dolores on a sunny morning. Two tucked his notebook into his jacket pocket, switched off the monitor, and turned back to Clarence. He'd forgotten about Clarence.

"I don't want to hurt you, Two, but I will." Clarence was pale and shaking, holding the little pistol with both hands. "You're going to kill me, I know it."

Two reached out to take the weapon, but Clarence stepped back sharply. "I've killed before, Two. I won't hesitate—I just want to leave."

"Man, put that thing down before one of us gets hurt. You wanna go to Polynesia—we both know that—and we've got no quarrel with you."

"No—I saw what you did to my client." Fear overtook Clarence as he realized One could appear behind him any second.

"No one said we'd do anything to you. We gave you your freedom by killing your client—free of charge. Now, for the last time, Clarence, put that away." Two's jaw tightened and he took a step closer.

Clarence backed away. "Don't move, Two. I don't want to do this—give me your keys. I'll go. I promise you'll never see me again. I'll never tell a soul about what you've—what *we've*—done." Blow immediately regretted his gaffe.

"'What you've done'—meaning what One and I have done?" Two took another step and reached again for Clarence's weapon. "It's weird how folks say shit when they're scared—call 'em on it and they'll say, 'Oh no, that's not what I meant.' . . . But it is, Clarence, that's exactly what you meant." He shook his head in disappointment, "Okay, last chance—give me the gun."

"The car keys—you have my word. I'll disappear forever."

Two glanced abruptly at the door. Clarence took the bait and glanced over his shoulder—Two lunged for the gun.

Startled, Clarence fired.

Two was smiling, shaking his head, and studying the hole in his jacket, which was smoking. "Now look what you've done . . ." Once again he looked at the door, and again Clarence fell for it. Two swung hard, knocked the pistol out of Clarence's hands, and sent it skidding across the floor.

TOM HAD JUST passed One the business card for the manu-facturer when they heard the shot. The reverberation echoed up the elevator shaft and hung like an echo in the air.

Tom was shaken. "What's going on?"

One rolled up the brochure and shoved it and the card in his pocket. "Get in your car and drive away calm and easy, like you're off to a meeting. You won't get hurt—but you gotta go now. God bless." One pushed him out of the office the way a father might a son reluctant to go outside and play.

From the sound, One knew the shot hadn't been fired by Two. Inside the elevator, he closed his eyes and prayed to a merciful God, after which he drew his .38 Special and waited for the elevator to land.

When the doors slid open, he checked to see that no one was there, then walked swiftly to the cremation room door. With his weapon at his side, he called out, "Two. Lemme hear you, brother..."

The sound of a cough. "I'm hit. Blow's down."

Of all the things One might have expected when open-ing the door, what he saw stopped him cold. Clarence Blow's body was draped over Two's shoulder and he was shoving the man feet first into the cremation chamber. A dark stain was spreading across the back of Two's new blue suit.

As One drew closer, he saw a small pool of blood on the floor. "What happened, brother?"

"Oh... Well, I'm fucked—sorry for my language. Blow was convinced we were going to do him in like his client. He pulled that peashooter over there and shot me when I tried to take it away; after that, I knocked him sideways."

"Chest shot?"

"Yeah—lower right ribs—probably nicked my lung—went clean through after that. I'm okay for now..."

"No doubt. You need some help with that?"

"No, I got this..." He was feeding Blow through the opening, bandy little legs and all. "Okay, maybe help me here..." Blow's lower torso and legs were crumpled inside the chamber, but his upper body and arms hung outside.

"I'm clear what your intention is—you sure you wanna go through with this?"

"I think so. Get him in there and I'll see...Maybe the warden'll call with a last-minute...what's that word?"

"Reprieve."

"Yeah, that..." Two leaned against the wall as One hoisted and shoved the rest of Clarence Blow's body into the chamber. He closed the door and Two triggered the lock.

"You remember what to do next?"

Two managed a brief, wan smile. "I think so...though his shot messed up my notebook. When we open our crematorium, guess I'll hafta use your notes."

"Okay, let's get to it. Soon as we're done here, we're on our way."

Based on the early going, Two was already a professional. He judged Clarence's body weight at about a hundred and thirty pounds to set the duration of the burn. One couldn't see which buttons Two tapped next—but when the pilot light jets came to life, so did Clarence Blow.

Clarence woke up screaming and pounded on the window. The pilots quickly ignited his clothes, distracting him as he attempted to beat them out. Both men stood watching, jaws dropped—they'd never seen anyone burn alive before. One waited for Two to stop the process.

Clarence's eyes were wide with terror as he thrashed about, but in less than twelve seconds a 2,100-degree inferno would consume everything, including his fear.

"Is the warden calling?" One asked, as the flames caught hold of the flesh on Blow's arm.

"Warden's gone fishin'. Take me home, Lester."

[78]

WHEN THE DETECTIVES ENTERED THE ROOM, RONALD SLATER feigned a sudden interest in the blank wall to his right. To get his attention, Vertesi slapped the already bloated folder on the table and pushed the button to start recording.

To get ahead of the latest proceedings, Slater's lawyer, Erin McNulty, huffed, "Now, explain why we're still here, and why you've already taken several hours of our time."

"We won't be doing that, Mr. McNulty," MacNeice said, turning to his client. "Ronald Slater, I have the unenviable task of informing you that, a short while ago, your brother Jeremy was found dead in his office."

Slater's face twitched. He shook his head several times before inexplicably flashing a grin. He looked at McNulty, who seemed stunned by the news. Left to fend for himself, Slater said, "I don't understand—what are you saying?"

"That in light of this news, you might need a compassion break."

McNulty came to life as if he'd been given a get-out-of-jail-free card. "Detective MacNeice, I request that my client be allowed to leave and grieve the death of his brother in a dignified way." Slater didn't seem to be listening; he'd returned to shaking his head.

"Unfortunately, we're about to charge your client for his role in the murder of three men, and the assault of a fourth. And, as our investigation is ongoing, more charges will likely follow."

McNulty sputtered for a few seconds about the law and fair practice, then cleared his throat. "Given that you haven't charged him with anything yet, is my client free to return to his family, to properly mourn the death—"

"Were you also Jeremy Slater's counsel?"

"I am...I was. Is my client free to leave?"

"No. As forensic evidence continues to arrive from Riviera Automobile Restoration and its subsidiary, Luxury Rental Vehicles, it's unlikely that your client will be going anywhere for a very long time."

Slater seemed incapable of grasping what was happening. In the absence of specific directions from his client, McNulty scrambled to pick one. "Detective MacNeice, you mentioned compassion; you must understand the trauma of this moment. If we put up a bond so Ronald can assist with the funeral arrangements—" McNulty stopped short. "Was it his heart, or a stroke?"

"Shot twice in the head, and something sharp driven

into his ear, though in which order each happened, we don't know yet."

"Christ almighty!" Ronnie Slater woke up. "Who did that?"

"Before I answer, Mr. Slater, can you describe your relationship with your brother?"

"Show some decency, Detective; how could you be so callous?" McNulty was building up to outrage.

MacNeice pulled two documents from the hefty folder in front of him. "This arrived a few minutes before we did." He pointed to a series of blood test results. "The blood found in the LRV Econoline van currently at Riviera is a match for a known victim, and there's also blood present from a John Doe." MacNeice pulled another report. "And these findings come from scum collected from Mr. Slater's stripping bath, also located at Riviera. Forensics has determined the samples are human and traceable to four people. Among them are the two that were transported in the Econoline van."

"Hey, I don't know anything about that." Slater's composure was disintegrating.

"There's more. Your office was recently painted, yes?"

"Yeah, so . . .?"

"Why was it painted?"

"That's obvious. We want it to look sharp."

"You're doing yourself no good. You see" — MacNeice removed a final document — "that room was painted because the wall took a shotgun blast, which we discovered when they removed twelve-gauge pellets from the drywall." Both men looked mystified at the rapidly mounting evidence. "And," MacNeice continued, pointing to the lower half of the document, "those replica toy cars — cleaned to remove any biological evidence — were in fact still rich with it."

He directed their attention to the last item listed on the report. "There's a scorch mark, barely visible to the naked eye, on the lacquered surface of your office table."

"Scorch mark?"

"Yes; the shotgun was fired just above the table."

"This is bullshit. What's going on here?" Slater was trying to enlist support from his lawyer, with little success. "Don't just sit there, Erin, do something."

"Before you do anything," MacNeice said, "there's one more thing. Later today, it's likely we'll learn what's at the bottom of your caustic soda reservoir and what was burned in your incinerator."

"Detectives, can I have five minutes alone with my client?"

"By all means." MacNeice slid the forensic evidence back into the folder. "Detective Vertesi, read Ronald Slater his rights, then time and stop the recording."

"Wait—you said we could pause this interview. Was that not for the grieving process?"

"It was. But, as must be obvious by now, your client will soon be under arrest. Considering that, you'd do well to encourage him to speak freely while he has a chance. Before I go, I do have one question for you, Ronald." MacNeice waited for him to look up. "Do you know Clarence Blow?"

However tough a negotiator Slater was in the antique car restoration business, the slight tightening around his eyes was all the confirmation MacNeice needed. He nodded and turned to Vertesi. "He's all yours, Michael..."

MacNeice had his hand on the door when Slater answered. "Blow's an accountant; he does the books for me and my brother..."

"An accountant—nothing more?"

Slater shrugged but didn't say anything further. Closing the door, MacNeice felt certain Slater was trying to buy time—but with the death of his brother and the evidence flowing in from Riviera, the window to save himself was closing fast.

Back at his desk, MacNeice sent a text to Swetsky and Aziz: "Give me an update."

He started sketching dotted lines in his mind, trying to find connections that made sense. Swivelling around to scan the whiteboard's photos, notes, names, diagrams, and places, his eyes fixed on the sketch of Clarence Blow, accountant to the Slaters—one of whom was dead, the other soon to be in a cell. Blow, and two American fugitives. Blow, formerly in possession of a short-barrel twelve-gauge. Blow, with access to Riviera and its stripping bath and incinerator. Blow, with access to LRV's fleet.

His cellphone rang, "What have you got?"

"Phew." It was Aziz. "Well...a dead fifty-nine-year-old male."

"Was he executed?"

"Oh yes...Mary Richardson extracted what looked like a fancy dagger from his ear—turned out to be a letter opener. It took out the right and left hemispheres—stopped shy of the opposite wall of his skull; the force, she assured me, took speed and considerable strength. And, for the coup de grace, two rounds to the forehead."

"Found by his wife?"

"Yes. Donna Slater, forty-three. She's a mess—a uniform just took her home. Claims she doesn't know anything about Jeremy Slater's business, other than that he's a very successful investment advisor. She's never heard of Clarence Blow and said her husband's relationship with his brother was amicable, but they travel in such different circles that they seldom see each other. She never discussed Jeremy's work with him because she finds finance boring. I believe she's telling the truth. She's an interior designer — she did her husband's office."

"Paper trail, computer, cellphones?"

"Forensics is sending a geek squad. It's odd — there don't appear to be any surveillance cameras. Slater's office is listed as the penthouse and it's inaccessible from the elevator without a code."

Ryan swung around, his telephone receiver in hand, and gestured for MacNeice to pick up. MacNeice told Aziz he'd call her back. Picking up his desk phone, he asked, "Who is it?"

"Constable Alvin Jeffers, officer on duty outside Professor Garrick's room."

"What you have got for me, Jeffers?"

"Sir, they brought Garrick out of his coma. He's very weak but insists on talking — doctor says we can have ten minutes but it's gotta happen soon."

[79]

WILLIAMS BROUGHT THE CHEVY ALONGSIDE A GREY UNMARKED car and lowered the window. "Any changes?"

"No traffic going into the crematorium lot, but ten minutes ago Cameron got into his car and drove off. I followed him. Nothing suspicious; he went home to Waterdown. He sat out on the porch with someone I assume is his daughter. He seemed relaxed, so I came back here."

"Otherwise, no signs of activity?"

"No, sir. I called in about two vehicles that went into the industrial park a couple of hundred metres ahead, but I haven't seen anything else. My turnaround time was probably twenty-five minutes, and I haven't checked the lot since I got back."

"No need. Get back to Waterdown in case he has a

meeting with our suspects out there. Give Cameron's address and plate number to the dispatcher. We'll circle the crematorium and then stand watch here."

Williams waited for the cop drive off before turning to Bichet. "This is probably nothing. But if it isn't, I want to be clear—no heroics, no boxing shit. We cool, Sergeant?"

"You're funny, sir. Yeah, we cool—you got me pegged as a firecracker, huh?"

"Oh yeah...I've even got your nickname—Short Fuse. It's a double entendre." Williams stopped the car at the entrance to the driveway, "Thing is, Lise, these guys don't do hand-to-hand combat."

"Understood." Bichet slid the sunglasses down her nose and looked off toward the treeline. "You really think something's going on here?"

Williams lowered his voice and delivery to that of a B-movie pitchman "There are four sides to every one-storey building, Sergeant. We've seen but two..." He eased the vehicle farther down the lane, gaining a better view of the parking lot with every foot advanced. It appeared to be empty. Closer to the rear of building, he inched the car forward.

"Want me to get out?" Bichet asked, gripping the door handle.

"Stay in the car."

She leaned so far forward that her head was over the dash. "Nothin' yet...Go a bit further, there's someth—"

The first shot struck the driver-side window—spraying cubes of glass over Williams and slicing across Bichet's back. She screamed, collided with the passenger door, and rebounded heavily against the console. Two more rounds hit the corner of the windshield—the first entered Bichet's headrest and exited through the roof. The second smashed through Williams's right wrist and grazed Bichet's neck. "Fuck. Fuck. Fuck."

"Fast, Lise—put it in reverse!"

She pushed herself off the console, using her momentum to work the gearshift—but instead of hitting Reverse, she hit Park and the Chevy jolted to a stop. Williams's right hand dangled from his shattered wrist, spraying blood across the dashboard and console.

Bichet's neck bled onto her collarbone as she slumped into her seat. Growling with rage and pain, she was trying to draw her weapon when she noticed something moving above her aviators. She raised her head for a clearer view, then froze. "Sir—check this shit."

Oklahoma State Penitentiary's "Five and Dime"—Taylor Daintry and Lester Wright—were standing fifteen feet away, squared off in front of them. Wright was supporting a pale and bloodied Daintry, who, once he had their attention, pushed free of Wright's grasp and assumed a gunslinger's stance, smiling at the gawking detectives.

Lester Wright's left hand hung casually by his side, his index finger on the trigger of a grey pistol. He seemed supremely nonchalant about the situation—like he was watching the lazy arc of a lawn sprinkler.

Daintry inhaled, coughed and spat blood, then tore off his jacket to reveal two shoulder holsters. He paused as if to let that visual sink in, then passed his jacket to Wright. With bloodstained hands and an exaggerated flourish, Daintry threw his arms out like he was preparing for his crucifixion. Then, in a blur, his arms folded and unfolded to reveal two chrome .38s pointing in their direction.

Some moments fly by; others take their goddamn time. It can be the same with thoughts. Williams thought of reaching for his weapon, but with his broken hand he couldn't, even as he kept thinking he should try. And then his thought ended with the click of a seatbelt—Bichet was going for hers.

Daintry was no longer smiling; the weight of the .38s seemed to be taking a toll on his outstretched arms. Still, he kept them trained on the detectives—and didn't notice Bichet had drawn her weapon.

But Wright noticed. He had fired the first shots and now had his handgun trained on her. Pursing his lips, he nodded a slow *no*.

Bichet understood. She let the firearm drop to the floor and raised her empty hands.

Seconds passed; the puddle of blood at Daintry's feet grew larger. Shaking from fatigue, he twirled the pistols and slid them cross-armed back into their holsters.

Wright draped the jacket over Daintry's shoulders. Taking hold of the wounded man's waist, he turned to leave. As a warning, he pointed his weapon at each of them before disappearing behind the crematorium.

Williams and Bichet looked at each other. She was bleeding onto the seat, blood smeared across her face and neck. Williams cradled his arm against the steering wheel and whispered, "What the fuck was that?"

Suddenly a white Escalade appeared before them and tore across the lot, then ploughed along a narrow footpath, whipping pines and snapping branches until it reached the other side and swung left, kicking up dust and disappearing from sight.

"Call it in, Lise . . ." Williams climbed out, showering the ground with small glass cubes.

"Officers down, officers down. Perps took off in white Escalade." She gave the plate number and their location, then dropped the handset.

Williams removed his belt and wrapped it tightly around his forearm before staggering to the trunk for the vehicle's standard-issue first-aid kit.

Making his way to the passenger door, he noticed a piece of folded white paper where Wright had been standing. He opened the kit. Inside were Band-Aids, a disinfectant cream, Q-Tips, a packet of aspirins, four tongue depressors, and two large gauze pads. "Pathetic."

Bichet got out of the car, removed her jacket and shirt, and leaned over the hood.

"Trapezius is torn, Lise. Blood's flowing freely from there and your upper back."

"Muscles severed?" she asked.

Williams used her shirt to clear the blood. "Neck—no. Back, I can't tell." He put a gauze pad on the wound, but it quickly soaked through, so he laid the remaining one on top. "I don't know what the muscles are above your bra. The ones running vertically next to your spine look like they've been slashed by a sword."

"Lattissimus dorsi . . ." she moaned. "Ribs and spine okay?"

The gauze pads were too bloodied to tell, so he rubbed her shirt over the gash.

"Fucking hell, sir."

"Sorry . . . Probably missed your spine, but not the ribs."

"Okay. You done back there, Monty?"

Funny, he hadn't heard that nickname since his grandfather died. "I'm done." He packed the soggy gauze into the wound and covered it with her shirt before pressing the shirtsleeve to her neck.

Seconds later, he was shivering and faint. He leaned against the car, pulled his own shirt free, and wrapped it around his wounded wrist. It was hot outside, but he was freezing. "Lise . . . you cold?"

"Shock, sir . . . Yeah, I'm cold — but the hood's warm. Keep that hand up high . . . They'll be here soon."

"Yeah, thanks, Sergeant . . . Sergeant?"

"Yes, sir?"

"I don't mind saying I was shit-scared."

"Me too. So weird they didn't finish it . . . especially with Daintry and that *Fistful of Dollars* routine."

"Lise . . . didya know I was a stand-up comedian?"

"No way. Go on, say something funny."

"I was a stand-up comedian."

Bichet erupted in a locker-room roar that was shortly overtaken by swearing.

Williams thought about screaming, but if anything, he was afraid he'd cry. He spotted a trio of small, fluffy clouds — it might have been their whiteness that made him recall the piece of paper. "Lise, look where Wright was standing. Do you see a folded piece of paper?"

Seconds passed. "No, sir . . . nothing."

Still shivering, Williams pushed himself off the car, and was hit by a wave of pain that made him nauseous. He almost swooned and took several deep breaths — then, like a Saturday-night drunk, he staggered forward.

"Monty . . . where you headed?"

"White piece of paper . . . It wasn't there . . . then it was . . . then it wasn't. I gotta find it."

Rounding the corner, he noted a silver Toyota parked on the far side of a ramp. As he drew closer, he spotted the paper three feet down the ramp, flapping lazily against the retaining wall. He watched as it skidded down another foot. It would only take a few steps to reach it, but the angle was steep, and he couldn't use his shot-up arm to support himself on the wall. So he did the only thing that came to mind—he turned around to use his left hand.

But now the down ramp was directly behind him. If there'd ever been a successful relationship between prudence and pain, it wasn't now. But it was only three or four feet, and if Williams waited, he knew there was a chance the paper would blow even farther away.

That first step was a shock. It felt like his heel would never touch concrete, and when it did, he took a moment to adjust to leaning forward to go backwards down the slope. When he'd taken two more steps, he paused; his wrist was throbbing with pain and still bleeding badly. His breathing was so forced that he thought he'd pass out, so to calm himself, he studied the trees in the distance—but the swaying of their branches only made him more nauseous.

He turned his head to see how close the paper was—which was an unrecoverable mistake. Disoriented, he grabbed frantically at the retaining wall. Free-falling backwards, it was futile to claw at a smooth surface. Before his head hit concrete, Williams saw his bloodied hand fly wildly above him like the broken wing of a great wounded bird.

[80]

MACNEICE'S GOAL WITH GARRICK CAME INTO FOCUS BEFORE HE'D reached his car. There was only one question to ask— and it wouldn't take ten minutes. It was the same question he'd have asked Rodney Conroy.

As he turned on to Main, a call came over the radio: "Officers down; officers down . . ." Though her voice was laboured, he recognized Bichet. The hair on his neck stood up; he hit the grille and tail emergency lights and called the dispatcher on the radiophone. "Get me DI Aziz; she's on her cell."

"Wilco; over."

Slalom racing through the traffic, MacNeice's thoughts returned to Bichet's voice. It had been strong—even pugnacious—but severely stressed.

The radiophone came to life; it was Aziz. "You're off to interview Garrick?"

"Williams and Bichet are wounded out at the crematorium—the call just came in—I'm on my way there now." .

"Oh god...Mac, we're about to turn this scene over to Forensics. Dr. Richardson left a while ago. Where do you want me?"

"Garrick wants to talk; you should interview him. His wife is there. You won't have much time—but you don't need much."

"What do you mean?"

"There's only one question to ask him—he didn't see his abductors, but we know who they are. Garrick must know *why* he was abducted, so the question is—who is he indebted to?"

"Understood. Anything else?"

"Montile and Lise will probably go to Dundurn General. John and Charlie should meet them there."

"One last thing—I'll be brief," Aziz said.

MacNeice swung onto the ramp to the 403 and accelerated. "What is it?"

"We had a breakthrough. John thought to wonder where Jeremy Slater's office toilet was. He found it—and a separate room behind a panel, triggered by a button under his desk. Inside was a wall of locked cabinets and a formidable-looking safe. Forensics will drill through the cabinet locks and think they can open the safe. If not, they'll blow it." She ended the call.

"We're in the octopus's garden..." MacNeice said softly.

"WHEN SOMETHING HAPPENS, something you didn't cause—but could have stopped—"

Are you responsible?

"Without doubt—I am."

Are you expecting me to disagree?

"I had a twinge, Kate—just for a moment. I should have acted on it but didn't."

That they shouldn't have gone out alone, even though Montile's not the cavalier sort...

"I miss you, Kate, more than words—"

You miss the idea of me, the touch and feel... my love. The last is ours eternal. As for the rest, you have that in front of you...

His cellphone rang. "Vertesi?"

"Slater had nothing to say. His lawyer's pissed off—I'm pretty sure they didn't spend their five minutes grieving. I handed them our division cards and told Moose to put Ronnie in the drunk tank with a bottle of water and a stale salmon sandwich."

"You think he'll come around to escape the cuisine?"

"Yeah, well, I would. Talking's his only choice..."

[81]

MACNEICE EASED THE CAR INTO THE CREMATORIUM'S LANEWAY and hit the brakes. Ahead, with its front doors and trunk open, Williams's Chevy provided visceral testimony against a backdrop of emergency response vehicles.

He went to survey the scene. Blood was smeared on — and in — the trunk; it streaked the passenger window and door, and much more was splashed on the dash, console, and driver and passenger's seats. It was painted along the Chevy's sides, and on the hood, a bloodied med kit and gauze pads lay next to Bichet's jacket. Her shirt was rolled up nearby, like a red-and-white tie-dye or a discarded mop.

Free of blood were the two half-inch holes in the windshield. Ahead of the Chevy he could see dark rust-red shoeprints that had been tracked in and out of a pool of blood.

Further into the parking lot, a firefighter was packing gear into the truck, and to his left an ambulance sat idling, its back doors open, no paramedics in sight.

MacNeice walked behind the building. A couple of cops immediately turned his way, and an OPP officer approached with his head down.

"DS MacNeice, Staff Sergeant Turek." He could see the concern on MacNeice's face. "DI Williams took a shot to the wrist—it's bad. He also toppled backward down this ramp. Paramedics suspect he's got a serious concussion, or possibly brain damage from internal bleeding. He was unconscious when we arrived and still out when he left—a medevac chopper took him to the brain centre in Toronto."

"And Sergeant Bichet?"

"Shot up a bit more—but she's lucky. First round tore across her back and hit some ribs. Paras think her spine and organs are clear. The second one hit her trapezius near the neck and went clean through." Turek pinched his left trapezius muscle. "She confirmed it was Daintry and Wright, and that Wright did the shooting. Daintry's wounded; there's a spent casing from a small-calibre pistol in the crematorium. Before Bichet left for Dundurn General, she kept asking why the pair hadn't finished them off."

"Anything else?"

"Yes, sir. Bichet said Williams went looking for a piece of white paper; she thought he was delirious. But when the first responders got down that ramp, they found it pinned under his shoulder."

"Don't keep me in suspense, Sergeant."

He handed MacNeice an evidence bag; the note inside was open: *Blow's in the cremator.*

"Where's Blow now?"

"Still down there. Paras are in communication with DGH's burn unit. Thomas Cameron, the owner, is down there too. He was brought in by the uniform sent to watch his house. Cameron said the computer was set for a test, not a full burn—has no clue whether that was intentional. We're just about to arrest him.'"

"Hold off on that...Any leads on the Escalade?"

Turek pointed diagonally across the lot. "Abandoned outside an empty building. From the state of the passenger's seat, it looks like Daintry was bleeding out...Shall I take you below, sir?"

"Not necessary. I've been here before." MacNeice stepped onto the ramp and felt sickened to see that Williams's blood had streamed its way down to the drain grate, and that several of his rusty-red handprints could be seen on the retaining wall—like those found in prehistoric caves.

MacNeice passed carefully through the steel door— can-opened by a chainsaw—and followed the sound of voices until he was in the room. Confronted by the smell of burnt flesh, he instinctively shortened his breath. Blood pooled around the cremator—its sleek door axed and lying on the floor.

He couldn't see the stretcher for those standing in front of it, but he recognized Thomas Cameron as one of the onlookers. His arms were wrapped tightly across his chest and he was weeping. MacNeice wondered why he wasn't cuffed until he noticed the thick-necked cop standing behind him.

Someone must have noticed MacNeice enter, because the attending cops and firefighters slowly parted, exposing something awful on the gurney. The words that came to his mind were *roast pig*. MacNeice gulped, risked a deeper breath, and moved closer. One of the two paramedics was on his cell, speaking in a monotone: "Understood. Right now. No intubation? Got it. Affirmative—morphine and oxygen." Ending the call, he tucked his phone into a thigh pocket.

MacNeice couldn't look away; it was like viewing an exotic creature before it disappeared forever. "He's not dead?" he asked, incredulous.

The older of the two paras answered. "Not quite. Ninety percent second-degree burns and the skin's sloughing off his back—we're leaving *now*."

As they rolled by, MacNeice held his breath and glanced down. Blow was naked but for a few blackened patches of clothing, the remains of a leather belt, and a holster. What was left of his shoes clung haphazardly to his scorched feet. Across his chest and stomach, hot pink lava-like rivulets had broken through the scorched flesh. Oxygen tubes perched in his nostrils. His forearms were frozen and folded in a defensive position above his body, fists clenched. And yet, Blow's face appeared, by contrast, untouched, merely flushed from embarrassment or a bad sunburn.

The paramedic explained, "When that oven lit up, buddy's instinct was to use his forearms to cover his face … that's the other ten percent."

They finished covering him with a silver foil blanket and hurried the gurney through the door; firefighters helped them minimize the body's movement on the ramp. The thick-necked cop took Cameron by the arm.

MacNeice stepped in. "I'll bring him up, officer; we won't be long."

The officer nodded toward the ramp. "I'll be right outside."

The room felt worse than empty. Just as you can't unsee something horrific, you also can't unsmell it. MacNeice took a deep breath and regretted it—the stench of burnt flesh filled his nostrils.

Cameron was staring at his shattered Scandinavian oven, his cheeks still wet with tears. MacNeice handed him a tissue from a packet, and for a moment Tom looked surprised to find it in his hand.

"Thomas, you're being taken into custody. You'll be charged—though the scope of the charges will take us some time to determine. But before the justice system kicks in, we should talk."

[82]

THE ROOM'S LIGHTING WAS SO LOW THAT THE MONITORS FOR Garrick's vitals offered most of the illumination. Once her eyes had adjusted, Aziz saw Elaine Garrick slumped in a chair, legs tucked up—asleep.

Arnie Garrick had three drips going, and an oxygen mask covered his face. Out of sight, the compressor's breathing intersected dreamily with the monitor's constant *do-re-mi* beeps. The blue bedding was neat but gave no hint that the person it covered was alive.

Aziz sneezed just as the door behind her swung open. "Bless you, dear," the nurse said.

"Sorry. I'm Detective Aziz," Aziz said. She read the nurse's nametag—Dora Aploon, RN.

"No worries, miss, I knew you were here." Tray in hand,

she proceeded to the bed. "Professor Garrick, wake up—you have a visitor." Her voice, a fill-a-hall contralto with a Cape Town lilt, sounded calm and motherly. "Professor, I'm here for some blood..." She switched on the bed's overhead lamp, mercifully directing its light up to the ceiling.

Elaine opened her eyes. Her face was expressionless, as if seeing Aziz from the safety of a dream.

"I'm glad you're here, Elaine..."

"Where else would I be?" She let her legs fall to the floor and slipped on her shoes. "I'm sorry, that was curt."

"You've every right—"

"No...I don't. I'm grateful to you and your colleagues—you didn't give up on Arnie."

"You must be exhausted, and I can't imagine how your husband's feeling, so I'll be as brief as possible."

"To be clear—this is Arnie's idea."

Nurse Aploon nodded. "I'll be back shortly...Mind now, you have ten minutes." She smiled as she exited the room.

Aziz turned to Arnie Garrick and was met with a blank stare, though his eyes sharpened as she introduced herself. "I'm here to take your statement, Professor. I've been told I have ten minutes, so, if you're ready..."

Garrick turned to his wife. She pulled a chair over to the bedside. "He knows about you and MacNeice. His voice is just a whisper, so you'll have to be close." Elaine leaned over and removed his oxygen mask.

Aziz sat down. Seeing Garrick up close was shocking. He was more grey than pink; his cheeks were hollow. His right eye was bloodshot. The orbital bones of both eyes were dark and theatrically defined. The rat bites on his neck had been stitched and covered with an antiseptic stain. His lips were so badly chapped it looked like he'd been lost in the Sahara.

Aziz opened her notebook. "Whenever you're ready, Professor."

He looked past Aziz to his wife. "Sorry, he needs water..." They juggled positions and Elaine put a straw in his mouth. Aziz noticed how focused Arnie was on Elaine, watching her as if she might evaporate any second. When he nodded, she removed the straw and stepped back.

"I'm a gambling addict..." In spite of the water, his voice was little more than a dry hiss. "Since university...I've never told anyone." A couple of tears leaked from his eyes. "Not even Elaine...I was too ashamed."

"And yet someone knew all about it..." Aziz said.

He nodded. "I used a separate account...When that ran out...I used funds from my Brant program." After pausing to regain strength he continued. "When that ran out...I borrowed from the man who took my bets. He's who you're looking for."

"He ordered your kidnapping?"

He nodded again. "Nobody else knew..."

"His name—and where we might find him?"

"Abbey Laundry and Dry Cleaning."

"I'm sorry?"

"It's a front...from here to Montreal. His name is Gregor Abatstvo...from Crimea."

"Again, the last name?" Aziz leaned closer.

He swallowed thickly. "Google Translate *Abbey* into Ukrainian."

"How much do you owe him?"

The tears in Garrick's eyes spilled over. Elaine turned

away. "Just over three million... I used the university funds... tried to bet my way out... but I lost that too."

"Hence the threatening phone call to your office..."

His eyes widened. "That wasn't Gregor—or any of the men I've met—but I heard that voice again after I was kidnapped."

"Do the names Clarence Blow or Jeremy and Ronald Slater mean anything?"

"No..."

"Do you have anything else to add?"

"Please keep us safe." He closed his eyes.

Aziz checked her watch; eight minutes had passed. She slid her pen into the notebook's binding and stood. "This took courage, professor... thank you."

Garrick's eyes remained closed as Elaine replaced the oxygen mask. After that, save for the hissing of oxygen and monitors beeping, the room fell silent again.

Elaine Garrick followed Aziz out of the room and waited for the door to close behind them. "Just a word, before you go...?"

Aziz cocked her head. "What is it?"

Elaine spoke softly. "Will you bring charges against my husband?"

It struck Aziz as a lawyer-up question, but she answered anyway. "Not from Dundurn Homicide. Gambling isn't a crime—fraud is. As he misappropriated funds, Brant University might seek damages, and charges could follow from that. However, if your husband is a valued member of faculty, they may waive the right to do so—he has an addiction—it might be possible, if he volunteers to do counselling and works hard to restore the funds and his reputation."

[83]

THE MORPHINE ADMINISTERED AT THE CREMATORIUM WAS intended to ease off slightly before Clarence Blow reached the Burn Trauma Unit. Too high a dose and he'd die, or he could vomit and drown—his airways were too swollen to cough up bile.

At the hospital, no one noticed when Clarence Blow's eyelids flickered open. He stared at the ceiling, the lights; no one has time to study the diamond pattern of fluorescent lenses like a patient on a gurney. The men in blue uniforms towered over him; one on a cellphone, the other talking to someone out of sight. He was comforted by having them at his side. Was he in pain? Not really. His back felt wet and warm, as if he were inside out. Everything else felt vaguely sunburned... He marvelled at the diamonds in the ceiling, how they morphed the closer they got to the fluorescent tubes.

All of a sudden the gurney was speeding along the corridor, turning corners at such a pace that the diamond screens blurred, and trying to focus on them made him dizzy.

The blue uniforms were replaced by a beautiful woman. He squinted, blinked, and refocused, trying to catch her face. "Wait. I think I know you..." She didn't respond; she was looking ahead like a warrior on a mission. "I know you..."

"We'll be there in a minute...don't try to talk."

"But...I know you." Still no response. Maybe she didn't recognize him.

She swung the gurney around a corner and for a second looked down at him.

"Please—I know you."

"Almost there, hang on."

"Polynesia—the beach." He was panicking.

Boom went the doors—he was in a cold room with huge bright lights, no more diamonds. There were people wearing masks, hats, gloves, and shiny white aprons. Some were busy-busy-busy; others peered down at him like he was an unusual oddity. Their masks moved; they were talking. The Polynesian beauty, like the blue-uniformed men, had disappeared.

One of the new people carefully removed a foil blanket he didn't know had been covering him. Almost immediately he began shivering.

They converged at his head from both sides. "What are you going to do? What's happening to me?" Horror struck the moment he realized no one was listening. And then something incredible happened—they opened his mouth.

He assumed they were wondering where the questions came from. He tried to answer but couldn't find his words— they'd been stolen.

His eyes were wide open—of that, he was certain—but the longer they stayed open, the harder it was to keep them that way. They drifted shut; he was falling asleep under a cold white sun.

[84]

BICHET WAS IN SURGERY WHEN SWETSKY AND MARACLE ARRIVED. The nursing supervisor would only say that she'd been conscious when she'd gone into the OR. The pair decided to wait for more news. They were huddled in the corridor drinking terrible coffee from paper cups when a heavyset constable approached doing the cop walk—arms wide to avoid any contact with his duty belt. "Hey—we just got to the Burn Trauma Unit with Clarence Blow. There's a Hail Mary on to save him—my sergeant thought you should know."

"What happened to him?"

"Somebody put him in a furnace and turned it on . . . we're pretty sure it's the same boys that shot up your team."

"Will he survive?" Maracle asked.

"The paramedic asked the BTU for permission to let him

die. Next thing we knew, we were racing over here — so, dunno." He shrugged.

Swetsky hung his head. "What happened to DI Williams? Nobody here knows."

"His right arm took a round, sir — it didn't look good — and he had a fall. He might've gotten a brain injury. Air ambulance took him to Toronto Western; that's all I know."

"Was he conscious?" Maracle asked.

"Unconscious the whole time . . . lost a lot of blood too, eh." The cop shuffled back down the corridor.

Swetsky dropped his cup into a nearby bin and leaned against the wall. The "officers down" call was on him. He shut his eyes and tried to let his thoughts drift . . . but the only thought that wouldn't budge was one about taking early retirement and going fishing, wherever the fish were big and the conversations small.

Maracle studied Swetsky; he didn't need a printout to know what was on the man's mind. He'd seen it before in Afghanistan with both enlisted grunts and seasoned officers; it was easy to think an IED could have been avoided if only they'd done — or not done — something else.

Maracle waited for him to open his eyes. For all he knew, Swets was one of those rare soldiers who slept on their feet. There weren't many; Maracle'd seen it twice — guys fast asleep like they were home in bed. When they woke up, they were spaced out, but not rattled or even surprised to be standing.

And that's how it happened five minutes later. With his head still leaning against the wall, DS Swetsky suddenly opened his eyes. "Charlie . . . you stay here. Divide your time between Bichet's surgery and Blow in the BTU."

"Wilco, sir. And you?"

"I'm taking the Chevy to Toronto. I don't want any second-hand information on Montile."

"Understood, sir." Maracle kept his tone casual as he added, "Sir...you know you're not responsible for this, correct?"

Swetsky shoved himself off the wall and exhaled. "Williams is a great cop—a careful cop—much more careful than I am." He looked down at his shoes again. "But I gave the order..."

"Yes, sir. But you didn't tell him how to execute it."

"Nice try, Charlie. Stay in touch—I wanna know the minute something breaks here." Swetsky turned to walk away, then paused. "D'you find it strange that BTU is the Burn Trauma Unit, and also the British thermal unit—that both use the same initials?" He didn't wait for an answer before heading for the exit.

SWETSKY WAS APPROACHING Mississauga when the radio-phone crackled. "Maracle, sir; the doc from the burn unit just came out. Instead of me doing broken telephone, here she is—Dr. Elizabeth Wisebrough..."

"Detective Superintendent, I'll be brief, but I'm happy to answer any questions you may have..."

"What can you tell me?"

"Just over forty minutes ago, Clarence Blow succumbed to his injuries. We planned to intubate him but quickly realized that was impossible. The only alternative was a tracheostomy. It was during that procedure that his heart stopped."

"Did he say anything when he came in, Doctor?"

"No. Though it was odd; his lips—while cracked and swollen—kept moving like he was speaking, but he wasn't emitting sound. Not unusual given his condition, but he definitely had something to say. Our intake nurse said he was trying to talk all the way to the OR."

"Guess we shoulda had a lip reader." When Swetsky's joke failed to get a reaction, he continued. "If we'd gotten him to you sooner, would he have had a fighting chance?"

She took barely a moment to answer. "No...I think not. A good chance of survival would have required him not to end up in a cremator."

[85]

BANG. BANG. BANG. BANG. "HANG ON..." MACNEICE HOLLERED INTO his phone.

At Division One, where the only sound was Ryan's fingers flying across his keyboard, the repeated metallic banging made Vertesi wince. It continued until MacNeice was outside.

"Jesus, Peter, Paul, and Mary—boss, where are you?"

"Sorry, I'm at a sheet metal factory near the Crematorium, reviewing security footage. If it's bad over the phone, it's much worse here. What have you got?"

"Slater wants to talk, boss—but he's got conditions."

MacNeice sat down on the concrete steps and took a deep breath. Through the trees he saw a forensics van stop behind the crematorium. "So your canned salmon sandwich strategy worked."

"Maybe, but here's the thing—he and McNulty aren't an item anymore. Ronnie's here on his own; the cop outside the holding cell said Slater fired off a few f-bombs at his lawyer, and after that they lit into each other. He couldn't hear it all, but a few minutes later, McNulty yelled, 'You're on your own, asshole' and knocked on the door to leave."

"Slater's willing to talk without representation?" MacNeice couldn't believe it.

"Says he can represent himself. How long will you be?"

"You've got the ball, Detective; run with it. Have Ryan bring you anything that comes in from the Riviera forensics team."

"Got it. How's it out there?"

"I'm on the road where they abandoned the Escalade; factory has a security camera that rakes across the front entrance, so we should see whatever they left in..."

"Good luck. An alert went to local hospitals and clinics for anyone showing up with a gunshot wound."

"I doubt they'll go to an ER, but they may have a doc lined up somewhere..."

"Boss, Aziz just got back. Here she is..." Vertesi handed over the phone.

Aziz launched right into her update. "Garrick's going to be slow to recover, but he gave up a name—Gregor Abatstvo—surname anglicized to 'Abbey.' He owns Abbey Laundry and Dry Cleaning. The professor says it's a front for a gambling racket. There are three of these operations; one is in Montreal, twenty minutes from Cheval Fou. Garrick was into Gregor for three million."

"Reach out to detective Girone in Montreal, ask him what they know about Abbey..."

"I've got a call in; should hear back shortly."

"Good. Ride shotgun with Michael in the Slater interview; he'll brief you."

MacNeice steeled himself to re-enter the cacophony of the factory, where everyone but him and a constable had massive noise-cancelling headphones. He was saved by his cellphone ringing again; this time it was Swetsky.

"John, where are you?"

"I'm with Montile. There are two issues. He's been through a barrage of tests and he's awake but still disoriented. I'm getting this from a nurse in neurosurgery. According to an MRI and a functional MRI, Montile's brain isn't damaged; as yet there's no swelling, no bleeding. So nothing definitive, but they're cautiously optimistic."

"That's a relief." MacNeice realized he'd been holding his breath.

"For his head, yeah. The hand surgeon saw him in the brain centre...I caught up with him after that. He's prepared to take Montile into surgery for assessment. He wouldn't commit until they assess the damage."

"When will that be?"

"Don't know. First up is the brain trauma. The wrist has been stabilized, so they have some time—but not a lot. Basically, he's in critical but stable condition."

The door behind MacNeice flew open—it was the constable. "Sir, we've got something..."

"I have to go, John. Stay with Montile till you know more." He followed the constable through to the equipment closet containing the CCTV and shut the door to dampen the noise.

A pale grey blur flew across the screen. "Pretty certain

that's the Escalade, sir. In ninety-four seconds you'll see them leaving," the constable said. A split-second on screen isn't much—but there it was: the blur of a smaller car headed in the opposite direction.

[86]

APPROACHING DUNDURN, MACNEICE TOOK THE FIRST EXIT OFF THE 403, looped around, and eventually came to a stop at Princess Point. He rolled the windows down; the hum of the nearby traffic arrived in waves. Traffic wasn't what he'd hoped to hear; he craved birdsong and didn't care which bird or song—just something wild and free.

He closed his eyes and listened to the engine's cooling crackle, the gentle lapping of waves. Somewhere off in the trees behind him, a crow called—and, like the crow, he waited for a response.

In that in-between time, he recalled a dream Kate had had three weeks before she died, ten days before a morphine drip rendered her comatose and presumably dreamless to the end. It was just before sunrise—she woke up whimpering. Once she'd drifted off again, he closed his eyes and fell asleep. It could have been a minute or an hour later that she cried out in terror.

He held her gently and said, over and over again, "I'm here, my love. I'm here . . . You're safe now." Her hollow eyes and weak smile quickly exposed his lie.

Back at Princess Point, MacNeice realized that Kate's nightmare had inserted itself into his concern for Bichet and Williams. He decided then and there to call Dr. Sumner, to set an appointment for the following week.

She picked up before the second ring. "Detective Superintendent . . ."

"Sorry, Doctor; I was just going to leave a message."

"Well, I've just been told my next appointment will be ten minutes late, so I'm happy to offer a sliver of time . . ."

He told her about Kate's nightmare; about how he'd searched for a compassionate response to correct the lie he'd told, and how he'd been unable to find one and instead said nothing.

"The lie that you could keep her safe?"

"Yes," he said. "She did manage to whisper back to me, 'I know, I know . . .'"

"What did she know?"

"I didn't ask. I just held her."

"But you thought you knew."

"That she was telling me she knew I couldn't help her."

"Possibly," Sumner said. "Though it's conceivable she might have meant *I know you love me and you've done all you can do to keep me safe.*"

MacNeice held the phone away from his face — to cover his shaky breathing and sudden rush of tears. He wished

Sumner hadn't answered; this wasn't the time for a session. He brought the phone back to his ear, "Maybe..."

"Do you have any idea why this memory came to you just now?"

"I was daydreaming, and let my guard down." He inhaled. "Two of my team were wounded today—guilt casts a very wide net." MacNeice's radiophone burped. "Sorry, Doctor, I've got to take this." He said goodbye and picked up the handset. "MacNeice."

"Wallace. I'm ten minutes late for an appointment but wanted to check in..." MacNeice smiled at the thought that he and the Deputy Chief shared the same psychiatrist. "My spider senses are tarantulas, Mac. Please tell me you've got this under control."

"We're in the heat of it now, sir. *Control* is a difficult word to apply."

"I understand—and I heard about your detectives. Not for now, but the Special Investigation Unit will want to know why they were out there on their own. Look, if you need further support..."

"I've got everyone deployed, sir. The rest is straight-up police work—I'm sure you understand."

"Stay safe, Mac. Remember, anything you need—call." With that, he hung up.

MacNeice turned his eyes to the water just in time to see a quartet of geese skidding to a landing off the opposite shore. He took a USB key with the split-second Escalade footage from his jacket pocket and turned it over a few times, as if holding it might give him an insight into where Wright and Daintry might have gone.

Across Cootes, the geese were back on the move,

paddling furiously to gain airspeed and altitude, leaving behind their silver wakes.

"'COME LIVE WITH me and be my love, and we will some new pleasures prove, of golden sands and crystal brooks, with silken lines and silver hooks.'"

You were such a tender oddity to recite John Donne to me.

"Cops don't do that, you mean."

I'd never fallen in love with a cop before . . . but I doubt very much that many think Donne's the way to a girl's heart.

"Let's just say I did my research."

Your own words would have taken you there . . .

"Kate, I shouldn't have said you were safe. I'm sorry . . ."

You're wrong. I was safe in your arms while I was dying.

[87]

LIKE THE GEESE, MACNEICE WAS READY TO GET BACK ON THE MOVE. He started the car, and his cell rang. "Tell me, Ryan."

"Abbey's plant—where the local outlets take their cleaning—is in Secord. I've got addresses for the Niagara Falls and Montreal plants, but I haven't located the owner's house."

"Give me Secord."

"124 Cascade Street—north of Barton, near the QEW. Do you want the phone number?"

"Not now . . ." MacNeice switched on the flashing grille lights and sped away from Princess Point. "I'll be at Division in seven minutes; meet me in the parking lot and I'll pass over a USB key. On it, I'm interested in the footage of the second vehicle—sharpen the image as best you can."

"Understood, sir."

"The Slater interview's still going?"

"Oh yeah...And it probably got more interesting; I just dropped off the latest from Forensics."

"Topline that for me."

"The stripping bath scum DNA is Dr. Evan Moore's. There are three more unidentified samples, but his was already in the system."

"Is that it?"

"No, sir. I'm quoting from photo captions...*Engineer's iron ring, discovered under incinerator cowling. Engraving inside, reads E.M. QNS – 1969.*"

"Call Bill Moore; ask him if Evan graduated from Queen's Engineering in 1969."

Pulling into the division parking lot seven minutes later, MacNeice followed the inside lane to where Ryan was waiting with an open hand. MacNeice slowed down and handed him the USB. "Confirmed, sir. Evan Moore, Queen's Engineering, '69. Oh, and Jack says hello."

Driving east on Main, he turned his thoughts to Cascade Street. However confident and insulated Gregor Abatstvo felt about his family's enterprise, he had to be twitchy with the news of Arnold Garrick's rescue.

When he finally crossed Barton on Lake Avenue, MacNeice killed the grille lights. Turning left on Cascade, he eased the Chevy toward number 124, a long, low brick building set back from the street. The facility was surrounded by a high security fence. Intermittently across its expanse were small metal signs warning that it was electrified. A dry-cleaning Fort Knox.

Three truck bays on the building's west side were sheltered behind large rolling doors, each distinguished by a large white numeral. An unremarkable three-storey office block anchored the far end of the complex, while the entrance off Cascade Street resembled a dispatcher's office — small and efficient — its windows covered with opaque film. Three large black vans were parked against the west side of the lot, the most visible of which had *Abbey* printed in white on the doors.

MacNeice drove to the end of Cascade and swung about. As he approached the building from the west, the security fence slid open. Feeling his heart quicken, he slowed to a stop. Two men, both wearing black suits and white T-shirts, stood waiting by the front office, arms crossed.

Moments later, a leviathan he thought was long extinct slid menacingly into view. MacNeice's jaw dropped; he eased the Chevy to the side of the road and got out. Switching his cell to camera mode, he made his way across the street and stepped enthusiastically onto the driveway. One of the men watched him warily.

"Well, well . . . *well*. Sorry, I really had to stop. Tell me I'm right — a 1960 Lincoln Continental Mark V?"

"Yes," the slimmer of the two men said as he walked around the vehicle and prepared to get in the front passenger seat.

"But it's beefed up, no? The original had a 429.9-cubic-inch V8, but looking at the size of those wheels, you're pulling more, no?"

The two men glanced at each other but neither spoke. The shorter, stockier man climbed into the back seat and closed the door. The slim one waited, eyeing MacNeice as he continued hyper-enthusing about the car.

"My uncle had one — but his was a Mark IV. He'd bring

American entertainers from places like Tonawanda and Cheektowaga; I love that word—*Cheek-tah-waga*—don't you? And he'd chauffeur them around in his Mark IV."

Slim shook his head as if MacNeice was speaking an unknown dialect, but he didn't get into the vehicle either. He was clearly waiting—not for MacNeice, but for another passenger.

MacNeice showed him the phone and started taking pictures. "Hope you don't mind—it's just that I've never seen a Mark V. Anyway, Uncle Jock would bring jazz stars—Duke and Basie, Eartha Kitt and Ella. Yeah...Ella slipped him a two-hundred-dollar tip; be about a thousand in today's money. They'd come up to visit a jazz pal who lived in Dundurn. It's true."

A man in his early sixties, trim and elegant in a silver-grey one-button suit, stepped into the camera frame—*click click click*—as MacNeice continued. "Those days, you didn't need a passport to cross the border..."

The new arrival skirted the car and moved, head down to avoid the camera, toward MacNeice. *Click click*. Slim was approaching too. MacNeice dropped the phone to his side. "Hey, mister. Sorry if I'm keeping you guys...It's just, I've never seen an M-five in the flesh."

Both men were closing on him and the guy who'd climbed into the back seat was now out of the car again and advancing. The older man stopped so close that MacNeice caught a whiff of his cologne. He stood there for a moment, apparently studying MacNeice's shoes, before looking up.

His head was shaped like an upside-down teardrop. He turned his icy blues on MacNeice and asked, in a clipped accent, "Where's your car?" He tilted forward for MacNeice's response as if he was hard of hearing. When he didn't get an answer, he looked around. "That Chevrolet over there... that your car?"

"Yeah... Well, it's a fleet car. What we call a company car."

"Yeah? So's mine." The man glanced over his shoulder and smiled at Slim. "Mine's prettier." He looked MacNeice squarely in the face, like he was recording his features for future reference. When he turned away, he nodded ever so slightly to Slim and walked back to the Mark V. The second black suit opened the door.

Slim stepped forward. "Goodbye. You go now, yes?"

"Sure... Hey, sorry, I was just—"

"Go now, yeah?"

MacNeice waved awkwardly, jogged back to his car, took several deep breaths, and then pulled away. Turning south on Lake Avenue, he checked his rear-view mirror. Seconds later, the Mark V swung left on the south service road, back toward the city or the Queen Elizabeth Highway.

MacNeice punched the radiophone: "Dispatch, this is DS MacNeice."

"Detective Superintendent."

"There's a white 1960 four-door Lincoln Continental, three occupants, proceeding west on the south service road from Lake Avenue, in Secord. Notify all units. I want it tracked from a distance—ideally with an unmarked car and the aerial unit."

The dispatcher repeated the message. "Any instructions regarding its occupants, sir?"

"Yes. Do not engage."

[88]

BACK AT DIVISION ONE, MACNEICE STOPPED BY THE CUBICLE TO hand his phone to Ryan. "Enhance and print all the images that show a large white car with some men. I'm particularly interested in the older man. I'll be in the interview room, but not for long."

"I didn't get a lot from that security footage, sir, but when I overlapped it with the Escalade, it's much smaller, like a compact..."

"Colour?"

"It could be any mid-range colour." MacNeice turned to leave, and Ryan added, "One more thing, sir—Abbey's Montreal and Niagara Falls plants are run by Gregor Abatstvo's sons."

As MacNeice slipped into the interview room, Aziz

announced, "For the record, Detective Superintendent MacNeice has joined the interview."

"How is this going for you, Mr. Slater?" MacNeice asked.

Ronald Slater shook his head. "How would I know?" He looked at Vertesi. "How's this going for me?"

"We could be doing better," Vertesi said coolly. "I've suggested several times that Ronnie should have counsel present, but he continues to decline. Correct?"

"There's no use . . . I need to make a deal. I want to be with my family and mourn my brother."

"Will you sit in, sir?" Vertesi asked.

"No . . . but I do have a few questions."

"Fire away." Attempting a brave face, Slater couldn't keep a small short-circuit twitch from the corner of his mouth.

"Do you have any recollection of restoring or rebuilding a 1960 Lincoln Continental Mark V?" MacNeice asked the question as if he was only mildly interested in an answer.

To cover his discomfort, Slater rubbed his eyes before studying the tabletop like a man trying to remember something.

"White inside and out. Big wheels; not spec, not even close." Slater did his best not to respond, so MacNeice added, "If you like, we can ask the men who work on your cars instead—though that won't help you."

Slater pushed himself off the table and crossed his arms. "Can I have a coffee?"

Vertesi also leaned back in his seat, suggesting that weariness or frustration was contagious. "I'll make it."

MacNeice put a hand on Vertesi's shoulder. "No, I'll make it; it'll take less than five minutes. In that time, Ronald, I want you to consider what other questions I might have for you." He smiled and walked to the door. "Sugar? Milk?"

"Black," Slater said, eyes focused on the tape recorder's tiny red light.

"DI Aziz, please step out with me..."

Aziz put down her pen. "DI Aziz and DS MacNeice leaving the interview."

WHILE THEY WAITED at the espresso machine, MacNeice asked, "Were you able to reach Eugene Blow?"

"It's all set up—he'll view the body tomorrow."

"Good. And how did Slater react to the forensics report naming Evan Moore?"

"Shocked...confused...nervous..." Aziz smiled. "And then he implicated Blow and his brother."

"Meaning they had access to the building but he didn't know what they were doing?"

"Close. Jeremy said he didn't know anything until after the fact; seems Blow went rogue."

Espresso in hand, MacNeice said he would join Aziz in the interview room shortly. "I've given Ryan some photos I took outside Abbey Laundry and Dry Cleaning, including images of Gregor Abatstvo and two of his men. That Lincoln Continental I just asked Slater about is Gregor's."

The lightness in Aziz's face drained when she realized what he was saying. "Mac, for God's sake, please tell me you weren't seen."

"I was...we spoke, briefly. About cars."

"You're joking. You must be." Frustrated, she ran a hand through her hair.

"I was overzealous and car crazy."

"Mac, you were bullshitting a killer." She shook her head

in disbelief. "You were driving an unmarked car! You think he didn't spot that?" Aziz dropped her head for a moment; she was furious when she looked up. "Give me something else to focus on, before I say something I can't take back."

MacNeice studied the crema dissolving in his cup. "Call Detective Girone again. Request that he show those photos to the maître d' at Cheval Fou."

"Yes, sir. Anything else?"

"Start a conversation with him about all three cities coordinating; if Garrick's right and Abbey's a front for gambling, we might pursue parallel investigations..."

"A three-city raid?"

"Yes." He poured the espresso down the drain and started over. "Fiza, I don't want this to—"

"To what? To interrupt our investigation? It won't. Unless, of course, Gregor's men hunt you down at your cottage. Hell, Mac—half the bloody city knows you live out there alone, surrounded by—by foxes, coyotes, rabbits, fireflies and...ghosts." She shook her head. "I apologize for the last one—make that birds." Exasperated, she turned and walked away.

VERTESI SENSED SOMETHING was wrong when MacNeice returned to the interview room alone, but he simply noted MacNeice's return for the recording. "Sir, you had some more questions?"

MacNeice slid the cup across the table. "I do, but first, the Mark V?"

"Yeah, that's my work..." Slater downed the coffee. "Here's what I know: The owner, Gregor Abatstvo accepted that vehicle in return for an American client's bad debt. It's heavy 'cause it was built for an ambassador. Thing has bullet-proof glass, armour-plated door panels, and dense, bullet-proof rubber tires. Paintjob was black, but Gregor's got this thing about cleanliness — so we did a complete makeover in Polaris White."

"Does it have any weaknesses?"

Slater nodded the way someone does when they alone know a secret. "Only one. Look, that thing's a beast, but even a beast needs to breathe, and it breathes through its grille."

"Interesting . . . How were you paid?"

Slater's long sigh suggested the oxygen was running out of his defence. "I was plugged into Gregor . . . I didn't know anything about Garrick. I did that car free of charge to clear my own debt."

"A debt for what service, and how much?"

"Gambling. Three hundred and seventy-five thousand."

"The two men with Clarence Blow — are they Gregor's men?"

"No . . . Blow was in over his head with some local talent. When that didn't work out, Jeremy asked if I could find him some professionals. I couldn't, but we both knew who could."

"Gregor. But your brother could have asked him directly."

"Jer didn't like getting his hands dirty; he managed Abatstvo's investments." Slater smiled as if that fact was of no consequence. "I thought he'd give us one or two of his guys — they're Russian or Ukrainian ex-military. Gregor laughed that idea off. For two hundred grand he'd deliver two professionals."

"Wright and Daintry."

"I don't know their names; ask Blow."

"That'll be difficult. I'm asking you."

"I never met them . . . Did they kill Jeremy?"

"We don't know." MacNeice wasn't finished. "You never met them and yet they borrowed your Econoline van, a Lincoln, and an Escalade, is that correct?"

"Jeremy called me, asked me to leave the keys for the Lincoln in the dropbox—I didn't know anything about the van. I gave him the dropbox combination, but that was it. The Lincoln was dropped off the night they came for the Caddy—same deal with the keys—and I haven't seen the Caddy since."

"You're very trusting, lending luxury automobiles to strangers. What was in it for you?"

"Triple the rental fee." Slater couldn't help smiling to suggest that he wasn't stupid. "In cash from Jeremy."

"How closely associated were you with your brother? What did you know of his involvement with Abatstvo?"

"Only that he and some guy in Montreal did investment management for the Abatstvo family. Jeremy's not a gambler. Neither am I—except that one time."

"By investment management you mean money laundering?"

"Maybe . . . *Laundry* is in Abatstvo's company name."

"Solely from betting . . ." MacNeice said.

"Not solely . . ."

"Meaning?"

"Jeremy said Abatstvo has a *very* diversified portfolio."

"Be specific, Ronald."

Slater sat back, crossed his arms, and shook his head

like he was having an internal debate about how much he'd already said and whether maybe it was time to shut up.

"Is this a crisis of conscience, or are you just scared to death?" MacNeice asked.

Slater tucked in his chin. "No shit—both. I've already given you a lot...enough. Agreed?" He looked for confirmation from Vertesi, who shrugged unenthusiastically in Slater's favour. "Come on, I've given you a lot...What's that word when cancer spreads?"

"Metastasis."

"That's it. You figure it out; do the math. Dad here, a son in Montreal, another son in Niagara Falls. You can't hit the old man and ignore those two." Slater was exasperated. "Obviously, I'm talking about self-interest; you'd do the same in my shoes. Straight up, you arrest the father in Dundurn—one or the other son will find me."

"Makes a good point, boss," Vertesi said, dropping his pen for emphasis.

"Then help us take down all three," MacNeice said with an air of indifference. "Gambling, money laundering... What else—drug money, human trafficking?"

"I don't know anything about that...Look, I know they offer yacht bunnies as a side service. I've seen 'em do it."

"Prostitutes?" Vertesi was a stickler for clarification; he pointed to the interview recorder.

Slater shook his head dismissively. "Yacht bunnies are young girls and boys. His right-hand guy called them that..."

Vertesi was undaunted in his pursuit of clarity. "Local talent for sex?"

"Not local—no one's putting out province-wide alerts or missing persons posters for these kids."

With a sinking heart, MacNeice clarified: "Foreign national minors."

"Yeah…" Slater nodded, then shrugged.

"Human trafficking." MacNeice refined his own clarification.

"If you say so…" Slater said.

MacNeice smiled grimly at Vertesi. "Last question, Ronald: why would Abatstvo drive around in such a conspicuous vehicle?"

"I asked him that when he picked it up. For business, he said. For everything else, he's got a Tesla." Seeing them glance at each other, Slater added, "It's that clean thing, like I said."

"So it's a white Tesla," Vertesi added.

"If someone saw him pull away in the Mark V — that was a business call."

MacNeice stood to leave. "If you have anything further to offer, it would be a grave mistake not to share it with Detective Vertesi."

"Just before you go, sir…" Vertesi raised a hand, "Ronnie, how do you know so much? Betting on a game doesn't give you access to inside baseball."

"First of all, everything I've said is true." Responding like a fighter on the ropes, Slater tried to take charge of a situation that had already slipped away. "Secondly, my brother and I aren't — weren't — close, but we have things in common. Blow was my accountant and his. Thanks to my brother, Gregor became my bookie…for a while. Then my client, for a while. Jeremy never told me what he was into Abbey for — but I sensed there was more."

MacNeice sat down but didn't pull his chair to the table. "Go ahead."

Slater's energy surged. "Okay. So, when you work on a car like that for almost two years, you meet with the client a lot. You've seen my operation...you know I go for a classy bottle of wine and I listen to people talking upstairs. Most of those conversations were between him and his guys, in Russian or Ukrainian..."

"Happy, sad, angry voices raised, conversations?" MacNeice asked.

"Normal sounding for them. To me they all sound angry. But—here's the but—there were phone calls where Gregor spoke in English. Most of them nothing special. But once I heard him talking to an American who was sailing in from Syracuse with a US senator, looking for a good time."

"Names?" MacNeice asked.

"No...So I come back to the office with a bottle of wine and Gregor tells me to deliver six bottles of 2017 Chateau Margaux to the dock..." Slater leaned on his elbows. "That boat was at least a hundred feet long. The crew was all dressed up like sailors; it was the captain who said 'yacht bunnies,' like I was supposed to know what that meant. As I'm leaving the marina, a black Abbey van pulls in. Driver opens the back and three boys and three girls climb out— they looked Asian. They're like thirteen, maybe fourteen, wearing what looked like school uniforms: white shirts, shorts or short skirts, blue ties, knee-high white socks and white loafers...going out for a bunny cruise."

MacNeice stood. "You didn't ask Gregor about that?"

"Ask about what? I didn't see anything; I delivered the wine and I left."

[89]

IT WAS FIRST THING IN THE MORNING, AND C.C. CAMERON WAS IN A room too small for his indignation. When MacNeice arrived, he sat back and locked his arms across his chest. "I had to wait all night to find out what's going on? Explain that to me." His cheeks were glowing, but so was his nose.

"I'm confused, Mister Cameron. Are you outraged for your son or for yourself?" MacNeice asked.

"You know what, Detective — whatever your name is — fuck you!" Cameron tightened the hold on his chest as if he was squeezing a beachball; the effort sent deep ruby blotches across his face. "What've you charged my son with?"

"The charges pending, but they're serious. That's all I can say. Your son's in need of a criminal lawyer."

Cameron shifted his posture and glanced at the recorder. "We being taped right now?"

"I've no reason to record this meeting. You're a concerned parent whose son is implicated in crimes ranging from kidnapping to homicide."

C.C. blasted out of the chair, throwing out his arms like a coach railing at a ref's call. "This isn't Tom! It's Clarence, isn't it?" He paced back and forth. "That little shit got him into this...Where's he now, eh? Is he locked up, or did he slip through your fingers?"

MacNeice turned to leave. "He's dead—burned alive at your son's crematorium. I'll let you cool down." At the door, he looked back. "Our meeting's over. If you have any influence, I'd use it to get Thomas representation. I'll let the desk sergeant know you're free to meet with Thomas for ten minutes, after which you'll be escorted from the building."

"You can't walk out on me. D'you know who I am?"

"You're Thomas's father, and for his sake, pull yourself together, man."

AS HE HEADED upstairs, MacNeice met Aziz, who was on her way down. "When I first spoke to Jean-Paul Girone, the detective from the Montreal Police Service, he hadn't heard of Abbey, but he just called back." She nodded for MacNeice to follow her outside, where they sat together on the bench.

"He took my question to Sûreté du Québec's Major Crimes Unit—turns out, they've been investigating the Abatstvo family for running a gambling racket..."

"Anything else?" MacNeice leaned back to study a band of feathery clouds.

"SQ then called the RCMP to ask the same question. The Mounties had a nascent investigation of Andrej Abatstvo for human and drug trafficking and prostitution but hadn't been able to build a case strong enough to impress the Crown Prosecutor. On their own, neither force had enough evidence to move forward, but once Girone asked about Rodney Conroy, SQ acknowledged that he'd been under suspicion for money laundering—in connection with Abbey." Aziz leaned back and they watched the clouds glide by together.

"That it?"

"Almost..." She closed her eyes and her voice softened. "Girone took a leap and called Rodney's widow. He asked if she knew anything about his connection to Abbey Laundry and Dry Cleaning."

"Good cop..."

"Here's one for the record... She said Roddy had developed a cleaning fetish. He was cleaning his golf and fishing clothes, T-shirts, shorts, sweatpants, and socks. She said he hadn't been like that when they met."

"Will wonders never..." MacNeice closed his eyes, enjoying being next to her. He imagined them in Gage Park, or under the trees of Luxembourg Gardens—though he realized that to anyone crossing Division's lot, they'd look like two cops asleep on the job.

He opened his eyes and glanced her way. "I'm sorry, Fiza. You were right yesterday."

She kept her eyes closed but her lips curled into the slightest of smiles. After a deep inhale and a long sigh, she returned to the case. "SQ, the RCMP, and Girone's boss at the MPS want to partner with us... Each has a stake, but they feel we—well, you—have the best grasp of Abbey's enterprise right now."

"At the very least, that's an overstatement. But before we discuss that, will you come for dinner at the cottage tonight—just me, the foxes, coyotes, rabbits, birds, fireflies—and you?"

She chuckled. "Let's see how the day unfolds. I think it's time to call Wallace."

"Past time. I've been using his name for helicopter and unmarked car surveillance. We'll also need Niagara Regional on side."

Aziz sat upright. "A sickening thought... Wouldn't Abatstvo have cops on his payroll?"

"He may be smart enough to try. And we've got four or five forces in play."

"Files may already be lost..."

MacNeice pushed himself off the bench. "Come on."

Back inside, he asked Ryan to call Aerial Command. "Find the chopper crew chief who was trailing the white Continental."

Vertesi swung into the cubicle to deliver an update on the remainder of the Ronald Slater interview. But before he could speak, Ryan nodded for MacNeice to pick up the landline.

"Flight Sergeant Ari Reisman, sir."

"You followed the white Lincoln?"

"Correct, sir, to a large estate on Carriage Trail in Burlington. We were subsequently relieved by a mocked-up telecom van. It's currently outside the property, ready to report on any movement."

"Other vehicles on site?"

"Three black SUVs; one was there when the Continental arrived, two arrived five minutes later. There's a helipad on that site, sir. I've requested that air traffic keep us informed if a bird attempts to land."

"Good call. Any additional structures?"

"A barn and a shuttered-up house. We're downloading the onboard footage and stills now."

"Thank you, Sergeant; send them over soon as you can." As he put the phone down, Maracle arrived. "How's Lise?"

"Pretty doped up, sir. ICU doc says three ribs are damaged. She'll likely need more surgery, but she's awake and in recovery."

"Was she coherent?" Aziz asked.

"More or less... she wanted to know about Montile. I told her what I knew. She said Montile saved their asses."

"Did she mention Wright or Daintry?" MacNeice asked.

"Only that Daintry was the coolest cowboy she'd ever seen, but she thinks he was bleeding out. Wright could easily have killed them both but didn't. She doesn't understand why."

"From the scene, I can..." MacNeice took out his cellphone.

"Why?" Aziz asked.

"Montile and Bichet were disabled. Wright doesn't seem the kind to kill for sport. Those men are professionals— leave the cash at Garrick's and, if it isn't in the contract, don't kill." He put the phone to his ear and looked over at Lester's mugshot. When Swetsky came on, he put him on speaker. "John, give us an update."

"Latest scan shows Montile's brain didn't swell, and so far there's no internal bleeding. Apparently he came to in the medevac and answered simple questions..."

"Sounds like Williams..." Vertesi quipped, to a withering look from MacNeice.

"Doc said that the fall may have saved his life...something about his torso and legs being above his head when he landed." Swets paused, then read from his notes: "The equivalent of getting two to four pints of fluid. Basically, he's very lucky."

"That's a relief..." MacNeice said.

"I spoke to the hand doc. Once they had the all-clear on the brain, Montile was wheeled into an OR. They cleaned out all the bone fragments and gunk to see what was left."

"And?" Aziz asked.

"Doc said he'd seen worse—I didn't ask where. Bullet hit Montile just above the wrist, but it didn't damage the small bones that provide flexibility. Two or three days from now, they'll discuss their next move. I asked him what that meant. One option is to fuse the joint, but he won't have any flexibility. I asked for another option, acting like the kid's father or something."

"Well, you are like a surrogate father..." Aziz said.

Swetsky hooted. "Yeah, right. Anyway, the other option is a bionic joint—a wrist replacement. Basically, that means his wrist would be made of titanium and plastic. If it works, it'll be flexible."

MacNeice winced. "*If* it works...?"

"No shit. I told him to do what was necessary to get Montile back to work—as if this had never happened."

"I'm sure he appreciated that, John," Aziz said, shaking her head.

"Yeah, whatever. Of course, I gotta get Montile to agree."

Ryan raised his hand. "DC Wallace on two, sir."

[90]

SECURITY FORCES DON'T OFTEN PLAY WELL TOGETHER. LAW enforcement, and all branches military, covet their own intelligence—but you won't find any police service ready to admit that one of the reasons for that secrecy is to counter the potential for criminal influence within their ranks.

Task forces are a possible exception—but mobilizing one over the course of a day would require crazy glue to cement extreme caution to unbridled daring. Which explains why, prior to hanging up on MacNeice, DC Wallace made it clear that he thought a task force would be an "unprecedented fuck-up" and that it would be dubbed a "colossal overreach" initiated by "a lead investigator consumed by grand illusions."

MacNeice was just relieved the idea wasn't met with an

outright no. Rather, Wallace demanded a meeting with all the Division One homicide detectives still standing. "Trust me," he'd added forcefully, "there'll be a show of fucking hands on this one." Which is how Deputy Chief Wallace came to be in Division One's interview room with MacNeice and four other detectives.

Swetsky arrived fifteen minutes before Wallace. The consummate team player, he was happy to stand with MacNeice. Five minutes before Wallace's arrival, Ryan rushed into the room with the latest forensics from Jeremy Slater's secret cabinets and safe. There was too much to absorb before the DC arrived, but Ryan had printed a half-dozen copies, including one for Wallace. They were still poring over the dozen pages of preliminary findings when the door opened. Everyone stood to attention.

"For chrissakes, sit down." Wallace removed his jacket, rolled up his sleeves, and dropped into a chair. "This meeting will be thirty minutes. If I agree with you, MacNeice, I'll call the mayor and give him the heads-up. Then you and I will request an immediate conference call with the Montreal Police Service, Sûreté du Québec, Niagara Regional Police, and the RCMP's Quebec and Niagara detachments. If that doesn't pucker your sphincter, you weren't listening." When no one responded, Wallace slapped the table. "Okay. Convince me."

Thirty-seven minutes later, the DC pushed his chair from the table and began pacing the room. After two laps he said, "Mac, make me one of those Italian coffees. Give me a minute with the team."

MacNeice nodded and left the room, not entirely sure what Wallace wanted — a cappuccino, a macchiato, an espresso, one shot or two? It didn't matter, as he knew the request was a ruse. Since his last big case, the one where he'd entered that farmhouse unarmed, Wallace had been giving MacNeice signals — some subtle, most not — that he had concerns about his top detective's mental stability. *Fair enough*, MacNeice sighed to himself.

He began a double-shot cappuccino — simply because it would take the longest to make. Returning to the interview room nine minutes later, MacNeice tried to read his team's body language. "Your coffee, sir."

"Thanks. Sit down." Wallace took a sip, unaware that he'd given himself a foam moustache. Everyone remained stone-faced except for Vertesi, who looked over at the tape recorder to stifle his grin.

"Mac, there's no division in this division — not one dissenting voice."

MacNeice nodded, relieved. "Do we make the call, sir?"

"I'm onside. But consider this: there's enough here to raid the home and business of Gregor Abatstvo, and Forensics will probably find more . . . But are you convinced that his sons — names again?"

"Andrej in Montreal, Micha in Niagara Falls," Aziz offered.

"That those two are in on this with their father? Montreal maybe — but we don't know anything about Niagara Falls . . ." Wallace raised the cup to his mouth. "Aziz, you're a criminologist — what do you think, are all three Abatstvoses bent?"

"Do I believe it's a family affair? Yes, sir. They likely bulk-buy their dry cleaning and laundry supplies and share in everything we suspect their father of doing here. I believe

Gregor provided each son with a territory knowing they'd be lucrative for the entire enterprise."

"Thank you, Detective." Wallace tapped his fingers on the table and turned to MacNeice. "What do we say about Wright and Daintry? What are we doing to apprehend them?"

MacNeice reminded him that Daintry was badly wounded and in need of immediate medical care. Hospitals and clinics throughout the region had been alerted and provided with mugshots of both. "But we can't rule out the possibility of a freelance surgeon—for a price."

"You think they'll make a run for the border?"

"They might, but it won't be easy. Reports have circulated in the US that they're both in Canada, and US Customs has been alerted."

"Okay, I've heard enough—you're all dismissed. Except you, Mac; hang back with me."

AN HOUR LATER, Wallace left the division. They had their task force, with coordinated raids set to take place the following morning at five-thirty a.m.

While committed, it didn't mean everyone was convinced. Niagara Regional Police, accustomed to investigating organized crime, remained somewhat sceptical. The Montreal police were in. On the call, Girone said the maître d' of Cheval Fou had identified Gregor Abatstvo and his men as Rodney Conroy's guests the night before he died.

The operation was assigned the name Clean Sweep/Table Rase and all parties agreed to operate on a strictly need-to-know basis. For its part, the Quebec RCMP would provide air and ground units—groupe tactiques d'intervention—at Andrej Abatstvo's estate, where it was suspected he kept illegals—while SQ and Montreal would hit the plant.

At Wallace's request, DPD Sergeants Washburn and Gretchen Britt—who introduced herself as TTL, for Team Two Leader—arrived at One Division to prep the detectives. Washburn had requisitioned five body-armour vests, each emblazoned with an enormous "DPD" on the back, and shotguns for Swetsky and Vertesi.

"Looks like we're going in alone . . ." Maracle said with a smile.

"Last line of defence, Charlie. If they make it past Washburn's people, God help us," Swetsky said.

Abatstvo's Burlington estate was set well back from Carriage Trail. Washburn assigned Swetsky and Maracle to the Burlington raid under Sergeant Britt's command, while MacNeice, Aziz, and Vertesi would follow Washburn to the Abbey plant on Cascade. Both teams were to rendezvous at four-thirty a.m.

[91]

WHILE JEREMY SLATER MAY NEVER HAVE EXPECTED HIS LIFE TO end as it did, he was smart enough to know that it might end abruptly — which would explain the invisible room. The blown safe revealed an enormous cache of money, stocks, and bonds. More tantalizing were the cabinets, which required a diamond-bit drill to open. Inside were dozens of binders, each four inches wide, standing cover to cover, alphabetized and dated by year — codified by a system known only to Slater.

Had the files been discovered a decade before, deciphering that code would have taken weeks, but with the high-speed technology available to Forensics' digital team, it took them two and a half hours. Each entry had been given a numerical and alphabetical code that accompanied the data it held. In the case of Abatstvo and Abbey, those entries went back five years. While a thorough analysis of the binders would take months, a team of three forensic accountants, armed with the codebreaker's key, had already begun to identify red flags.

It was that initial red-flagged data that Ryan had circulated just prior to the meeting with Wallace. Most intriguing and worrisome, given the task force's impending plan, was that a full scan of the data later failed to directly connect Gregor's business to those of his sons.

On the other hand, there were several names — not disguised — trailed by the letter D in brackets: A. Garrick (D), R. Conroy (D), and a third, M. Jessop (D). MacNeice asked Sergeant Evanson to do a North American search for a missing person with the third name, M. Jessop.

MacNeice wondered: D meant what? *Dead, death, disposed? Disappeared? Done? Deactivated?* Forensics was just getting started and there was no way to know how many names, with or without an accompanying (D), might be logged for the previous years. Though he hadn't expected otherwise, MacNeice was nonetheless relieved that an E. Moore wasn't on the list... Nor was there any mention of Steadman and Raymond, whose DNA had also been identified at Riviera.

At 8:35 p.m., as MacNeice and Aziz made their way together to the stairwell, she said, "Rain check on dinner with you and your forest friends... agreed?"

"Agreed, on one condition — we do it as soon as possible."

SLEEP CAME QUICKLY, but like a fickle friend it soon slipped away, leaving MacNeice staring at the ceiling, considering all that could go wrong in the hours that lay ahead. Up the lane from the stone cottage stood a sodium lamp that no one ever tended to, but its yellow glow came on at eight p.m. and went off at eight a.m. No matter the season. MacNeice could just see it from his bedroom window. The light was a constant, and there's something to be said for constancy.

Shortly after midnight, MacNeice got out of bed and poured a double grappa. Rather than drinking it in the kitchen or living room, he returned to his bedroom and slid the curtain open so more of the light would spill over the landscape of bedding that covered his legs.

Thinking back to the Ronald Slater interview, MacNeice recalled how proud Slater had been of restoring Abatstvo's Mark V, and of seeking Abatstvo's help in finding professional muscle—killers for his brother. Slater hadn't realized, or didn't care, that his words had solidified his role in the deaths of five men, making him an accessory, which would unquestionably send him to prison. It was as if he'd believed that cooperating fully meant all might be forgiven…

MacNeice drifted off. But Slater's tale about the Mark V wouldn't leave him alone. He bolted awake at 2:45 a.m. and reached for his cellphone. His first call was to the dispatcher, and from there to the telecom van outside Gregor's residence.

"Yes, sir, how can I help?" The spotter spoke softly, the way you would if you didn't want to wake someone sleeping nearby.

"The white Lincoln Continental—is it still at the house?"

"No, sir. Left at 11:10 p.m. Three men inside. Around the same time, a white Tesla pulled in; it's behind the big house."

MacNeice went into the kitchen and poured another grappa, this time a long single shot, which he bolted back. Grappa had been his velvet hammer for years — melting away nightmares, dissolving the days into something tolerable at night. Why it was failing him this time?

Back in bed, he wondered why the Mark V had returned to the plant and why the men would remain there. Perhaps the multi-storey block was constructed for apartments, not offices.

At 3:14 a.m., MacNeice felt sleep taking him. After committing one last thought to paper — *Hit the grille . . . hit it hard* — he let it.

[92]

"**H**UMOUR ME, FOLKS," WASHBURN SAID, AS ONE OF HIS TEAM handed out Kevlar vests and helmets. "Though you likely won't need them — if things go sideways, you'll be happy you got 'em." Another officer handed out earpieces and receivers. "You'll hear everything, but you can't transmit."

Someone else, a giant who looked as if he might bust out of his combat gear, handed around coffee in paper cups. "It's a double-double. Pretend you like it, even if you don't," he advised.

The Division One detectives, already wearing their vests, helmets, and earpieces — accepted the cups. While they sipped, the tactical team continued with last-minute equipment checks and quiet confirmations of strategy.

Washburn approached MacNeice. "There'll be two EMS crews and a DFD pumper idling on Lake, just south of Barton. If required, they'll come on the run. Similar assets are ready in Burlington — and there's more on standby. Reisman's aircrew will be overseeing the heliport, and roadblocks are already in place on the service road and Carriage Trail."

"Wash, I can't recall if I mentioned the electrified fence at Abbey's plant?"

"You did; I was there late and flew a night-eye above the facility. That fence explains the wedge on our tank; it'll cause some sparks, but nothing more. Once we're through, use your Chevy to block the driveway."

"Will do. I called the surveillance van earlier." MacNeice set his coffee cup on the tank's running board.

"I heard." Washburn clapped him on the shoulder; MacNeice noticed he had the call signs for his team members encased in plastic on his right sleeve. "It's difficult to sleep before a big game. We don't know how many are inside the plant other than those three, but we do know there's no night shift for the laundry service."

MacNeice was going to mention the Mark V's one weakness, but before he could, Washburn drew a circle in the air. "Time to punch in; mount up." Six heavily armed street soldiers in black uniforms, armour, balaclavas, and helmets disappeared inside the tank with DPD-TACTICAL printed along its side. Five more climbed into the matte black extended-chassis DPD-5 van with its blacked-out windows. The tank powered around the lot and stopped for Washburn, who saluted MacNeice. "Stay low; keep those helmets handy." With that, he hoisted himself inside and closed the door. With the van close behind, the tank moved away slowly. As it did,

MacNeice took a deep breath. He was certain they were heading into combat.

He and Aziz took the Chevy's front seats, while Vertesi cradled a shotgun in the back. No one spoke. MacNeice lowered his window and caught a sound he never liked: night birds screeching as if they were in pain. By the time the Chevy hit Main, he'd closed the window to concentrate on the black shadows ahead.

[93]

APPROACHING BARTON ON LAKE AVENUE, WASHBURN BROKE through the static of their earpieces. "Comm check, roll call." Each team member—assigned names from NATO's phonetic alphabet—confirmed. The one exception was Washburn; he was simply "Wash" or "boss."

Moments later, the slow-moving convoy encountered DFD pumper number six. Its crew members stood behind it with coffee cups in hand. Some nodded; others offered solemn fist-pumps. Next in line were the two EMS vehicles with crew inside, each flashing the emergency lights.

"Wish I hadn't chugged that coffee..." Vertesi said.

MacNeice noticed that the tank and van were accelerating as they approached the intersection of Cascade and Lake.

Washburn's voice was calm and brief: "Tuck it up, Mac."

MacNeice was quick to close the gap, but when the tank and van turned left on Cascade, they were listing so dramatically he eased off the accelerator, concerned that one or the other would flip over. Neither did; in fact, they'd no sooner stabilized than they made a hard right into Abbey's driveway.

The armoured van's wedge exploded the electrified gate, sending sections of it skidding across the asphalt as a blinding ripple of sparks raced harmlessly along what remained of the fence. The tank slowed as Washburn jumped free, before accelerating toward the three-storey building. The van swung right and came to an abrupt stop outside the front office door.

MacNeice manoeuvred the Chevy to block the driveway. Using the Chevy as a shield, they waited, their three helmets lined up like turtles on the vehicle's roof.

Through their earpieces, they heard Washburn command, "First position—go-go-go," his voice as calm as it was urgent. The tank and van teams disembarked and lined up quickly along the building's outer wall, each with an assault rifle, behind two officers with battering rams. "Alpha, Delta, check those vehicles on the west side."

"Roger that."

In the pre-dawn light—even with an additional spill from the building's night lighting—the teams were little more than fast-moving phantoms. The security alarm was triggered the moment both doors were breached. As the teams filed inside, Washburn turned to his right. "Romeo— kill that alarm."

Seconds later all was quiet, save for the sound of tractor-trailers hauling freight along the nearby highway.

"Office—clear. Landline dead, boss."

"Copy that." Washburn found the master switch and turned on the fluorescent overheads. The office, truck bays, and factory blinked hesitatingly to life, as if they weren't sure it was a good idea to do so.

"This is Charlie; looks like the laundry room . . . going in."

"Mike, cover Charlie."

"Roger, I'm on it."

"Clear those truck bays—be thorough, now." Washburn turned his attention to the office filing cabinets and was surprised to find them unlocked. He flipped randomly through folders in several of the drawers and scanned the paperwork left on the desk before whispering, "Mac, a quick peek— front office looks cleaning-biz legit."

"Oscar; we got movement, boss . . . above and below."

"Below?"

"Yeah, boss, behind a steel door . . . Permission to ram?"

"Negative. Stand by; I'm coming through."

"Copy."

Washburn moved quickly along the truck bays, where racks of clothing on hangers stood near bulging canvas slings on dollies, each with marked-up tags. Papa was checking the shipper's office beside the third bay.

"Romeo here; all bays clear, boss."

"Copy."

"Papa here; shipper's office, clear."

From this point on, the back-and-forth chatter came fast and without names. "Washrooms clear." "Supply room clear." "Steel door ahead, boss." "Boss, there's more movement."

"Identify."

"This is Oscar; something's being dragged across the floor . . . something heavy."

"Oscar, which floor?"

"Could be the second or third—can't tell, boss."

"Update me, Charlie."

"Huge space . . . sewing machines at the south end, laundry room full of equipment . . . then dry-cleaning workstations."

"Mike, second that."

Suddenly the lights went out. "NVG. NVG. Report if you turned out the lights." What followed was a ripple of rapid overlapping voices: "Negative". . ."Negative". . ."Negative."

Another staticky pause. Aziz looked over at MacNeice. "Night-vision goggles," he said.

"Bloody tense stuff," Aziz said.

"Someone's playing with their heads," Vertesi said under his breath.

"Cleaning supply room clear."

"Oscar here; someone's on a cellphone above us."

"Bravo here, Wash; we got a steel door between us and the tank crew."

"Ram it," Washburn said, as Charlie and Mike emerged from the dry-cleaning room.

"Roger that."

Over the line the detectives could hear the deafening sound of a battering ram. MacNeice and Aziz winced. "It's getting real," Vertesi said, laying the shotgun on the Chevy's roof. "Scout's motto: be prepared."

When the banging stopped, the door was still intact. Oscar hammered the door with the butt of his weapon. "Hang back, Bravo; we'll take it from our side."

Washburn covered his ears against the noise. "Alpha, Delta—those vehicles clear?"

"Delta; van engine compartments and the Lincoln's hood are cold and dewy; listened for sounds inside—negative. Continental's windows are blacked out; windshield fogged. Need a stethoscope to know for sure, Wash."

"Copy. Mac, you heard that—stay alert." Washburn let his comment dangle before adding, "Alpha, Delta—get eyes on the rear of the building."

"Roger; on our way."

MacNeice turned to Aziz and Vertesi. "If you see a white Lincoln Continental heading our way, focus your fire on the grille—not the body, not the windshield or wheels. If we can't stop it, wait till he commits to a turn. He'll likely go left to Lake Avenue; the other way's a dead end. Whichever he chooses, run in the opposite direction."

Washburn checked his watch—elapsed time, nine and a half minutes. "We're through," Bravo said, shoving the damaged door aside with a loud metallic squawk.

"Delta; nothing behind the building; small windows; a hallway, stairwell—whoa, wait a minute."

"Alpha; we got lights on. Do you copy? Lights are on."

"Copy. No basement door or windows?"

"No sign of a basement, boss."

"Not exactly code . . ." an unidentified voice added.

"Windows on east and west sides, covered with black film—but somebody's home. Lights are on, all floors. Is that us?"

"Negative." Washburn looked up at the ceiling—no heating or air-conditioning vents. They were standing in a dead space. "Alpha, Delta: best you can, cover that roof."

"Roger."

Washburn ordered everyone to stop. The lobby had steel

doors on three sides—two had been blown and the last was
the entrance to the three-storey block. As their gear stopped
rustling, he heard the sound squirrels make when they're
moving inside a wall. Washburn knelt and laid a gloved hand
flat on the floor. Though it was faint, he could feel a vibra-
tion like steel wheels crossing concrete.

"Delta; boss, we got thick black smoke coming from the
chimney—"

"Roger that. Ram that door now! First shot is theirs. After
that, engage, engage." Washburn paused. "Tank crew—
Oscar, Tango, Victor, Lima—hit the basement. Once neutralized, fall in line above; understood?"

Everyone responded affirmatively. "Delta, Alpha, on my
call, send smoke through those windows, then come on the
hurry up."

"Roger that."

"This is Alpha. Wash, weird chem smell's coming from
the chimney."

"Thanks for the heads-up. Gas masks on. Do we still
have lights inside?"

"Affirmative."

"Soon as the door blows, flip your NVGS."

[94]

WHEN NO ONE WAS SPEAKING, THEIR EARPIECES BUZZED WITH static. MacNeice covered his free ear to block the calls of passing shore birds; it was like listening through a sound fog.

He needn't have worried. Seconds later, all hell broke loose.

They heard Washburn's commanding baritone call: "Police. Put down your weapons and come —" What followed sounded like he was in a battle on four levels; the humble little earpieces clearly distinguished incoming from outgoing fire. Seconds passed without a report, then the chatter kicked up.

"This is Oscar. Four on the basement floor, one wounded."

"Charlie — go right, go right."

"Behind that wall—fire through it. Wait—No, don't do that...Shit."

"He's on the move, Bravo—coming your way."

"Bravo here, eyes on..."

"Heads up, Papa—"

"This is Mike; grenade, third floor north; fire in the hole..."
WHUMP!

The explosion rang in the earpieces, followed by several rapid pops from an incoming automatic weapon.

"Fuck. Papa's down, Papa's down! Romeo here; shooter eliminated." Papa wasn't wailing, but he let out a stream of profanity, each burst ending in "fuck."

"This is Wash. Secure the area. Cut Papa's comm feed."

For the detectives it was like standing in the middle of a gun battle without being shot at. With sunlight starting to streak between the shadows of a late-August morning, the setting couldn't have been stranger.

"Alpha, Delta, smoke those windows now."

"This is Victor; second floor east; five women against the wall—non-combatants—do not shoot."

"Don't shoot—copy."

"Someone's on the stairs. Identify."

"That's me, Lima."

"Romeo; they were burning some kinda drug, Wash, lots of it."

"Tango; centipede ties on four in basement, one wounded. I'm coming up; hold fire."

"Delta; smoke rounds bounced off, zero penetration, zero penetration—windows are intact."

"Alpha here; boss, Lincoln just started up; it's gonna be on the move."

"This is Wash. MacNeice, ready up. The Continental is coming."

They heard it before they saw it. The smoke bombs that had ricocheted off the windows produced a thick cloud that was now rolling across the parking lot. Alpha and Delta fired into the Mark V — to no effect. It emerged from the smoke, heading slowly toward the entrance. Tactical soon stopped firing, concerned that strays would hit the detectives. "Alpha; boss, no effect from our rounds; vehicle moving to the gate."

"Understood. Mac? Heads up now."

MacNeice took a deep breath and leaned on the Chevy's roof. "Hold fire till it's closer to the gate."

The Continental stopped ten yards shy of the gate, beyond which was the Chevy. The driver, who was barely visible behind the windshield, revved the engine several times. It thundered and rocked like a beast about to charge.

"How many rounds in that shotgun, Michael?"

"Five, boss."

"The moment that thing moves, unload on the grille."

"This is Victor. First floor secure."

"Oscar; second floor, two left, playing whack-a-mole. Sending stun grenade —"

Bang! The detectives flinched.

"This is Wash. Alpha, Delta, how many in that vehicle?"

"Alpha; can't tell. Musta been on the floor or in the trunk."

"Delta here; it took fifteen or twenty rounds. Might as well have been shooting peas through a straw."

"This is Wash. Mac, no heroics. You and your people get out of the way of that thing."

"Charlie; second floor secure. Two down."

"Tango; active shooter in that office. Wait for me."

"Roger, Charlie" There was a rapid series of shots, followed by silence. "Neutralized."

Aziz was peering along the firing line from her weapon to the Continental. "If I have a vote, Mac, I'm with Washburn."

"Thing looks supernatural, in a Sci-Fi kinda way," Vertesi added.

"Wash here. Report in. Repeat, give status."

"Basement, secure."

"First floor, secure."

"Second . . . now secure."

"Third, secure."

"Papa's stable; tourniquet on. Need medics."

"Wash here. Alpha, Delta, into the tank pronto-pronto. Take that goddamn automobile out. Go in hot — copy that?"

"Copy. Hot we got."

MacNeice saw them sprinting to the armoured van, but before they were inside, they'd disappeared behind a cloud of smoke.

For a longer runway, the tank went to the far end of the lot. They heard it swing about, but the complaints of its massive wheels was soon overtaken by the sustained howl of its unleashed engine. Unlike the Mark V, this sound wasn't for show. This beast was on the move, and in seconds it would blast free of the smoke. The driver in the Continental must have heard it too — because the machine with the wide-mouth grille came to life.

"Michael, steady now . . ."

"Delta to detectives — coming fast and hard. GET OUT NOW!"

The tank emerged from the fog like a runaway train with a black iron cowcatcher. The Continental's driver must have seen it fill his rear-view mirror; he'd already floored the accelerator, but he was achieving little more than burning rubber. For all its security and protection—and its horse-power—it was just too heavy to sprint.

As the black machine closed in, MacNeice screamed, "Run—left!" He pulled Aziz with him; Vertesi ran, still aiming at the Continental's grille.

The tank met the Mark V's tail with such deafening force that the iron wedge cut straight through to the front seats. Whether it was simply mass plus velocity plus impact or the car's vaunted armour plating had been oversold, the car shuddered forward and down the driveway.

In an act of what MacNeice later referred to as "youth-ful exuberance," Vertesi rushed into the Mark V's path. He screamed something only he could hear, levelled the shot-gun, and fired two quick rounds into that shark-mouth grille before jumping out of the way. A geyser erupted from the grille as the tons of metal, buckling and grinding, thundered past him and slammed into the Chevy. The tank plowed the whole twisted mess across Cascade in an enormous fusion of black, white, and blue mangled steel.

"Delta, Alpha, neutralize that driver." Seconds later, the pair were out of the tank and pointing assault rifles at the driver's door.

Wide-eyed, Delta looked back at the tank, his face betraying the joy of the moment. "Well, that was—"

"Historic fubar!" Alpha said. "Outstanding."

Washburn approached with three more of his team. The Mark V was bleeding fuel. Smoking and steaming, it wore the buckled Chevy like a hood ornament. The driver wouldn't, or couldn't, open the door.

Washburn walked alongside the Continental and tapped the roof with his .45. "If you can hear me, the show's over. Best come out now."

Beyond the hissing of its blasted radiator and the crackle of overheated metal and the smell of gasoline on asphalt, of burning oil and rubber, the oddest sensory element MacNeice noticed was the insistent call of a nearby hawk.

Leaning casually against the rear door, Washburn might have been waiting for a shake and burger. He waited another ten seconds before the door cracked open an inch or so, and Delta and Alpha wrenched it the rest of the way.

Slim was slumped sideways in the seat, his head was tilted awkwardly; Washburn recognized immediately what had happened. "How fast were you going, Delta?"

"On contact, fifty-six miles per hour..."

Laughter, hoots, and hollers erupted in everyone's earpieces. Washburn tapped the roof with his palm. "This is a vintage automobile, son, from a time before they invented headrests. Our friend here has whiplash."

Seconds later, the ambulances and DFD's pumper came to a stop beside the wreckage. Papa walked out on his own and paused to marvel at the automotive wreckage before he was led away by the paramedics.

When the driver finally emerged, he was in a neck brace and had a cop under each arm. The first person he spoke to was MacNeice. "You like Mark V, mister? You can buy now cheap, yeah."

Washburn clamped a paw on Delta's shoulder as more

EMS crews arrived. "Extract that tank from this vehicle to let these folks through."

Delta glanced at the tank. "Assuming she'll let it go; she's pretty attached..."

[95]

"**M**AC, BEFORE WE GO INSIDE, YOU AND YOUR PEOPLE JOIN ME IN the van.**"** Washburn sat behind the wheel; Aziz and Vertesi climbed in the back, MacNeice in the front.

Looking through the rear-view, Washburn said, "DI Vertesi, you're the kid who's used to scoring the game-winning touchdown; I understand that." He turned around to look at him directly. "But you're not a kid. And I don't tolerate behaviour like that on my watch. Never again. Understood?"

"Yes, Sergeant — it won't happen again."

MacNeice could hear in Vertesi's voice that he'd gotten the message. Turning to Washburn, he asked, "You've heard from Burlington?"

"Yessir. DS Swetsky's down. He's probably at DHG by

now; para thinks he may have had a heart attack—he was stable when they left the scene."

The colour drained from MacNeice's face. Behind them, the tank was bucking violently to free itself of the Mark V. When it did, Delta reversed in a slow arc and parked on the lot's west side. His curved path was strewn with Continental minutiae and essential debris.

MacNeice asked, "When did you get the call?"

"Just as things went quiet here. The estate raid was different—the old man surrendered almost immediately, with his wife beside him."

"The barn and the house?"

"That's where things got thorny. Shots fired, no one hit. When Britt's team rushed the building, six individuals blew out the back door and ran like mice in every direction. Swets spotted a fella doing an end run for the street—he took off after him."

"Bad idea. John's not built for a foot race," MacNeice said.

"Actually, Britt said he was gaining on the kid when he went down."

"Maracle?"

"He followed our team into the barn, so he missed the great escape. But Reisman's chopper came in handy. Two of those boys musta been sprinters, 'cause in no time they were half a mile away, beating through gardens and hedges until the flight sergeant guided OPP cruisers to corner them."

"So it was a success?" Vertesi asked.

"Too soon for the parade, but sure as shit, nobody runs like that for no reason"—Washburn nodded at his team, who were lining up the remaining suspects—"or fight the way these folks did. That house out in Burlington was loaded

with computer work-stations. Britt thinks it's mission control for the whole network."

"Any word from Montreal or Niagara Falls?" Aziz asked.

"Not yet."

The forensics team, which had only just finished at
Riviera, pulled into the lot, positioning their vehicles near
the three-storey building.

"If you want a look-see, now's the time. We've got a van
coming for the women. The team's keeping them separate
from these fellas."

They were met by the forensics team leader. "There's
a box of gloves and footwear for you..." He stood at ease,
making it clear that it wasn't a choice. Watching Washburn
wrench the baggy little booties over his combat boots was
worth a day at the dairy.

Inside, what immediately struck MacNeice was the
smell—an acrid toxic stew. It hit his senses so hard he
could taste it. Sharper than smoke, sulphur, or cordite, it
was almost metallic... and bitter.

Washburn explained. "Smell's interesting; it's a combination of burning plastic bags and little glow-in-the-dark
tablets they called Chernopills. Add to that the weapons
fired from both sides, our stun grenades... The place
also has a sprinkler system that either failed or has been
disabled."

"How many injured?"

"Four; one deceased. Another four were in the basement—non-combatants doing the burning. The young
women were upstairs. We'll bring them out once the gun-
men have been taken away."

"What were the women doing here?" Aziz asked.

"None of them speak English well, but one said she's an entertainer."

"Maybe they're the yacht bunnies," MacNeice added.

"The second floor has bedrooms?" Aziz wasn't interested in euphemisms.

"Third floor has six bedrooms with bathrooms and a communal kitchen. The second has two apartments and a red velvet meet-and-greet room—featuring a giant jar of Chernopills. First floor's all offices." When Aziz appeared surprised, Washburn shrugged. "Abbey's cleaning business seems legit."

MacNeice's cellphone rang. "Sergeant Steiner, sir; I'm outside."

Though he had no idea why Steiner was there, MacNeice welcomed a reason to leave the building; Aziz followed him out. Abatstvo's men were cuffed and filing into a large van with blacked-out windows, Steiner standing off to one side. He came forward when he saw MacNeice.

"What is it, Sergeant?" MacNeice asked, removing his booties and gloves.

"We've got a body you should see, sir."

"Another body...?"

"Out in Lincoln, in that old orchard. I was told that your vehicle wouldn't be going anywhere, so I came down to collect you—it's not far."

"Did you ID the remains?"

"Looks like Daintry. Dropped off sometime last night."

"Lead the way, Sergeant." Aziz and MacNeice exchanged glances as they walked toward the gate. "Was he found by Doctor Thomas's people?"

"No, sir; those remains were taken out to the university yesterday. Neighbour's dog found him."

"What time?"

"Just after four thirty this morning..."

"The neighbour didn't see anyone—or a vehicle?"

"No, sir..."

Before they headed out, MacNeice went to retrieve what he could from the Chevy. The impact had snapped both axles; the off side of the car was resting on wheels that now looked like large rubber coasters. There was no need to open the trunk; its lid was torqued and buckled open. Inside, his battered briefcase and muddy boots lay in a jumble of latex gloves, booties—and an umbrella that had sprung open on impact.

The passenger door took some time, but with help from one of the cops they wrenched it open. From the glove compartment, he retrieved his binoculars, CDs, a copy of e.e. cummings collected poems, and *Birds of North America*—from which he had identified thirty-something birds in the field, an admittedly paltry number. Seeing it reminded him to add the northern goshawk. He stuffed it all in his briefcase and left the boots, umbrella, gloves, and booties.

FOR A FEW miles they didn't talk, not about the events at Abbey or the body they were about to see. MacNeice and Aziz turned their heads as they passed the road leading up to the stone cottage.

"Sir, do you still have Jack?" Steiner asked.

"No. He's out in BC with Dr. Moore's family."

"I'll never forget that day..."

"No..." MacNeice's voice trailed off; he didn't know what else to say. Losing Jack had left an ache too tender to touch.

His cellphone ring was a welcome interruption. "Talk to me, Charlie."

"It wasn't a heart attack. Swets had a severe case of acid reflux. I'm at the DGH. He's okay."

"What was the cause?"

"Doc says six inches of kielbasa and John's version of brewed coffee at four a.m." Maracle laughed. "And after that breakfast of champions, chasing a guy half his age."

"Once a cast-iron constitution..."

"That it was, sir. I also saw Lise. She's itching to get out; asked about Williams. So I called Toronto Western and got through to Montile. He's gonna be in overnight; they want to do another MRI of his head and more X-rays of his wrist. He's in a hard cast but ready to return for desk work. He's already requested the wrist replacement."

[96]

NEARING THE ORCHARD, MACNEICE WAS SURPRISED TO SEE THE pathologist's van. "Dr. Richardson's here?"

Steiner nodded. "Got here just as I was leaving to find you. She was out in Grimsby for a boater-floater fished out of the water."

Richardson stood at the escarpment's edge, looking out at the lake, an updraft gently tugging at the linen duster she wore as a field coat.

The detectives paused at the edge of the former orchard as Steiner went off to talk with the regionals.

"It's sad, being back here . . ." Aziz said.

"You know . . . it used to be *He had it coming.*"

"Now you can't allow yourself the thought?"

"Not even close."

They made their way through the now-familiar maze of divots, as foreign-looking in the morning sun as an octopus on the deck of a trawler. They passed between the massive split oak and the pile of charred fruit trees where Rodney Conroy had been found.

MacNeice spotted Daintry propped up against the oak's large, snaggy root pillow near the precipice.

"Mac, Aziz, before we begin, join me here." Richardson turned back to the panorama and added, "That chap behind us was set down—alive, dying, or dead—to enjoy this view. He, or the one who left him, understood important things like life, I reckon. How many bodies have we seen together, Mac? Dozens—more? In tawdry rooms, in rat-tracked alleys, thawing out in Cootes, buried beneath concrete...?"

"Too many, Mary."

"Quite so. You agree, Detective Aziz. You needn't answer—I can feel it." Richardson smiled at the lake in the distance, or perhaps at the farmland and vineyards below. "Well, then, to our task..."

They turned together to examine Taylor Barrow Daintry, whose arms were relaxed and open beside him, his hands palms up as if to catch the morning dew. His legs were splayed out before him—left to eleven, right to one—and his head rested on the tree's still-tender roots, delicate enough to suggest they were veins.

Daintry's face was sublimely peaceful, the colour and smoothness of porcelain; his eyes were slightly open, with lips parted as if he were about to whisper someone's name. Below his shoulders, his white T-shirt was soaked in blood the colour and viscosity of cherry syrup. It had stained his blue suit pants right down to his once-white Stan Smiths.

"When I arrived, he looked like he'd been glossed by a fine mist..." Mary extended a branch she'd been using as a walking stick to ease Daintry's jacket open. "Small-calibre wound, though obviously effective. The position of it suggests this young man didn't have a chance. He'd have bled out, whether under the lights of an emergency room or out here gazing at the lake."

MacNeice noticed the shoulder holsters and pearl-grip pistols—both bloodied—and was relieved they hadn't been used on Williams or Bichet. Richardson released the stick and looked at the detectives.

"I take it we're still actively pursuing his running mate?" she asked.

"Yes," MacNeice said. Though he didn't really believe having a mug shot on board every cruiser within five hundred miles qualified as "active pursuit." They were left waiting for Wright's next move, and it didn't help that he was on his own—no more Five and Dime.

"I won't accomplish much out here beyond external examination of that wound—so if you'd like to accompany me to the van, I'll get my bag and you can leave."

"Sounds good, Mary. It's been a long morning and it's not yet ten." He glanced over at the old oak's root ball and wondered if the gorget was once again resting under Jeremiah Stokes's chin. He also wondered if Lester Wright believed that his partner's spirit and the spirits of the oak and that old warrior were mingling now at the escarpment's edge.

Back at the road, MacNeice asked Steiner to give them a lift.

"Certainly, sir. To Cascade or Division One?"

"Neither... On the way down Highway 20 there's

a narrow lane on the west side. You can drop us there."
MacNeice could feel Fiza's eyes on him; he imagined her
discreet smile.

Steiner did a slow U-turn and Aziz looked off toward the
lake. It was the ideal setting for a last breath.

As they passed the cops stringing up DO NOT CROSS tape,
MacNeice mused aloud. "A vehicle moved through here last
night, Sergeant. It's a lonely road; the sound of an approaching car might've drawn someone to the window. Have these
men conduct another door-knock—from Highway 20 to
the other end."

"Will do, sir. I'll go with them."

Halfway down Highway 20, MacNeice pointed out the
cottage lane. Steiner switched on his grille and dome lights,
waited for the northbound traffic to clear, and swung about.
"Want me to take you up, sir?"

"No, this is perfect; a walk will do us good. Thanks for
the lift, Sergeant." MacNeice got out, holding his beat-up
briefcase, and opened the rear door for Aziz. Steiner turned
off his emergency lights and headed back up the Mountain.

[97]

EVERYTHING CHANGES THE MOMENT YOU ENTER A FOREST IN August. Fifty feet in, sounds outside soften and fade. The light, like the temperature, is cool. August air lacks the freshness of spring. And yet, the earth releases its reserves of moisture to let you know it'll survive.

They walked on quietly side by side, dodging potholes, taking in the world around them. MacNeice felt Aziz relaxing into a trail walker's pace, one that comes naturally if you let it. She was looking at the canopy above—either seeking signs of birds or just marvelling at the myriad variations of green. She paused and pointed to a cluster of fat-faced mushrooms poking out of the ground cover. Further on, she stopped to study a large patch of moss surrounding a near-perfect circle of stone that resembled an old monk's tonsure.

MacNeice spoke tentatively at first. "When I was a kid, I'd walk with Silver—my dad's dog—through the forests of Georgian Bay. One summer, I had a project—I called it a secret, only because I was too embarrassed to tell anyone."

"Tell me..."

"I loved watching Silver smell everything—nothing escaped him. So I brought a pencil, a notebook, and a government tree-identification chart... and together we went into a forest quite different from this one. My goal was to smell every species—spruce, cedar, hemlock, maple and oak, birch and aspen. I'd step right up to each tree and take a deep breath. I kept that notebook for years"—he shook his head at the thought—"certain that one day it would come in handy."

"And?" she asked.

"Well, I learned that every tree smells different. Sometimes dramatically, but mostly it's so subtle I couldn't find the words to describe it. To make up for that, I sketched all the bark patterns..."

At a steep turn, he took her hand to help her over a bumpy stretch that Streets and Sanitation had repaired only a year before. Once beyond it, he let go—and immediately regretted it. The road ahead resembled a long arcade under the interlocking branches overhead. It ended in a small clearing where the sun fell, warm and uninterrupted.

Something moved off to the right, scurrying out of sight into the ground cover. Moments later and a few feet away, a shy salamander retreated from a rock. Chickadees flitted about on all sides, anticipating the possibility of food. A shiver of a breeze shook the poplar leaves, and farther off, a woodpecker was tapping.

"Can you hear that above us?" he asked.

"Yes. One branch is rubbing against another?"

"My father would say that trees have family quarrels. Everything listens and sees, only asking that we do the same."

A few turns later, they arrived at the plateau. Nestled off to the left was his stone cottage.

He opened the door, put down his briefcase, and asked, "Can I make you breakfast?"

"You actually do breakfast?" she asked doubtfully.

"When I can...I'm spoiled by Cristiana, my housekeeper, who comes up from Secord twice a week to make sense of this place. As I've never kept much in the fridge, she began shopping for me. She was here yesterday; I've got heirloom tomatoes, fresh eggs, breakfast sausages, toast...and coffee from Clappison Corners."

"Almost a full English breakfast—lovely."

"Why don't you sit outside and get reacquainted with my feathered and furry friends. I'll make a cappuccino—and put in a call for a replacement car."

THEIR CONVERSATION FOCUSED on birds, breakfast, and the ancient escarpment. It was a preoccupation for MacNeice, something he considered to be fundamental and primordial. "It's a humbling reminder of the passage of time, Fiz... that even if you live to be a hundred, you're doing so in the shadow of half a billion years."

"A somewhat daunting thought..."

"Not to me; I stand in awe of it. Occasionally I'll rest a hand on its face. There's something, an immutable energy..." MacNeice was struggling to find the words when his phone interrupted him.

"Heads up, boss." It was Vertesi, speaking in a whisper. "Wallace came to Cascade for a media scrum; he's looking for you."

"Anything else I should know?"

"No, it's all good. Gotta go—"

Aziz was leaning back in her chair. She'd arranged a line of crumbs on the edge of her plate, waiting for a bird with the courage to collect them. "I could get used to this..." She smiled. "I mean, breakfast in a forest."

"I know what you meant." He handed her a jar. "For your toast—direct from Paris."

She read the label. "*Fraises des bois*—strawberries of the forest. Oh my."

A chickadee arrived; tilting its head this way and that, it hopped closer to the plate.

When Aziz opened the jar, the bird retreated—but not for long. She'd just finished spreading jam on her toast when her phone rang. "Bonjour, Jean-Pierre..."

MacNeice was happy to listen. Even if he couldn't catch everything, it reminded him of the Café Laurent and "My Funny Valentine." But his reverie was cut short when his cell rang. "MacNeice..."

"You're AWOL, Detective." Wallace tried to sound angry, but it was clear that he wasn't. "I'm down at Cascade—it'll take time before we know the full extent of Abatstvo's enterprise, but we've got enough to charge him with racketeering, drug dealing, human trafficking, and ordering Garrick's kidnapping. Burlington's the family bank and home to his muscle—they're all here illegally, with overstayed visitor visas."

"Aziz is on the phone to Detective Girone in Montreal—have you heard anything from them?"

"Partials; all good. Niagara had a closer link to Dundurn than Montreal. Again, it's early, but we do know Niagara was running an illegal casino—strictly for American clients. In Dundurn they offered 'gymnastic entertainment' in the form of young girls and boys on cruises around the lake."

"And the drugs?"

"Abbey developed Chernopill as a next-generation ecstasy. Their hype line is that it's 'guaranteed radioactive'. The sons are the drivers of that one. Look, I was expecting we'd find skeletons in Abbey's closets—and that may be yet to come—but arresting them for what we do know is a good start, and taking the lead on this is a first for Dundurn."

"Forensics might also find a trail linking Abatstvo and Jeremy Slater to Clarence Blow for the homicides..."

"True...Anyway, Mac, I just called to congratulate you and your team, and pass on the mayor's acknowledgement as well...Where the hell are you? I can hear Aziz and birds."

"Daintry's dead, sir. We went out to confirm his identity. We're at my house, waiting for my replacement unit. Mine was—"

"Yeah, I saw your vehicle. Okay, later..."

MacNeice wondered how Abatstvo had managed to run a diverse criminal enterprise in three cities without being charged for one of their several sins. If Chernopills had already hit the illicit market, how had they escaped the attention of drug squads or public health officials?

His phone rang again; it was Sergeant Evanson from Missing Persons. "Sir, we may have an ID on your forest

John Doe. Martin Allen Jessop, forty-seven, from Allentown, Pennsylvania. Reported missing by his wife two days after our forest killings. Jessop owns three Ford dealerships — Allentown, Harrisburg, and Trenton. He told his wife he was going to Ford headquarters in Dearborn for their new product meetings."

"And that wasn't true . . ." MacNeice lifted his glass of water and, without thinking, he looked for the ripples Venganza had said would be there — and they were. He set the glass down without a sip.

"Correct . . . According to Ford and to Jessop's secretary, no such meetings were scheduled. And while his business was successful — regional sales leader for the last five years — he was heavily in debt. Local cops and the FBI think he emptied the till and left the state, maybe the country. I've downloaded publicity photos of him and have requested DNA samples — that's it for now, sir."

A few minutes passed, and two house sparrows that had been watching nearby came to join the chickadee. With the arrival of another chickadee, the race was on; the birds began frantically driving their beaks into the crumbs.

"Greedy little buggers, no?" Aziz said, looking over at MacNeice.

He smiled, gave a slight shrug, and flicked a small wedge of crust off the plate toward a newly arrived sparrow. "Fiza, I want to be honest with you . . ." He laughed awkwardly to cover taking a deep breath. "I want tonight to make up for the first night we would have spent together in Paris."

Aziz reached for her own glass of water. She drank and set it down so softly the birds didn't flinch.

"If you're uncomfortable, you can stop me anytime —"

"No, go on..." A smile flickered nervously across her lips.

"At the end of my stay in Paris, I dreamt about you..."

"Working a case?" Then she seemed embarrassed by her attempt to diminish the electric charge of the moment. "I'm sorry..."

"Actually, you were singing."

"Ah, a fictional dream... Sorry again."

"It was as real as you are right now. Though fictional—as all dreams may be—it continues to haunt me."

"Go on..."

"So much rides on what I say next, and even if—" MacNeice snapped his head around. Two vehicles were straining up the mountain lane. "Wait here; don't move."

Once inside, he released the strap on his weapon and stepped out the front door. He waited with his hand on the grip for the first one to turn the last corner. What appeared was a midnight-blue heavy Chevy, followed by a DPD cruiser. He looped the strap over his weapon and waved.

A young man from the DPDS fleet pound got out. "Apologies for the interruption, sir."

"No problem, thanks for bringing it so quickly."

"Well, I got to see it do hill climbing..." He handed MacNeice the keys and added, "Boss managed to send you one with a CD player—I haven't seen one of those in years."

"I'm old-school."

"Is there a way out if we keep climbing up?"

"Sorry, there's no up up there. You'll have to swing about and head down."

He watched the cruiser turn around and waddle back down with its brake lights on, then went inside. Aziz was in the kitchen rinsing dishes. "Other than a few crumbs, the table's clear..." She dried her hands on the dishtowel. "I'm sorry we were interrupted..."

"Yeah, I was just getting to the good part."

"And I do want to hear it — *tonight*. Now, though, I suspect we're both more than a bit distracted, and I want to debrief you on that call from Girone."

"Understood. I want to be clear though, Fiz — this is about romance."

A wide smile took over her face; she stood on her toes and kissed him on the cheek. "But if we stay here much longer, I'll be in your bed — and then where will we be?"

"In bed, together."

[EPILOGUE]

FIFTH IN LINE BEHIND FOUR SUVS WAS THE PERFECT POSITION. IT allowed him to study the US Customs agent's body language and temperament. Was he jacked up on caffeine? *Doesn't appear to be.* Was he butt-tired after a long shift? *Could be.* That's why he had arrived a half-hour before shift change. Was the agent a mean spirit, determined to take out his resentment on the powerless arriving at his window? *Hard to tell.* Did he appear affable with those in the Canadian vehicle directly ahead? *No.* He was doing a relaxed version of standard procedure—keeping an eye peeled for the next vehicle in line.

The burly, ginger-haired agent studied the five-year-old Dodge Charger, noting the ATL COMPANY 11 sticker on its windshield and Atlanta Fire Rescue plate below. *Good eyes*, the driver thought. He opened all the windows to the

eighty-degree heat to make it easier to scan the interior—
and to suggest he had nothing to hide.

Hanging against the window behind him was his turn-
out coat, his name embossed in fluorescent letters across
the shoulders. Easing up to the window, the driver handed
his passport over with a toothy smile. "Good day, officer.
How're y'all doing?"

"Could use a good AC." He opened the passport, looked
down at the driver, then scanned it into the computer.
"What've you been doing in Canada, Malcolm? I see your
firefighter coat; you been fighting fires up there?"

"Not exactly." Malcolm chuckled. "I was asked to test a
new chem-fire retardant . . . I'm the Atlanta Fire and Georgia
Fire Academy chemical specialist."

"Huh . . . Did it work?" the agent asked, passing an eye
over the car's interior.

"Close. It's not there yet, but it could be a game changer."

"Good to hear. You bringing anything in that I should
know about?"

"No, sir. It was a wall-to-wall fire detail. Now I'm just
happy to be headin' home."

"Back down the I-75 . . ."

"Tried and true."

The agent handed his passport back. "Well, you drive
safe now, and thank you for your service." He tapped the
car's roof, his eyes already shifted to the pickup next in line.

Malcolm—Lester Wright—pulled away slowly. An hour
later, he left the I-75 to head west on America's longest highway—the I-90 to Seattle.

Eighty miles on, he took an exit at random, stopping at a
strip mall for a burger and fries. When he'd finished, Lester

dropped his garbage in a bin, then sat behind the wheel of the Charger watching a young family at a picnic table. They looked happy, laughing together as if they'd somehow escaped all the life-defining damage that had altered the lives of almost everyone he'd ever known.

He sighed, opened the glove compartment, and pulled out a US Postal Service pre-stamped padded envelope. He held it reverently, as if it contained some magical power — as if, in fact, it was alive. A USPS mailbox stood outside the drug store next to the McDonald's. But sealing the envelope seemed so final — Lester wanted to read the letter one last time.

He flipped over the faded Dundurn Blues Society poster and scanned the handwritten note. The top half was difficult to read through the dried blood smudged on the page, now more brown than red, but also because of the shaky hand that had written it . . .

Wright needed to see it — he needed to read it — one last time.

> *My dear Dolores . . . I can't make it home to you after all. I want you to know I love you and wish you are by my side at this here time. Lester took good care of me to the end. He's gonna send all my earnings for the work I done. Goodbye — I love you. Taylor*

> *Dolores —*
> *It's me, Lester.*
> *I left Taylor in a peaceful place. He was a fine and loyal man who thought of you all the time. Enclosed you'll find his passport in the name of Frank James Cooper (the real name of his favourite actor, Gary Cooper).*

As the funds are in an offshore account, I've enclosed Frank Cooper's bank cards, social security, passwords, and signature—all you'll need to retrieve the money.

It would make him very proud if you used a portion of it to buy a property in Alberta, up in Canada. When we worked there, Taylor saw a ranch he thought would be perfect for you. He asked me to include a listing for the property—also enclosed. I happen to know it's still for sale.

When we were up there, Taylor learned a song, one he sang over and over—he really wasn't hard to listen to. He always said he'd sing it to you. I suppose you could use Youtube to find it. It's called "Four Strong Winds."

Taylor was a true friend, Dolores, but, like me, a sinner.

God bless him, and you.

Lester Wright

[ACKNOWLEDGEMENTS]

I DON'T KNOW where these stories come from, but I do know how many disciplines and people I rely upon to help me bring them to life. To each of them, I owe a great debt.

First among them is my partner, Shirley Blumberg Thornley, my first reader. Without her support, encouragement, and knowledge of my principal characters—I'd be lost. Her belief in me makes me a very lucky man.

Middlemen wouldn't have happened without the support of House of Anansi's Leigh Nash and Douglas Richmond. I am truly grateful to Leigh for her leadership, and for her editing of this book. Special thanks to Jenny McWha!

Scott and Krystyne Griffin are champions in the publishing world—and, fortunately for me, of these MacNeice

Mysteries. Thank you for your commitment to poetry and independent publishing in Canada.

I'd also like to acknowledge Bruce Westwood, Chris Casuccio, and Michael Levine of Westwood Creative Artists for their continued support.

While these books are a works of fiction, I rely on truth to tell the tale. Doctors John Bienenstock, Dody Bienenstock, Gerry O'Leary, Karel O'Brien, and Rae Lake have answered all my questions about science, psychiatry, and medicine.

I wish for every living soul a champion like Peter Herrndorf (1940–2023). Canada has lost a giant with his passing. I've lost a friend, mentor, and enthusiast of all things MacNeice.

Roberto Occhipinti, Roman Borys, and the late, great Andy Dawes have added significantly to my appreciation of music, and to MacNeice's playlist.

John Michaluk's aphorisms inform my "true north." Bill Gordon and John Seliwoniuk help keep my passion for Hamilton alive. Special thanks to Professor David Sandomierski.

H Is for Hawk is a book I've yet to read. But, after listening to an interview with its author, Helen MacDonald, I was inspired to write the scene in the forest. Thankfully, Stephen Lechniak provided more insights into the magnificent, and very testy, northern goshawk.

And finally, my thanks go to Marsh, Ian, Chuck, and their families, for being there when I need love, laughter, and the innocence of grandchildren.

Murphy the Wonder Dog

© 2018 Malcolm Lewis

SCOTT THORNLEY grew up in Hamilton, Ontario, which inspired his fictional Dundurn. He is the author of five novels in the critically acclaimed MacNeice Mysteries series: *Erasing Memory, The Ambitious City, Raw Bone, Vantage Point,* and *Middlemen.* He was appointed to the Royal Canadian Academy of the Arts in 1990. In 2018, he was named a Member of the Order of Canada. Thornley divides his time between Toronto and the southwest of France.

NOW AVAILABLE
from House of Anansi Press

The MacNeice Mysteries

Book 1

Book 2

Book 3

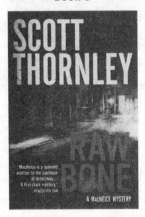

Book 4

houseofanansi.com